10

Valeria's Cross

This powerful and emotionally evocative story transported me to a place where people's passion and commitment to Jesus Christ was something they were willing to die for. I was deeply entrenched in the historical setting and challenged by the message in this novel. *Valeria's Cross* will stick with me because of its powerful message of hope and commitment.
—Michelle Sutton, bestselling author of over a dozen novels, including *It's Not About Me* (2008) and *Danger at the Door* (2009)

Valeria's Cross

Kathi Macias and Susan Wales

Abingdon Press fiction
a novel approach to faith

Nashville, Tennessee

Valeria's Cross

Copyright © 2010 by Kathi Macias and Susan Wales

ISBN-13: 978-1-4267-0215-0

Published by Abingdon Press, P.O. Box 801, Nashville, TN 37202

www.abingdonpress.com

Many of the persons and events portrayed in this work of fiction are the
creations of the author, and any resemblance to persons living or dead
is purely coincidental, except for well-known historical figures and events.
The authors have taken the liberty to change the order
of some of the battles and events to enhance the story.

Published in association with Hartline Literary Agency,
and the literary agency of Alive Communications, Inc.,
7680 Goddard Street, Suite 200, Colorado Springs, Colorado 80920,
www.alivecommunications.com

Cover design by Anderson Design Group, Nashville, TN

Library of Congress Cataloging-in-Publication Data

Mills-Macias, Kathi, 1948-
Valeria's cross / Kathi Macias and Susan Wales.
    p. cm.
ISBN 978-1-4267-0215-0 (binding: pbk./trade pbk., adhesive perfect : alk. paper)
I. Wales, Susan. II. Title.
PS3563.I42319V35 2010
    813'.54—dc22   2010006510

All scripture verses are taken from the King James or Authorized Version of the Bible.

The letter of Theban Legion is adapted from *The Golden Legend, or Lives of the Saints* (1483)
translated by William Caxton.

Printed in the United States of America

1 2 3 4 5 6 7 8 9 10 / 15 14 13 12 11 10

Acknowledgments

Though *Valeria's Cross* is a book of courage and adventure,
it is ultimately a love story. And so I dedicate this book
to the love of my life, my husband, Al,
and to my First Love, my precious Lord Jesus.

Thank you to Voice of the Martyrs for their updated version
of *Foxe's Book of Martyrs*, which first introduced me
to the Theban Legion and birthed the idea for this book.

—Kathi Macias

To my friends, Betty Motes and J. M., for the trip to
Diocletian's castle in Split, Croatia, and many of the other
magical places on the Mediterranean Sea. *Old Broads at Sea*
was my inspiration to write this story about the emperor's
daughter, Valeria, and his wife, Prisca.

This book is dedicated to my mother, Mimi;
my daughter, Megan;
and my granddaughter, Hailey Blu,
for inspiring me to tell stories.

—Susan Wales

1

Shame on you! Valeria chastised herself as she serpentined through the secret passageway that led to her mother's boudoir. Had the agonizing thought of leaving the palace during the exciting winter social season reduced her, the emperor's daughter, to a common spy? Absolutely! Overhearing snippets of her parents' conversation in the hallway, she knew she had no choice; eavesdropping was her only weapon. Valeria was determined to discover why her father was so insistent that she accompany her mother to Egypt.

Near the end of the tunnel, Valeria broke through a maze of cobwebs to reach the secret entrance to her mother's room. She pushed the door, rusted shut by years of neglect, but it would not budge. As a young girl, she had frequently played in the tunnel, but a couple of years ago, she had put away her childish ways. Frustrated, she kicked the door repeatedly until at last it opened. A puff of dust blew into the room and settled over the Turkish carpet like a storm cloud, but there was no time to clean. The echo of her mother's singsong voice drifted down the hallway, warning of her imminent approach. Valeria scurried to a hiding place behind the damask draperies—just

in time! The door swung open, and her parents, Emperor
Diocletian and his beautiful wife, Empress Prisca, entered the
room.

Valeria's heart raced. She knew she should not be eavesdropping, but it was too late to turn and run. Besides, she
needed to discover her father's reasoning for the trip, and
then perhaps she could persuade him to allow her to remain
at home and attend the winter ball.

After all, her mother's dressmaker in Milan had created a
stunning velvet gown for the event, specifically designed to
match the color of Valeria's eyes, as well as the aquamarines
in the bejeweled crown her father had presented to her on her
fourteenth birthday. What more perfect occasion to show off
her latest finery than the winter ball at the palace?

"You simply must not tell her," she heard her mother
protest.

"But if I do not, the child will surely drive me mad," her
father countered.

"You are a mighty warrior, my dear. Surely you can withstand the harpings of a fourteen-year-old girl."

The emperor sighed. "Truthfully, I would rather fight a battle with the most ferocious barbarian in the empire than to
deny a request from our strong-willed daughter."

Behind the curtain, Valeria suppressed a giggle. Her incessant harassment of her father was obviously working. It should
be only a matter of time until she wore down his resistance
and he granted her permission to stay in the palace with the
servants while he and her mother were away.

Prisca laughed. "What right do you have to complain? You
know she inherited her strong will from you. It has certainly
served you well."

"Alas, it benefits me as a man, and more so as the Roman
Emperor, but Valeria is a young woman."

"As the daughter of the mighty Roman Emperor, Valeria will marry a powerful man. She will need her strong will."

Diocletian's voice reflected his good humor. "Is that spoken from the voice of experience?" Before Prisca could respond, the emperor teased, "I love the way your eyes spark with fire when you are angry, my love."

Valeria muffled a giggle as she pushed the draperies aside to peek at her mother's reaction. She felt her face grow hot as she watched in horror; her father pulled her mother close and placed his lips on hers. She squeezed her eyes shut and scolded herself for spying on her parents during such an intimate moment. How she wished she could disappear!

A few moments later, her father's sandaled footsteps sounding across the marble floor as he walked away, Valeria was showered with relief. Then she heard his voice boom throughout the bedchamber. "Why not just tell her the truth?"

"Because I want our daughter's childhood to be innocent and carefree."

Diocletian chuckled. "In the meantime I will have to live in fear of her aggravating me."

"So be it. I do not want our daughter frightened at such a tender age."

Valeria was even more perplexed now. She had to know what could be so dreadful that her parents wanted to protect her from it. Curiosity overcame her, and she stepped out from behind the curtains.

"Valeria!" the couple cried in unison. The shock on their faces was evident, as her mother jumped up from the divan and walked over to her daughter.

"What were you doing hiding behind there?" Prisca demanded.

Valeria ignored the question, and asked, "What is this ominous threat that you are afraid to tell me about?"

Her parents looked at one another for a moment and then burst into laughter.

"Come here," her father coaxed, reaching out for her.

Valeria remembered protocol and fell prostrate before her father. She wondered if he were still smiling or if his initial humor had turned to anger, but from her vantage point all she could see was the jeweled hem of his robe and his pointy red slippers encrusted with diamonds. One thing the emperor would not tolerate from any of his subjects, including his daughter, was the refusal to bow down before him, so she had to remain perfectly still until he dismissed her.

There were no servants in the privacy of her mother's room, and Valeria felt her father's hand reach for her to help her to her feet.

Accepting his invitation, Valeria took his hand. Diocletian pulled her close and peered over the top of her head as he announced to his wife, "There is no greater fear than fear of the unknown. I must tell her." He paused, as if waiting for his wife's approval.

"Oh, do tell, Father," Valeria begged, filling the silence as she pulled away from him and shot her mother a pleading look.

"Very well," Prisca agreed, as she resumed her seat on the divan and patted the spot beside her.

Once the women were seated, Diocletian explained. "As you know, I am leaving for Gaul in a few weeks to join my troops in order to quell an uprising by the Burgundy rebels."

"I do know, yes. And I will miss you terribly, Father."

The emperor smiled. "I will miss you, too, my darling. But if you must know, I am sending you and your mother to Egypt, not for pleasure but for your protection."

"But I thought our palace in Nicomedia was the safest place in the Empire," Valeria argued. "You have told me so on numerous occasions."

"At one time this was true, but our reconnaissance spies have heard rumors of a plot by the rebels to invade Turkey. With all the uprisings throughout the empire, and the majority of the army, as well as me, away in Gaul, our castle in Nicomedia could be in imminent danger. Should our home be invaded, your lives and the servants' could be in jeopardy. I cannot risk such a threat."

Valeria hung her head. "Please forgive me, Father. I had no idea you were saddled with such an enormous burden."

Her father lifted her chin with his thumb and index finger. "You are not to worry your pretty head about me, nor anything else for that matter. You and your mother will be safe and happy at the palace in Egypt. Some of the finest armies in the empire are stationed there."

"Thank you for your concern for our well-being, my lord," Valeria answered, humbled by her father's care, though still doubtful that Egypt would be nearly as pleasant as he claimed.

2

Accompanied by a fleet of a dozen ships, the royal ship was extravagantly fitted for the empress and her daughter's comfort on their journey to the island of Elephantine in Upper Egypt.

Valeria spent most of her time on deck, basking in the sun and viewing the picturesque Greek Isles along the route. One moonlit night after dinner the ship's captain stopped to exchange pleasantries with Valeria and Prisca. The women marveled at the stars that twinkled across the black velvet landscape of the sky.

The captain pointed upward. "See the brightness of the North Star tonight? That same star has led ships to their destinations for centuries. It is the star that led the wise men to the Christ child." After his explanation, the captain tucked his chin in what Valeria imagined to be embarrassment over his mention of Jesus. It was no secret that Diocletian was a devout pagan with little tolerance for the Christian religion.

Prisca quickly reassured the captain. "My husband employs many Christians for their loyalty and integrity."

The captain lifted his eyebrows, appearing surprised.

Valeria understood that her mother was trying to put the captain at ease, so she added, "Father speaks highly of the

Christian soldiers in his army too. He says they are honest and loyal."

The captain's jaw relaxed, and he smiled. "It is God's command . . . to do everything with excellence, as if unto our Lord."

"An intriguing impetus," Prisca observed. "I should like to learn more about your faith and this Jesus you worship."

"Then you are traveling to the perfect place," the captain assured her. "The Coptic monks in Aswan are considered the greatest biblical scholars and teachers in all the Roman Empire. Madame could perhaps arrange a meeting with them."

Prisca smiled. "Perhaps I shall," she said, turning to Valeria. "Are you ready to go below? I am tired, and it is time for me to begin my bedtime beauty rituals."

"Oh, Mother, could I please stay and stargaze awhile longer?"

Prisca hesitated and then spoke to Valeria's lady-in-waiting, Eugenia, who was seated nearby. "Valeria is behind in her studies. She has my permission to stay if you will give her a Roman astronomy lesson."

"I am sorry," Eugenia answered, "but I am not qualified to teach astronomy."

Prisca raised her eyebrows.

"What I mean is . . . I am hardly the person to do so, Madame. I do not believe—"

Prisca's eyes narrowed, and her reprimand was sharp and to the point. "Were you not taught astronomy as a child?"

"Of course, but I cannot—"

"What you are really trying to say is that you object to our method of teaching astronomy. Is that it?"

Eugenia hung her head.

"I will not tolerate your religious beliefs interfering with the education her father and I have chosen for our daughter."

"Forgive me, Empress." Eugenia bowed before her mistress, her eyes lowered in obvious embarrassment. "I will gladly provide Valeria's lesson."

Prisca, still stiff with anger, nodded before turning to her daughter. "Good night, love," she whispered before she went below, her entourage of servants following.

When they were gone, Valeria reached over and touched Eugenia's hand. "By morning, Mother will have forgotten this little altercation."

Eugenia, only a few years older than Valeria, bit her quivering lip and blinked back her tears, but forged ahead with the lesson. First she fetched some papyrus and sketched two constellations before pointing to the sky. "You see the North Star, the one the captain pointed out earlier? It is actually the tail of Lesser Bear, Ursa Minor."

"Son of Jupiter," Valeria interjected. She looked up at the sky and then ran her fingers over the illustration Eugenia had sketched for her.

"Very good." Eugenia smiled at her eager pupil. "Across from it is Larger Bear, Ursa Major—the boy's mother, Callisto."

"Stop." Valeria held up her hand. "Jupiter's wife is Juno. Where does Callisto fit?"

"Let it suffice to say that Callisto was Jupiter's 'wife on the side.'"

"You mean his mistress? Are you insinuating that Jupiter was an adulterer?"

Eugenia's eyes opened wide. "How do you know the meaning of the word?"

"Stop treating me like a child. I am fourteen years old!" Valeria flung her head to one side, and her copper-colored hair cascaded like a waterfall down one shoulder.

Eugenia rolled her eyes and continued. "Callisto was not always a bear. An insanely jealous Juno turned her into one."

"Can you blame Juno? If Jupiter were your husband, would you not do the same?"

"Me?" Eugenia grinned. "I would have turned Jupiter into a bear myself."

Valeria laughed. "What happened next?"

"Juno tricked Callisto's son into killing the bear—his own mother."

"I suppose that is one way to get rid of the other woman, but the poor boy must have been devastated."

"Yes, but Jupiter took pity on his grieving son. He placed the boy and his mother in the sky so they could live together forever." Eugenia paused and concluded Valeria's lesson. "From the North Star we can always know the direction we are facing. It will help us find our way. The North Star never sinks below the horizon, so you can always locate it."

Leaning closer, Valeria whispered, "You do not believe a word of the lesson, do you?"

Eugenia lowered her lashes. "My Father in heaven created the moon, the stars, and the sky—not Jupiter."

"My father believes he is Jupiter." Valeria laughed nervously. "At least, the embodiment of the god upon earth. Do you believe he is?"

"I would rather not discuss it," Eugenia said, standing to her feet. "It is late."

"Now I understand why you preferred not to teach an astronomy lesson." Valeria grinned. "In honor of your god."

Eugenia appeared distressed. "I have failed my God. My Christian friends will die before they deny him, but I . . . I do not even have the strength to refuse to fill a young girl's head with the lies of pagan gods."

"But how can you be so sure they are lies?"

"With your mother's permission, one day I shall tell you." Eugenia dried her tears with her handkerchief and reached for Valeria's hand. "For now," she said, as she kissed the girl's fingertips, "it is bedtime."

❧

Once their traveling expedition reached the river, their luxurious cruising boat was dry-docked, and they stepped aboard the *feluccas*, the sailing vessels of the Nile.

As the hours slipped by, mother and daughter stood in awe, craning their necks to see the pyramids, the temples, and the palaces on the riverbanks. They marveled at the ancient mastery of engineering and perfection in design against a backdrop of sand dune cliffs and the lush green banks that gave way to russet mountains, set afire by glowing sunsets.

The women were fascinated by the wildlife, especially the vast herds of camels bunched at the shore. They were fearful of hungry crocodiles and enormous hippopotami that swam close to the boat and had to be coaxed away by the sailors. Valeria screamed every time she spotted a menacing snake the length of a small boat slither off the riverbanks and into the water.

On the final day of their journey, Valeria sensed a change in her heart. "Something is coming," she told her mother.

Prisca raised an eyebrow. "Not another herd of hippos, I hope."

Valeria laughed. "I am not sure what it is, but I feel a great sense of adventure awaiting us at Father's palace on Elephantine."

"I must write to your father with this news. It will truly make him smile."

Before they could continue their conversation, the boat reached the city of Aswan, and the women gasped as one of the sailors pointed to the Island of Elephantine in the distance. They beheld the magnificence of Diocletian's fortress rising up like a jewel out of the banks of the island. Fringed by palm trees, the palace glittered in the sunlight like a priceless diamond.

3

$\mathscr{V}$aleria was besotted with Egypt. She adored the beautiful gardens, which overflowed with fragrant flowers, and vegetables and fruits beyond the size and flavor of any she had ever tasted. What she cherished most were the early morning strolls she and her mother took through the gardens and on the golden beaches. She delighted in plucking seashells from the sand and dipping her toes into the water. The warm sunshine had soon colored her pale skin with a peachy glow.

Getting settled into the palace had taken far more time than the women had anticipated. There were Roman dignitaries to entertain, and prominent Egyptians hosted parties given in the women's honor. Four weeks passed before Prisca was able to arrange to meet the Coptic monks recommended by the ship's captain.

When the day arrived, Valeria pouted. "Why should I have to go study with the monks? I can hardly keep up with my lessons now."

"I have arranged for us to go late mornings so you can study with your tutor earlier and then spend the rest of your school time with the monks."

Valeria shrugged. "As long as it is part of my studies. But I have heard the monks are old and crabby." She pinched the end of her nose. "My friend Aneksi told me they smell as musty as the catacombs."

"You can take your handkerchief filled with cinnamon."

"You have an answer for everything."

"Where you are concerned, that is true." Prisca clapped her hands, and the servants appeared. "We are ready to depart."

First the women and their entourage of ladies-in-waiting, servants, and soldiers boarded several feluccas and crossed a narrow section over to Aswan, where the monastery and the church were located. Once they reached the city, the women boarded ornate chariots with drivers, while the remaining soldiers mounted horses.

To her surprise, Valeria soon found she was enjoying herself. She chuckled at the spirited Egyptian horses that flew ahead of the carriages, their riders desperately trying to control the frisky beasts. As their entourage passed through the cobblestone streets in their golden chariots, it attracted a lot of attention. The citizens along the way cheered. Women and children ran for bouquets of flowers and tossed them in their path; others simply stopped what they were doing and stared. Soldiers on horses pushed a few protesters from their path.

"Long live Emperor Diocletian and his Empress Prisca," a chorus of voices rang out as the chariots rolled past.

"I find Father's popularity here surprising," Valeria noted.

"Rome offers Egypt protection from the barbarians from the north and the savages south of here," Prisca explained.

"Look," Valeria said, quickly distracted as she pointed out one of the beautiful homes in the area. "Even the simplest of structures are constructed of limestone or granite."

"These elegant houses are far more appealing than the flat-roofed homes built of mud and sun-dried bricks that we observed along the Nile," Prisca added.

An Egyptian guide who walked alongside the carriage interjected, "Every obelisk and statue throughout the empire is carved from red granite or yellow limestone taken from local quarries. Even the pieces in the mosaics of Rome and beyond originate from our quarries."

Once the royal party arrived at the monastery, the carriage came to a halt in front of the gate. The oblong-domed church, an imposing structure, was divided by a natural wall from the monastery. Lookouts towered strategically at the four corners of the buildings. The lead soldier dismounted and knocked at the massive arched gate and announced their arrival. Valeria thought if the church and monastery were only half as exquisite as the colorful mosaic walls, it would be well worth the trip, even if they found the religion a disappointment.

Alara, a young Nubian with skin the color of dark chestnuts, appeared at the gate. He took a deep bow before them. "Welcome to the monastery, ladies."

Valeria smiled at the beautiful young man with dark eyes and well-toned body, but Eugenia quickly reprimanded her. "This man is a monk. Please do not torture him with your tantalizing smile."

Valeria blushed, wondering how Eugenia had the power to read her mind. Yet even under Eugenia's watchful eye, it was hard not to stare at this strikingly attractive man.

Seemingly unaware of his admirer, Alara guided them on a tour of the church, which contained the most intricate mosaics the women had ever seen. The walls inside the church and other buildings were filled with mystical and colorful hieroglyphics, painstakingly drawn centuries ago. The octagonal domes of the church were painted with murals of Jesus and his disciples.

Once they had toured the magnificent church, Alara invited them to step outside into the courtyard. He led them through an arcade covered by a succession of arches that connected the church to the monastery. Through the archways, the women saw that the monks were cultivating vegetables and fruits.

"Would you like to go down into the garden grotto?" Alara asked.

The women declined, explaining that their own religion taught that these underground caves contained evil spirits.

When they crossed the gardens into the monastery, the women discovered it was a community in itself, busily humming with workers—not just scholarly monks, but brothers who were craftsmen, artists, carpenters, and potters. Alara paused at the kiln where the women observed several industrious monks in various stages of creating exquisite pottery from the red clay indigenous to the area. The women were delighted when they were offered several pieces as gifts. They thanked the monks and went on to the next room, which was a workshop manned by several carpenters. These craftsmen gave them hand-carved wooden crosses, inset with mosaics.

The aroma of the bakery caused the women's mouths to water, and they were soon enjoying a sample of homemade bread fresh from the clay ovens. Their servants' arms were quickly laden with loaves and cakes, filled with nuts and dates, to take back to the palace.

Next Alara gave them a peek into the monks' living quarters. Each cell contained six beds carved out of the natural limestone. "How does one sleep on stone?" Valeria wondered aloud.

Alara laughed. "They are quite comfortable, and the stone is beneficial for the back. The monks do not afford themselves luxuries, for our Savior Himself had no home or bed."

"Then I am sure I do not care for your religion, for I prefer luxurious surroundings," Valeria declared.

"Ah, you misunderstand, dear lady. God does not expect everyone to choose the same path. You will not have to sacrifice luxury unless God calls you to do so. If He does, you will want nothing more because He will either provide the strength you need to live without it or take away the desire."

Valeria made a face.

Alara smiled at her. "Some of the older monks do not choose the luxury of living at the monastery. The founder of our order, Antony, and many of his followers prefer to live in underground caves."

Prisca gasped. "With the evil spirits?"

"Even if evil spirits resided in the underground caves, the Bible teaches, 'Greater is He who is in us than he who is in the world.' There is nothing to fear."

Valeria's eyes opened wide. "You believe you have a god living inside you?" Before Alara could reply, she added, "So does my father. He believes he *is* God and demands that everyone address him as Lord and God."

Alara's handsome face twisted into a pained look, but Valeria was not surprised that the young monk remained silent. What could he say? A derogatory statement in the presence of the empress and her daughter concerning the emperor would have been unwise.

"Father believes he's Jupiter. So who do you claim to be?"

"I do not claim to be a god. Christians believe there is only one God and just by inviting Jesus into your heart, the Holy Spirit will come and dwell within you, giving you strength and peace."

Alara smiled and changed the subject. "Come and let us visit the monastery. Before you leave, we will schedule your Bible studies, where you will find the answers to your questions."

As they continued down the limestone hallways, they passed room after room filled with rows of papyrus. Prisca stopped at the door of one of the rooms and asked, "What is written upon all these papyruses?"

"Those are writings pertaining to Scripture," Alara explained. "Many are Saint Mark's interpretations. The Apostle Mark founded the church during the reign of the Roman emperor Nero, and a great multitude of Egyptians embraced the Christian faith. But even before Christianity, Jewish and Greek scholars joined forces with the Copts to translate the ancient Holy Scriptures."

"Who will teach us the Holy Scriptures?" Prisca asked.

"The biblical scholars in the monastery will instruct you. You will love the poetic and inspiring Psalms penned by King David. And your daughter, as a young pupil, will grow in wisdom and garner valuable life lessons from Proverbs. The Holy Scriptures are rich with history, and many of the prophecies that were foretold of Jesus are written there."

Prisca's eyes lit up. "Oh, is it possible that the monks can tell my future?"

"Biblical prophecy is unrelated to fortune-telling," Alara explained.

"I am not sure that I understand the difference," Prisca confessed.

"You will after you study the Word of God," Alara assured her.

The tour ended as they arrived at a door in the back of the temple overlooking the garden. Alara knocked and then introduced the women and their servants to Brother Bishoy, who led the group into a large library, with a barrel-vaulted roof and filled with arcades and pendentives. Shelves of papyrus lined the walls. In the center of the room were several tables and chairs, some occupied by monks so deep in study they were unaware of the women's presence.

"Welcome," Bishoy said, as the servants scurried around, finding chairs for the women and their attendants. "Please sit down."

Valeria studied the priest in his long flowing robe, tied at the waist with a simple rope. A pair of bright red shoes peeked out like mice from beneath his robe. Brother Bishoy's vestments were brightly colored, but tattered. His long, crooked fingers were smudged in ink. Tufts of white hair sprouted out of his mostly bald head, but his bright smile lit up his otherwise homely face.

After they were seated, Prisca spoke on behalf of the women and thanked the monks for agreeing to enlighten them.

"There have been hundreds of scholars throughout the Roman Empire who have come here to study," Bishoy informed them with a smile.

"We are hardly scholars," Prisca stated. "Just two women intrigued by your religion."

"Two very important women," Brother Bishoy added, bowing his head slightly.

The sound of a monk clearing his throat came from a nearby table, causing the women to glance in his direction. Seated at the desk was a man even more disheveled than the one who had welcomed them.

"Antony, the old monk who lives in the cave?" Valeria wondered in a whisper to her mother.

There were no papyruses stacked upon his table, but his hands moved furiously over stone tablets on the table before him.

"Is he reading with his fingertips?" Valeria asked.

Brother Bishoy answered her question with an introduction. "This is Didymus, one of our monks who will be teaching you. He is blind."

The women greeted Didymus with cheerful salutations. Absorbed in his work, he did not look up, nor did his fingers stop moving across the tablets of stone. He simply nodded his head.

"Didymus is reading the Scripture carved upon the tablets," the priest explained, "a method of reading created by the Copts for those who cannot see with their eyes."

Prisca stood and walked to the desk, then ran her own hand over one of the tablets.

Didymus suddenly stopped and reached for Prisca's hand, clasping it in one of his own. With the other, he reached up to touch her face.

Bishoy intervened. "Do you mind if Brother Didymus explores your face?"

Prisca answered the question by leaning forward. She reached for the priest's hand and moved it to her face.

"Ah, very beautiful," the blind priest sighed. After a brief pause, he inquired, "May I speak?"

"Please," Prisca said and visibly squeezed his hand.

"God is going to use you and your daughter mightily. You will one day change the world."

Prisca laughed. "You flatter me, old man, but have you forgotten that we are mere women? Surely we do not have such power."

"God will grant you that power . . . if you follow Him." The man held up a gnarled finger and wagged it in Prisca's face. "But you must heed these words one day when life becomes more difficult than either of you think you can bear."

4

$\mathcal{V}$aleria was haunted by the words spoken by the old monk, but she was also intrigued, so she accompanied Prisca without a word of protest when they returned to the monastery. Their first studies went so well that their group returned daily to learn from the monks. With all the miracles recorded in the Bible, it was hard for Valeria not to believe in this Savior. Before long, both she and Prisca made the decision to convert to Christianity and accepted the forgiveness that the monks explained had been purchased for them through the life, death, and resurrection of Jesus Christ.

Valeria was eager to meet other young Christians, so she accepted an invitation from Cornelia, the daughter of a respected Roman senator. The girls had met at a luncheon hosted by Cornelia's mother in honor of Prisca and Valeria, and they had become fast friends. Now they were attending an athletic event in Thebes at an arena similar to the Coliseum in Rome, though it was far more ornate and much smaller. The finest athletes in the area would compete for the prizes, and the girls were excited to join the other spectators.

They climbed the steps of the large circular arena and found a seat in the center mezzanine. Valeria instructed her bodyguards to watch from above so she would not attract a lot of attention from the crowd. From her vantage point, Valeria was able to focus on a young Roman soldier who had successfully completed a race on one of the tracks below. The crowd cheered wildly for the handsome athlete, as Valeria strained her neck to get a better look. Never had she seen such a handsome man! Though tall and slender, every muscle of his bronzed body appeared to have been carved by a master sculptor. While most of the Roman soldiers had their hair closely cropped to their heads, this one's shiny black hair curled around his face, framing dark eyes that seemed to sparkle with sunbeams, even from a distance. When he stepped up on the podium to accept his medallion, his smile ignited Valeria's heart.

"Do you know the athlete who just won the race?" she asked Cornelia.

"No, I do not," Cornelia swooned, "but he is the most handsome man I have ever seen."

"Just remember, I saw him first," Valeria said.

"But what if he wants me?" Cornelia teased.

"You cannot have him," Valeria laughed.

"Should we not let him choose?" Cornelia smiled, raising a brow.

"Absolutely not. He is mine!"

"Well, I shall not sit here and wait for him to come to us," Cornelia announced. "I am going down to the field to meet him."

"I dare you," Valeria challenged, and then laughed in amazement as she watched her friend depart. If Cornelia wanted the handsome young man's attention, she should have no problem getting it. She was a beauty, tall and lithe, with a complexion the color of warm honey, highlighted by her rosy cheeks and lips and eyes the color of topaz. Her blonde hair was braided and tucked neatly into a chignon at the nape of her neck. As she sashayed down the steps of the stadium, her diaphanous linen gown, covered with a gold striped tunic, lapped at her slender ankles and attracted many admiring looks from within the crowd.

Part way down, Cornelia turned back. Smiling mischievously, she waved, her gold and topaz bangles jangling at her wrist. Then she continued down the steps two at a time.

Valeria watched, envying Cornelia's courage. Her friend would probably walk right down to the field and introduce herself to the attractive athlete. But then she noticed a throng of admirers had surrounded the handsome young man. It seemed Cornelia must wait her turn.

Valeria turned to a group of Egyptian girls seated in front of her. Perhaps one of them might know his name. She studied the bronze-skinned girls until she had picked out the friendliest of the bunch, a pretty Egyptian with raven hair that swept up into an intricate knot atop her head, with bangs that fringed her dark eyes. Fashionably dressed in an elegant lime green sarong, she was so animated that when she spoke to her friends, her emerald and gold hoop earrings danced about her ears.

Valeria tapped the stunning girl on the shoulder and introduced herself.

"Nice to meet you," the girl answered in response. "I am Nanu." She brushed Valeria's cheek with a kiss, the customary greeting.

Valeria skipped the pleasantries and got right to the point. "Do you, by chance, know the name of the Egyptian athlete who just won the race?"

When the group of girls broke into laughter, Valeria was puzzled. "What is so amusing?" It was at times like this that Valeria felt humiliated and longed to tell her offenders she was their emperor's daughter. But this new spirit who lived inside her heart nudged her before she had a chance to react.

"Forgive us," Nanu explained, once she caught her breath. "Yes, we know him—very well."

Valeria's heart soared. "Who is he? What is his name?" Suddenly she felt the heat creep up her neck and into her face. "Oh, dear, I hope he is not your sweetheart."

The group of girls giggled, but Valeria paid them no mind until Nanu said, "I adore him, but alas, he is not my paramour; Mauritius is my brother." The girl touched Valeria's arm. "No need to feel embarrassed. There is scarcely a young woman in this stadium who has not declared her love for him."

"I should have known," Valeria replied, studying the girl's face. "The resemblance is . . . remarkable. You are as beautiful as he is handsome."

"Thank you." Nanu's black eyes flashed, as she, in turn, studied Valeria. "You are stunning yourself. Such a lovely face! And your hair . . . it is the color of the Nubian lions."

"Nubian lions?" Valeria paused to think. "Why do they sound familiar?"

Nanu lowered her eyes. "During Nero's reign, the Romans transported the lions from the nearby Nubian jungles to fight the Christians in the Coliseum."

Valeria winced. "Oh, how awful!"

"Trust me, it is not an export Egypt is proud of, especially those of us who are Christians. But Nubian lions are the most beautiful creatures you will ever see . . . from a distance, of course."

Valeria nodded. Encouraged by Nanu's friendly manner, she asked, "Does your brother have a sweetheart?"

"Oh, no. Mauritius has many admirers, but he is far too committed to his Savior and to Rome to seek a wife. He has no time for courtship."

Valeria's heart leapt at the realization that Mauritius was a Christian, though she tried to temper her excitement. "What is your brother's position in the Roman Army?"

"He is the captain of the renowned Theban Legion."

"My father says that the finest Roman armies are here in Egypt." Valeria had chosen her words carefully, not yet ready to reveal her identity; that confession would come soon enough, particularly if she was blessed to meet Nanu's brother.

"Your father is right. There is no finer legion in the Roman Empire than the Thebans. It is comprised entirely of Coptic Christians."

"Really? My mother and I are studying Christianity under the Coptic monks at a monastery in Aswan."

"Mauritius and my fiancé, Baraka, have studied with them for years, until recently, when they had to undergo their rigorous military training."

Her hopes of running into Mauritius at the monastery dashed, Valeria noted, "You are so young to become engaged."

"I am fourteen, which is not considered young in our culture. Girls in Egypt marry as young as twelve or thirteen. Baraka and I plan to marry before the legion is called to battle."

Surprised by the Egyptian girl's friendliness, Valeria thanked her. Then, just as Nanu said she hoped they would meet again, Cornelia returned and announced, "His name is—"

Before Cornelia could utter his name, the group of Egyptian girls sang out in unison, "Mauritius," and then laughed, leaving Cornelia looking baffled.

Valeria blushed again. "Nanu, this is my friend, Cornelia. And Cornelia, this is Nanu." She paused, and then added, "She is Mauritius' sister."

Cornelia's eyebrows lifted in obvious surprise, but she recovered quickly, and after the introductions were made and the girls had chatted for a few minutes, Valeria and Cornelia returned to their seats.

"Did you meet him?" Valeria asked as soon as they were alone.

Cornelia shook her head. "Someone told me his name, but there were far too many admirers surrounding him for me to get closer. I only got a tiny glimpse of him, but he is even more handsome up close. There was an intensity about him that is difficult to put into words. But I can tell you this: his eyes exude love. When he looked my way, I felt . . . like I really mattered."

"He must have liked you," Valeria admitted, feeling somewhat slighted.

"No, it was not in any personal way. There was just so much love and kindness in his eyes. Forgive me if I sound sacrilegious, but when he looked my way, I had a strange sensation, as though I were looking into the eyes of Jesus."

"Oh, I should have gone with you!"

"Why? You met his sister, which is far better. Did she agree to introduce you to him?"

Valeria shook her head. "Nanu was adamant that Mauritius had no time for courting. She explained he was far too busy with his military training and his dedication to his faith."

"Did you even ask her to introduce you to him?" Cornelia prompted, propping her hand on her hip.

When Valeria blushed yet again, Cornelia sighed. "I have a lot to teach you, especially about men, my friend."

Valeria felt her defenses rise. "I know about men!"

Cornelia smirked. "Is that so? Have you ever kissed a man? Or even flirted with one?"

"Eugenia accused me of flirting with Alara, one of the younger monks at the monastery."

"That is nothing to boast about, Valeria."

"But he was so handsome."

"Forget the monk. Here is what you do about Mauritius. You must persuade his sister to invite you to her home."

"How will I do that? I do not know if I will even see her again."

Cornelia leaned close and spoke in a conspiratorial tone. "Ask one of the servants to find out where Nanu lives, and then send a messenger to her home with an invitation for her and her mother to have lunch at the palace with you and your mother. Enclose a note explaining that you would like to return the kindness she showed at the athletic event."

"But what if they refuse?"

Cornelia rolled her eyes. "No one will refuse an invitation from the empress and her daughter. Besides, every one in the area is curious to see inside the palace. I know that firsthand because everyone nags me to tell them about it, now that they know I have been inside with you." Cornelia laughed. "Believe me, they will come."

"But I do not want Nanu or Mauritius to know my identity yet. I want him to care about me for who I am, and not because I am the emperor's daughter."

"Nanu seems a bright girl. She has probably already discovered your identity. Besides, do you want to lose your chance at Mauritius? Listen, if you had seen those women down below, clamoring for a chance to speak with him, you would not hesitate. You must use any moral measure to attract his attention."

"But what good will that do if his only interest is God and country?"

"After one look at you, my dear, he will quickly change his mind."

Valeria hesitated. "I will consider it."

"There is no time for that. Rumor has it that the Theban Legion could be called to Gaul any day now. Worse yet, what if your parents decide it is time to arrange a marriage for you?" Cornelia put one hand over her brow and fanned herself with the other. "I can think of nothing worse than to be married to a man you do not love."

Valeria shuddered, but as the emperor's daughter, it was imperative for her to maintain her dignity and pride. Another thought flitted into her mind, and she smiled. She had found the answer. Just this week Valeria and her mother were studying prayer at the monastery. If she could not finagle an introduction to Mauritius from Nanu, she would ask God to arrange one.

5

The next morning, Valeria awakened to the sight of her mother standing at her bedchamber door, waving a letter in her hand.

"A messenger arrived at dawn with news from your father."

Valeria threw back the bed linens and jumped up. "Is Father all right?"

"I assure you, he is fine, but he has asked us to return to Nicomedia at once."

With no attempt to hide her disappointment, Valeria plunked back down on her bed. "But we cannot leave now; I love Egypt!" Just yesterday Valeria had seen the man she was sure she wanted to marry. They simply could not leave before she had a chance to meet him.

Her mother sat down beside her and placed an arm around her shoulders. "I understand. I, too, would prefer not to leave."

"Then why must we go? Can you not convince Father that we should stay in Egypt? He told us Nicomedia was unsafe."

"The circumstances have changed over the past few weeks. Your father has asked us to return so we can host the victorious general, Galerius, at the palace."

"Oh, him." Valeria was not impressed and demonstrated her feelings with a careless shrug.

Her mother's look was stern. "Do you understand the importance of these battles in Gaul? General Galerius and his legion won the first few skirmishes, and your father wants him to take some time off to relax and enjoy himself before the major battle begins."

Valeria sighed. "The general is all anyone talks about these days. But why can he and his family not stay at the palace without us? There are plenty of servants who can take care of them."

"Who would entertain them?"

"The citizens of Nicomedia would be delighted to host a war hero, especially one so famous."

"This may be true, but your father would never allow it. And General Galerius would be highly offended if we were not in residence during his visit."

Valeria stuck out her lower lip, a gesture that obviously did not go unnoticed by her mother.

"And you, young lady, had better tuck that lip back in and practice your bow, because we are going home to entertain our famous guest."

Valeria swallowed a grin, determined not to yield to her mother's persuasive arguments. "Why not invite General Galerius here? The weather in Thessalonica is dreadful this time of year. Here the commander and his family could enjoy the sunshine and the scenery, not to mention the fresh fruit and vegetables from the garden."

"You sound like our Egyptian guide," Prisca quipped, as she tucked an unruly lock of hair behind her daughter's ear. "But it is apparent that you have inherited your father's brains, young lady. Hosting the general and his family in Egypt is a brilliant suggestion."

❧

Prisca was successful in persuading the emperor to change his mind, so she and Valeria remained in Egypt. A month later, Galerius and his family joined them in Elephantine.

Soon after the arrival of the general and his family, Valeria passed Galerius in the hallway. Was it her imagination, or had he deliberately brushed his body against hers?

"Excuse me, my lady," he apologized. "What a beautiful woman you have become, a peach ripe for picking in the springtime. How old are you?"

Valeria blushed, her answer barely audible. "Fourteen." It was the first time anyone had referred to her as a woman.

"The beautiful daughter of the great emperor must have scores of suitors."

Valeria dared not answer; Galerius moved closer. He reached for her hand, which was clenched into a fist at her side, then lifted it to his lips. Valeria shivered at the unfamiliar sensation, a strange mixture of revulsion and excitement.

"Ah, my kiss has caused you to tremble," Galerius chuckled. Valeria struggled to breathe and to keep her hand far from his lips, but she was unable to extricate it from his grip.

"I really must go," Valeria pleaded. "Eugenia is waiting for me."

As if in answer to an unspoken prayer, Eugenia suddenly appeared in the hallway. Galerius dropped Valeria's hand, and the poor girl sighed with relief.

"I have been searching for you," Eugenia announced, her voice authoritative. "Your tutor is waiting in the library."

Following Eugenia, Valeria hurried away, relieved to escape the clutches of Galerius.

"What did he say to you?" Eugenia asked when they were out of hearing distance.

"That I was pretty." Valeria laughed nervously. She decided not to make an issue of the uncomfortable encounter because of Eugenia's tendency to overreact. From now on, however, Valeria determined she would avoid their guest.

"Do not allow the general's honey mouth to flatter you," Eugenia warned. "He may be handsome, but it is inappropriate for you to be alone with such a charmer—especially a married one."

Valeria was incredulous. "You find him attractive? And charming?"

Eugenia blushed. "There is no disputing that fact."

"Well, I find him revolting."

This time Eugenia laughed. "Oh, you are still such a little girl, dear one!"

Following her encounter with Galerius, Valeria avoided the hallways and enjoyed breakfast alone in her private garden. Though she noticed him every morning, watching her from his bedroom window, she managed to evade him. Yet his stares made her uncomfortable. Even during dinner he spied on her out of the corner of his eye, but she pretended not to notice.

This particular morning, Valeria hurried down the marble steps into the magnificent gardens surrounding the palace. Servants appeared out of nowhere, as Valeria glided toward the table for breakfast. Eager to please, they fluttered around the princess as she took her seat on the divan before the table

laden with delicacies. A dark male servant filled her tumbler
with grape juice from a golden pitcher. Valeria smiled in gratitude, then pointed to a sumptuous apricot that crowned the
platter of fruit. Within seconds, it appeared in slices upon her
plate.

A loud voice boomed throughout the garden—Galerius!
Valeria ducked behind the flowers arranged in a cobalt vase
on the table, but to her surprise, Galerius did not even glance
her way when he and his entourage passed by. Instead, he
proceeded through the garden, flanked by four bodyguards,
toward a stranger who had just arrived atop a magnificent
ebony horse.

In the short time Galerius had been their guest at the palace, Valeria and the servants had come to despise him. And
yet Valeria enjoyed the company of his daughter, also named
Valeria, which caused some confusion in the household. The
girl was only a year or so younger than Valeria, and they both
enjoyed the company of the Egyptian youth. But the younger
Valeria's parents, both pagans, strictly forbade their daughter
to accompany the group of women to the monastery.

Valeria strained now to see the visitor in the garden, who
had dismounted and stood erect, waiting. When she realized he was a soldier, she called to a nearby servant, "Official
business? Perhaps another war has broken out." The servant,
appearing disinterested, nodded and set a bowl of honeyed
pottage in front of her. She picked up her spoon but set it
down again, squinting as the mid-morning sun glinted off the
metal helmet held in the hand of the tall, broad-shouldered
warrior. There was something about him . . .

Valeria rose from the table and peered through the box-
woods for a closer look at the young soldier who waited among
the roses. His back was turned halfway toward her, his eyes

fixed on some distant point of reference. Was that a cross emblazoned upon his helmet? She peered closer. Yes, it was!

Although there were many Christians in the Roman Army, Galerius' hatred for them was well-known. Why would he choose to meet with this particular soldier? If the general had agreed to see him, Valeria presumed this young man was a distinguished warrior, which intrigued her all the more.

Though she could not see his full face from her vantage point, the outline of the handsome stranger's aquiline features and his muscular build made her heart flutter. She thought he looked like a living statue of Apollo, and though she was tempted to stay where she was until he turned and revealed his face, she convinced herself to return to the table. There was no sense risking attracting Galerius' attention. Besides, she would still have a nice view of the attractive soldier from the divan.

Lifting her goblet, she sipped the grape juice, hoping her pulse would slow and her hands would stop trembling. Excitement churned in the pit of her stomach, and the strange and unfamiliar sensation frightened her. Perhaps this soldier, unlike the athlete she had seen a month ago, was interested in marriage. The visitor remained oblivious to her presence, so she took full advantage of her brief invisibility to study him, trying to imagine his thoughts. Was he remembering his last battle, or anticipating the next? Did he have a wife who longed for him at home while he was away at battle? The thought disturbed her, so much so that she quickly and quietly returned to her earlier spot among the bushes.

When Galerius approached the soldier, Valeria ducked so he would not see her. From there, she watched the young man fall to his knees, cross his right arm over his chest, and pound his heart with his fist in a salute to a superior officer.

Galerius motioned for the soldier to stand. Both men reached out their arms and touched their fingertips in the traditional Roman greeting. Valeria listened intently while he addressed the young visitor. "Captain Mauritius, the great Emperor Diocletian has summoned your Theban legion into battle in Gaul. Are you prepared?"

Mauritius! Could it be? Valeria's heart banged against her ribs. She had nearly given up hope of meeting him . . . and yet, she had prayed, had she not? Now God had brought him to her garden!

Valeria watched the men converse until Galerius strode away, perhaps on his way to the Great Temple of Ramses to make his daily sacrifices. She abandoned her meal and hurried to the other side of the hedges. This could be the only opportunity she would have to speak with Mauritius, who had resumed his pensive pose, possibly contemplating his new orders while he waited for a stable hand to fetch his horse.

The closer Valeria got, the more handsome the soldier appeared. As daughter of the Roman emperor, her privileged life had afforded her introductions to hundreds of rulers and kings, but she thought Mauritius far more regal than any man she had ever met.

Of course, she had no intention of admitting that to him. For now Valeria would be content to hear his voice. She had heard so much about Mauritius since the day she had seen him in the arena, but they had never met—until now.

Valeria stood behind the bushes for a moment, mustering up her courage to speak to the captain. At last she stepped forward and cleared her throat. "Captain Mauritius?" Her voice squeaked, causing her cheeks to flush with embarrassment, but she stood her ground.

Valeria had expected Mauritius to jolt from his reverie and spin around in the direction of her voice, but he did not.

Slowly he turned, as if he had known all along that she was there, watching him. Perhaps he had.

Mauritius smiled, revealing the whitest teeth she had ever seen. His dark eyes twinkled with a delight that appeared close to amusement, and he dipped his head in a slight bow.

"Captain Mauritius, at your service." He chuckled. "And who might you be, lovely lady?"

Valeria could not speak. His eyes! Valeria had never seen any quite like them. It was as though he could see inside her soul. And his voice! Joy resounded in his words, as smooth and warm as honey, yet authoritative, as she would have expected from a man in his position. If she had thought he was attractive from a distance, he was more so now that he faced her with his square jaw and chiseled features, his dark curls moving slightly in the breeze. The golden cross that hung from a heavy chain around his neck sparkled in the sunlight.

"I asked your name," he repeated softly.

Still Valeria could not utter a single word.

"Please, do not be afraid," he coaxed, holding out his hand.

She offered her trembling hand in return. Her mouth felt dry, and she wondered if she would be able to speak. She cleared her throat.

"I . . . am . . . Valeria. I am delighted to meet you."

"And so am I . . . delighted to meet you." His smile seemed warmer now, more genuine, as he stepped closer, lifting her hand to his lips for a kiss of greeting and respect. His kiss produced the same strange sensation she had felt when Galerius kissed it, only this time it was not commingled with revulsion.

"I heard Emperor Diocletian had a beautiful daughter," he said, "but I never imagined I would have the honor of meeting her."

"How did you hear of me?"

"Since the day your ship arrived in Egypt, is there anyone who has not heard of the young woman with eyes the color of turquoise and hair as golden red as the mane of a lion?" He reached up and pulled a sprig of boxwood from her hair and handed it to her.

"Who told you about me?" She twirled the evergreen between two fingers on her free hand.

"Nanu."

Valeria smiled. "Ah, yes."

"But she did not tell me you were so incredibly lovely that you would take my breath away when I gazed upon your face."

Valeria's cheeks warmed at the compliment, and she quickly withdrew her hand when she realized she had allowed it to linger a moment too long.

The young couple stared at one another, wordless. At last, uncomfortable in the silence, Valeria spoke.

"I suppose I had better go inside and report to my tutor. He is probably waiting for me."

"But we have only just met." Mauritius' dark eyes clouded with disappointment, and the tone of his voice took on a hint of pleading. "Please stay."

"I suppose I could . . . for a moment more," she agreed with a smile.

His eyes were dancing again, but he suddenly appeared shy, as if he were searching for the right words. Finally he asked, "Do you like Egypt?"

"More than any place I have ever visited. But, really, I must go now. My tutor will be searching for me." Mauritius was far too handsome and outspoken for her to feel comfortable in his presence without a chaperone. She felt panicked in her need to escape from him, yet she could not pull herself away.

"You must not keep your tutor waiting." He smiled as he dipped his head in farewell. "I shall look forward to seeing you again soon—with your permission, of course."

"But you are leaving for Gaul," she said, a hint of desperation in her voice.

"My troops do not even know that yet. How is it that you are privy to such information?" He grinned. "Were you hiding in the bushes when the general presented our orders?"

Valeria knew she was caught but could think of nothing to say in her defense. Instead, she turned on her heel and took a slight step away from the handsome soldier with the laughing eyes. To her surprise he reached for her and took her hand.

"I will be in Thebes for several more weeks before I have to leave for Gaul," he said, gently turning her toward him. "With your father's permission, I would like to see you again . . . and again." He smiled, and her heart jumped.

"As would I . . . like to see you," she said breathlessly, wondering even as she spoke how she could say such a thing to someone she had only just met. Then, before she could say or do anything more to further humiliate herself, she turned and hurried away. When she thought she was out of his range of vision, she abandoned her control and danced on the pathway, her skirt swirling about her ankles.

"I shall see you soon, beautiful dancing lady," he called out to her.

And then she heard the servants' laughter mingling with that of Mauritius'. Was this any way for an emperor's daughter to behave?

Fighting tears of humiliation, she vowed she should never see the handsome soldier again. He simply held too much power over her, and she could not risk disgracing her family.

But she had to see him again, because at that moment she knew in her heart that she wanted to marry Mauritius—and she would not wait long to see it happen. She would find her mother and persuade her to speak to her father about the matter. Unless the young man decided he did not want her for his wife, or her father objected to her marrying a Christian, Valeria knew that Mauritius would soon be hers. She hugged herself and imagined for a moment what it would be like for him to hold her in his strong arms.

Valeria smiled. There were definitely advantages to being the emperor's daughter. Besides, there was nothing to be ashamed of; her feelings for Mauritius were pure.

She could feel his eyes following her as she ran into the palace to find her mother, but she no longer cared that he was watching. She spun around and waved at him one last time, and he threw his head back, curls tumbling, and laughed.

A fine soldier like Mauritius! Father was going to love him; she was sure of it. Then life truly would be perfect.

6

*H*er assessment of her father's acceptance of Mauritius was more than a bit premature and overly optimistic, but her mother was at least receptive to the idea. With Diocletian gone, Prisca invited Mauritius and his family to dine with them the next evening. After dinner, Valeria asked Mauritius and Nanu to take a moonlight stroll in the garden. Valeria's excitement waned when her mother insisted that Eugenia accompany them. Much to Valeria's disappointment, there was no handholding, but she considered even walking beside Mauritius a gift.

The next morning, after completing her studies, Valeria spent the afternoon in the arena with Nanu, watching Mauritius and Baraka, Nanu's fiancé, compete in the athletic events. Afterward, the young people had dinner with Valeria at the palace. Eugenia was not feeling well, so after dinner Prisca gave them permission to walk alone in the garden if the young people stayed together. Almost immediately Baraka pulled Nanu behind the hedges, away from Valeria and Mauritius.

"What are they doing?" Valeria asked.

"The same thing I am about to do to you," Mauritius replied, smiling as he bent to give Valeria a kiss, this time on the lips. He kissed her gently, and then stepped back.

"Please do not stop," Valeria begged, her head swimming with daydreams of utter delight. She pulled on his tunic to bring him back close to her, but he only pecked her forehead.

"No more kisses," he scolded her.

"But I want to kiss you over and over again."

Mauritius touched her face with his hand, sending sparks throughout her body. "I love you, but . . ."

"You love me!" Her heart skipped a beat. "I love you, too, Mauritius," she declared . . . and then she did the unthinkable. She stood on her tiptoes, threw her arms around his neck, and kissed him.

After a moment, he had to step back to extract his lips from hers. "We must wait until we are married to kiss with such passion, my love."

"Married? Are you proposing?"

His smile melted her heart. "Valeria, I knew from the moment I saw you in the garden that God had brought you to me for my wife. But you are the daughter of an emperor, and that complicates our relationship."

"My mother will take care of my father if that is what you are concerned about."

"But I have not even met your father, and I must ask his permission for your hand in marriage. This will likely be a long and arduous process."

"But Father will love you, just as I do," Valeria assured him.

"He may like me, but most royal marriages are arranged. Still, I am confident that God, who brought us together, will make a way for us."

Valeria smiled. "If God could part the Red Sea for the Israelites, He can surely sway my father's favor in your direction."

"I am sure of it," he agreed, kissing the top of her head. "I see you have learned your Bible lessons well from the monks. Come, let us ask my sister and Baraka to join us for a walk on the beach."

When Valeria told Prisca of Mauritius' proposal, she even offered to help with the wedding plans and trousseau, assuring Valeria that she would approach Diocletian about the situation when the time was right. But each time Valeria asked when that time would be, her mother reminded her that patience and prudence were necessary virtues. Valeria found it difficult to concentrate on these virtues when she longed for Mauritius' kisses.

Mauritius knew by now that Valeria had told her mother about them and enlisted her help in gaining Diocletian's approval. He often echoed Prisca in his warnings to Valeria, who had come to believe that patience was highly overrated and that action was preferable.

On the morning of Baraka and Nanu's wedding, Prisca granted Valeria permission to take part in the traditional Egyptian wedding customs.

"Why does Eugenia have to come along?" Valeria sulked, standing next to the divan where her mother lounged.

Prisca smiled. "You are the emperor's daughter, but even if you were not, I would still insist on a chaperone."

Valeria moaned. "Most Egyptian women are married by age twelve. If you were not so slow in asking father for permission for me to marry, Mauritius would be my husband by now, and I would not need a chaperone."

Prisca flashed Valeria a stern look.

"Forgive me, Mother." She crumpled to her knees and laid her head upon her mother's lap. "I cannot bear the thought that Mauritius will soon leave for Gaul. Even the hours we spend apart seem like decades, and it will be months before he returns."

Prisca soothed Valeria, stroking her hair. "When we are planning your wedding, time will pass quickly. It is a thrilling time in the life of a young woman."

"Without Mauritius there can be no excitement in my life," Valeria declared. "You are confident that Father will grant us permission to marry?"

Before Prisca could answer, Eugenia appeared at the door. "Mauritius has arrived early. Are you ready?"

Valeria's hands flew to her hair. "Oh, I must look a mess."

"You look lovely," Prisca assured her as she wiped a tear from her eye. "Where did all the years ago? It seems like yesterday you were a babe in my arms."

Valeria brushed her mother's cheek with a quick kiss before she stood and hurried out into the marble hallway with Eugenia. Her mother's moist eyes had not escaped her, but she was in too much of a hurry to see Mauritius to stop and console Prisca. Now pangs of guilt pricked at her heart. Valeria was devoted to her mother, and she understood it was difficult for her to let go of her only daughter. With her father away so often, the two women had become inseparable, but with thoughts of seeing Mauritius, she could not force herself to turn back.

"The palace is bustling this morning," Valeria noted as she and Eugenia made their way to the front hall where Mauritius waited.

"Have you forgotten that your mother insisted on hosting a wedding celebration for Nanu and Baraka?"

"I suppose I did." Valeria smiled. "I must confess that Mauritius has been my only thought."

"Did I hear my name?" Mauritius called out to her before he was in her sight.

Valeria ran toward the sound of his voice. When she saw him, she rushed into his outstretched arms. He quickly lifted her off the floor and twirled her around.

"We must hurry or we will miss the festivities," he warned.

It was a busy morning as friends and family moved Nanu's possessions into her husband's room at his parents' home. Valeria may have been the emperor's daughter, but she worked as hard as anyone. Once the job was complete, there was little time to freshen up before they were expected at the church.

The servants at the palace were waiting for Valeria when she arrived. Everyone pitched in to help her dress for the wedding. She had insisted on wearing a simple green linen tunic so as not to outshine the bride.

Since Mauritius had to accompany his family to the wedding, Valeria went to the church with her mother and Eugenia. The wedding was unlike any of the weddings the women had ever attended.

The Zaffa, the Egyptian wedding march, began. Traditional music filled the church, and belly dancers and performers with flaming swords preceded the bride and groom. Valeria joined in the lively celebration, clapping her hands wildly and swishing her hips. Mauritius smiled when he spotted her across the aisle and did some clapping and dancing of his own, which made Valeria laugh until she cried.

When Nanu came into their view, the women sighed. The happy bride was exquisite in a simple white linen dress overlaid with an intricately woven bead-net of blue and green faience beads; her ebony hair was encased in a matching bead-net with flowers crowning her head. Her jewelry was fashioned from lapis and gold.

The custom for the groom's family was to propose to the bride before the couple spoke their vows. Baraka's large family gathered around the couple and made their proposal to Nanu. She accepted with hugs and kisses.

Valeria's emotions ran rampant during the solemn wedding ceremony. Many of the young Egyptian women rushed to the altar before their soldiers sailed off to battle in Gaul. Yet the emperor's daughter would not be among them. Royalty had its benefits, but for now it seemed the negatives far outweighed them.

Her heart was stirred by the religious service, but to her surprise, it also burned with envy when Nanu and Baraka spoke their wedding vows. The words were poetic and meaningful. Instead of her friend Nanu, Valeria wished that she were the bride and Mauritius her groom. During a poignant part of the ceremony, Mauritius turned and smiled at her, and her body trembled with a deep longing for him to be her husband.

During the wedding celebration, which Prisca had insisted on hosting for the couple at the palace, Mauritius whispered into Valeria's ear to meet him afterward down by the beach. Then he went off into another room. The Egyptians had long observed the custom of men and women celebrating in separate rooms.

"Oh, how I hate this custom," Valeria complained to Eugenia, who tried to coax the lovesick young woman to enjoy herself. Though eager with anticipation at the thought of being alone with her future husband, Valeria could not relax during the wedding festivities. She became anxious and found herself wishing the party would end, but it continued on past midnight.

Mauritius motioned for her as the bridal couple finally sailed away in their felucca in the moonlight. Valeria watched him walk toward the beach, so she mingled with the crowd before taking a discreet path to the seashore. Each step, no matter how carefully placed, seemed to echo like a gong, outdone only by what she was certain was the loud pounding of her heart. When a pair of young lovers wandered down toward the seashore, Valeria hid in the bushes to keep from being seen.

But at last she was there, creeping onto the beach, her eyes darting back and forth in the darkness. She slid out of her sandals and wiggled her toes in the sand, which was still hot from the day's sun. It was a balmy night, and Valeria felt exhilarated as she walked along the edge of the row of sequoia trees where they had once kissed. But he was not there. Though she was glad the trees blocked the moonlight, lessening their chances of being seen, it also made it more difficult to locate Mauritius.

As it turned out, she did not have to find him. Before she realized he was standing in front of her, she felt his hand cover her mouth. He pulled her behind a sequoia tree. The sharp intake of her breath confirmed Mauritius' wisdom in preventing her from screaming in surprise. As her adrenaline ebbed and she came to terms with the fact that she was at last in the embrace of the man she loved, she relaxed, enjoying the feel of his muscular arms and broad chest, even as her cheek pressed against the Theban cross he always wore around his neck. Oh, if only her mother would send a messenger to her father soon so they could at least make their betrothal public knowledge before Mauritius was called away to the battle in Gaul!

"We must be quiet," Mauritius whispered. "If they find me here alone with you, I'll be drawn and quartered before sunrise."

Valeria nodded. Without Nanu and Baraka as chaperones, Prisca would have insisted Eugenia accompany them, but Valeria longed to be alone with Mauritius in hope of receiving his passionate kisses. Mauritius removed his hand from her mouth, but he made no move to release her from his embrace—which suited Valeria just fine. She was exactly where she wanted to be, whether her mother approved . . . or not.

Her eyes had adjusted to the darkness by then, and up close she could see her intended's face as he gazed down at her, his dark eyes reflecting the longing she felt in her heart. When his lips spread in a dazzling smile, she knew she would have collapsed if he had not been holding her up.

"You are as beautiful at night as in the daylight," Mauritius whispered. "The memory of you in my arms will carry me through the battle of Gaul—and any others I must endure to finally have you as my wife."

Valeria's heart leapt in alarm. "Memory?" she asked, reminding herself to keep her voice low, even as her pulse began to race once again. "Why would you say that? Surely it is not time for you to leave for Gaul already! It has been only a few weeks since—"

Mauritius placed his finger over her lips. "Shh," he cautioned. "Do not be upset, sweet Valeria. God willing, I will return to you—soon."

What was he trying to tell her? Then, with her gaze locked into his, she knew. He was leaving, going to Gaul. The time had come, and they had not even spoken with her father or announced their betrothal.

Her heart felt as if it had sunk into the sand at her feet. Hot tears pricked the back of her eyelids. How could she let him go when they had just found one another?

She opened her mouth to demand the answer, but Mauritius shook his head. "I know, my love. I have asked myself the same question. But there is nothing we can do about it. My calling is to serve God first, and then my country. If I am needed on the battlefield, I must go. Besides, my emperor orders me there. It is not an option, beloved."

Valeria knew he was right, and she loved him all the more for his loyalty and strength of character. But she felt no such constraints on her own emotions. She wanted to cry out, to scream in protest, to demand that her father rescind the order and allow Mauritius to stay behind—but as quickly as the emotion overwhelmed her, the responsibility of their respective positions negated it. Mauritius was right. He had to go . . . and she had to let him, without complaint or protest. But she could not do it without tears.

"When are you leaving?" she sobbed.

"We sail at dawn."

Droplets spilled over her eyelids and onto her cheeks. She whispered, "Oh, Mauritius, how can I send you away like this? If only I were your wife—"

Mauritius withdrew his finger from her lips and slid it to the side of her face, tracing her cheekbone as tears glistened in his own eyes. "Do you really think it would be any easier if we were married?" He shook his head. "Leaving for battle is difficult—for the one going and the one left behind. But sometimes it must be done. And this, my lovely Valeria, is one of those times."

He lowered his head and kissed her then, lightly and gently, but her lips felt as if they were on fire. How was it possible to love someone so much and still survive when separated?

When he pulled away, his face only inches from hers, she asked, "How long will you be gone?"

His jaws clenched before he answered. "Until God brings me back to you. That is all I can tell you, my love, for only He knows what tomorrow will bring."

Swallowing a sob, she cried softly, "Oh, Mauritius, how will I bear it?"

"The same way I will. We will pray each day—each moment, if need be—for the strength and courage to do what we must, and for God to grant that we be together again . . . in His time."

Once again, his lips touched hers, and Valeria thought she would die with the exquisite pain of loving him. And then he released her.

"I must go," he whispered. "The longer I stay, the more difficult it is to say goodbye. And the more we risk being caught. We have to do this the right way, Valeria. We must gain your father's permission to marry, and perhaps my service in Gaul will enable us to do that."

"What do you mean?"

"If I can be a hero in your father's eyes, he will surely grant me your hand in marriage."

"But you must give me your word that you will be careful and not take any unnecessary risks. I would surely die if I lost you," she cried.

Mauritius lifted his cross and kissed it. "I have God's protection."

"And my prayers."

As he pulled away, Valeria clung to him, her sobs escalating as she spoke. "Do not go," she pleaded. "Please, Mauritius! Not yet . . ."

But Mauritius pulled away and did not look back. When Valeria could see him no longer, she threw her hand over her mouth to prevent her cry from escaping. Once she had collected herself enough to speak, she whispered into the night, "God be with you, Mauritius, my love!"

❧

After many days at sea, the Theban Legion landed near Rome. They marched through northern Italy, across the St. Bernard pass, and encamped near the Swiss border to await their orders from their leader, Maximian, Diocletian's co-emperor of the Western Roman Empire. It was barely a week until they began heavy fighting against the Gauls.

While other Roman legions suffered major defeats at the hand of the Gallic barbarians, the Thebans marched, victorious in every battle. As a result, Captain Mauritius captured the attention of Emperor Diocletian. Usurped by Mauritius, General Galerius seethed with jealousy, not only for the young captain's exemplary military skills, but for Valeria's love as well. At their first encounter, the girl had ignited a passion in him unlike any he had ever known.

Galerius was a man who stopped at nothing to get what he wanted. Had Valeria not been the emperor's daughter, Galerius would have forced himself into her sleeping chambers and stolen her virginity when he was a guest at the palace in Elephantine. Fortunately for Valeria, his lust for power burned hotter than his sexual desires. The fact that she was Diocletian's daughter provided the ambitious Galerius with all the restraint he had needed to resist the nubile creature. He was confident that the plan he had devised for his future would soon get him everything he wanted, including Valeria.

❧

Valeria and Nanu were inseparable after the men they loved left for Gaul. They spent their days together studying with Prisca at the monastery or at parties with other Egyptian girls, who were also forced to entertain themselves in the absence of the men they loved. On the days they stayed at the palace, Valeria and Nanu, who were both adept at needlework, spent hours with the ladies sewing Valeria's trousseau. But Valeria's favorite pastime was taking long walks upon the beach, where she retraced the steps she had taken with Mauritius. Meandering along the beach, she relived every kiss he had given her and repeated every word he had whispered to her. On one such walk, Nanu took Valeria's hand in hers.

"My dear sister, I have exciting news for you today."

Valeria's heart leapt with expectation . "Are they coming home? Mauritius is on his way back to me!"

Nanu nodded. "I am sorry, but no. However my news should still make you smile."

"Then please, do tell! The suspense is killing me."

Nanu took her friend's hand and placed it upon her own stomach to reveal her surprise. "I have a baby growing inside of me."

Valeria squealed. "Nanu! This is wonderful news. You are going to be a mother, and I am going to be an aunt—once I marry your brother, of course. Oh, if only he would return to me so I could!"

Nanu touched her friend's face. "You will be our baby's aunt, regardless."

Valeria embraced her. "I am so happy for you. Have you sent a message to Baraka?"

"Yes, and he has written to me that he is overjoyed with the news of our child. He says our baby makes him fight even harder so he can return home to me as soon as possible."

"So you have known for some time." Valeria's face fell. "Why did you not tell me?"

"I wanted my husband to be the first to know that we were having a child."

Valeria nodded. "I understand. Creating a baby together is such an intimate, beautiful experience that a husband and wife should share the news before telling anyone else. But how can you be sure the news has reached Baraka?"

"Just this morning a ship brought letters from Europe, and I received a letter from him. You will probably have one from Mauritius too."

Valeria smiled as hope filled her heart. "Mauritius must know he will soon be an uncle. I am sure he is as happy as I am about the news. Will you forgive me that I must cut our walk short to see if a letter has arrived from Mauritius?"

"I will walk back with you, but you must slow down. Remember I have a baby inside of me now." She patted her tummy affectionately.

Valeria slowed her pace and put an arm around Nanu. "Tomorrow morning we shall begin to sew clothes for your baby too. It has been so long since Mauritius and Baraka left us that if we keep creating clothes for my trousseau I fear there will not be enough drawers and chests in the land to hold them!"

Nanu giggled, and then looked down at her expanding waistline and sighed. Her eyes glazed over with a faraway look as she spoke. "I hope Baraka will come home in time for our baby's arrival."

Valeria grabbed her hand. "Of course he will. But if he does not for any reason, I promise you, my friend, I will be at your side holding onto your hand tightly as you bring this child into the world."

The days of Nanu's pregnancy flew by. The women filled these long months with their usual activities, spending more time on their needlework than on their studies with the monks. As a result the baby's layette was so complete that there were more clothes than a child could possibly wear in a lifetime. Yet with the baby due any day now, the women had accepted the fact that perhaps the child's father would not be home in time to greet the newborn.

Weary, Nanu began to fret. "I cannot do this alone," she complained.

"I have told you that you will not be alone. Eugenia and I will both be there with you," Valeria promised, though she, too, worried that their men had not yet returned.

The next day Valeria appealed to Alara, the young monk, during their studies. "Why are our faithful prayers for the return of the men we love unanswered?"

Alara was sympathetic, but he assured the young women that while they may not understand God's reasons, they could trust His plan for their lives.

Valeria shrugged. "I suppose we have no choice. We will wait on the Lord."

Valeria was up later than usual that evening, reading a letter from Mauritius, until she finally drifted off to sleep, clutching the missive in her hand. Barely an hour later, Eugenia came into her room, softly calling to her.

"What is it?" Valeria asked, pulling herself from a deep sleep and alarmed that Eugenia was the bearer of bad news.

"Nanu sent a servant to tell you she is having her baby."

Remembering her promise, Valeria rubbed her eyes and jumped out of bed. "But it is the middle of the night," she complained

"A baby waits for no one, not even the emperor's daughter. Come, you must get dressed. Hurry!"

Eugenia and the servants helped Valeria dress. In less than an hour the women were at Nanu's side, watching her writhe in pain. Valeria tried to comfort her hysterical friend, but to no avail. Exhausted and concerned, she whispered to Eugenia, "Is Nanu going to die?"

Eugenia laughed. "She will be fine. This is typical of what happens when a woman has a baby."

Valeria turned up her nose with distaste, thinking that perhaps she never wanted to have a child of her own.

Several hours later the baby boy arrived, but Valeria was not there to welcome him. Moments after her arrival, she fainted and had to be carried to a nearby room, where she now slept soundly. Eugenia sat beside her and patted her back.

"Wake up, beautiful dreamer. There is someone you must meet."

Valeria pushed herself up with her elbows. "What happened?"

"You fainted."

Valeria's hand flew to her forehead. "I broke my promise to Nanu! Is she angry with me?"

"I doubt if Nanu is aware you were not there."

Disappointed that she had missed the big event, Valeria scampered into the other room with Eugenia close behind. She gasped when she saw Nanu propped up on pillows, cradling her child at her breast. It was such a beautiful sight that Valeria burst into tears, as her previous concerns about not wanting a baby herself evaporated. Not only did she want one baby, but many—and she and Mauritius would surely have them!

Valeria soon learned that having a baby meant little time for the mother to do anything other than care for the helpless little one. Nanu was either feeding, bathing, or playing with her son, Babafemi, whose name meant "loved by his father." Valeria struggled with her feelings of jealousy for Babafemi. Although she thought a baby was the grandest thing, she quickly became bored with watching the tiny creature. Nanu, however, never seemed to tire of it. She refused to leave Babafemi. Every breath he took was a miracle so far as Nanu was concerned, and she was not about to miss a single moment of her son's life.

"You will understand when you have a baby," Eugenia reassured Valeria. "You will feel different when it is your own child."

Valeria shook her head with doubt that she would ever allow herself to be a prisoner of a baby like her friend had become since Babafemi's arrival. Without Nanu as her constant companion, Valeria complained that the time crept by far more slowly and her longing for Mauritius to return had increased tenfold. Despite attempts by her mother and Eugenia to keep her occupied in lessons and her studies with the monks, plus endless social activities, Valeria moped around the palace so much the older women became worried about her.

As Babafemi grew older, Nanu came around more often, bringing her baby and her nurse with her, but not often enough as far as the emperor's daughter was concerned. Valeria sulked until Babafemi began to walk and talk, and then she took more of an interest in the boy and grew to love him. Babafemi adored his aunt as well.

Although her relationship with Nanu had changed, Valeria soon became comfortable with the idea of a threesome. Eugenia smiled as Valeria's conversation was filled with the news of Babafemi's latest accomplishments, even as Valeria's studies continued.

✒

General Galerius scowled as he surveyed the battlefield and observed the Theban Legion. He figured that if he could persuade Diocletian to give him Valeria's hand in marriage, he would divorce his wife, marry the emperor's daughter, and ultimately succeed Diocletian as emperor. His plan had been infallible until his rival Mauritius had threatened it by first winning Valeria's heart, and then Prisca's favor. Now the young captain had won Diocletian's respect on the battlefield, threatening Galerius' future.

But Galerius had searched for the Egyptian's Achilles heal, and he had found it—his allegiance to his God. Galerius kept a close watch on Mauritius when the Theban Legion arrived in Gaul. When Diocletian ordered that the entire Roman Army participate in pagan sacrifices so the gods would turn the battle in their favor, Mauritius, on behalf of the Theban Legion, had refused.

"You must punish them," Galerius had insisted to Diocletian and his co-emperor, Maximian, the ruler of the Western Roman Empire.

Diocletian was adamant in his response. "I will not risk losing the finest soldiers in the empire."

Sensing Galerius' anger, Emperor Maximian stepped between the two men and voiced his opinion. "We need the Theban Legion to win the battle with Gaul. It is impossible to trust the loyalties of the local soldiers. Many of them are fighting against family members, and when there is a choice, a man will choose his brother."

Galerius was furious but was forced to swallow his anger. After a few days, he reassured himself that this was only a minor setback. His ingenious plan would not only spoil Prisca's matchmaking attempts but Mauritius' military future as well. To seal his own fate, Galerius would stop at nothing—even if it meant destroying Mauritius. So Galerius watched and waited for the opportunity.

After weeks of a succession of crushing defeats on the battlefield, Diocletian summoned Galerius and his co-emperor,

Maximian, to dine with him in his tent one evening so they could collaborate on their future plans. The last to arrive, a weary Galerius, removed his helmet and handed it to a servant. He reclined on a divan, surrounded by servants, who brought platters of food and decanters of wine for the leaders.

"We have suffered heavy casualties and lost the majority of our battles," Galerius reported, dipping a hunk of bread into his porridge and stuffing it in his mouth.

"Not all of them are lost," Maximian added. "Have you heard of the Theban Legion's victories? They have yet to lose a battle."

Galerius frowned, folding his arms. "All I know about the Thebans is their constant refusal to participate in the sacrifices."

Diocletian nodded. "Their fierce allegiance to their God is rivaled only by their expertise as soldiers. Have you observed their military strategies?"

Galerius agreed, "Fine soldiers, indeed, but they have made the gods angry, and I am convinced this is why we are losing so many of our battles."

Diocletian rubbed his chin. "But the Thebans have been victorious in their confrontations. How do you explain this theory?"

Consumed with jealousy, Galerius preyed upon both Diocletian's and Maximian's pagan paranoia. "The Thebans may be winning their battles, but since they arrived, our overall losses have increased tenfold."

"So what are you saying?" a worried Diocletian asked as he set his wine goblet down on the table. "Their allegiance to their God is obviously working in their favor."

"Perhaps that is true. Their God may enable them to win the battles, but we are losing ours, because our gods are angry that the Thebans are refusing to join in the pagan sacrifices."

"Then we must demand their participation in our sacrificial rites," Maximian insisted, with Diocletian nodding in agreement.

But the following day their discussion was quickly forgotten when the course of the battles abruptly changed direction in favor of the Roman Army. Within weeks they had won the bloody confrontation, defeating the rebels of Burgundy.

The Theban Legion went about the business of resting and refreshing themselves from the arduous campaign, awaiting their discharge orders to return to Egypt. All the army was celebrating in the large city of Octodurum situated on the Rhone River, except Galerius, who brooded in his tent. Time was running out for his plan to succeed, and he feared that Mauritius might rob him of his future.

The Egyptian Christians went to hear the victory speeches and partake of the feasting and revelry—so much as their faith and good conscience would allow. When Baraka entered the inn, where his legion was dining on platters of suckling pigs, beef, mutton, cabbages, and an array of other foods, Mauritius saw him and waved him over to his table.

"My brother, how soon can we leave for Egypt?" Baraka asked.

"Ah, are you so anxious to see my sister that you cannot greet me properly?" Mauritius teased him and stood to his feet. He embraced Baraka and said, "Congratulations on a battle well fought and superbly won. How are you, dear brother?" He held Baraka's face in his hands and kissed him on both cheeks.

"Exhausted. The Barbarians were fierce competitors, but alas, I am grateful that God has protected us and blessed us with a mighty victory." Baraka grabbed the goblet in front of Mauritius and drank from it.

"I thought this was wine," he said, spitting it out. "What is this stuff?"

Mauritius roared with laughter. "Ale, a popular Gallic libation."

"It's terrible," Baraka groused. "Is there any wine around here?"

Mauritius lifted a bottle with one hand and a goblet with the other and filled it with wine. He handed it to his friend and then lifted his ale in a toast. "To our Almighty God, our country, and the women we love." The men's goblets clinked.

Baraka soon rubbed his hands together as the wine warmed his insides, and then asked again, "When are we leaving?"

"As soon as we receive our orders." Mauritius blushed. "I have also requested a private audience with Emperor Diocletian, and I am awaiting his reply. I hope he will see me before our orders are signed and we must depart. Pray for me, brother."

Baraka grinned and slapped him on the back. "Aye, you are a brave man."

Mauritius frowned. "You think the emperor will not grant it—his permission for me to marry Valeria?"

Baraka laughed. "Do not look so glum, my brother. I was only joking. Your leadership and the way you fought on that battlefield did not go unnoticed by anyone, including the emperor. He will be honored to have you for his son-in-law. No, he will not refuse you." He laughed again and winked. "A fine emperor you will make one day!"

"I have no desire to become emperor," he assured Baraka. "I wish only to marry his daughter. There could be no greater prize in my life than to receive Valeria's hand in marriage."

"I will pray for you," Baraka promised, and then hurried off to find his regiment for the feast.

When Mauritius rejoined his fellow officers, Candidus questioned him. "Is there any truth that Emperor Maximian has ordered the entire army to participate in the pagan rituals tomorrow?"

Mauritius shrugged. "We have not received any orders yet."

Another commander named Exupernis joined their conversation. "I have heard dreadful rumors that tomorrow's sacrifices will be human—Gallic Christians."

"Human sacrifices!" Mauritius winced. "Are you sure?"

Exupernis shook his head. "Let us hope we are not among them."

"For months the emperors have ignored our refusal to participate in the sacrifices," another officer commented. "So why would tomorrow be any different?"

"Tomorrow's rites honor the gods for our hard-won victory, but they are also tantamount to the divinity of the emperors," Mauritius noted. "With their egos involved, there is no way to predict what can happen."

"What will we do if the rumors are true?" Exupernis asked.

"We managed to escape the pagan rituals during the conflict," Candidus reminded them. "Now that we have conquered Gaul, perhaps it will not be an issue. By now they will be drunk on wine and ale. They may not care."

Mauritius took a deep breath before answering. "Yes, but there is one thing we should consider. As long as the war was ongoing, we were invaluable to the emperors. Now that it is over, they will be unconcerned whether they offend us or not."

"Then what is our strategy?" Exupernis asked as he stuffed another piece of mutton into his mouth. Before they could finish their conversation, an eerie silence settled over the establishment. All heads turned toward the entrance where three soldiers and a young man, who appeared to be a messenger, walked through the door. The men searched the dimly lit room until their eyes landed on Mauritius.

Exupernis took a deep breath and sighed. "The orders have arrived."

"Perhaps it is a message from Emperor Diocletian granting my request to speak with him," Mauritius hoped aloud. His companions around the table shrugged.

Pushing their way through the crowd, the soldiers stopped directly in front of the Theban leader and stood at attention, waiting. Mauritius nodded his permission for the messenger to speak.

With his eyes aimed slightly above the military leader's head, the messenger unrolled a papyrus scroll and read the orders. The proclamation was short but clear: Mauritius and his men were not to be spared the required attendance. The Theban Legion was required to attend the rituals.

Mauritius stiffened. He replied without hesitation, "With all due respect, please tell the emperor that the Theban Legion will not attend tomorrow's ceremonies. Our allegiance is to our God. And while we are loyal Roman soldiers, we will not be present at a ritual where our fallen Christian foes are sacrificed to the gods."

The messenger paled. "But . . ." He paused for a brief moment and then regained his composure. "But, sire, you killed many of your Christian brothers in battle. What is the difference?"

Mauritius shook his head. "Aye, it is one thing to kill a brother in war, but to condone their sacrifice to the pagan gods is unconscionable."

"But . . . what shall I . . . tell the emperor? Commander Mauritius, Emperors Diocletian and Maximian have ordered the whole army to participate in the pagan sacrifice to the gods tomorrow."

One of the other soldiers who stood beside the messenger suggested, "If you attend, there is a chance that the other officers will not force you to participate. But if you do not obey your orders and report to Octodurum, I fear it will be far worse for you."

An impatient soldier in the group spoke up. "Report with your troops to the base camp outside Octodurum tomorrow at dawn. Those are your orders. May we take our leave, sire?"

Mauritius granted their leave and then watched the soldiers disappear into the night.

"Perhaps we should go and take our chances," Candidus suggested.

Shaking his head, Mauritius replied, "We cannot witness such a travesty."

They returned in silence to their table, and within a few minutes the Thebans' victory celebration ended.

The men of the Theban Legion returned to their campsite and spent the night in prayer, hoping that tomorrow would not bring a confrontation with the emperors. Mauritius met with his co-leaders, Exupernis and Candidus, around the fire. They concluded their best plan was to withdraw the troops from Octodurum. In the middle of the night, the officers marched the men to Agaunum in southwestern Switzerland, where they made camp.

At daybreak, General Galerius waited and watched. With no sign of the Theban Legion, he was the first to report to the emperors that they were absent from the roll call. Diocletian, who felt a deep respect for the exceptional soldiers, sent orders to the Theban Legions' camp to return to Octodurum.

Captain Mauritius met the messengers himself. "The Theban Legions' first allegiance is to our God; our second is to Rome. Nothing will ever reverse our loyalties."

One of his own soldiers urged the captain, "Sire, please let us go, and perhaps they will ignore our nonparticipation in the rituals, like they have previously."

One of the other messengers, who was sympathetic to the Christians, suggested, "And if they do force you to make the sacrifices, why not make the sign of the cross like many of the other Christians do, to exonerate yourself?"

Mauritius would not compromise. "We have fought valiantly for Rome; let us worship our God as our reward, as you have the freedom to worship yours."

Exupernis, who stood at his side, asked the soldiers, "Is there any truth in the rumor that the emperors have offered human sacrifices?"

One of the soldiers hung his head. "Aye. The smell of burning flesh is horrific. Even Gallic children are being thrown in the fire."

Mauritius and Exupernis exchanged sorrowful looks, each making the sign of the cross.

"What shall we tell the emperors?" another of the soldiers asked.

"Tell them we will not come," Mauritius declared. "We cannot."

Throughout the day, Diocletian sent repeated orders, but with each order the Theban Legion respectfully declined.

Incited by both Galerius and his co-emperor, Maximian, Diocletian grew weary at each refusal, and it was not long until his agitation turned to rage. In a fit of anger, he exclaimed to Emperor Maximian, "We will decimate them! We will kill every tenth man."

After the sacrifices were completed, the trumpets blew, and Emperor Maximian ordered the entire Roman Army to descend upon Agaunum to fulfill the emperor's declaration of decimation.

Sometime later, as a soldier approached Mauritius to report that their lookout in the mountains had seen the Roman Army headed their way, Mauritius heard the clamor of approaching horses' hooves in the distance. He called his troops together to pray while they awaited the army.

Never in his wildest dreams had Mauritius imagined it would come to this. Just days ago he had been revered as a conquering hero with hopes of marrying the emperor's daughter. But when a band of messengers arrived ahead of the army at Aguanum, it was perfectly clear. Now in the distance the Roman soldiers were ready to carry out the orders—the Theban Legion would be decimated.

Mauritius turned his eyes on Candidus. As their gazes locked, Mauritius was sure he saw a glimmer of terror in the eyes of his otherwise fearless warrior-friend.

*

Inspired by the Holy Spirit, Mauritius climbed upon a boulder and announced the order as an opportunity to die for their Savior. By the time he spoke the words, "Every tenth man will be put to the sword," the legion cheered, eager to offer their lives to die for the One who had promised them eternal life. Mauritius encouraged his men in death as though they were going into battle. With songs of praise on their lips and a refusal to compromise their first allegiance to Christ, to a man the Theban Legion stood strong against the emperor's command to sacrifice to the Roman gods as an act of loyalty to the empire.

When the army arrived, the leaders wrote the names of every tenth soldier upon strips of papyrus and placed them in the caps of the centurions. The six hundred ultimately chosen to die stepped forward without protest. They laid down their weapons and offered their necks to the swords of the Roman soldiers. Mauritius and the others, who were spared, praised God and rejoiced with their comrades in their moment of death.

Mauritius pulled away from his soldiers and watched with great sadness as the bodies of his martyred comrades were dumped in the Rhone River, turning its waters red. Then he returned to the survivors and rejoiced with them. When they were issued another order to participate in the sacrifices, they refused, persisting in proclaiming their loyalty to Christ.

The Roman leaders conferred and ordered a second decimation. This time Mauritius flinched when he saw that Baraka was among the doomed men. *What shall I tell my sister?* he wondered, choking up as he imagined the scene.

With great courage, Baraka laid down his weapons and motioned to Mauritius. He slid a lapis ring emblazoned with a gold cross off his finger and pressed it into Mauritius' palm, closing his friend's fingers over it. "Please give this ring to your sister," his voice trembled. "Tell her when our son becomes a man to please give the ring to him to wear in memory of his father, who loved him very much."

Mauritius nodded, too emotional to speak, and curled his fingers around the ring in the palm of his hand.

Mauritius' voice broke as he swore to Baraka, "My brother, I vow to you before God that I will raise your son as if he were my own . . . if God allows me to survive."

"Please do not be sad for me. I consider martyrdom a great honor," Baraka assured him, smiling. He clutched his chest. "Only for those I leave behind is my heart heavy."

"We shall all be together again one day in heaven," Mauritius assured him. He then embraced the man whom he had loved since they were boys, kissing him on both cheeks. "God be with you, my friend."

"And also with you," Baraka replied, and then he stooped, lowering his head upon the stone.

As the soldier lifted his sword, Baraka sang praises to God until his blood poured over the rock, splattering upon the sandals of Mauritius, who turned away in sorrow.

Mauritius and the other soldiers remained strong, but upon hearing their songs and praises, Maximian recoiled with such fury that he demanded yet another decimation.

Afterwards, Mauritius conferred with his fellow officers, Candidus and Exupernis. Three decimations. It was time to stop the killings. They grieved for their fallen comrades, especially for their families, who were left behind.

"It is time to stop the butchery. Our surviving men are eager to return home to their families," Mauritius pointed out.

With prayerful consideration, the officers composed a royal remonstrance, dictating it to an aide, who wrote the words on a papyrus and addressed it to the emperor. It read:

Emperor, we are your soldiers but also the soldiers of the true God. We owe you military service and obedience, but we cannot renounce Him who is our Creator and Master, and also yours even though you reject Him. In all things which are not against His law, we most willingly obey you, as we have done hitherto. We readily oppose your enemies whoever they are, but we cannot stain our hands with the blood of innocent people (Christians). We have taken an oath to God before we took one to you, you cannot place any confidence in our second oath if we violate the other (the first). You commanded us to execute Christians, behold we are such. We confess God the Father the creator of all things and His Son Jesus Christ, God. We have seen our comrades slain with the sword, we

*do not weep for them but rather rejoice at their honour. Neither
this, nor any other provocation have tempted us to revolt. Behold,
we have arms in our hands, but we do not resist, because we would
rather die innocent than live by any sin.*

They sent the note to Maximian with great hopes that it
would soften the emperor's heart.

. Captain Mauritius stood in wait with his head high, surrounded by his fallen comrades. With his nostrils, he inhaled
the unmistakable stench of death. He watched as the Roman
soldiers disposed of the bodies. One of the Roman generals,
who could no longer bear the sight of the Rhone River running with blood throughout the land, had ordered a great pit
be dug for the bodies.

The sun blazed hot above the field where so many had
fallen—bravely and valiantly, just as they had lived their lives.
Sweat trickled down the cheek of Mauritius, but his hands
were occupied, furiously swatting flies, drawn by the bodies
not yet disposed of in the pit.

The Roman soldiers shuddered at the sickening sight of
the carnage. But not Mauritius and his Theban Legion, for
they knew that Christ's resurrection had swallowed up death,
and the souls of his friends did not occupy these decaying,
earthbound shells. Although many wept for their colleagues,
praises could be heard above the wailing.

When Emperor Maximian read the remonstrance, he raged
uncontrollably and sent a messenger to Diocletian of the plan
he had formulated in his anger.

Diocletian disputed it. "But these men are Roman soldiers.
They defeated the Gauls, almost single-handedly. Maximian is
surely mad if he wants to slaughter the entire Theban Legion."
Diocletian waved his hand, "Three decimations is sufficient
punishment."

Having his own agenda, Galerius dared to warn the emperor, "If we intervene in Maximian's orders, then the gods will severely punish us. I tremble at what could happen to us. Even after this great victory, we are likely to never see our homeland again."

His paranoia far outweighing his strength of character, Diocletian signaled the messenger. "Give me those orders." With a shaking hand, the emperor sealed the death warrant with his ring.

In the distance Mauritius saw the messenger returning. The scroll he carried in his pouch would surely contain their fate. Riding beside him was General Galerius himself.

Mauritius prayed that God would spare his men and him, grieving that he might have to leave his precious Valeria behind, praying that if it were true, she would take the news without too much pain. He was not leaving behind a child, a legacy, like many of his friends, but he was confident that his love for Valeria would live forever in her heart, until she took her last breath.

When the soldiers arrived, the reply on the papyrus was unrolled and read to the Theban Legion. To their surprise, their remonstrance had an opposite effect on the evil Maximian.

As the Roman soldier delivered the orders that every member of the Theban Legion would be slaughtered, Mauritius accepted his fate with sadness to leave this life, but with joy over entering into the next for an eternity. The troops who had come to execute the order then drew their swords. To their surprise there was no fight or refusal to die. The Thebans laid down their weapons and offered their necks to the soldiers.

The officers were the last to die. While he waited, Mauritius caught the eye of one of the soldiers, a Christian he knew and who had participated in the sacrifices by making the sign of the cross. He motioned for him to come near. When the young man knelt down beside him, there was an exchange and a Roman officer feared he had slipped the captain a weapon, but when the young man assured his superior he was only praying with Mauritius, he let them be.

Raising his voice in worship, Mauritius began to sing and was quickly joined by the remainder of his legion. Though he imagined the vain Diocletian and Maximian would think they mocked him as they sang while being slaughtered, he continued to worship as, one by one, voices around him were silenced. When at last he was the only man still standing, he committed himself into the hands of his Lord and prepared to join Him.

7

*I*n the middle of her French lessons, Valeria turned to Eugenia, who sat nearby, concentrating on her needlework.

"Listen," she said, tilting her head. "Do you hear the rustle of sails?"

"No, I do not. Now, please, get back to your studies."

"But I hear sails flapping in the breeze. Can it be? Have the soldiers returned?" Valeria placed her hand over her heart. "Are the boats bringing my true love back to me at last?"

Eugenia shot a helpless look to the exasperated tutor. "You must finish your studies, Valeria, and when you are done, you and I will go out on the terrace and watch for any ships coming into the Aswan port."

"If you insist," Valeria said. "But I have to stop soon because Nanu and Babafemi are expected at noon. Will you ask the servants to serve our lunch in the garden so we will have a front row seat?"

Eugenia blushed. "Oh, I forgot to mention that Nanu sent a messenger earlier. Babafemi has a stuffy nose, so they will not be coming to the palace today."

"Babafemi was sneezing yesterday, so I am not surprised. This means we are free to go to the harbor to watch the ships arrive."

Eugenia shook her head. "Get back to your lessons."

"But I already know how to speak French," Valeria protested, turning to the tutor for his acknowledgement. The man shrugged, doubtless wanting to avoid getting in the middle of the dispute between the two women.

"You have not yet mastered your pronunciation of the French letter 'r.' Besides, if you do not allow me to finish my needlework, you shall have no wedding trousseau," Eugenia warned her.

Determined to win this argument, Valeria replied, "Dozens of dressmakers in Milan are sewing as we speak. The dressmaker's assistant has sailed down from Milan and is with Mother in her chambers this very moment, enticing her with an array of silks and embroidered trims from the Orient. May I please have just one peek?" Not waiting for permission, she sprang to her feet and hurried to the window. With one hand on the curtain, Valeria begged, "Please, Eugenia!"

"Young love," Eugenia sighed in resignation. She dropped her needlework on a nearby table, then joined Valeria and pushed the curtains open wide.

"See, I told you they were here," Valeria rejoiced, pointing to the fleet of boats coming into the last port of the Nile, packed full with Roman soldiers.

Eugenia tucked her head inside the window and settled alongside Valeria, as they craned their necks in an attempt to see who was inside the feluccas.

Valeria was careful to squelch her own enthusiasm since she knew Eugenia would not see her husband, Octavius, until they returned to Nicomedia. But it was hard to contain her joy over the possibility of seeing Mauritius again in a matter of days—maybe even hours. She sighed. *And soon, we will be married.*

Valeria hopped down from the window and spun around, unable to contain her joy. "I must find Mother and tell her!"

"But—you promised," Eugenia called after her.

Valeria heard her lady-in-waiting catch up with her just outside her mother's door.

"Knock," Eugenia called out, but Valeria ignored her, bursting through the ornate doors that led to her mother's sitting room.

"Mother! Quick! Please, come and look out the window with me. The soldiers have returned. They—"

Valeria stopped when she noticed a trio of Roman soldiers seated across from her mother. "Oh, please forgive me for intruding. I was unaware you had guests. Of course, you must already know the soldiers have returned." Humbled only slightly, Valeria surmised the soldiers were here to tell the empress that the war had ended.

Valeria waited for her mother to reply, but an awkward silence filled the room. Prisca was facing the soldiers, so Valeria was unable to read her expression, and she worried that her rude behavior had angered her mother. "I shall depart and allow you to return to your business," Valeria apologized as she backed toward the door.

"Please stay," her mother called to her, her voice trembling as she spoke.

Frightened by her mother's uncertain tone, Valeria rushed to her side. She was even more alarmed when she saw that Prisca's eyes were red and swollen and her trusted servants were dithering around her. One lady-in-waiting was at the empress's side, holding smelling salts under Prisca's nose.

"What is wrong?" Valeria demanded. Suddenly she realized her mother's upset had to be related to her father. Valeria felt nauseated. The room began to spin, and her vision dimmed to gray. "Is Father . . . ?" Valeria could not bring herself to complete her thought.

Eugenia wrapped her arm around the young girl's waist to steady her.

"Your father . . . is alive," Prisca answered, choking back a sob. "But, alas, he is not well."

At the news that her father was alive, Valeria threw her arms around her mother in relief and then turned to the physicians. "Will my father recover?"

The eldest physician spoke for all three. "The emperor is in excellent health physically, so with the proper rest and treatment, we are hopeful that he will."

"Hopeful? But you cannot be certain?"

When no one answered, she pleaded, "Will someone please tell me what is wrong with my father?" Overwhelmed, she fell to her knees as if in supplication, her dress crumpling around her.

The older physician rubbed his chin, as though searching for the right words. Finally he cleared his throat and explained. "The battle in Gaul took an enormous toll on the emperor. With the adverse weather conditions and the large number of casualties, Diocletian collapsed under the strain of it all." He paused and then added, "I fear there is no kind or gentle way to tell you this, but . . . your father has gone mad."

Even as the words swirled around her, Valeria refused to accept them. It made no sense. The emperor's soldiers had been triumphant!

"My father is strong," she argued. "What do you mean, he has gone mad?"

Two of the doctors bowed their heads, but the older doctor looked Valeria in the eyes. "Your father has suffered a breakdown. In his present state, he is unable to function normally.

He cannot eat or sleep. He is suffering from extreme exhaustion and anxiety. Recently, he has exhibited signs of paranoia, all of which are of great concern to us."

"Where is my husband now?" Prisca interrupted.

"He is on his way back to the palace. His special guard and personal physician are secretly transporting him back to Nicomedia."

Prisca frowned. "Secretly?"

"Ladies, please understand the ramifications of the emperor's illness as it pertains to the empire. If word gets out about his condition, it will only invite further uprisings or betrayals, even from his own men who are greedy for power. Only Diocletian's most trusted advisors are privy to the details of his illness."

"We must leave for Nicomedia at once," Prisca announced. She pushed the smelling salts away from her nose and stood to her feet unassisted, then instructed the servants to prepare for the trip.

The palace at Elephantine was immediately aflutter with activity. Returning to her room, Valeria was saddened at the news of her father's condition and heartbroken by the resoluteness of her mother's tone, for she knew if Mauritius was on one of the ships returning today or if he did not arrive soon, she would surely have to leave before she had an opportunity to welcome him.

When a single tear trickled down Valeria's face, Eugenia dabbed it away with a linen handkerchief. "Do not worry, my child. Your father is the strongest man I know. He will surely recover from whatever ails him."

Valeria was too ashamed to admit to Eugenia that though her heart was full of concern for her father, it was the thought of leaving before seeing Mauritius that most plagued her.

When Eugenia left her alone, Valeria paced, begging God for mercy. When her anxiety peaked, she sent word to Eugenia to come at once.

"Why are you still dressed?" Eugenia asked. "You must get to bed and rest for the long journey ahead. Many of the servants will work through the night so we can sail by noon, perhaps earlier."

"But Mother said tomorrow night."

"Your mother is sick with worry over your father and wants to leave as soon as possible. We are leaving a part of the staff behind to complete the relocation, and they will come a few days later. Why did you call me here?"

"I want you to accompany me to Thebes."

Eugenia's eyes widened. "Do you have any idea what time it is? We cannot go to Thebes at this hour of the night. Besides, we have work to do."

"You cannot persuade me otherwise. I am going to Thebes to tell Nanu goodbye. I will not leave without asking her if she has had any word from Mauritius."

Eugenia hesitated and then sighed. Within minutes she was ready. As they walked down the beach, Eugenia scolded Valeria. "I have ordered a servant to prepare the felucca. I will make the trip with you, but I must warn you that your behavior is inappropriate. I plan to report this incident to your mother once we have returned, and you will be severely punished, young lady."

"Please walk faster," Valeria coaxed, ignoring Eugenia's admonition.

Eugenia shook her head but did not speak again until the servants helped them board the felucca. When they arrived in Thebes, Eugenia sent a servant ahead to Nanu's home to announce Valeria's arrival. A house servant answered and was soon joined by Nanu's father-in-law, complaining until he heard the visitor was the emperor's daughter. Within seconds, Nanu appeared at the door. When she spotted her friend standing behind Eugenia in the darkness, she cried, "Valeria, what are you doing here?"

Valeria embraced her friend, explaining between sobs, "I had to see you. Is there no news of Mauritius or Baraka and the others in the Theban Legion? Surely if they had returned today, Mauritius would have come to see me."

Nanu took her into her arms and comforted her. "Oh, dear one, please do not cry. You can be assured that you will be the first to know when Mauritius returns. I know my brother better than anyone, and he will come to see you even before he goes to my parents' home."

"Many Roman soldiers arrived in the harbor today. Why do you suppose the Thebans were not among them?"

"All of the soldiers cannot return at once. I am sure the Thebans will be home soon. Now please, go home, and I will visit you at the palace tomorrow."

"I will not be there," Valeria sobbed, explaining that they had to leave for Nicomedia immediately, though she did not reveal the reason. "I will not be here for Mauritius' homecoming."

"Then we will come to see you in Nicomedia. Please, do not worry. We shall all be together soon. Come, the boy is sleeping, but I will take you to his crib so you can kiss Babafemi goodbye."

After Valeria had kissed the sleeping boy and they returned to the hallway, she pulled Nanu aside. "Will you please give Mauritius this letter?" Valeria asked, placing it in Nanu's hands.

"Of course. And I am positive he will set sail for Nicomedia at once when he learns you are not here. Why, I will even pray that God will bring him back tomorrow before you leave. Goodbye, my sister."

As the women hugged goodbye, Valeria's heart warmed at the thought that Nanu already considered her a sister.

When the royals boarded the feluccas the next day, Mauritius was nowhere to be found, nor was any member of the legion. None of the soldiers who returned had any news of them. At Valeria's bidding, Eugenia sent one of the servants to the port early that morning to check the incoming military rosters for Mauritius' name, but neither he nor any member of the legion was recorded there. A Roman officer suggested that the legion, known for its organizational skills, had probably remained in Gaul to wrap up the campaign.

Valeria's disappointment was evident, but when she saw Alara at the dock, her face brightened. Yesterday Prisca had sent a messenger with a letter to Alara, explaining they had to leave. She also wrote that she regretted that they must discontinue their lessons and requested that the monks pray for Diocletian.

Alara joined them on board. "I could not leave without telling you ladies goodbye. Such a sad day for us," he commented.

"I am so distraught that I must leave before Mauritius returns," Valeria confessed to the young monk. "Will you pray for me?"

"Of course. Have I not always believed that the love you and Mauritius have for one another is truly ordained by God?"

Valeria thanked him for the reminder. "Will you come to our wedding?"

"I shall be honored to witness such a blessed occasion."

Tearfully, Valeria and Prisca thanked Alara and bid him farewell. As their felucca set sail up the Nile, they looked back one last time at the magical land where their lives had been changed forever. Then they turned their heads in the direction of home, not knowing what awaited them there.

✑❧

The return trip up the Nile was far different from their exhilarating arrival in Egypt. Valeria ignored the scenery and spent most of her time on the deck, watching for a passing ship that might be transporting Mauritius and the Theban Legion down the river. When they reached Alexandria and boarded their royal ship on the Mediterranean Sea, Valeria went below and did not return to the deck until the captain announced late one afternoon that they had spotted the coast of Italy in the distance.

When Valeria went on deck, Eugenia was already there, gazing at the coast. Valeria's faithful servant and friend had remained quiet throughout the trip, lost in her own thoughts.

"Have you had any news of your beloved Octavius?" Valeria asked. Before Eugenia could answer, Valeria's heart froze in terror. "Look, Eugenia! The gods are angry!"

The women stared, terrified, as the distant mountains regurgitated a great wave of fire. The glowering flames shot high into the heavens before tumbling back onto the earth. Gray and black smoke intertwined, swirling angrily into the sky, before darkness returned to the earth. Even through the veil of smoke, Valeria could see the sky was ablaze.

"We shall surely die," Valeria whimpered. "I shall never see Mauritius again!"

Eugenia gathered her mistress into her arms and prayed, calling on the name of Jesus. As she did so, the captain hurried by, stopping briefly to reassure them.

"Ladies, there is nothing to fear. It is Mount Vesuvius, the volcanic mountain behind the island of Pompeii."

"But the gods have wiped the constellations from the heavens. Surely it is the end of the world," Valeria cried.

"The moon and stars are still there," the captain explained. "The sky only appears dark because it is covered in smoke. These eruptions occur periodically, but they usually stop after a short time. Besides, we are a safe distance from the hot lava."

After the captain had excused himself, Eugenia took her seat and motioned for Valeria to join her. Still trembling, Valeria was flabbergasted that Eugenia appeared so calm. As though she could read her mind, Eugenia said, "The gods are not angry, my lady." She paused and then added, "There are no 'gods,' remember? Only the one Almighty God."

"I am sorry. I know that with all my heart, but old habits are hard to dismiss. Still, I cannot help but believe this eruption is a bad omen," Valeria worried.

"Then you must trust God that His will be done and forget about the pagan omens."

Valeria was not allowed to see her father when they returned home. Since Prisca rarely left Diocletian's side, Valeria scarcely saw her mother either. Worse yet, there was still no word of Mauritius. Eugenia tried to distract Valeria with wedding plans, but to no avail. Her anxiety remained at a high level until her mother appeared in her room one morning.

"Good morning, darling."

Valeria, who was already awake, sat up in bed. "What is it? Do you have good news about Father, or . . . Mauritius?"

Prisca, who looked exhausted, collapsed into a chair beside the bed. "I will not lie to you. The past few weeks have been challenging, but your father's condition is improved this morning."

"What is wrong with him, Mother? I do not understand."

"He is haunted by horrific nightmares when he sleeps and menacing visions while he is awake. I believe his condition is due to exhaustion. I am faithful to pray for him as he sleeps."

"When can I see him?"

"That is why I am here. After his night of good sleep, your father feels well enough to dine in the great hall tonight, and he wants you to join us there for dinner."

Valeria felt a spark of hope. "Have you spoken to him about Mauritius? Did he tell you if Mauritius asked for my hand in marriage?"

"Oh, no, darling! And I trust you will not mention Mauritius either, or ask any questions about the battle in Gaul. Remember, your father is not well. Let him talk. When he is better, which I am sure he will be soon, we will proceed with the designing of the grandest wedding gown ever seen in the empire." Prisca touched her daughter's face. "You will look more radiant than any bride who ever lived, I assure you."

The mention of her wedding dress lifted Valeria's spirits, if only slightly. "Oh, I pray we find Father well enough to tell us about Mauritius. I have not received a letter or a message from him, and no one seems to have heard of him. You do not think that Mauritius has forgotten about me, do you?"

Prisca put her arm around her daughter and kissed the top of her head. "Never. Do not worry about a single detail, dear one. Throughout the war, I have been praying for great favor for Mauritius and his men. I am sure the good captain's leadership and military expertise caught your father's skilled eye."

"Oh, Mother," Valeria cried, suddenly alarmed, "you are not worried that Father will not permit the marriage, are you?"

A look of surprise flashed in Prisca's eyes. "Where is your trust, Valeria?"

Valeria blushed. "But Father may be concerned that Mauritius is a Christian. You know how devout Father is with his own pagan worship."

"Consider that most of his servants are Christians. Your father admires their integrity and the excellence of their work. Above all, I can assure you that he only wants your happiness, as do I."

"Have you told Father of our conversion?"

Prisca was the one to blush this time. "It was something so special I could not find the words to put on paper. I preferred to tell him face-to-face."

"And have you?"

"No, but my decision to wait was motivated by wisdom, not fear."

"Then you are confident that Father will grant permission for me to marry Mauritius?"

"Would I be planning your wedding if I were not?"

✍♥

Later that evening, the flames crackled in the large fireplace as the royal family gathered together to celebrate Diocletian's homecoming. It was the first time the emperor had dressed and left his room since returning from battle. Valeria's hand flew to her mouth to muffle her gasp at his appearance. His purple robe hung on his frame like the drooping feathers of a dying eagle. The emperor appeared as prideful as ever with his heavy diamond diadem atop his wobbly head. In his shaky right hand he carried a large scepter, which almost landed on Valeria's head when she bowed down to kiss the jeweled hem of his robe. When a servant stepped forward to help Valeria to her feet, he left her hand dangling in midair, reaching instead for the weak-kneed emperor's arm to keep him from toppling over onto his daughter. Now that she had a closer look at her father, Valeria became even more alarmed. He looked haggard, his hair whiter, and his face lined.

Diocletian shuffled across the floor to his divan with the help of a trusted servant. Valeria wiped away a tear, recalling how her father had loved to prance about in his pointy silk and diamond slippers. The shoes now flopped about his shrinking feet. But it was the now-absent twinkle in his eyes that most alarmed her.

Once the servant had helped Diocletian recline on his divan, Valeria sat beside him and exclaimed, "Father, it is wonderful to see you."

Diocletian was silent but placed his hand on her head and stroked her hair. After a few minutes, Prisca motioned for Valeria to come sit with her. When Valeria left his side, the emperor ordered a servant to help him to his feet. He hobbled over to the great hearth, facing the warmth of the fire. It was obvious he was trying to stand straight and erect, his hands clasped behind his back as if in military readiness, but he swayed back and forth.

"We need to discuss Captain Mauritius," he said suddenly, his back still toward them.

"So you met him," Valeria squealed, as she jumped from the divan and joined her father by the fire.

"One of the finest and bravest soldiers I have had under my command," Diocletian admitted.

Valeria beamed, smiling in her mother's direction. She felt as though her heart would burst with happiness.

"He sent me a message requesting an audience with me," Diocletian began, "just before the victory celebration."

Valeria's heart leapt at the announcement, and then fell again when she recognized her father's cold tone of voice and the realization that her father did not say whether he had granted Mauritius' request. Suddenly frightened, she returned to sit beside her mother, who took her hand. Valeria found the courage to ask, "I take it you are concerned that Mauritius is a Christian."

"I have no problem with the Christians as long as they obey my orders."

"Then you do not object if Mauritius and I marry? He is obedient to his faith and dedicated to Rome. He is the most ethical, honest, and moral man you will ever meet."

Diocletian turned. "Can a man serve two masters?" he demanded.

Valeria frowned. "The Scripture says—"

"Forget the Scripture." Diocletian waved his hand as though he were erasing her words. "What do you suppose Mauritius would do if his two allegiances conflicted?"

Valeria spoke with conviction. "His first allegiance is to God, but his second is to Rome."

"And to remain faithful to his God, would he disobey an order from Rome?"

"What are you saying, Father? Did Mauritius' service displease you?"

"Displease me?" The emperor's voice rose to a near roar as he repeated himself, shocking Valeria at the strength he exhibited. "Displease me?"

He scowled, and Prisca squeezed Valeria's hand. Even the servants cowered as Diocletian yelled, "Your Mauritius humiliated Emperor Maximian, and he humiliated me."

"But how?"

"By refusing to obey our orders."

Bravely, Valeria spoke up. "When you have more time to get to know Mauritius, you will understand and respect the loyalty he has to his God. I love him with all my heart, Father. Will you please give him a second chance?"

The emperor grew quiet and less agitated. He hung his head and mumbled, his brief show of strength seemingly dissipated. "Three chances we gave Mauritius. Three times he refused to obey our orders. We did not make the choice; Mauritius made it for us."

Valeria was confused. "His decision to marry me? What are you saying, Father?" Valeria wriggled loose from her mother's clasp and stood to her feet. "Did he choose not to marry me because you told him he would have to deny his God for your permission?"

"This man you love . . . Mauritius. No, he did not choose to marry you; he chose to die for his God."

Valeria's vision dimmed, and her ears buzzed as her father continued. "They have been killed . . . all of them. The entire legion, not in battle, but in rebellion against the emperor and the empire."

The noise in her head was deafening now, as blackness closed in. If her father was still speaking, she could no longer hear him. The only words that swirled in her mind as she felt herself go limp were "killed . . . all of them." Did "all" include their leader, her Mauritius? For if it did, her life was over as well.

✍

Day blurred into night, and Valeria neither knew nor cared how much time had passed since she first learned of her beloved's death. That the entire legion, including its valiant captain, had been killed by order of Valeria's own father was more than she could absorb, and so she pushed that detail to the back of her mind. It was all she could do to make herself inhale and exhale, just knowing she would never again, this side of eternity, see the love of her life. To accept that her father had been instrumental in the death of Mauritius would drive her insane. Even the warnings of the Coptic monks that suicide was a sin would not deter her from taking her own life.

And yet, though she had locked herself away in the darkness of her room, refusing to eat or speak to anyone or even to allow the drapes to be opened to let in the sunshine, she remembered her father coming in to tell her she must forget her feelings for the man who refused to serve and obey his emperors by sacrificing to the Roman gods.

Then, after a few days, Diocletian came to her again and stood with her mother beside her bed to tell her news so horrible that she prayed for death. "I have picked a more suitable husband for you," he announced, "a man who is revered throughout the empire. As soon as he rids himself of his present wife, you will marry him. You are old enough to wed, and this match will be of great benefit to us all."

Valeria could not believe the words she was hearing. She tried to read her mother's reaction, but Prisca stood stoically, refusing to look her daughter in the eye. It was obvious she too had been crying . . . whether for the loss of the son-in-law she had hoped would be hers, or because another would take his place. Valeria had no way of knowing, but her heart squeezed with fear and anger simultaneously.

"You cannot force me to marry anyone," she cried. "Do you not understand, Father? The man I love is dead—murdered!" She clenched her teeth and glared. "I refuse to marry—ever!"

"You will marry General Galerius, and he will become my adopted son."

An image of the lecherous man flashed through her mind, and she recoiled with horror. "I would rather die!"

His face reddening with anger, Diocletian raised his hand. Surely he would not—

Even with Prisca struggling to stop the blow, her father's hand landed upon Valeria's face, slapping her with such intensity that she screamed in pain. Her horror was surpassed only by the utter disbelief she saw in her mother's eyes. Even for days afterward, her mother burst into tears every time she saw her daughter, who wore the imprint of her father's hand upon her face.

But worse than the physical reminder of the emperor's proclamation was Valeria's knowledge that the man she had been promised to marry was Galerius. How could her own father, even in a mentally unstable condition, consign her to such a fate? Death—even hell itself—would be preferable to living with such an ogre. It had to be her father's illness that had spurred such a decision. Surely he would come to his senses and rescind his order!

When Valeria heard the light rap on her door, she ignored it. It was either Eugenia, trying again to convince her to eat something, or Prisca, coming once more to attempt to comfort her and talk her out of her depressed state. Why answer the knock when Valeria knew neither attempt would be successful?

Then the heavy door opened, its slight creak announcing the entrance of a visitor. Valeria refused to open her eyes to identify her uninvited guest. The light steps were familiar, however, and Valeria quickly recognized her mother's presence even before Prisca opened the drapes and then sat down on the edge of the bed and took Valeria's hand in her own.

Her mother's touch was gentle but firm as were the words she spoke. "This behavior must stop," she said, and Valeria knew Prisca was serious. Not that it mattered; Valeria had no intention of stopping anything. She would lie there in bed, neither eating nor drinking nor speaking to anyone until she starved herself to death or died of thirst, whichever came first. That was not actively committing suicide, was it? It was simply dying of a broken heart.

"Valeria, you must look at me."

Valeria was torn between respect for her mother and the grief that had become such a part of her. Even opening her eyes was more effort than she wished to exert, but when Prisca repeated her command, Valeria finally conceded.

She lifted her lids only enough to be obedient and peeked at her mother. She was astonished at the dark circles under Prisca's eyes. It had not even occurred to Valeria that her mother was also a victim of Diocletian's madness.

"Are you . . . all right?" Valeria managed to croak, her voice as unfamiliar to her as the light of day she had tried so hard to avoid.

Prisca's eyes filled with tears. "How can I be all right when my husband has lost his mind and my only child has withdrawn from the living to mourn the dead?" Her tears spilled over onto her cheeks. "Oh, my dear Valeria, you must not allow yourself to continue in this devastating depression. I cannot bear it!"

"I am . . . sorry, Mother." Valeria swallowed, her tongue thick and her throat parched, each word an effort. "I did not mean to . . . hurt you."

Prisca stroked Valeria's face. "Do you not understand, dear one, that you are my heart? When you hurt, so do I. If your father were in his right mind, he would be hurting too."

When Valeria stiffened at the mention of her father, Prisca withdrew her hand and held up a finger. "Stop. I know you need someone to blame for what has happened, and I do not deny the horror of it. But do not turn on your father. He loves you more than you can know, and it is his anguish over this situation that has driven him mad."

"He caused it," Valeria said, still straining to speak. "He and his cohorts ordered Mauritius murdered. How can I not despise him? I never want to see him again!" Valeria felt warm tears trickling down her cheeks onto her neck and hair. "How can I ever forgive Father for what he has done? My life is over, and my father is to blame. As for marrying that horrible Galerius, the subject is not open for discussion, so do not even think about broaching it. I love you, Mother, and I am sorry my grief has caused you so much pain. But not even for you will I consider such an unthinkable suggestion."

Valeria felt exhausted, having delivered in moments more words than she had spoken in days, but at least her mother knew where she stood. And she had no intention of acquiescing.

Slowly Prisca released her daughter's hand and rose from the bed. "I understand your feelings, my dear," she said, her voice still soft but more composed now. "But you are wrong about one thing. Your father's announcement that you are to marry General Galerius is not a suggestion. It is a command, one that neither you nor I can disobey."

With that, Prisca turned and walked from the room, leaving Valeria in tears to consider the words that had sealed her fate.

8

*E*ugenia poked her head through the doorway of Valeria's bedroom. "Good morning," she chirped and pushed back the heavy damask draperies that surrounded the ornate bed.

Valeria again wondered if Eugenia had a sixth sense about her. Only seconds before, Valeria had awakened from a dream of Mauritius that even now continued to hold her captive with its sweet memories. She sat up, her disheveled hair about her shoulders, realizing that the man in her dream was gone. Eugenia's singsong greeting cheered her still-aching heart.

"I stopped by earlier but you were asleep," Eugenia noted. "Thanks be to God that you are resting again, child. I have gone to church every day to pray for you."

Valeria welcomed a distraction from her sadness. "Thank you for your prayers." She swung her feet off the bed and sunk her toes into the thick Persian rug atop the sparkling pink marble floor, outlined with pure gold.

Eugenia turned and clapped her hands, and a cadre of servants appeared. It had been days since Valeria had allowed them to open the gold damask curtains. Today she nodded in approval because she wanted to see the ornamental gardens outside her window. Some of the women carried armfuls of bouquets from the garden to arrange in the vases. Valeria's senses were piqued as the sweet fragrances of roses, narcissus, lilies, and iris wafted throughout the rooms.

The servers from the kitchen were a welcome sight as they appeared with her breakfast. Valeria's appetite had returned with a vengeance, and this morning she was so famished that she plucked a bunch of grapes that cascaded off a servant's mosaic tray piled high with sumptuous apples, pomegranates, and quinces. At the table, Valeria ate bread, cheese, and eggs. She nodded her thanks to the young woman, who refilled her jeweled goblet with grape juice.

"You are overdue for a bath," Eugenia announced. She knelt beside the bed and slid jeweled pink silk slippers onto Valeria's feet. She usually stood by while the other servants attended to these tasks, but since the recent events in her young mistress's life, Eugenia had personally attended to some of Valeria's more immediate needs. Valeria had noticed those small demonstrations of love but had been too sad to acknowledge them.

"I have not seen you smile in weeks." Eugenia commented.

"I'm smiling because last night I dreamed of Mauritius."

"You must stop torturing yourself and accept that Mauritius has died."

Unflinching, Valeria ignored Eugenia's warning. "I was hoping my present circumstances were just dreams and Mauritius was still alive, but then I was awakened by the starlings singing outside my window, reminding me I was back in Nicomedia and that my tragic fate was real."

"Try not to be so dramatic, please."

Valeria sighed. "Would it shock you if I told you that when I went to bed last night, I prayed I would die in my sleep?"

"The way you have been acting lately, nothing would surprise me."

Valeria sighed. "And why not? Lately it seems that God has turned a deaf ear to my prayers. He no longer cares about me."

"You must not talk like that, dear one, but trust in the Lord with all your heart." Eugenia made the sign of the cross over her own heart and sat down on the bed beside Valeria. "He will make your paths straight. Everything will turn out well, you will see."

"I do not believe you. What I learned in Egypt about the Lord . . . it is all rubbish." Hot tears squeezed their way out of Valeria's eyes, as she asked, "How could a loving God take Mauritius away from me?"

Eugenia snatched a linen handkerchief from her pocket and dabbed at her mistress's tears, and then pushed an unruly strand of gold-streaked auburn hair from Valeria's face, gently tucking it behind her ear. "There, there, my darling girl, do not cry. Have you forgotten that we set sail tomorrow to complete your wedding trousseau?"

If Eugenia's reminder was meant to cheer Valeria, it failed miserably, instead only increasing her anxiety.

Eugenia tried again. "In Istanbul there will be great trunks of jewels for you to choose from for your wedding crown, and cloths spun of golden thread in Milan for you to buy for your dressmakers to fashion your gowns." Eugenia chatted endlessly. It was obvious she was trying to pique her young mistress's interest, as Valeria had once adored beautiful things. "And I have a surprise for you too! Your mother has mentioned that we may travel to France so we can personally purchase the galloon from the godly hands that embroider it."

Valeria shrugged, as curiosity overtook her tears. "And what, pray tell, is galloon?"

"Threads made from strands of gold stitched into lace for trims and borders. It surrounds the hem or the sleeves of some of your finest gowns."

"Ah, I know what you mean. It is ornate, yet delicate. But what makes French galloon so special that Mother wants to travel to France?"

"This galloon is hand-stitched by a group of young women in an old castle, who have dedicated their lives to God," Eugenia explained. "They live together in a community in the valley of Loire in France that was founded by Mary Magdalene, and they call themselves her disciples, spending their time in prayer and in God's Word."

"Are they the female equivalent to the monks?"

Eugenia nodded. "These women make the galloon for the church vestments, altar cloths, and also for fine clothing. They use the money they make to support themselves and the poor."

"How does Mother know about them?"

"The Empress is their best customer. Her dressmaker in Milan buys galloon and lace from the women for your mother's gowns. The dressmaker has made a special request to them to tat the lace for the wedding gown of the Christian daughter of the emperor. Last week they sent word to your mother that they are praying for your marriage, so she wants to visit them and select the trims herself—and to thank them, of course."

She lowered her voice. "And wait until you hear what the ladies are sewing, especially for you. They are secretly stitching crosses into the design of the galloon." Eugenia laughed. "Your pagan husband-to-be will not even know the crosses are there . . . right in your wedding garments."

Valeria's sarcasm was evident in her reply. "That *is* a blessing because if Galerius sees the crosses at the wedding he will explode and rip my clothes right off me, and then I will stand naked in front of God and everyone."

"That is not funny, Valeria."

Valeria refused to stop her foolishness. "Oh, what a sight that will be! Everyone in the empire will gossip about me: 'The naked girl was stripped of her clothes with only her auburn hair to cover herself.' We must not cut my hair before the wedding, dear Eugenia, because it is all I will have to hide behind on my wedding day after my bridegroom tears my clothes from me."

"Stop that ridiculous chatter. It is beneath you."

"Even if he does not rip off my clothes at the ceremony, you and I both know he will tear them to shreds in the bedchamber." Valeria was serious now.

Eugenia shook her head. "Ah, Valeria, the general is a mere man, not a monster."

"I am not at all sure about that, but if I had to place a wager, I would put my gold on 'monster.' Besides, I have heard that all men are brutes in the bedroom."

Eugenia sighed. "Where do you get these outlandish notions?"

"I have heard the whispers and giggles of the servant girls."

"It is not true—at least, not of all men."

"But everyone knows that Galerius is a monster—even you."

Although Eugenia did not respond, Valeria could see the apprehension in her friend's eyes. Valeria was well acquainted with fear, as she battled with it daily. That she would have to endure a loveless marriage to the horrible pagan terrified her.

"If the uprisings in the empire continue, General Galerius should be away at battle most of the time," Eugenia said. "Now, stand up, please." She tied the cord around Valeria's robe at her waist, and then touched her young mistress's face. "You will be fine. Your mother and I and other women in the court have all faced our wedding nights with some trepidation, but after a few days have passed, you may enjoy your marriage bed."

With tears once again brimming in her eyes, Valeria held up her hand. "Please, stop, Eugenia. I know you mean well, but nothing you say can help me get through this wedding or my honeymoon."

Eugenia's face softened. "You may not trust what I say, but you must listen to me. Consider that your father is the most dreaded and fierce warrior in the empire. Yet every time he leaves for battle, your mother weeps at his departure. For weeks afterwards she is morose, and when she hears he is on his way home, her heart overflows with joy."

Valeria knew it was true. She thought of how her mother moped around the palace when her father was away. But once a messenger arrived with news of his return, Prisca came alive. Her singing and laughter again filled the halls of the palace. "I know this is true of my mother, but what does that have to do with me?"

"Consider if the bedchamber is such a terrible place, would your mother not rejoice when your father was away and tremble with fear when she heard of his return?"

Valeria cocked her head at Eugenia. "My father may be a fierce warrior and a stern emperor, but he has a loving and kind heart toward Mother—as I once thought he did toward me."

"And he still does, my dear, whether you choose to believe it or not." Eugenia raised an eyebrow. "Might the same be true of Galerius?"

"Sometimes you have such a short memory, Eugenia. Do you recall the lascivious stares he sent my way when he and his family were our guests at the palace in Egypt?"

It was obvious Eugenia was holding her tongue, so Valeria continued, "Do not deny you saw him. I overheard you complain to Mother about his inappropriate behavior. You told her the evil man was stalking me like a hungry lion."

Eugenia blushed as she twisted her handkerchief in her hands.

"Now do you understand why I feel as I do?" Valeria pressed.

"Your mother and I will pray. We will help you," Eugenia promised as she wrapped her arm around Valeria's shoulders.

"But how can either of you help me? What will I do when you are far away, and I am alone with that awful man?" Valeria's tears began afresh. "When Galerius comes to me on my wedding night, there will be no one to help me behind the locked doors of our honeymoon chamber."

Eugenia tightened her embrace of the princess. "God will be with you behind those doors. You remember the words from the Scriptures that you learned in Egypt . . . 'I can do all things in Jesus Christ who strengthens me.'"

"If there really is a God, perhaps He will be with me too. . . ."

Eugenia was adamant, releasing Valeria and then placing her hand over her own heart as she spoke. "Not perhaps, but truly."

"One thing is for certain. I will be alone with my memories of my beloved Mauritius."

Eugenia opened her mouth as if to scold Valeria, and then stopped, obviously deciding to change the subject. "It is time for your bath," she said gently.

Three servants drew the rose-scented water for her bath, while still others carried the freshly pressed lavender stola and a bright pink pala of wool that Valeria would wear that day.

As they stood at the marble tub, Valeria asked, "And what about the poor wife of Galerius, tossed away like garbage? Galerius even stole her daughter from her." She sighed. "I envy you, Eugenia . . . married to a man you love so deeply."

Eugenia paused. "Not always."

Valeria blinked in surprise. "But you were mad with love for Octavius when you first met him."

"Yes, I was," she answered, "and I am still as much in love with my husband today. But it is a different kind of love."

Valeria was curious. "What do you mean?"

"It is impossible to explain, but our love is deeper now. I have a much stronger respect for my husband too."

"But no passion?"

"Oh, yes. The passion may not burn continuously as it did in the beginning . . . and thank heavens it does not because there would be nothing left of either of us if it did." Eugenia laughed. "Octavius and I have our moments of passion that are far more intense than when our love was new. I am confident you will discover those moments of passion one day."

"Undoubtedly I would have experienced passion with Mauritius, but with Galerius . . . never." Valeria shook her head and closed the subject, as the servants in the bath disrobed her and shielded her body from view with a towel. She pushed aside the pink and white lotuses that floated upon the water with her toe and stepped into the fragrant marble tub of sweet-smelling oils and potions of frankincense, orange, and cinnamon. With the help of two servant girls, she lowered herself into the soft, luxurious warmth of the scented water, submerging her shoulders until the water lapped about her throat. Closing her eyes, she inhaled the aroma of the essences and felt herself relax, despite the tension that gripped her neck and shoulders and simmered in her gut. She knew Eugenia was right—at least so far as Valeria's need to once and for all bury her hopes and dreams for a love-filled marriage to Mauritius. But never would she accept her servant's reassurances that Valeria might one day come to feel love or passion for the vile man she was being forced to marry.

How could Father even consider consigning me to such a fate? she fumed, letting her arms drift weightless at her sides. *First he listens to Galerius, and then he issues an order that he knows will make a martyr of my beloved. Father then informs me I must marry the despicable creature that helped initiate Mauritius' death. Mentally ill or not, how could my father allow such a thing to happen? Does my happiness mean nothing to him?*

She sighed, as reality invaded her self-righteous musings. She had lived as royalty long enough to know that though her father might indeed care about her and wish her great happiness, political expediency trumped familial love and good wishes. It was politically expedient that she marry Galerius, despite the fact that she could not bear the sight of him, and therefore she had no choice.

Unless—

"Good morning, darling!"

Valeria gazed up at her mother, who stood over her, smiling, as if she expected Valeria to share her enthusiasm for the coming day. And yet, despite Prisca's cheery demeanor and her obvious efforts to hide the shadows under her eyes, Valeria beheld the sadness behind her mother's cheerfulness.

Forcing the corners of her lips upward, Valeria said, "Good morning, Mother. You look lovely, as always."

"And you look more relaxed than I have seen you in days," Prisca responded. "Though I was hoping you would be dressed and through with your morning devotions so we could take a walk together."

This time Valeria's smile was not forced. "I do believe you must have been born walking. Do you never tire of strolling the grounds? As beautiful as they are, you should know every bit of shrubbery and blade of grass by memory. But then, I suppose that is one of the things that keeps you so young and beautiful."

Prisca chuckled. Though Valeria suspected her mother's laugh was forced, it still comforted her. Where her father was sometimes gruff and reserved, Prisca was loving and positive. Even today in her grief, the empress managed to inspire her.

If ever there was a mismatch, Valeria decided, it was between her parents. And yet the great Emperor Diocletian and his wife were deeply in love and devoted to one another, despite the conflict that had arisen since Prisca had become a dedicated Christian and Diocletian remained a devout pagan worshiper of the Roman gods.

As Prisca lifted the hem of her gown just enough to lower herself to a sitting position at the edge of the large sunken tub, Valeria spotted a simple trim of galloon. Inspired by the sight of it, her heart raced as the beginnings of a plan flitted through her mind . . . .

"I see you are studying the galloon on my gown," Prisca said. "I passed Eugenia in the hallway and she told me how distressed you were by my plans for us to travel to France following our trip to Istanbul and Milan, so I have decided to send a messenger there instead."

With a scheme already formulating in her head, Valeria quickly protested. "Oh, no, Mother! I want to go to France to see the women and pray with them."

"But Eugenia said—"

"Forgive me. I was acting like a spoiled child. I must confess that I am intrigued by Eugenia's vivid description of the women at the priory, and I want to go to France after all. Please, can we go?"

Her mother lifted an eyebrow. "Do I detect a bit of excitement about your upcoming wedding?"

"Not the wedding. Never! But you know how I love pretty things! It was you who taught me to appreciate beauty, Mother." Valeria smiled, a reflection of her growing scheme to escape her fate.

"Very well, to France we shall go," Prisca agreed. "Now, will you walk with me or not? I am in no hurry. I can sit here and wait as long as you feel the need to pamper yourself. And I will happily stay and share your morning devotions with you as well, though I have long since had my own."

"Please take your walk, Mother. Perhaps you and I can take another one later. I think I will spend extra time relaxing in my bath this morning."

"But you must not forget that we need to prepare for our trip. Just think! We shall visit Istanbul, Milan, Rome, and France. It will be delightful!"

"How could I forget such a grand adventure with my mother?"

Prisca rose to leave, completely unaware that this trip would change their lives forever.

9

*O*nce their ship escaped the rough waters of the Adriatic Sea, Valeria lounged on the deck under the ornate canopy, surrounded by servants, who were eager to please. How she loved Mediterranean voyages! With so many sights to savor, Valeria remained on deck for as many hours as Prisca would allow. In her heart, however, she still grieved—first, for the great loss she had sustained through Mauritius' martyrdom, and second, because she knew that if all went according to plan, this would be her last trip across the turquoise waters.

The day they arrived in Marseilles was truly magnificent. Blue skies surrounded a fiery, blazing sun. As they neared the dock, a friendly sailor informed the women that Greek settlers from Phocaea had landed in 600 B.C. in Lacydon, a rocky Mediterranean cove, and had set up an emporium in the hills on the northern shore.

"At the end of the port, the workers are cultivating cannabis for the manufacture of the finest rope in the world," the sailor explained. "The ropes on this very ship are indigenous to this area, which is why many sailors refer to Marseilles as Canebière."

When the royal travelers disembarked, another large crowd waited for a glimpse of the beautiful empress and her daughter. The masses of people seemed to close in on them, and Valeria, feeling a surge of panic, feared she and her mother and Eugenia might be crushed to death. At the last moment, however, their alert guards forced the people back and cleared the way for the women's entourage.

Farther into the crowd, Valeria caught the blue eyes of a young man with tousled blond curls, making his way through the masses in her direction. *If there truly were such a thing as a Greek god*, she mused, *he would be one*. Tall, with bronzed skin and muscles that bulged beneath his tunic, he was so unlike many of the short, dark Roman men, even her beloved Mauritius. Despite the guard's best efforts to hold the man back, he drew closer to Valeria.

"Please, I have a gift for you," he called out in a voice that was so commanding even Prisca turned toward him.

"I will take the gifts," a Roman soldier declared, pushing the man away with his spear.

The attractive man hesitated and then said, "I believe the young lady will want to see me. I was with Mauritius in Gaul."

With that announcement all three ladies halted, as Valeria cast a pleading glance toward her mother. Prisca bristled with apparent disapproval, but nodded.

Flanked by two stocky Roman soldiers, the young man was escorted to within a few feet of where the women stood. Valeria's heart raced with anticipation at what he would tell her.

When he was but a few steps from Valeria, the guards stopped him. "State your business," one of them ordered.

"I have a gift for the emperor's daughter, Valeria," he said boldly, reaching toward her. In his hand Valeria saw a piece of intricate gold cloth. Carefully, the young man unwrapped it, revealing a golden Theban cross on a heavy chain.

"What is this?" Valeria cried out with joy. "Could it be? I know this cross! It is the cross that hung around Mauritius' neck, is it not?"

The young man nodded. "It is none other."

Prisca stepped forward, her eyes squinting as she studied the offering. "How do we know this cross belonged to Mauritius? Did every Theban soldier not wear something similar?" She lifted her eyes and glared at the handsome Swiss. "And just what is your price, young man?"

Before Valeria could speak in his defense, he announced, "There is no price, my lady. The cross is my gift to your daughter."

"Look!" Valeria pointed. "He also has Baraka's ring. See the cross on the lapis stone?"

The young man nodded. "Baraka was among the first to die, and Mauritius promised him that he would deliver the ring to his wife and son."

The young man was not close enough to hand Valeria the cross or the ring, though she desperately wanted to take them from him. Yet she dared not move without her mother's permission.

"Mother, please," she pleaded.

"Has the news of my daughter's impending marriage to General Galerius not reached you?"

"I have heard of the marriage, your highness, but I made a vow that I would deliver this cross to your daughter. I fought in the battle of Gaul and am now on a sabbatical at the Saint John monastery in the village at the foot of the mountain in Saint-Baume."

"Then you have no doubt heard that we are visiting the priory there?" Prisca asked, raising an eyebrow.

He nodded. "One of the sisters from the priory informed me of your arrival, and I had planned to request an audience with you there, but today as I was running errands in the village, I heard the commotion of your arrival, so I hurried to greet you. I believe this is truly a divine appointment."

Prisca's face softened at his words, and she nodded. "I suppose your bravery entitles you to give this gift to my daughter. Come."

With the guards leading him, the young man stepped closer and then fell to his knees in respect for the empress and her daughter.

"You may stand," Prisca ordered.

Valeria feared her heart would leap from her chest as the young man faced her. She trembled when she took the jewelry from his outstretched hand. Grasping the pieces at last in her right hand, she held them to her heart, as the tears began to flow. "Thank you, sir," she mumbled. Her mind raced with dozens of questions that she dared not ask in front of her mother. How grateful she was for the handkerchief Eugenia handed her!

Valeria composed herself and fixed her gaze once more on the handsome messenger who had brought her such a price-less gift. When Prisca again granted him permission to speak, he said to Valeria, "I did not come to make you weep. I was a Roman soldier who fought in Gaul. I prayed with Captain Mauritius as he took his last breath. Before heaven, you were in his final thoughts. When he asked me to deliver this cross and ring to you, I thought it impossible, but he assured me that God would help me find a way. And so, He has."

"You mentioned earlier that Mauritius had a message for me," Valeria said.

"Yes. He said to tell you not to despair because he is waiting for you in heaven, where you will be together for eternity."

Struggling to hold back her tears, she begged, "Please, tell me more!"

Before the young man could continue, Prisca intervened. "Enough. You must go now."

"Mother, please," Valeria interrupted. "I must hear every detail of Mauritius' last hour on this earth. But first, what is your name, sir?"

The young man glanced nervously at Prisca. She hesitated, and then, with a shrug of her shoulders and a wave of her hand, granted him permission to speak.

"I am Felix. I was born in Turicum, but since the war, I have settled in Valais."

"Valais! I have heard this is where Mauritius is entombed."

The young man nodded. "A shrine has been erected in his memory and in honor of the courageous legionnaires who also gave their lives rather than deny their faith."

"I must go there one day," Valeria said, her heart aflutter at the thought. "What else can you tell me?"

"Mauritius died bravely," he said, tenderness in his voice. "He was joyful, singing hymns and praising God. But he wanted you to know that his love for you will never die and will live in your heart forever."

"Those are the most beautiful words anyone has ever spoken to me. And I feel it . . . his love." Valeria placed both her hands over her heart.

"He was adamant that you understand you are to live your life, fulfilling the great purpose that he believes your heavenly Father has for you."

Valeria's tears returned, this time tempered with joy. "And did Mauritius mention what that purpose might be?"

The man lowered his eyes, and he spoke in a whisper. "Only that he believed God would use you to stop the persecution of Christians."

"But . . . I have no power," she protested. "I cannot—"

"But you will."

"I appreciate your confidence and faith in me, sir, but I don't see how—"

"Mauritius said that God will show you the way," Felix assured her. He paused. "And now that my mission is accomplished, I must return to my retreat at the monastery."

He bowed to the ladies, and Valeria wished him well. "I will never forget your kindness," she called after him.

Stop the persecutions. Valeria laughed to herself. Surely God would not give her such a formidable task. As she watched Felix melt into the crowd, she realized that her brief encounter with him had brought a spark of healing to her heart. It was as though Mauritius had reached down from heaven and touched her.

10

*W*hen at last they reached their destination, Valeria gasped as the picturesque village came into view. The town was encased by three towering mountain ranges: Mont Aurelien, Mont Sainte Victoire, and the Santa Baume. The village itself was surrounded by rows and rows of vineyards, making it appear wrapped in a green bow.

"Much of your father's wine comes from this valley," her mother pointed out. "Look, there is the castle ahead, high upon the hill."

The carriage wound around the mountain, moving upward with each turn. Valeria marveled at the sight of the magnificent stone ediface with towering peaks jutting out of the mountain like diamonds.

Soon the women were inside the priory. The sisters were excited to have royal visitors, and they served a bountiful feast with fine wines and delicacies to welcome the empress and her entourage.

After dinner, Sister Mary Therese, the head of the priory, gathered the women around a crackling fire in her study and enthralled them with stories of Saint Mary Magdalene.

"Following the death of Jesus, Mary Magdalene and several other of our Lord's disciples continued His ministry in Jerusalem, where they attracted large crowds. Eventually, the authorities felt threatened, and they arrested them, male and female."

"How did they get to France?" Valeria asked.

"It is a miraculous tale, my dear. A trial ensued, and the group was sentenced and herded like cattle into a boat with no sails, oars, or supplies. Their captors set the boat adrift at sea."

A younger sister with dark brown eyes added, "Their captors assumed the prisoners would drown in a storm if they did not first die of thirst or starvation. They thought that no one would survive in an aimless vessel."

"They could have been eaten by a gigantic whale or a hungry shark," Valeria interjected.

"But God protected them, and none of those things happened," Mary Therese reminded everyone.

Valeria was intrigued. "Where did the boat finally land?"

"At Sainte-Marie-de-la-Mer. Mary Magdalene was among the passengers, as was Lazarus and his sisters, Mary and Martha. Once they landed on the coast of France, they prayed and decided to separate and evangelize the surrounding area. They persuaded a prince to allow them to live in his castle . . . this very one. Eventually, Mary Magdalene yearned for solitude. She shut herself away in a cave in the Saint Victoire Mountains, where she devoted the next thirty years of her life to prayer."

"I feel that same longing in my heart," Valeria announced, the outburst visibly surprising everyone around her. "I wish to dedicate my life to prayer."

The sisters reacted with surprise, but Prisca's brows knitted together as she studied her daughter.

Mother is smarter than I give her credit for, Valeria worried. *Does she suspect?*

After a brief moment of awkward silence, Mary Therese spoke. "We should all devote our lives to prayer, but some of us, such as you and your mother, are called to pray in the world instead of the seclusion such as we sisters have chosen."

"Yes, of course," Valeria agreed, chastising herself for the poor timing of her outburst. "We can pray wherever we are."

"Your mother is a fine role model for you," Mary Therese continued. "She is married to the most powerful man in the world, and she continues to pray for his soul and for the empire as she goes about the tasks of her daily life. Her first concern is her Lord, and then her husband, according to God's plan. God gives us all different roles in life."

Valeria nodded in agreement. "Please continue your story of Mary Magdalene," she urged, anxious to deflect her mother's suspicions.

The older sister smiled. "Very well. Mary Magdalene remained in the cave for thirty years until her death. Her relics were then placed inside a crypt in the castle. Shall I take you to see it?"

"Oh, yes," Valeria cried.

The women were excited as they navigated the stairs to the crypt. "The opportunity to see the remains of a woman who was with Jesus thrills my very soul," Valeria whispered to her mother. "Thank you for bringing for me here. I shall be forever grateful to you, Mother."

"And I am happy that you came, my darling." Prisca squeezed her hand as they marveled at the intricately carved, fine-grained marble sarcophagus that encased Mary Magdalene's remains.

"This marble was mined from the Imperial quarries of the Marmara Sea, near Byzantium," one of the younger women elaborated.

Mary Therese spoke in a reverent tone as she described Mary Magdalene's remains. "The reliquary holds the skull of Mary Magdalene. In the center, a glass tube holds a fragment of her skin, the *noli me tangere*. This is the place on her forehead where Christ touched her with his finger the morning of the resurrection."

Valeria shivered with excitement, but she was exhausted from the day of travel and felt relieved when the women showed her to her quarters. The women had made a great effort to make her room beautiful and comfortable, and Valeria was touched by the details. The sisters' handiwork added a touch of elegance to the drab décor. A young woman named Colette pushed back the lace curtains from the tiny window so Valeria could see the rose garden. She bent down to smell the flowers on the table, and then sunk down into the bed without even pulling back the covers or removing her clothes. Her encounter with Felix was exhilarating, but it had left her an emotional wreck. Longing for dreams of Mauritius, she clutched his golden cross to her chest, closed her eyes, and promptly fell asleep.

☙

Valeria awakened early, while it was still dark outside. With the help of her servants, she dressed and tiptoed past Eugenia's room and then her mother's suite. Wandering the halls, she found her way to the large kitchen, where the nuns sat around long tables. She was determined to speak to the head of the priory, Mary Therese, before her mother appeared.

The sisters seemed surprised to see Valeria so early in the day but invited the emperor's daughter to share in their prayers and a simple breakfast of fruit, bread, and cheese. Ravenous, she also devoured a plate of eggs, while the nuns giggled at the voracity of her appetite. When Mary Therese came into the dining room, she informed Valeria that her mother was having breakfast in her room and would meet her in the chapel later.

Valeria seized the opportunity. "May I speak with you privately, Mary Therese?"

"We are expected in chapel. Come with us, and I will meet with you afterwards."

Valeria hesitated. "My mother will be there. I am afraid that her presence will make it impossible to speak with you."

"Come along, dear. The good Lord will provide a time for us to talk to one another."

Valeria sighed and accompanied the women to the chapel, where they sat on the hard stone pews for their morning devotionals. When it came time to kneel for prayer, she was grateful for the soft cushion embroidered in gold—the women's handiwork—provided for her novice knees.

The women's voices rang out in praise, echoing in the cavernous chapel, deeply touching Valeria's heart. She admired the women's exquisite handiwork that hung in their place of worship. Since she was a young girl of seven, Valeria had loved her needlework far more than any of her lessons. Her delicate fingers could stitch the most intricate of designs, but it was nothing to compare with the work of these talented and devoted women.

Her attention was diverted back to the service as a young nun read from the Scriptures. Valeria knew she could find happiness here, but first she had to convince Mary Therese that the Lord had indeed called her to join them. Once Valeria had accomplished this, she would enlist the help of the older woman to elicit her mother's permission to enter the order of Mary Magdalene so she could dedicate her life to prayer instead of becoming the wife of General Galerius. With that thought firmly in place, Valeria felt at peace.

After chapel, Prisca appeared and asked to see the trims for Valeria's trousseau, but Valeria was determined to avoid the drudgery of the tortuous task. It would be a waste of time to select trims for her trousseau for a wedding that would never happen.

"May I have a word with you, Mary Therese, before we select the trims?"

"Your mother is eager to preview them," she answered. "Please, come inside."

Valeria sighed but followed the others into a large sunny room where they spent the morning previewing yards of gold galloon and delicate lace. Once they had selected the trims for Valeria's trousseau, Prisca reached inside her large tapestry bag for a stack of gold coins and made a generous donation to the priory.

"Thanks be to God," the head of the convent declared, lifting her hands in praise. She hugged both Prisca and Valeria and thanked them for their generosity.

It was lunchtime, and a spread of cheese, fruit, vegetables, and grilled fish was served in the garden. As anxious as Valeria was to speak with Mary Therese, she admitted to herself that she enjoyed the beauty of the outdoors and the fellowship with the women.

After lunch, when her mother excused herself to lie down in her room, Mary Therese motioned for Valeria to follow her into her study. She patted the spot on the divan beside her and said, "Please tell me what is troubling you, child."

"Nothing is troubling me. I simply feel that God has called me to join the group of women here. I want to dedicate my life and service to Jesus and become one of Mary Magdalene's devoted followers."

The nun took Valeria's hand. "This is a surprise. Have you spoken to your mother about your decision?"

"I wanted to discuss it with you first. Perhaps you could help me tell my mother."

"So you have felt God's call to live a life of prayer and seclusion, have you?"

"Oh, yes! The Lord spoke to me concerning this before I even left our palace. I have thought of nothing else on my journey here, and then, when I arrived . . . I cannot explain it, but I felt that I had come home at last." Tears stung Valeria's eyes as she struggled to sound as pious as possible.

The older woman rose from her seat and knelt before Valeria. "My dear child, God has called you to something far more important than a life of prayer and solitude here, and it includes your upcoming marriage."

Valeria's heart crashed to her feet. "But I am a Christian. Do you not agree that I should not marry a pagan? The Scripture forbids it."

"I am impressed that you have studied God's words, but have you read that you are also to honor and obey your father and mother? The Scripture also states that obedience is more important than sacrifice."

"But I cannot marry Galerius. I simply do not comprehend why my mother and father are commanding me to marry such an evil man."

"You shall be an Esther, my dear. I believe that God will empower you to change your husband's heart. You have the potential to change the laws of the Roman Empire. You must dedicate yourself to prayer concerning the matter."

"But I have spent hours and hours in prayer, and I believe I am to join my Christian sisters at the priory."

"You were born for a purpose in this life. Surely you realize that God can use you more in the world than locked away in the castle here. God gave you the parents you were born to for a reason."

Summoning an earnest look, Valeria continued to plead her case. "But the news that the emperor's daughter has chosen God over a royal, pampered life in a luxurious palace will send a powerful message to the people of the empire."

Slowly, Mary Therese rose to her feet. She straightened the folds in her long, drab skirt and walked to a window. "Few young women have the opportunity that you will have to change the world. You are a woman of influence. If you have not done so already, read about the life of Esther in your Scriptures, and you will understand your purpose. The life of Esther will be a good role model for you to follow. Surely, your marriage to Galerius is a greater calling from your Lord and Savior."

Valeria refused to concede so easily. "You must know how the women in the palace are treated. I will become a mere object for my husband's affection—a trinket for him to play with until he tires of me."

"It is your job to ensure that your husband does not tire of you."

"How can I do that? He will care for nothing I have to say."

"Have you considered the great influence your mother has over your father? I know your mother, and I believe that one day, because of the respect your father has for her, he will turn from his evil ways. And then there will be one person responsible for your father's salvation . . . your mother."

"And you think I can convert Galerius." Valeria scoffed at the ridiculous thought. "Surely you know his mother is the high pagan priestess, Romula. Galerius was marked for Satan when he was in her womb."

"And why do you believe your father has chosen Galerius for your husband?"

"Once Galerius was successful in the battle of Gaul, he rose to astonishing heights in my father's eyes. Until then, my father was ambivalent toward Christians. He even employed mostly Christians in the palace because he believed them to be trustworthy and their work excellent. But once Galerius became Father's number-one general, everything changed."

"Surely one man cannot wield that much influence."

"There is no doubt Father's sudden change of heart toward the Christians is due to Galerius' influence. Galerius' mother is the high priestess at the Temple of Jupiter. She is a fanatical pagan, and he is just like her."

"Having grown up under the influence of such religious zealotry, it is no surprise to me that Galerius' feelings toward other religions is hostile," the woman admitted.

"This is why I cannot imagine marriage to the man. Surely, the Lord does not expect me to endure such a fate."

"God is greater than your circumstances."

"Oh, please," Valeria cried, dropping her head into her hands and beginning to sob. "Please, you must save me from this horrible fate!"

"It is just as I thought. Your desire to join us here has nothing to do with a calling or your desire to serve. Valeria, are you called to serve at the priory, or are you running away from home?"

"But he's a wretched, horrible man," Valeria cried, ignoring the woman's question. "You must help me!"

She returned to Valeria's side and touched the top of her head. "You, my dear, have been chosen by God to find Galerius' heart. He does have one, you know."

"But he has no soul," Valeria protested.

"Enough. You have my word that I will pray about the matter of your joining our community, but I do not believe this is the purpose God has decreed for you. God is waiting for you to relinquish your will to Him so he can work mightily in your life."

"I want to yield my will to God's, but how can I under these circumstances—facing such a dreadful marriage?"

"You will find there is great peace and power in relinquishment, my child. When you leave the choice to God, he always gives you His best. I can assure you that God will supply all the strength you need."

But even as Mary Therese spoke her words of wisdom and advice, Valeria was already moving on to her next plan, plotting her escape to Switzerland. Surely Felix would not refuse her, would he?

11

"Wake up," Eugenia called, penetrating Valeria's consciousness. "Did you forget we are going into the village today to see the fabrics the merchant brought from the Orient? You must choose the silks for your trousseau."

"I am sorry, but I cannot go," Valeria moaned, her hand shielding her eyes from the rising sun.

"You have no choice in the matter, young lady."

"But my head aches, and I feel chilled," Valeria complained. "You and Mother will have to go to the village without me."

Eugenia put her hand on Valeria's forehead. "You do not feel warm. Perhaps you are just tired."

"I am exhausted, but I also feel miserable. Will you please go with Mother and help her choose the fabrics for me?"

"But if you are not feeling well, I should stay with you."

"There are plenty of servants to take care of me. Besides, the women can look in on me too. Please go with Mother for me, will you? Without you, Mother might select stodgy old things that I would not like."

"Your mother has beautiful taste. She does not need me."

"Oh, but your tastes are more youthful."

Eugenia hesitated, touching Valeria's forehead and cheeks again. After a moment, she acquiesced, declaring that she would ask the women to serve Valeria a breakfast in her room.

Moments later a worried Prisca, having heard the news from Eugenia, entered Valeria's room.

"I just need some rest, Mother," Valeria insisted. "Please go to the village without me." When at last Prisca agreed and left, Valeria smiled. Neither of the women were the least suspicious.

From her window, Valeria watched her mother and Eugenia walk through the garden to the gate. *This could be the last time I will ever see them*, she thought. She raised her hand in an effort to say goodbye to the two women she loved most in the world. Overcome with emotion, she let out a small cry as she watched them disappear from her sight. She had deceived her mother and her friend. But what choice did she have?

✑

Valeria soon made her way into the kitchen to talk to the women who were putting away the breakfast dishes, convincing them she was now feeling much better. During the course of the conversation, she intentionally mentioned how much she admired the black wraps the women wore outdoors. As she had hoped, one of them quickly retrieved a cape for Valeria. *Surely, God is in my plan*, she comforted herself. *He will assure that it succeeds*.

Returning to her room, Valeria dismissed the servants by explaining she needed to rest. The moment they were out the door, she slipped around the corner to her mother's room, where she found the tapestry bag that held the gold.

Within moments she had filled her skirt with gold coins. Once back in her room, she tied the coins into stacks of gold in her handkerchiefs and slipped them into her traveling bag. She then slicked her hair back into a severe bun, tucking her curls underneath with hairpins. Although the weather was moderate, she flung the hooded cape around her shoulders. No one would recognize her now. Just before she tiptoed out the side door of the castle, she mumbled a prayer.

Traversing the cobblestone streets of the village, Valeria was relieved that she did not attract attention. A few people nodded in greeting, but even when she stopped a farmer to ask directions to the monastery at St. John's, he barely glanced at her.

Valeria soon arrived at the monastery. She spoke her best French and inquired of the monk at the gate if Felix from Valais was a guest there. The monk nodded and ordered an errand boy to fetch him. Valeria paced nervously as she waited, praying she would not be discovered. To her delight, Felix appeared within minutes.

"Good morning," she said, greeting him with a radiant smile and unwinding the scarf from her neck so he would recognize her.

With a look of confusion, Felix studied her face. "Good day, Madame. Have we met?"

Valeria's courage seemed to melt away, as she answered with a weak "yes."

"Forgive me," Felix said, "but I cannot recall your name. Should I?"

Unable to speak, Valeria unpinned her hair and let it tumble about her shoulders. At the sight, the corners of Felix's lips turned upward. "It is you! I should have recognized those azure eyes. What are you doing here? But, wait. How rude of me! Please, step inside the gate. Have you visited the monastery before? Would you like for me to show you around? Is that why you have come?"

Valeria smiled. "I would love to see the monastery—later. But first, what are your plans? Are you leaving for Switzerland soon?"

He returned her smile. "You almost missed me. I leave tomorrow before dawn."

She clapped her hands together like an excited child. "Ah, then God is indeed in the details!"

"He is always in the details. Come, sit down and tell me why you are here." Felix pointed to a bench under an arbor of purple wisteria, then took her bag and carried it. "What have you got in here . . . gold?" he teased.

Valeria laughed, knowing Felix would be flabbergasted at the truth.

He placed the bag on the ground, and they sat side by side on the garden bench under the arbor.

"Now, tell me what brings you to the monastery this beautiful morning."

Valeria took a deep breath and decided to get right to the point. "I came to inquire if I might travel with you to Valais to see the Basilica that holds the remains of my beloved Mauritius."

Felix raised his eyebrows, a look of surprise evident in his blue eyes. "Your mother would allow it?"

Valeria nodded. "She plans to stay at the priory for a few more weeks, and, truthfully, I have become deathly bored with all of the details of the fashions that we traveled to France to purchase."

"Then you are different from most young girls."

"*Au contraire*," she declared, laughing. "I adore beautiful things, but too much of anything can grow tiring. Besides, traveling to Valais will provide a nice diversion for me. And paying respects to Mauritius prior to my marriage would not only comfort me in my grief, but it will bring closure for me before I begin my life anew with General Galerius."

"But surely your mother knows a journey to Switzerland can be extremely treacherous." He studied her. "There is only one route from France to Valais, and it winds over and through the Alps."

"Oh, I am quite accustomed to adventure. Have you not heard that I traveled the Nile?" She thought she sounded quite convincing, and could only hope and pray he would believe her story. She raised a questioning eyebrow. "Do you not want me to travel with you?"

He took her hands in his. "I should cherish your company, Valeria, but the sea is far different from the mountains. You were raised on the coast, so you are quite accustomed to sea travel. At sea, you have leagues of mariners to protect and navigate you safely over the most treacherous waters and to guide you through the eye of the perilous storm. But the Alps are teeming with danger—wild animals, avalanches, and thieves, to name a few."

"I am prepared to take those risks, for I know that our Father in heaven will protect me."

He sat quietly for a moment before speaking again. "I am traveling with only two servants and a companion, but perhaps this is not an issue since dozens of your servants will certainly accompany us."

Valeria ignored his comment and tried to elicit his commitment. "So I have your permission to accompany you to Valais?"

"It will all depend on how many of your servants will come along and if any of them have mountain-climbing experience."

It was an appropriate concern and one that Valeria knew she must overcome to enlist Felix's help. She sighed, resigned to the truth. "To be honest, I did not plan on bringing any of my servants or even my companion on the trip."

He cocked his head. "I thought so. Your mother does not know you are here, does she?"

Valeria blushed.

"I suspected as much. If your mother were behind this trip, she would have sent a messenger to make this request. Are you running away, Valeria?"

With no reason to continue her charade, Valeria nodded and tried a second approach.

"You must know that my father has ordered me to marry Galerius, the general who was instrumental in Mauritius' death." Tears spilled from her eyes, but she had no hand-kerchief because every one she owned was in her bag, filled with gold coins. She was grateful when Felix dug into his pocket and came up with one of his own and offered it to her.

Dabbing at her eyes, Valeria sobbed, "I think it is too much to expect me to marry that monster."

"Ah, I have met him, but I have faith in you . . . and in God that you can melt Galerius' evil heart." With compassion written on his face, Felix put his arm around Valeria's waist. "It seems unconscionable to me that you should be consigned to such a fate, but at the same time, I know you can trust God. He wants only what is best for us, according to His plan."

"But how can a loving God condemn me to something so terrible?"

"I have no answer for your question, but if it is not God's perfect will for you, He will intervene in a miraculous way. It is exciting to wait and see what God will do on your behalf."

Valeria shook her head. "I have prayed about the matter since my father told me I must marry Galerius. When Mother told me we were coming to France, I believed God wanted me to join the followers of Saint Mary Magdalene."

"That is certainly a viable solution."

"I thought so, but Sister Mary Therese does not agree."

"Did she say why?"

"Only that God had a far greater purpose for me."

"This is what Mauritius believed, and knowing God's nature, I must admit I believe it too. The end of your story has not yet been written."

Frustrated that none of her schemes was working, Valeria buried her head in the young man's chest and pleaded for mercy. "You must help me. I cannot bear to become the wife of such a horrible pagan."

Just as Valeria had hoped, when she looked up, Felix's eyes had filled with tears. She lowered her head once again and wept, as he held her in his arms and gently stroked her hair. After a moment, he lifted her chin, gazed into her eyes, and brushed a strand of hair away from her face. Valeria was sure that he was about to kiss her, but when she moved closer, he turned away. To her surprise, she was disappointed. Her attraction to him alarmed her! Perhaps was it because when she was with him she felt closer to Mauritius, since Felix was the last person to have seen him and touched him. Yes, of course; that explained it.

"There is no man who could resist you," he said, his voice husky.

"Except you?"

"Including me."

She touched his arm. "Please take me away with you. We could be married, and—"

He released her and stood to his feet. "Have you forgotten that your father is the Roman emperor? Do you think he would not search to the ends of the earth to find us and bring you back home and then brutally execute me?"

Valeria knew marriage to Felix was her last hope, so she had to give the performance of her lifetime. Jumping up, she pleaded, "Felix, when I saw you in Marseilles, I knew God meant for us to be together. I can make you happy. I promise you that I will be the best wife on this earth."

"And I do not doubt for a moment that you would be a good wife. But we are Christians, so you must understand that I cannot support any decision that would go against your parents' wishes. I am sorry, but it is just not possible without their permission."

"But you were a friend of Mauritius'. Surely you must know that he would want you to rescue me from this horrible fate."

"Mauritius would insist that you honor your parents and trust God in all circumstances. He would never condone your disobedience. All I can offer is to pray for you."

"But with Galerius, my life is in danger. Consider that you would be saving my life," Valeria pleaded.

"Even if I agreed to take you with me, we would not get far. I am not afraid to die, but they would execute me, and I cannot say what would happen to you. You are the daughter of the emperor, so your life is not your own. The man you marry is your parents' decision, and they have spoken. I know you can make a life for yourself if you will just die to yourself and allow God's plan to unfold. I am confident that if you could speak to Mauritius at this very moment, he would tell you the same thing."

Valeria paused, her heart sinking at the implications. "Then this is goodbye?"

He squeezed her hand. "I will pray for you . . . every day I am on this earth. You have my word."

She swallowed. So this was God's answer. Her options were gone. "And I shall pray for you," she whispered at last.

He reached up and touched her face with such tenderness that Valeria trembled.

"Please," she said softly, as she blinked away tears.

He shook his head. "Your faithfulness will change the world, Valeria."

"So I have been told, though I cannot imagine how."

Felix kissed her forehead. At last she stood to her feet, accepting that her struggle had come to an end and she would somehow do what was required of her. Stealing one last look at Felix, she blew him a sad kiss and hurried out the gate.

12

The residents of the palace were in a jovial mood when Valeria and Prisca arrived home in Nicomedia. Servants smiled and joked as they prepared for the great celebration. Diocletian, who had completely recovered from his illness, would formally announce the upcoming marriage of his daughter and his esteemed general at the party.

Everyone of importance in the empire had received an invitation, and anticipation was high. Senators and foreign dignitaries would also be in attendance. Though a marriage of political convenience, the emperor was pleased with the match—so much so that he also planned to announce the appointment of Galerius as his Caesar.

By Saturday, the day of the festivities, Valeria had tried on dozens of gowns before settling on a turquoise silk with a brocade robe, trimmed in ermine and the exquisite gold galloon stitched by the women from the Mary Magdalene priory. Despite the haunting sadness that plagued her because her betrothed was Galerius and not Mauritius, Valeria was pleased when she noticed that the turquoise silk perfectly matched her eyes.

That evening, as Valeria dressed for her appearance at the elaborate feast, Eugenia came into her room and presented her with a pair of gold-trimmed sandals. Valeria slid her feet into them and then stood in front of the mirror, fussing with her upswept hair.

Eugenia smiled. "You look breathtaking."

"And so do you, my friend. You are a vision in pink."

Shyly, Eugenia thanked her mistress.

Removing her hairpins and holding them between her teeth, Valeria mumbled, "Tonight I prefer to wear my hair down." She placed the hairpins on the dresser and tossed her head, causing her gold- and copper-colored hair to tumble down her shoulders.

"Lovely," Eugenia conceded. "Although your mother prefers you wear your hair *chignon*."

"But tonight is my night," Valeria replied, smiling at her friend. "I'm welcoming my husband-to-be home from yet another successful campaign."

Eugenia raised her eyebrows. "Do I detect a trace of excitement in your voice?"

Valeria shrugged. "Excitement, no, but I have accepted my fate and have pledged to make the best of it. Now, instead of plotting my escape, my days are spent on my knees, begging my heavenly Father to bless me with undying love and devotion for my husband."

"And to think I imagined all that time spent in prayer was a plea for God to 'take this cup' from you."

Valeria laughed. "You know me so well, my dear friend. I will admit that most of my prayer time has been spent begging God to spare me, but since no angel has dropped down from heaven to rescue me and no stray arrow has pierced Galerius' heart in battle, I believe I am destined to marry him."

"Give General Galerius a chance," Eugenia advised. "He may surprise you."

"I cannot say I am hopeful," Valeria sighed, "but I have pledged obedience to my Father in heaven. Felix convinced me that it could be exciting to see what God will do in the marriage on my behalf."

Eugenia nodded and expressed her pleasure with a smile. "Now, come, my darling girl. It is time to go to your mother's quarters and then proceed to the great hall. Your fiancé awaits you." Eugenia kissed Valeria on the cheek before they exited the room. As the friends walked down the long stone hallway to Prisca's suite, followed by an entourage of servants, Valeria squeezed Eugenia's hand. She had always believed that Eugenia could somehow protect her, but once Valeria was married, she knew she must face her husband on her own.

Once at their destination, a servant let them inside the empress's luxurious and ornate boudoir, where dozens of hand-maidens fussed with Prisca's gown and hair. Upon seeing her daughter, Prisca smiled warmly.

"Come, let me have a look at you." She extended a jew-eled hand to Valeria, and Eugenia pushed the hesitant girl forward.

"Turn around, darling," her mother ordered.

Valeria obeyed, spinning slowly so her mother could see her from all angles.

"Perfection," Prisca exclaimed, "except for your hair. My hairdresser will put it up on your head."

"But, Mother, I prefer to wear my hair down tonight."

Prisca's smile faded, replaced by a slight frown. "It should be your lover who has the pleasure of taking down your hair."

"But you promised that he will not become my lover until we have spoken our vows," Valeria reminded her.

"It is symbolic," Prisca insisted, pursing her lips in obvious disapproval. Valeria knew her mother did not like being challenged in front of her servants and friends, but she was not yet ready to give in to her request.

"I promise I will wear my hair in an intricate weave on my wedding day," she bargained. "But for tonight, may I please wear it down?"

Ignoring her daughter's pleas, Prisca clapped her hands, and within minutes, a cadre of hairdressers had swept Valeria's mane atop her head. As the last hairpin was inserted, Valeria bit her lip and fought back the tears that had gathered in the corners of her eyes.

"Your father will be here in a moment to present you with tokens of his affection," Prisca said, "so please do not appear weepy and morose when he arrives."

Moments later, when Diocletian entered Prisca's chambers, all the women except the empress and Valeria were ordered out of the room. Dutifully, Valeria bowed before her father and then rose to greet him with a kiss on each cheek.

"Hello, Father," she said, smiling. "You look wonderful—well rested and tanned. I trust you are feeling better."

"I have recovered fully, and I have never felt better in my life. And you? Did you enjoy your trip to France?"

"It was wonderful. You know how I adore traveling by sea."

Diocletian smiled. "Your mother and I are elated about your marriage to Galerius. He is a mighty warrior and a fine leader. I trust he will lead your family as well. He has become a trusted advisor to me, and I love him like a son—which very soon he will be. I hope that you and Galerius will bless us with many grandchildren, and that your firstborn will become an heir."

"Now, darling," Prisca teased, "it is a bit soon to talk about grandchildren."

Valeria returned her father's smile. She knew the great regret of Prisca's life was her inability to present her beloved husband with an heir to the throne. Perhaps if Prisca had given Diocletian a son, her daughter would not be forced to marry a man she did not love. Eugenia had confided in Valeria that much of her mother's time in prayer was spent asking God for a son for Valeria. "If it pleases you, Father, I pray my firstborn will be a son."

Diocletian nodded and then clapped his hands together, as servants stepped forward, carrying an assortment of decorative boxes. "Your mother and I have gifts for you. We prefer to present them to you now so as not to upstage your husband-to-be when he presents you with your engagement presents tonight."

"You are not obliged to give me any more gifts, Father," Valeria protested. "And I have heard gossip that you have made Galerius one of the wealthiest men in the province—perhaps the entire Roman Empire. As his wife, I shall benefit from this wealth too."

"Ah, but you are our most precious jewel," Diocletian said. "And speaking of jewels . . ." Turning, he motioned to the servants to present the gifts.

"Each piece is more beautiful than the one before," Valeria gasped, as the parade of gift-bearing servants passed by. "They glitter like a sparkling sky at night!"

"Take your pick," Prisca said. "Which one will you choose to wear to your engagement party?"

Valeria's head felt as if it were spinning. How could she choose? Yet she knew she must. "The diamond necklace would look best with my dress," she said at last.

Diocletian removed the necklace from the box and fastened it around his daughter's throat, while Prisca slid the matching bracelets onto the girl's slender arm. Another servant stepped forward to fasten more diamonds to Valeria's ears. Her father had the honor of placing a diamond crown upon her head. When the jewels were in place, the emperor and empress stood back and admired their daughter.

"There is no one prettier in the entire Roman Empire," Diocletian exclaimed.

"Except for Mother," Valeria added quickly, smiling and taking Prisca's hand.

Her father laughed. "I have not forgotten your mother," he exclaimed. "Never! She is the love of my life." Grinning at his wife, he opened another box and took out a necklace of emeralds and diamonds that rivaled the ones he had given Valeria. The jewelry perfectly matched Prisca's dark green gown, which was trimmed in mink and gold. Diocletian fastened the necklace behind Prisca's neck, while a servant appeared out of nowhere to hang the matching emerald earrings on her ears. The earrings were as big as gold coins and dangled seductively on each side of her lovely face.

Diocletian, obviously pleased with himself, kissed his wife and then his daughter. "Ah, I am the luckiest man in the empire! I am Jupiter! I rule the world. Come, let us join our guests."

Moments later, the royal family made a grand entrance into the great hall of the palace, as a loud blast of trumpets heralded their arrival and the crowd cheered. Even the musicians and dancers ceased their performances.

Once the music resumed, Valeria's eyes surveyed the great hall in search of her fiancé. She finally spotted him seated at the banquet table, with belly dancers swishing their hips all around him. Though the sight of him made her stomach churn unpleasantly, she was encouraged to note that he did not appear quite as repulsive as he had in Egypt. As her father escorted her closer, she noted that her fiancé's curls were closely cropped upon his head, and he was immaculately groomed and dressed in a toga trimmed in royal blue and gold.

Valeria smiled to herself. It amused her that the man had obviously cared enough to spend time planning and getting ready for the evening. Was it possible that he cared that she be attracted to him? Her heart softened at the thought.

But when she arrived at the table and stood face-to-face with him, he leered at her until she felt herself grow pale and weak, though she refused to faint and somehow remained on her feet.

"Come here, beautiful one," Galerius said, standing and helping her get situated on the divan.

Valeria's servants surrounded her, giving place to Galerius, who stood so near she could almost feel his hot breath washing over her. Eugenia sat behind Valeria in order to attend to her every need.

Galerius leaned over her and whispered in her ear. "So, now you are mine. All mine, to do with as I please."

"We both know that we were forced into this marriage," Valeria whispered back, a chill snaking up her spine. "Could we please make the best of it and call a truce?"

Still leaning over her, he reached down and wrapped his arms around her. No more was there any doubt that she could feel his hot breath on the back of her neck. "Does marriage to me not excite you?"

She refused to move away. "Are you demanding that I answer your question?"

He grabbed her chin and firmly turned her face up to his. "Yes."

"Then, no," she said, forcing herself to hold his gaze. "Marriage to you does not excite me. In fact, I consider it a tragedy."

He raised his eyebrows, appearing amused. "A tragedy, you say?"

"The greatest tragedy of my life," Valeria shot back, and then wished she had not spoken so frankly. "I am at your mercy," she added, the haughtiness gone from her voice, "just as are your soldiers and your enemies. And so I beg your mercy where I am concerned, sire."

He laughed again. "Ah, Valeria, I took you for a fighter. I expected a real hellcat with claws. I believed you would take me years to tame. But, alas, I am disappointed that you beg for mercy."

"My father has ordered me to be your wife. Do you not know that I am an obedient daughter?"

"Do you take me for the sort of man who would tolerate a lifeless wife in my bed?"

"No," she answered, daring once again to defy him, "but I hope you understand that I am a woman who *does* want a lifeless husband in hers."

Galerius roared with laughter, attracting attention throughout the great hall, while Valeria blushed, regretting her words. When at last he stopped laughing, he ignored the words she had spoken and reached into his pocket and produced an engagement ring. Grudgingly, she admitted to herself that it was quite lovely, an exquisite diamond set in gold. Her hand trembled as he slipped it on her finger, explaining, "This ring should be worn symbolically on the third finger of your left hand, for there is a nerve that runs from this finger directly to your heart." He lifted his gaze from her hand to her eyes. "I pledge my troth to you," he swore, crossing his chest with his right hand and then pounding his heart.

"And I pledge my life to you," Valeria whispered, choking back a sob as she spoke the words.

Having observed Galerius' actions, Diocletian immediately stood to his feet, with Prisca next to him. "Hear ye, hear ye, citizens throughout the Roman Empire, friends in Nicomedia, and countrymen and ladies." With his arm around his wife, the emperor raised his jeweled gold cup high. "This day marks the betrothal of our daughter, Valeria, to my Caesar, Galerius. May the gods bless their marriage!"

"Here, here!" the crowd cheered. "Long live the Emperor!"

Galerius pulled Valeria to her feet and drew her to his side. He placed his arm around her waist so tightly that she wondered if he would cut off her breath. Together they smiled and waved to the thousands of dignitaries, citizens, friends, and family members in attendance.

Then the celebration erupted into an orgy of sorts. For the rest of the evening, Valeria's future bridegroom ignored her until the party had ended, focusing his attention on the exquisite food and drink and the never-ending parade of dancing girls. As the gala event drew to a close, Galerius brushed Valeria's cheek with a rather impersonal kiss, for which she was greatly relieved. Perhaps he would show little interest in her once they were wed, and she could lead a quiet life dedicated to prayer.

Back in her bedchamber, alone, Valeria admired her ring. Yet even as she did so, she realized she would give it and all the jewels she owned to bring Mauritius back.

13

It was a perfect June day, enveloped by blue skies and wispy clouds. A silver tray of strawberries was set before Valeria as sweet fragrances from the season's many flowers wafted through the palace windows. Today was her wedding day, but despite the lovely setting, Valeria felt numb. She could scarcely see the beautiful sights or smell the lovely aromas. Even the sweetest berries were tasteless, and Valeria could not concentrate on Eugenia, as she reviewed the day's schedule with her. Despite her brave talk about having accepted her fate, it seemed her life would end today as she stepped into the deep abyss of marriage to a man she despised, a man who seemed determined to torture her. How could all the prayer and submission in the world cause her to love such a man?

As she dressed for the ceremony, with dozens of servants fussing with her face and fixing her hair, she imagined how different this day could have been had she married Mauritius.

Suddenly, she had an inspiration. Why, this was exactly how she would cope with her impending marriage! She would close her eyes and imagine that Galerius was Mauritius. She could escape from her body in her mind, and go to Mauritius in her dreams. Galerius' touch would belong to Mauritius!

By the time Prisca was escorted into Valeria's chambers to help her daughter dress for the wedding, Valeria was not so glum. In fact, her mood bordered on cheerful.

As it was the Roman custom for a mother to help to dress her daughter for her wedding, it was now Prisca's job to add the finishing touches. "The most important part of your wedding dress is this belt," Prisca explained, fastening an orange sash around Valeria's petite waistline. "I am tying this belt into the knot of Hercules, the guardian of the wedded life."

Valeria was horrified. "Mother, this is a pagan custom, and we are Christians. Please, do not speak these words." She grabbed the belt before her mother could complete the knot and flung it from her. Whispers came from the servants who were huddled across the room.

Prisca calmly ordered a servant to retrieve the belt. "I am obedient to my husband," she explained. "He instructed me to have you wear this belt, and so you shall."

"But where is your obedience to God, Mother? Did you not teach me that obedience is more important than sacrifice?"

As her mother once again placed the belt around Valeria's waist, she said, "You must not untie this knot. Only your husband can do so."

Valeria did not want to embarrass Prisca in front of the servants a second time, so she stood silently and allowed her mother to complete her task, though tears pricked Valeria's eyes.

"She cries because she is happy," Prisca assured the servants before ordering them from the room, motioning Eugenia to stay.

Prisca kissed her daughter and recited the explanation of the ritual of marriage to her. "Marriage transfers a woman from

KATHI MACIAS AND SUSAN WALES

her father's authority to her husband's. This control extends even to life and death. Everything that is yours becomes the property of your husband once you speak your vows. Your body is no longer your own. It is your husband's to do with as he pleases, and you must submit your body to him. Your husband will offer you a goblet of wine when you go to the marriage bed. If you will drink wine or mead, it will calm your fears and relax you, and you will feel less pain."

"Pain? No one has warned me that my body would ache as my heart does." Prisca and Eugenia did not respond, and Valeria tried to calm her terrified, racing heart.

The final task was placing Valeria's veil upon her head and securing it with jeweled hairpins and a diamond-studded crown of gold. Valeria remained still while her mother stood on a stepstool and, with Eugenia's assistance, adjusted her daughter's lace veil. Prisca then tucked a sprig of evergreen behind Valeria's ear. "A symbol of a long marriage," she explained.

With Valeria's preparations finished at last, Eugenia opened the door and invited the servants to come back into the room to see the bride.

Valeria stood on the platform before an ornate mirror, resplendent in the white silk and lace gown embroidered with tiny threads of gold. Her arms covered in lace, she slid them into a sleeveless white robe, also embroidered in gold, which trailed for more than a hundred feet. Outlined in gold and silver galloons and bordered with ermine, the robe was embroidered with lilies of the valley and studded with diamonds and pearls.

"You look like an emperor's bride," Eugenia told her, planting kisses on both her cheeks as the servants oohed and aahed. But Valeria could not share their joy, for she had imagined this day so many times in her dreams and this time, there would be no happy ending.

"A prayer, everyone, before we leave," Prisca insisted. "May God bless this union, and may it bring great peace and honor to the Roman Empire."

Prisca and Eugenia, along with Valeria's many bridesmaids and ladies of the court and their servants, then made their way down the marble stairs toward their guests.

As Valeria started down the aisle toward Galerius, she felt no emotion. Escorted by her parents and carrying a bouquet of orange blossoms and herbs into the great hall of the palace that was bedecked with thousands of blooms, she walked on a fine carpet scattered with rose petals. When she came face-to-face with the man who was about to become her husband, she forced a smile. Roman law required that consent to the marriage be shown publicly, so Valeria accepted Galerius' outstretched hand and stood by his side before the pagan priest. She then chanted her vows by rote, while praying that her new husband's intentions were not as sinister as she imagined.

After the words of consent, the bride and groom sat on stools, facing the altar. The priest handed the groom a loaf of barley bread, which Galerius broke and ate. He broke a second loaf over the head of his bride.

"This act signifies the groom's breaking of the virginal condition of the bride," the priest announced, "and his subsequent power and control over her."

The priest then offered up the wedding cake to Jupiter. Once the high priest had made the offering to the Roman god, he served the sweet cake to the bride and groom, and they fed it to one another. When it was eaten, the priest presented Galerius and Valeria to the wedding guests as man and wife. A great cheer arose in the crowd, as the couple exchanged a simple kiss, and then everyone applauded.

Though repulsed by the pagan ceremony, Valeria forced a smile. When Galerius kissed her a second time, she closed her eyes and pretended she was kissing Mauritius. This time, the kiss made her tingle, and she smiled to herself, knowing she could endure anything with this secret game of hers. Perhaps she would survive her wedding night after all.

As her mother had warned, the wedding feast continued for hours. Wine flowed like a river, and food was served on hundreds of silver and gold trays until the wedding guests ate themselves into a frenzy of indigestion. Entertainment in the form of song, dance, and dramatics was presented at every station. Valeria danced with her father and Galerius until she was exhausted.

The party continued into the wee hours of the morning. When Galerius appeared to notice that his bride was fading and commented accordingly, he quickly bid everyone goodnight on their behalf, already taking charge of his wife.

Normally, after the bridal dinner party, the bride was escorted to her husband's home. This ceremony was essential to the completion of the marriage, so it could not be omitted. However, since Galerius' home was far away in Thessalonica, the people joined in a procession to a bedchamber in the palace that had been prepared for the wedding night. Prisca held her daughter in a tight embrace, and the groom took his bride with a pretended show of force from her mother's arms. The entire procession then paraded to the bedchamber, where the guests showered the newlyweds with almonds for good luck.

Before entering the bridal chamber, Valeria recited the consent chant one more time. Then, amidst the cheers of the wedding guests, Galerius lifted his bride into his arms and carried her over the threshold. The doors were then closed to the general public, while the family and special guests were invited to come inside to watch as the bride lit a fire with a special torch that had been carried in front of the procession. The torch was then blown out and tossed among the guests, who scrambled for it, believing it was a token of health and happiness.

At last the guests bid the couple goodnight, though her parents and Eugenia remained behind. Eugenia helped Valeria slip out of her robe, and then removed her crown and veil. Standing in her wedding gown, Valeria felt naked, until Eugenia and Prisca led her into a chamber and dressed her in her evening clothes for sleeping. The soft silks felt comforting against her bare skin. They placed a robe around her shoulders, and she slid her feet into soft-soled sandals. With Prisca and Eugenia on either side, Valeria returned to the bedroom.

Eugenia whispered a quick prayer into Valeria's ear and kissed her before she took her leave. In a tearful farewell, Valeria then kissed her parents goodnight. When the emperor and empress had gone, Galerius closed and locked the heavy door behind them. The newlyweds were alone, and Valeria was his prisoner.

Galerius turned from the door and eyed his bride with such hunger that she gasped. Without a word, he untied the ribbon on her robe and removed it. Valeria covered the bodice of her diophanous bedclothes with her hands. How she wanted to cry for help, but the servants stationed outside the door would hear and spread the gossip throughout the palace, maybe even the city, so she bit her tongue in an effort to remain silent.

"And now you are mine . . . at last," Galerius gloated. When he lifted her into his arms and carried her to their marriage bed, she steeled herself, determined to be strong as he used one hand to pull back the heavy draperies surrounding the bed. Valeria noted that the maids had turned down the bed and scattered it with rose petals in preparation for the newlyweds' arrival. Galerius wasted no time. He lifted the covers and nearly shoved her under them.

Next, he propped her head up with plush embroidered pillows, and then lifted the crystal carafe and poured the fine wine into two heavy gold chalices that sat on the bedside table. He offered one to her, which she took and sipped. When she winced and made a face, he laughed. The wine was bitter, but she remembered how her mother had explained it would help her endure the unpleasantness and pain of the evening, so she gulped it down. When she finished, Galerius placed their cups on the table by his side of the bed. Then he stood, staring down at her while she tried not to recoil in fear.

After an uncomfortable silence, Valeria finally asked, "Is something wrong? My mother told me that you would remove my bedclothes, but you do not touch me, sire. Are you waiting for me to undress?"

He laughed. "I am a gentleman, and I never touch a lady without her consent."

"Then I suppose you will never touch me," she answered flippantly, wishing immediately that she could take back her foolish words. When she saw the look of anger on his face, she winced and closed her eyes, wondering if he would strike her.

He did not. Instead he replied, "Very well. Then we shall go to sleep."

His response was so unexpected that Valeria simply nodded, wide-eyed. She watched as he went to his side of the bed and lay down beside her.

Once he was settled under the covers, Valeria removed the extra pillows from under her head and tossed them on the floor, and then slid down under the covers, keeping a safe distance between them. She waited in the silence of the room, but when nothing happened, she finally spoke. "You may touch me, sire."

"I shall not," he declared, his back to her now as he faced the wall. "I am a prideful man, and I will not touch you until the day you beg for me to do so."

Valeria was shocked at this unexpected turn of events. Neither her mother nor Eugenia had prepared her for such a scenario. *Am I truly to beg him? No! Never will I stoop so low.*

Her mind flooded with a myriad of conflicting thoughts. What would everyone think of her if the marriage were not consummated? The thought horrified her, but she had no choice but to wait.

The wine now flowed through her bloodstream, and she felt a bit tipsy. After a few minutes, she dared to try again. She touched his arm with her fingertips. Was it the wine or did she want him? The strong desire she felt caused her to ache for his touch . . . a strange erotic sensation indeed! When he did not respond to her advances, she asked, "Sire, do you want to touch me?"

"One day you will burn with passion for me," he said. "On that day you will beg for me, and our marriage will be complete. I will not touch you until then."

Never! I shall not beg him.

She turned away, reminding herself how much she despised him. Throughout the night she dozed fitfully, awakening with Galerius at her side, but never once did he approach her. *Perhaps I should be thankful,* Valeria tried to convince herself. But as much as she hated to admit it, a part of her longed for her husband's touch—and that was the biggest surprise of all on her wedding night, the beginning of the honeymoon she had so feared and dreaded.

14

Valeria slept until noon, though she had no idea what time it was when first she awoke. Slowly opening her eyes, she tried to focus, but the surroundings were unfamiliar. Then she remembered. Out of the corner of her eye, she peeked at the other side of the bed. Galerius was gone.

The heavy damask draperies were still closed around the bed and the room, and Valeria wondered how long her new husband had been absent from her side. Rising from her bed, she walked to the window and flung the draperies aside. The sun shone gloriously, almost directly overhead, and she had a clear view of the courtyard.

The sudden rap at her door startled her.

"Who is it?"

"Eugenia."

With some hesitation, Valeria unlatched the door. After her disastrous and more than slightly perplexing wedding night, she dreaded facing her friend.

"Good afternoon," Eugenia greeted her as she entered, but her smile faded quickly. "Your hair is still up?"

Valeria felt the heat of shame crawl up her neck to her cheeks, as her hand flew to touch her hair. "With the telltale signs, I suppose there is no need for you to pry now. As you can see, I had no wedding night."

"If I did not know you better, I would guess you are disappointed."

"Not disappointed," Valeria countered, "but maybe a bit rejected."

Eugenia's eyes grew wide. "Then it was not you who refused?"

Humiliated, Valeria shook her head.

"It must have been an enormous relief for you."

"True. But now I am concerned that my lack of a wedding night will disturb and concern my parents, especially Father. If anyone finds out, it would bring such shame on my family!"

"They will not hear it from me," Eugenia assured her, and then chuckled. "But I do recall that your father was expecting you to make a grandson for him on the night of your wedding."

"I am glad you are amused. I certainly am not. If I am forced to be this man's wife, then I may as well be married in the full sense of the word so I can at least produce a child."

Eugenia's smile faded as she began to pull the pins from Valeria's hair. "It is not unusual for a bride and groom to be so weary after the wedding festivities that they agree to wait until the following evening to consummate their marriage," she explained.

"Then why did you and Mother not tell me of this possibility?"

Eugenia began to brush her charge's long hair. "We preferred not to offer you any false hope."

"Ouch!" Valeria cried, as her head jerked to one side.

"Sorry. I missed a hairpin." Eugenia did not miss a beat. "Your wedding was beautiful. At breakfast I heard people saying that you were the most beautiful bride in all the Roman Empire. The ladies were also gossiping about General Galerius and how devastatingly handsome he is."

Valeria harrumphed. "That must have pleased him. Have you seen him this morning?"

"He is with your father, who has called an impromptu meeting of the dignitaries who were here for the wedding."

"Good. Then I can have my lunch alone on the terrace without being disturbed. Would you care to join me?"

Eugenia's hand stopped for a moment. "But everyone is waiting for you to come downstairs for lunch."

Valeria felt the warm blush of embarrassment returning. "How can I face them after . . . what I have just told you?"

"Silly girl, no one will know."

"But Galerius will know. And he will make me feel so small."

"No one can make you feel small. You are in control of your own feelings." Switching gears, the faithful Eugenia laid down the brush and looked Valeria in the eyes. "Now, what would you like to wear?"

Valeria shrugged. What did it matter? Oh, how she dreaded facing Galerius! Would he mock her? At the thought, a feeling of indignation and resentment began to replace her dread. How dare Galerius treat her with such contempt! She knew just what to do to make him sorry he had rejected her.

Determined to appear more beautiful and tempting than ever, she declared, "Please bring me the green toga and the emeralds my parents gave me as a wedding gift."

Eugenia smiled and went to do her mistress's bidding.

Once Valeria had bathed in fragrant oils and dressed, even her skin glistened.

"You look magnificent," Eugenia announced.

When she and Eugenia went downstairs for the luncheon, all in attendance ceased their conversation and gazed at the lovely bride. In moments the great hall was abuzz, and Valeria blushed again—this time with pleasure, as she knew her beauty was the subject of their comments. She also imagined that they were speculating about her wedding night. If they only knew!

Then she spotted Galerius. Her heart leapt when she realized he was smiling at her, and she immediately scolded herself for her reaction, reminding herself that she loathed the man. When he came to greet her, she wondered if he was mocking her.

"I trust you slept well," he said as he bussed her check with an obligatory kiss.

"Yes, thank you," she answered, careful to maintain a cool and aloof tone. "And you?"

"Very well, thank you."

Before she could think better of it, she blurted, "I will see you in our bedchambers tonight?"

Galerius raised an eyebrow. "That depends."

Horrified by her brash question and incensed by his taunting response, Valeria clamped her lips shut, stiffening as he escorted her to Diocletian's table and then helped her bow down before her father.

The emperor beamed, obviously in good spirits. "Ah, I see that my little rose is in full bloom this morning." He affectionately patted her stomach. "And how is my little grandson?"

Valeria's blush returned, and she cast a questioning glance in her husband's direction. As Galerius escorted her to the ladies' table, he whispered, "Remember, my dear wife, it is you who finds me repulsive, so do not mock me with those accusatory eyes." He squeezed her forearm, but Valeria refused to react. Galerius settled her on the divan next to her mother and then kissed the top of her head before rejoining the men.

"How are you?" Prisca whispered, taking her daughter's hand.

"Fine."

Her mother's eyes focused on her. From the tone of her next question, it was obvious she did not believe Valeria. "And how was last night?"

Turning her gaze from her mother's face, she answered, "We slept; that is all."

Prisca tightened her grip of Valeria's hand. "That is not so unusual, you know."

"Eugenia assured me of that, but it would have helped if you had warned me of this possibility."

"First, may I say how blessed you are to have such a sensitive husband who would allow you to sleep in your exhausted state after the wedding? Many men are such animals that they would have shown little concern for your feelings. This tells me a lot about your husband's character. Tonight will be different, and you shall become a woman at last."

Valeria nodded again and forced a smile, though she doubted her mother's words. But there was no time to dwell on the possibilities, as a select group of the dignitaries and their wives, including the most powerful rulers and senators, were being escorted into another, more intimate hall. Prisca and Valeria were included in that select group, and so they followed their husbands, while the majority of the guests remained in the grand hall to continue the festive celebration.

Once settled into the smaller setting, with men at one table and women at another, Prisca and Valeria turned their attention to the men's conversation, only to find that Galerius was speaking. How arrogant he appeared! Valeria refused to admit that she was intrigued with his speech and inspired by his passion. It was obvious to her that he was brilliant where politics were concerned.

As Galerius continued, Valeria watched, forgetting for just a few moments that he was the same man she had married against her wishes and who had then humiliated her by rejecting her in their marriage bed. Instead, mesmerized by his speech and manner, she quickly found his command of power intoxicating. Galerius was not only intelligent, but he possessed something her father did not have . . . an uncanny ability to inspire everyone around him. Even Valeria had to admit that the two men were a perfect combination.

Unfortunately I am the one who does not fit into this picture, Valeria realized, suddenly feeling very despondent. *There simply is no place for me here in this world. I belong in heaven with Mauritius. Why has God left me here to endure such sorrow?*

"The Roman Empire is far too vast for one ruler to control," Galerius declared, pulling Valeria back to what had become her reality, "but no emperor prior to Diocletian has had the selfless ambition or the genius of our beloved leader." Rousing cheers and applause greeted his proclamation, interrupting his speech for a brief moment.

Diocletian rose to his feet, immediately interrupting the crowd's praise. "The reason I have called this meeting at our luncheon today," he said, his voice booming across the great hall, "is to make yet another announcement."

Valeria raised her eyebrows, surprised, even as she saw Galerius flinch. He was obviously caught as off guard as she by her father's words. Her husband quickly took his seat and deferred to the emperor after a salute to Diocletian.

Valeria's father continued. "I have decided to form a tetrarchy, the rule of four."

"Four rulers?" One of the senators spoke with a note of surprise in his voice. "Will this not reduce your power?"

"Ah, but for a man who is also a god, it is not a problem," Diocletian explained. "I am Jupiter, all-powerful. I am the Alpha and the Omega, no matter how many rulers exist in our kingdom."

Valeria recoiled at the arrogance of her father's pronouncement, noticing that her mother did the same, though she hid it well.

"One day he will understand," Valeria whispered. "You must keep praying, Mother, as will I."

"And for Galerius as well," her mother added.

"As of today there will be four rulers over the empire," Diocletian announced. "Two Augusti will continue to rule as emperors—one in the east, the other in the west, as we have done. Each Augustus will adopt as his son a junior emperor, a Caesar, who will help rule his half of the empire with him and eventually become the emperor's successor."

Valeria watched the muscles in Galerius' face relax. He knew now what was coming, and he glanced her way and caught her eye, smiling triumphantly as if to say, "This is not just my future, but ours." Valeria returned his smile, surprised as she sensed her anger toward Galerius dissipating, though she was not yet ready to admit it.

"And who might these men be?" another general called out.

"Come, Maximian," Diocletian ordered.

Maximian, Diocletian's co-emperor, bowed prostrate before the senior emperor, and then rose and the men embraced. With his arm around Maximian, Diocletian spoke. "It should come as no surprise to you that I am appointing Galerius as my Caesar, my junior emperor, and my adopted son. And when I die or retire, Galerius will succeed me."

Cheers and applause once again rang out in the great hall, and Valeria clapped vigorously with the rest of them.

Diocletian then deferred to Maximian, who announced, "Constantius shall become my Caesar, my junior emperor, my adopted son, and my successor."

Applause erupted again.

"Excellent choice," shouted a senator from the Danube. "Both the Caesars are military men of Danubian origin."

The dignitaries from the Danube area went wild—whistling, clapping, and stomping the floor. When Diocletian raised his hand to continue, the cheering ceased. "Each of the tetrarchs will have his own capital city, in a territory under his control. The idea will be to create a system by which heirs to the throne are appointed by merit and will rule as Caesars long before the place of Augustus becomes vacant. They will have the responsibility of appointing the next Caesar by merit. This system will assure that the best men for the job ascend to the throne."

"My lord," a general questioned, "will the tetrarchy split the empire?"

"Absolutely not," Diocletian declared. "The empire will be divided into four quadrants, but it will remain one unit, ruled by four men."

Valeria was surprised to notice that her mother appeared increasingly bored, while she herself found the conversation fascinating. She wished she could join in but, of course, a woman would never be allowed to speak unless she was called upon.

A high-ranking military officer posed a question, "My lord, do you feel this districting will quell the uprisings throughout the empire?"

"It will certainly help," Diocletian assured him, "but as you know, the empire is still a vast territory."

Galerius requested permission to speak and stood to his feet when Diocletian nodded. "The problem of the uprisings lies within the provinces. With so much nepotism in the regions, rebellion is inevitable, but it is imperative that we reduce the power of the provincial governors. What do you propose, Lord?"

Diocletian smiled at his new son-in-law. "Ah, spoken like a Caesar under my rule. What do you recommend, my son?"

Valeria marveled at her father's wisdom. She was certain he knew how to accomplish this objective, but he was facilitating a chance for Galerius to shine in front of the guests.

Valeria's husband did not hesitate. "We must weaken the governors' powers."

"And how would you suggest that we do this?"

Galerius held up a wine goblet and ordered a soldier to drink half of the wine. Then he replenished the cup with water and passed it back to the soldier. "Drink it again," he said, "and tell us how it tastes."

The man did so and then answered, "Ah, very weak. With the water in the wine, it has only half the strength of the undiluted wine."

Galerius, still smiling, stated, "We diluted the wine by adding water. Using this same theory, we will add more governors, which will ultimately weaken the power of the existing rulers."

"Where do you propose that we add these governors?" another senator asked.

"In the Roman Empire we have fifty provinces. We will shrink the boundaries and establish one hundred provinces and appoint additional governors for each province."

"Ah," the senator observed, "so the present governors will be responsible for smaller provinces of fewer people."

"Exactly."

Diocletian smiled, standing shoulder to shoulder with Galerius now. "And that, my friends, will make it more difficult for any of the governors to launch a rebellion."

Everyone in the room clapped and cheered. Once the applause died down, a senator from Rome posed a question to Diocletian. "Lord, how do we keep the provinces from joining forces to rebel against the empire?"

"A very good question, indeed. Consider this: a ruler can delegate authority but not responsibility. Responsibility must be inspired. Galerius, my son, how do you propose that we inspire responsibility in the lives of our governors?"

Valeria felt proud that there was no hesitation in Galerius' response. "When we meet with the fifty governors to inform them of our plan, we will assure them that we want to lighten their sphere of responsibility. Believe me, they know how difficult it is to protect their provinces, and I believe the governors will feel a sense of relief.

"Next, we assure them they have proven worthy of our trust and, for this reason, we want to increase their power by appointing them to keep a watchful eye over their bordering provinces and report back to us on a quarterly basis." Galerius chuckled. "Of course, they will not know that we are telling their neighbors the same thing."

The audience clapped their agreement, and a senator from Rome stood. "But according to this theory, do you not believe that you have weakened your power by appointing four rulers?"

"I lead by example," Diocletian proclaimed. "The empire is far too vast for one ruler, which is why we have had so many wars in the past. I plan to use my own division of power as an example to the governors when we reduce their territories. Since I have divided my own territory, the governors will have no right to complain when I divide theirs."

"I believe this brilliant act will produce a peaceable kingdom," declared another senator from Rome, who raised his cup. "I propose that while we have all gathered in Nicomedia, we have a coronation for our newly appointed Caesars. All in favor?"

"Aye, aye!" Approvals rang out in the hall.

As the lively discussion drew to a close, Galerius and Diocletian joined Valeria and Prisca for the lavish lunch.

"The coronation will delay our trip to our palace in Thessalonica," Galerius informed Valeria. "But I am sure that will make you happy because you can stay with your mother longer."

Valeria's smile was less forced than it had been earlier. "Wherever and whenever you go, I shall be happy to accompany you, my lord."

Galerius' eyebrows shot up in obvious surprise. "Submissiveness is not becoming to you, Valeria."

Feeling rejected yet again, Valeria swallowed the retort that yearned to escape. Instead, she looked into her husband's dark eyes. "You were very impressive on the podium."

He seemed almost as surprised by her compliment as he had been by her humble attitude. "Really?" he asked.

"Your ideas were brilliant, and your delivery inspirational. It was obvious in the way the crowd responded with such enthusiasm. You have a gift, Galerius."

This time he paused before answering, and Valeria was not sure what emotions she saw playing across his face. "I do not believe I have ever heard you speak my name before."

Valeria felt the annoying flush trying to return. "I said your name at least a dozen times when we spoke our vows," she reminded him. "But if it is that important to you, I will say your name more often."

"Thank you." He took her arm. "Shall we take our seats at the banquet table?"

Valeria nodded, accompanying him without further conversation. Throughout the luncheon, he ignored her, but when she noticed that the other men also ignored their wives, she resorted to making small talk with the women, relieved that they were too polite to ask about the details of her wedding night.

After lunch the women retired for an afternoon nap, but since Valeria had slept until noon, she was not tired and decided to take a walk in the garden. "Eugenia, will you please accompany me?" Valeria could tell by the dark rings around Eugenia's eyes that her friend begged for a nap, but she also knew she could not walk the gardens alone.

As they strolled through the flowering bushes, Valeria confessed, "I am more prepared to meet my fate tonight. As Galerius spoke to the dignitaries this morning, there was something appealing about him."

Eugenia eyed her questioningly. "Are you telling me that you find power an aphrodisiac?"

"Oh, stop teasing me, will you? It is not power that I find attractive, but his inspiring manner."

"I must admit, I, too, was quite impressed with General Galerius."

"What did you think of the other Caesar?"

"Constantius?" Eugenia giggled. "We must have the same thought."

"That he has the longest nose and sharpest chin God ever put on a man?"

"I am glad you said it and not I. I could never be so rude."

Valeria rolled her eyes. "Oh, now I feel guilty! But you must admit, Constantius is an odd-looking man."

"Yes. And pity the poor girl who will be forced to marry him."

"That would be Maximian's stepdaughter, Theodora."

"You should be thankful that Galerius is so handsome."

"Not so to me," Valeria countered quickly. "There is only one who is handsome in my eyes."

"Then you are blind. Mauritius is no longer of this world. Let him go."

Valeria stopped in front of a red rose bush and stared at its radiant blooms as she spoke. "Love never dies, Eugenia. Only people do."

"When love is all that is left of someone, you must give away that love and not keep it all for yourself."

"Give away his love?" Valeria turned from the fragrant roses and fixed her gaze on Eugenia, patting her chest as she spoke. "Never. I will always guard it, here in my heart."

"You are a hopeless romantic!" Eugenia rolled her eyes. "But never mind. Do you know what I heard about Constantius?"

Valeria covered her ears. "Please do not tempt me to gossip."

"But this is not exactly gossip. Actually, the news is encouraging, but you must not tell anyone."

Valeria was curious now. "I promise."

"Constantius' present wife, Helen, is a Christian."

"Is that so unusual? Mother and I are Christians, but that makes no difference in Father's persecution of the believers."

"There is more. I have heard from a reliable source that in secret, Constantius is a Christian too."

Now this was newsworthy, and Valeria lowered her voice. "Do Father or Galerius know?"

Eugenia shook her head. "Hardly. If they did, they would have put a stop to his confirmation as Caesar. You must never tell."

"Never." Valeria crossed her heart. "One thing puzzles me, though. How could a Christian man agree to leave his wife in order to become Caesar, for that is what Constantius has done, is it not?"

Eugenia nodded and shrugged. "If he truly is a Christian, perhaps he believes he is called to serve and make changes in the empire once he becomes an emperor, though the abandonment of his wife is quite sad." She paused and fixed her eyes on Valeria. "No sadder than your situation, of course."

"So you do pity me! I knew it."

"I never pretended not to feel sorry for you. But I have told you that you must accept your fate and relinquish your life—not to your husband, but to your Lord."

"I believe I have done that," Valeria declared. "And I am finally ready to accept my fate . . . tonight."

"You said that last night." Eugenia smiled. "We shall see what happens when the sun sets."

15

*E*ugenia's teasing remark echoed in Valeria's head throughout the following days. Though part of her was relieved that she had been spared the horrible wedding night she had feared, she was also becoming more and more insulted by the fact that Galerius had not even attempted to touch her since the day they had spoken their vows. What would people—particularly her father—think if they knew that she and Galerius were married in name only?

Since they had arrived at their palace in Thessalonica, her husband was unconcerned about appearances and had not even visited her room. Night after night she lay awake in bed, waiting for him to appear, wondering if this might be the night she finally conceived a child. But Galerius never came. Embarrassed, Valeria had not yet confided in Eugenia, despite her friend's constant prodding.

"Everything is fine," Valeria continually assured Eugenia, though it was obvious her longtime friend did not believe her.

Valeria had not seen her husband at breakfast. Each day Galerius went out early, leaving Valeria to eat alone. No matter what time she ventured downstairs, he was never there. But her pride would not allow her to invite him into her bed.

Why do I care? she reminded herself. *This is the man who was ultimately responsible for Mauritius' death. How can I possibly encourage his advances? And yet . . .*

One morning Valeria arose at five, determined to have breakfast with her husband. To her dismay, his place was empty, even at that unfathomable hour. None of the servants knew where he was, and her curiosity consumed her. *Where does he go each morning? I have to know!* At last she decided to confide in Eugenia.

"He is probably at the temple for the early morning sacrifices," Eugenia suggested. ·

Admittedly, an early morning visit to the temple sounded logical, but Valeria wanted confirmation. The following day, she arose at three and dressed. The black cape from the sisters of Saint Mary Magdalene's priory provided the perfect disguise. She tossed it over her shoulders and pushed the hood down over her head. Down the hallway she tiptoed and then slipped into an alcove, praying that the servants, who were preparing the palace for the day, would not see her lurking in the shadows. She leaned against the wall and mumbled a prayer, as she waited for Galerius to appear outside his chambers.

As the clock struck four, she heard his door open, and he stepped into view. *At last!*

Valeria waited until Galerius was far down the hallway and then discreetly followed, hiding in the shadows whenever he paused or she heard the slightest noise.

Once outside, Galerius walked alone. *Where are his servants?* Valeria wondered. It was dark as she stepped onto the cobblestone streets to follow her husband, with only a hint of moonlight to light her path. For blocks Galerius continued, with Valeria following behind. Each time he paused, she ducked into the nearest alley, stretching her neck around the corner building so as not to lose sight of him.

To her surprise, when they passed the temple, Galerius did not enter. Instead he continued toward the other side of the city, headed for the seaport. *Perhaps he swims in the ocean every morning,* she thought. *That may be how he keeps so fit.*

She stood in the shadows and watched him walk down the beach. *Perhaps he enjoys the solitude of the ocean every morning.* With the mystery seemingly solved, Valeria considered returning to the palace. She was tired and hungry since she had skipped her breakfast. The sun was just beginning to lighten the horizon, and if she continued tagging along, she would most certainly risk being seen. But as she turned to retrace her steps, she heard a woman call out, "Galerius!"

Valeria halted. The voice was familiar. Refocusing on her husband, her eyes followed as he crossed the sand toward the ocean. At the water's edge, Valeria spotted a woman, waiting for him. When he reached her, they embraced, and Galerius leaned down and kissed her—passionately.

So, she fumed, *my husband is unfaithful to me! What sort of trollop is this woman?*

"Good morning, my darling," Valeria overheard the woman say.

"You look lovely," Galerius said, touching the woman's cheek. He kissed her again, more tenderly this time.

Valeria tiptoed closer to the sand so she would have a better view. When she caught a glimpse of the woman's protruding stomach, she gasped, barely able to restrain herself from voicing her thoughts aloud. *She is . . . with child!*

"I miss you terribly. My heart aches for you," the woman confessed, her voice weepy as she spoke.

"And I, you," Galerius responded. "I regret to tell you that I must take our daughter soon, but you have my word that I will try to have her transported out of the palace to visit you every chance I get." He paused before continuing, "And you know that when our child is born, I must take it as well."

The woman sobbed, and Galerius embraced her again, his voice choked with emotion. "Oh, my darling, what have I done to you?"

The woman gazed up at him. "You have no choice. The gods have chosen you. Go in peace, my love, and do not look back. I will survive. I will make another life for myself."

"Is there anything you need?"

The woman shook her head.

Peeking out from her hiding place, Valeria's worst fears were confirmed. The woman was Galerius' former wife.

Shocked and devastated, Valeria suddenly realized she wasn't the only victim in this politically expedient marriage. And yet, had Galerius not been the instigator behind the entire situation? Had he not leered at her from the beginning, even while he was still married to the woman who now clung to him in the early morning light, and who carried his child, apparently conceived after Galerius' betrothal to Valeria? No wonder Galerius found it so easy to avoid consummating his marriage to Valeria, as his manly desires were being met elsewhere.

Whatever the facts that had led to Valeria's marriage to Galerius and whatever the reason it had not yet been consummated, it was obvious the man still cared for his first wife, and there was no doubt that she loved him. Oh, the injustice of it all! What a monstrous price to pay for the Roman gods and empire! Valeria had already taken the woman's husband; how could she take her children as well?

Confusion swirled around Valeria, and she felt so overwhelmed she was tempted to fall to her knees and cry out to God for forgiveness. *Surely it is a sin to take this woman's husband*, she thought, even as she turned away and took her first steps back toward the palace. *What a self-centered, whining young woman I am! How dare I think I am the only unhappy person in this equation! In reality, there are others who have suffered more than I. I promise, Lord, that I will make no demands of my husband, for it is obvious that his heart still belongs to his first wife.*

When Valeria returned to the palace, Eugenia met her at the entrance. "Where have you been?" she demanded. "I have been worried sick!"

"I awoke early and could not sleep, so I went for a walk."

Eugenia's eyes narrowed suspiciously. "Alone?"

Valeria nodded, too exhausted and emotionally drained to say anything more. "Forgive me," she began, feeling light-headed. "It was such a beautiful morning, and I—"

As the darkness closed in, Eugenia's voice faded, and Valeria abandoned herself to her temporary means of escape. When she awoke, she struggled for her bearings, relieved when she finally recognized Eugenia's face. "Where is he?" she asked.

Eugenia frowned. "Who?"

"My husband."

"Downstairs," Eugenia replied, suspicion lurking in her eyes. "He came in moments after you returned. I told him you had collapsed and said I would send for him when you awakened. I will send a servant immediately."

"Please, no. Not yet. There is something I must tell you."

Eugenia paused. "Are you with child? Is that why you fainted?"

Hot tears pricked Valeria's eyelids and spilled over onto her cheeks. "Not at all. In fact," she whispered so the servants could not hear, "if you must know, I am still . . . a virgin." Then she broke into sobs, allowing Eugenia to gather her into her arms while she cried. As Eugenia stroked her hair, Valeria told her the entire story, including what she had seen and heard that morning.

"Galerius is still in love with his wife," she said, tying her tale together as she drew back and gazed at her friend. "And she is carrying his child!"

Eugenia blotted Valeria's tears and pushed her hair from her eyes. "Hush now," she whispered. "You are Galerius' wife. And we shall never mention this conversation again. Do you understand?"

Valeria frowned, confused by Eugenia's reaction, but nodded obediently.

"Galerius made a choice to leave his wife," Eugenia continued. "He felt a call on his life from his so-called gods. For a man like General Galerius, it is all about duty to the Roman Empire and devotion to his gods. An integral part of his duty is to be your husband—though I suspect that you were a great enticement to him as well. He may have some affection for his first wife, but it is obvious that he has wanted you since the first time he laid eyes on you. It is now your responsibility to make this marriage happen and to earn his deep and abiding love and respect. You are a very beautiful and tender young woman, Valeria, so this is a simple task for you. It is also an order, not a suggestion."

"But the baby—"

"Hush," Eugenia interrupted. "That will work out. We will not discuss it further."

Eugenia rose and exited the room. In a short while, Galerius was at Valeria's bedside, holding her hand and kissing her forehead. "I know why you are upset."

"You do?"

Galerius nodded. "While standing at the water's edge, I caught a glimpse of you before you turned to rush away. I am truly sorry. It was never my intention to cause you any pain, but she is the wife with whom I have shared my life, and she is the mother of my children. It has been very difficult for my heart to let her go."

Valeria, moved by the compassion that came from her realization that others suffered as much or more than she, reached up and touched his cheek. In response, he took her hand and kissed her fingers. "But the baby," she whispered. "The one yet to be born."

The sadness in his dark eyes was overshadowed only by his determination. "Our child," he said. "Yours and mine. We shall raise it as our own, and my daughter, Valeria, will be coming to live with us as well. I also have another son, Maximinus Daia, my sister's son, whom I adopted."

Valeria gulped. "Will he live with us too?"

"He will only visit occasionally, but he is my lieutenant."

Valeria blushed. She could not recall the young man, but she was too ashamed to confess to her husband that she could hardly remember any of the details of her wedding day.

"Is there a problem?" He raised his eyebrows questioningly, and she realized he was asking for her compliance. Hesitantly, she shook her head no.

"Good," he said. "Then it is settled. I have made a choice, and I am totally committed to you. You are my wife, and I can assure you that the past is past." With both her hands now in his, he placed them over his heart. "From this day forward, I will give you my whole heart. I will never be unfaithful to you again."

When she trusted herself to speak, Valeria said, "I am so sorry that this world we live in requires you to leave the woman you love, and who loves you, and to take her children from her."

"She is very resilient, and she will make a life for herself. It is your heart that concerns me now."

"If you can give me more time," Valeria whispered, stunned that the words she spoke were true, "I know I can love you."

His voice was husky. "How much time?"

"Enough for you to grieve the death of your marriage," Valeria said, resisting the temptation to add "and for me to grieve the death of my beloved Mauritius," instead adding what she was sure God wanted her to say: "And then, I can promise you, my husband, that I will do everything I can as your wife to earn your love and devotion."

Tears pooled in Galerius' eyes, stunning Valeria, as he said, "Ah, but I have wanted you from the first time I saw you, sweet Valeria. There is no man or god in the universe who could resist the temptation of your beauty and tenderness. That I still care for the happiness and well-being of my first wife does not negate that fact." Leaning down to where she lay against the pillow, the man she now recognized as her husband kissed her tenderly, and Valeria felt the stirrings of passion that she knew would one day ignite and become a reality.

"Please let me know when you are ready," he said, and then squeezed her hand and walked from the room.

✍❧

Since that day, she knew Galerius had been faithful to her. They met in the dining room every morning for breakfast, where he amused her with tales of his battles and the antics of his daughter, often making Valeria laugh with delight and anticipation of the day when she would have children of her own. The fact that Galerius' daughter had come to live with them at the palace only increased her longing for mother-hood, and even tempered her trepidation at preparing to take his former wife's newborn child as her own.

It was during one of these breakfast discussions that Galerius informed her that he had to leave for battle the following week. Her tears surprised them both.

Galerius rose from his divan and knelt beside her, gathering her into his arms. "Do not cry, my beloved wife. I will return to you. You have my word."

Valeria longed to believe him, but experience had taught her that not all warriors returned from battle. That evening, when Galerius came to the door of her chambers, he found it unlocked. When Valeria heard the door open, her heart stirred with desire.

Entering her dimly lit room, Galerius wore only a robe of purple velvet. He slipped his feet out of his gold sandals and left them by her bed. When Valeria saw him remove his robe, she lowered her eyes. When she stole a shy glance at his body, she was surprised that she felt no revulsion as she had anticipated. Instead, she was so stirred by its beauty that her heart pounded underneath her gown.

Without a word, he walked over to the court cabinet and poured them both a goblet of wine.

"Please sip the wine. It will relax you," he said, offering her the goblet.

She pushed it away. "I have waited for you for a long time. I want to be fully conscious our first time together so I can cherish the memories for a lifetime."

Visibly moved by her words, he touched her face, causing her to tremble.

Valeria's hair was down, tied with a silk ribbon to prevent it from falling into her face. Her husband reached up and untied it, watching as her curls tumbled down her chest.

Galerius eased her onto the bed and then eased down beside her. "You are certain . . . that you want me?" he whispered.

Her pleading kiss provided his answer.

When Galerius pulled away and reached for his robe, Valeria let out a little cry and begged, "Please do not leave me—not now!"

"I have presents for you," he smiled, digging into the pockets of his robe.

"But . . . all I want is you," she said breathlessly. "I do not need any presents."

"Oh, but you will like these gifts."

Out of his pocket he pulled the most exquisite diamond necklace Valeria had ever seen.

She gasped. "It is beautiful!"

He fastened it on her, kissing the back of her neck. "Roll over," he told her, and she complied, curious at what was going to transpire.

Reaching back in his robe, he clasped a small ornate bottle and opened it. A sweet musky fragrance filled her nostrils.

"Mm, perfume," she murmured.

He poured the oil into his palm and rubbed his hands together, and then he dribbled a few drops that felt cold upon her back.

Without a word, her husband massaged her neck and back with the fragrant oil, causing her to moan with pleasure.

When he finally pulled her close to him, Valeria melted into him. At last their marriage would be consummated before her husband was forced to leave her.

And so it was.

Afterward, Valeria delighted that God's design for marriage was one of the most beautiful and sacred moments of her life thus far. When she closed her eyes she was shocked that she had not pretended Mauritius was her lover, but it was her husband she wanted. Now, as she lay in the arms of Galerius, she was puzzled that she felt such a strong affection for him—so strong that she begged him to lie with her again. Had her mother been right after all . . . that God would give her a love and passion for her husband?

After Galerius left for battle, Valeria's loneliness surprised her, yet she was grateful to God that he had given her such affection for her husband even if it was not what she had felt for Mauritius. She felt as though a piece of her soul were missing. She vowed that each day he was gone, she would pray for his protection and salvation. After all, if God could perform such a miracle as to cause her to care for a man she had once despised, surely He could also cause that man to bow his knee and worship the one true God.

16

It was while Galerius was away in Upper Egypt that his son, Candidianus, was born to his first wife. Almost immediately the child was taken from his mother and presented to Valeria. Though her heart ached for the other woman's loss, she also rejoiced at the gift she had been given. With the help of a wet nurse, Valeria would care for little Candidianus as if he had been born to her.

The day the baby arrived at the palace, Eugenia brought him to his new mother.

"Meet your son, Candidianus," Eugenia smiled, pulling back the soft muslin blanket to reveal the tiny creature.

"Oh, he is so beautiful," Valeria cried, gazing at him in awe as Eugenia continued to hold him. "Look at his eyes! And those eyelashes are darker and longer than any I have ever seen on a child. And his cheeks, how rosy!" Valeria touched the baby's hand, and he curled his tiny fingers around hers. "Look, Eugenia. Oh, I couldn't love this baby more if he truly were my own." She ran her fingers gently through his dark curls and kissed the top of his head.

"Would you like to hold him?"

"May I?"

"Of course, silly girl. You are his mother."

"But the baby will know I am not his mother. What if he protests?"

Eugenia shook her head, ignoring Valeria's concerns.

Valeria held the baby gently, cuddling him to her bosom. "Hello, precious baby child," she cooed. "Eugenia, he is looking into my eyes." Valeria kissed the baby's forehead. "Mm, he smells so nice too."

Eugenia laughed and lifted the child's little foot. "Is there anything sweeter than baby toes?"

"Look at his fingers, how long they are," Valeria observed. "He's going to grow into a big boy . . . an emperor." She smiled at the little bundle in her arms and held him closer as she sang one of the songs her mother had sung to her when she was a child.

"Oh, no, he is falling asleep," she cried.

"A baby is supposed to sleep." Eugenia laughed. "Give him to me, and I will take him back to the nursery."

"No, please. He can sleep in my arms."

"Little Candidianus will sleep for at least three hours. Your arms will grow terribly tired."

"I could sit here for three days, and they would never grow weary."

Eugenia smiled. "How my girl has grown."

"I am not your little girl anymore," Valeria snapped. "You forget I am a married lady."

"And from what I see a very happy one."

Valeria smiled. "And a mother. I could not be happier."

"Children are a blessing from the Lord," Eugenia replied as she admired the scene—Valeria and her baby.

Eugenia tiptoed out of the room, and when she returned the little one was still sleeping, and Valeria had dozed off too.

Eugenia left the room again, but soon she heard the wails of a hungry newborn and hurried back to Valeria's chambers.

Valeria was frantic. "I am so glad you are here. Something is wrong with the baby! He's crying incessantly, and his face is turning red."

Eugenia laughed and washed her hands in the water basin before taking the baby. Gently, she placed her finger in the baby's mouth, who grasped it with his lips and made sucking sounds.

"What are you doing to my baby?" Valeria cried.

"Pacifying him. The baby has awakened hungry from his nap. I will take him to his wet nurse."

"Please do not take him away from me."

"He has to eat," Eugenia reminded her.

Valeria looked down at her breasts. "It is unnatural that I cannot feed him."

"Even if you could, you probably would not," Eugenia told her, wrapping the baby tightly in his blanket. "Most royals have wet nurses to prevent their breasts from sagging."

"Well, I would never. I want to feed my own baby. I do not care if my breasts sag down to my knees," Valeria proclaimed, and then she started to cry.

"What is wrong?" Eugenia asked. "Let me deliver this baby boy to his wet nurse before he starves to death, and then I will be back to comfort you."

Valeria soon discovered that her skirt was wet where the baby had leaked through his clothes. The bodice of her tunic was also damp with the child's saliva. But the only thing that concerned her was the baby's contentment.

When Eugenia returned, Valeria had changed her clothes and was sitting in the solarium with a faraway look in her eyes, staring out at the garden. Eugenia waved her hand in front of Valeria's face to get her attention. "Are you feeling better?"

Valeria shook her head. "Every ounce of my being longs to feed and care for this child, and then I think of his mother, having had her newborn snatched from her arms. Oh, how her body must ache for her child!" She began to cry again.

Eugenia pushed Valeria's hair out of her eyes. "You have such a tender heart, dear one. Just as you have accepted Mauritius' death, the baby's mother will accept the loss of her child. At least she has the satisfaction of knowing her child is alive and will be well cared for and loved."

Valeria twisted her handkerchief. "First I take her husband, and now her baby and her daughter. How must she feel? And how can I be completely happy when I am haunted by the knowledge that I have stolen another woman's life? I am living the life that is rightly hers."

"She will find happiness. You said yourself that Galerius told you that she would make a new life for herself."

"The poor woman's only sin was to fall in love and marry Galerius, a man who was so hungry for power and lust that he abandoned her. Why does she have to suffer? She is innocent, yet she is the person who is being punished."

"I do not have answers to your questions," Eugenia told her. "But I do know that we must pray for her to find peace and happiness."

Valeria felt comforted by this thought. "Perhaps I could write to her, too, and tell her how much I love the baby and give her reports on how he is growing."

"What a beautiful thought! God will bless you for your kind and unselfish heart." Eugenia hugged her.

Valeria pulled away, and then stood up and headed for the door.

"Where are you going?"

"I am going to watch the nurse feed my baby."

For the next few weeks, Valeria spent every waking moment with her son. She was up with him every three hours and sat by the wet nurse as Candidianus was fed. When the servants bathed him, Valeria helped. She was so obsessed that some days she forgot to eat; other days, Eugenia had to remind her to bathe. Holding the baby in her lap for hours, she sang and read to him. The only time Valeria took care of herself was when the baby napped. Eugenia was able to coax her out into the garden one warm afternoon for some sunshine and exercise, and the color quickly came back in her cheeks. Now that the weather was nicer, she encouraged Valeria to walk with the baby every afternoon and enjoy the garden.

Valeria spent more and more time in the garden, tending to the flowerbed she had planted. Even as she nurtured her new baby son, she nurtured the plants that brought forth such beauty. When her husband's daughter, the younger Valeria, arrived to live with them at the palace, Valeria discovered that they shared a love for gardening. The two Valerias spent a lot of time outside with the baby, often bickering over who would hold him.

Valeria relished her life, though she still longed for her husband to return and give her children of her own.

One sunny afternoon, as Candidianus slept in the nursery under the watchful eye of his nurse and Valeria knelt beside her beloved plants and dug in the dirt, Eugenia came out to announce that Valeria had a guest.

Valeria jerked her head upward, surprised at the interruption. "But look at me," she protested. "I am a mess. Who is it?" Suddenly, her heart leapt, and she jumped to her feet. "Galerius! Is he home?"

"Oh, I am sorry, my darling." Eugenia's smile faded. "No, I am afraid it is not your husband. Forgive me. But come; I assure you that you will be delighted to see your guest."

Valeria sighed, disappointed but curious as she removed her gloves, tossed her hair behind her shoulders, and followed Eugenia into the palace and straight to the great hall where their guest waited. Once again her heart leapt with joy, at the sight of her mother, sitting on the divan and surrounded by her ladies-in-waiting. Valeria squealed with delight and ran to Prisca, who rose from her seat and gathered her daughter into an embrace.

"I am so glad you are here, Mother, but also surprised," Valeria cried. "How I have missed you!"

"And I have pined for you, my darling. How are you? Turn around and let me have a look at you."

Valeria twirled, laughing as she did so. "You caught me working in the garden, so I doubt I look my best at the moment."

Prisca's smile was warm. "You are glowing. Why, you look more beautiful than I have ever seen you!"

"That is because I am deliriously happy," Valeria said, surprised at the level of truth in her statement. "Though I miss my husband and am anxious for him to return safely, I am now caring for his two children."

Her mother raised her eyebrows. "Are you . . . with child of your own yet?"

Valeria's heart sunk a notch. "How I wish I were," she sighed, "but I am a mother nonetheless! Galerius' children are so delightful, and I enjoy having them here."

Prisca's face shone. "Darling, my heart sings for your happiness. Marriage and motherhood certainly agree with you."

Valeria smiled. "And to think I believed I could never be happy again! What a miracle God has done in my heart! Not only have I grown to care for my husband, but I adore his children as well, especially the baby. What a beautiful child—pretty enough to be a girl." She laughed. "And his daughter even shares my name—Valeria! She is a young woman already, and yet so childlike. Although we are so close in age, I still consider her my child. Come, let me show you my beautiful baby boy."

"But there is an important matter I need to discuss with you first."

"Please, I cannot wait another moment to introduce you to your grandson." Valeria took a reluctant Prisca by the hand and practically dragged her into the nursery.

Valeria lifted Candidianus from his crib and held him high in the air. She tickled his chin and kissed his nose before she handed him over to his grandmother, who cuddled him and cooed.

"Oh, he is a beautiful baby," Prisca exclaimed, though little Candidianus started to fret at the realization that he was being held by a stranger.

"The most beautiful baby in the world," Valeria added. "There, there, do not cry, little one. This is your nonna." When he continued to fuss, she took the child from her mother and gave him to the wet nurse, who was waiting to feed him. Both mother and grandmother kissed the baby before they left.

"Come," Valeria said to her mother, "and tell me this important matter you need to discuss with me. We do not have long before the baby will finish feeding, and he will want his mother."

Prisca's smile faded only slightly, but Valeria recognized the frown that creased her brow. "Your stepdaughter is one of the reasons I am here."

It was Valeria's turn to frown. "What do you mean?"

Prisca hesitated. "You and I are to take her to Vienna."

"Whatever for?"

"She is to be married," Prisca announced, her smile widening once again. "Another wedding! And this time, you are the mother of the bride. But do not worry, my darling. I have already taken care of all the details."

Valeria's mind was racing. "Does Galerius know?"

Prisca nodded. "He and your father have arranged it."

"But the girl is not ready for marriage."

"Neither were you, yet look how you have blossomed." Prisca grabbed her daughter's hands, but Valeria was not comforted.

"I will not allow it. I will not do this to her."

"It is not your decision."

"But I am her mother now, and I do not want her to marry. She is like a sister to me, and a daughter. I love her, and I cannot bear to lose her companionship. She and I have such fun together, gardening and caring for Candidianus."

"Darling, it will be fine." Prisca smiled at her daughter. "Valeria, I am so proud and happy for you. What a wonderful mother and wife you are! I knew if you gave Galerius a chance that God would enable you to love your husband. And He will give you the strength to say goodbye to young Valeria. Besides, once your husband returns home, you will have little time to spend with her anyway."

Valeria had to admit that her mother was right, though she restrained herself from revealing how far short her love for Galerius fell when compared to what she had felt for Mauritius. She had to admit that her marriage to Galerius had worked out far better than she had expected, but she still pitied her young stepdaughter. How would she tell her what had been decided without her consent?

"We shall tell her at dinner," Prisca announced. "We must depart for Vienna in two days."

Two days! So little time to prepare! Then another thought grabbed Valeria's attention. "Mother, you never told me the name of the man who will become her husband."

Prisca smiled. "You are right, my dear. Come, let us sit down, and I will provide you with all the details."

They settled onto a plush divan, and Prisca took Valeria's hand in hers as she spoke. "Your father's co-emperor, Maximian's son by birth, Maxentius, is the bridegroom."

Valeria was somewhat relieved. "At least he is someone we know well. Will Father and Galerius attend the wedding?"

"It will depend on the success of the campaigns in Syria, but I would hope so."

Despite the possibility of being reunited with Galerius at the wedding, Valeria still felt a growing sense of dread at being the one to break the news to her stepdaughter that she was betrothed to Maxentius. At dinner that night, Valeria took a deep breath and blurted it out, prepared to counter the younger woman's objections. To the contrary, young Valeria was ecstatic about her upcoming wedding.

"What shall I wear?" she asked, her eyes dancing at the announcement. "Will my gown be as lovely as the one you wore when you married my father?"

"It shall be even more magnificent," Valeria assured her.

"And will I have lots of babies?"

"As many as the Lord allows," Valeria assured her, puzzled at the girl's eagerness.

Turning to Prisca, whom young Valeria already considered her grandmother, the newly betrothed girl declared, "I can hardly wait to meet my husband. Please tell me, is he handsome?"

Prisca smiled warmly. "Yes, he is most attractive."

"Handsome, yes," Valeria blurted out, "but I have observed that Maxentius is also a bit haughty."

The girl looked surprised, "Oh, but he will not be haughty with me because I will be his wife."

"Of course not," Valeria assured her with a smile, wishing she had not been so quick to voice her opinion.

"Do you know why Maximian did not appoint his son as Caesar?" the young Valeria asked.

Prisca shook her head. "I am sure there must be a good reason. I suppose I could ask Diocletian."

"Please do. I want to be a Caesar's wife too." The excited girl clapped her hands.

Valeria and her mother exchanged surprised glances, unable to contain their laughter over the young bride's unrestrained enthusiasm.

❧

Valeria was in Vienna, sitting on the terrace and finishing breakfast with her mother and stepdaughter, when she looked off into the distance and spotted Galerius and his entourage approaching. Forgetting protocol, she excused herself from the table and hurried down the stairs, where she waited at the entrance of the bridge that crossed the moat. When Galerius drew near, she bowed before him. Galerius dismounted and handed his reins to the groom, and Valeria waited patiently as Galerius' servants removed his armor. Then she opened her arms in welcome and he gathered her into his arms, planting a passionate kiss on her lips.

"You have come at last," she exclaimed, holding his face in her hands. "I have prayed you here safely, counting the moments until I would see you again."

"And here I am," he laughed.

"I must take you to meet our son! Little Candidianus is beautiful and such a joy to me. Thank you, my lord, for giving me a baby. He is long and lean, sure to be an emperor."

"Aye, and I shall enjoy giving you many more . . . a whole army of boys!" He laughed at her exuberance over motherhood.

"I should also like a girl to dress in beautiful clothes—and to replace the daughter I am losing. Young Valeria and I have grown so close. I can hardly bear to say goodbye. Come, I shall take you to meet your son."

"Wait! I must bathe, and then I will meet you in your chambers. Together we will see the children before we go to the dining room for the noon meal."

Back in her room, Valeria's servants helped her bathe. Soaking in fragrant oils, she chatted with Eugenia, who brought her several choices of outfits. Valeria selected a pale blue silk gown and a matching toga, fastened at one shoulder with a large sapphire and diamond pin. In her hair she wore a gold headpiece studded in sapphires, lapis lazuli, and deep coral, with matching gold and jeweled sandals.

"You are a feast for hungry eyes," Eugenia exclaimed, her own eyes twinkling mischievously. "And I am quite sure your husband is ravenous! But now I must hurry and dress for my own husband."

"Oh, please stay," Valeria begged. "Keep me company while I wait for Galerius to come for me so I can take him to meet his son."

Eugenia laughed. "Find someone else to entertain you. Or perhaps this is a good time for you to practice your patience. I must hurry."

Valeria frowned. "I do not recall seeing Octavius ride in with Galerius," she commented, suddenly envisioning the scene in her mind.

A hint of disappointment clouded Eugenia's face, making Valeria's heart ache. "Do not worry," she told her friend, hugging her. "There were hundreds of soldiers with Galerius, and I had eyes for only one of them. For all I know, Octavius could have been by my husband's side."

Eugenia's smile was tentative. "I am sure you are right, but I must say I never thought I would see the day you would be so pleased to see Galerius that you would lose your head in his presence."

Valeria laughed. "That I care for him at all is a miracle indeed! Now, you had better run along and get dressed. As soon as Galerius arrives, I will inquire of Octavius and send word to you of his whereabouts."

After Eugenia left, Valeria became so bored and anxious that she joined the ladies who were completing the needlework for her stepdaughter's trousseau. Needlework had always given Valeria a sense of accomplishment, but today she quickly lost interest and decided to go and see her mother.

"Oh, my dear, you look stunning," Prisca declared when Valeria entered her bedchamber. "I have missed you so much!" Prisca squeezed Valeria's hand. "It's been so lonely without you at the palace. When I spoke to your father this morning, he informed me that he and Galerius are leaving again and will likely be away for quite some time."

"What? How will I ever have a baby if Galerius is gone so much?" Valeria fought tears as she leaned back and gazed into her mother's eyes.

"We shall pray that God will give you a child while Galerius is here." Prisca pulled Valeria into her arms and held her, stroking her hair, causing the younger woman to once again feel like a child in need of comfort.

"Oh, I never told you my surprise," Prisca commented. "Since your father and Galerius will be away for an extended period of time, he has given me permission to live with you while he is gone."

"Oh, Mother, that is wonderful news! I shall be so happy to have you with me. And you shall grow to love my little one, even as I do. Though I still long to bear a child of my own, I know that God has given us the opportunity of raising a future emperor in Candidianus. I have great hope that one day Christianity will be the religion of the Roman Empire—if not through my father or husband, then my son will make it so."

Before the women could continue their conversation, a young servant girl entered the room and stood waiting for their acknowledgement and permission to speak.

"My husband is waiting for me in my room?" Valeria guessed.

"No, Madame. It is Eugenia. She needs to see you in her room right away."

"She wants me to come to her room?" Valeria felt a prickle of irritation at the near command. There were times when Valeria felt Eugenia took advantage of their close friendship, forgetting all protocol. "Tell Eugenia that if she wants to see me she must come to me."

The servant blushed. "Please, Madame. It is urgent."

Valeria looked at her mother, who gave her a slight push. "Go. Eugenia would never issue such a request unless something was terribly wrong."

Valeria followed the girl down the long hallway to Eugenia's room, where she found her friend crumpled on the bed, weeping into her pillow.

Valeria rushed to her bedside. "What is it? What has happened?"

"Octavius is not here," Eugenia cried. "He did not return with the others!"

"Do not jump to conclusions," Valeria soothed. "Octavius is probably at the bathhouse. Can you imagine how dusty the men are after such a long journey? It takes them time to make themselves presentable."

Eugenia shook her head. "No, I saw his comrades down-stairs. I even approached one of them, but he refused to look me in the eye. When I tried to speak to him, he turned the other way. I asked another soldier, but he told me he had not seen Octavius."

Valeria's anxiety level increased. Surely there was a logical explanation. "I will find Galerius and ask about his lieutenant. There is no need to shed tears, Eugenia. Octavius may have remained in Egypt to take care of unsettled matters. I know you would find this a great disappointment, but most of the soldiers had to stay behind."

"But Octavius now rides by your husband's side, and every-one knows that Galerius despises Christians. Why could you not have allowed Octavius to remain with your father, where he was loved and respected?"

Valeria laid her hand on Eugenia's shoulder and waited until her friend made eye contact. "Because I begged Father to release Octavius to serve under Galerius so you would not have to live apart from your husband."

"But why, when you knew how much Galerius despises Christians?"

"Octavius knew that too. He is a wise man, and he would do nothing to jeopardize his position."

"But Octavius was safe with Diocletian. Why did you med-dle in our lives and put my husband's life in danger?"

"You certainly did not complain at the time. Had I not intervened, you would rarely ever see your husband."

"But if he were with your father, I would at least know he was safe. If your husband has done anything to Octavius, I will never forgive you."

Valeria's concern turned to irritation. "Do not speak to me with such disrespect."

"Ladies, ladies, please stop your bickering," Prisca called from the doorway.

Valeria turned, surprised to find that her mother had followed her to Eugenia's room.

"You two are jumping to conclusions. Arguing will not solve your dilemma. I will send a servant to inquire of my husband concerning Octavius' whereabouts. I suspect that Valeria is correct. He probably had to remain behind in Syria. Someone has to watch over things, and Octavius is known for his loyalty and trustworthiness."

Valeria's irritation melted away, as she once again considered her friend's distress. "I am sorry, Eugenia," she said, leaning down to embrace her. "Mother is right, I am sure."

"I am sorry too." Eugenia sniffled and sat up on her bed. "I must get dressed in case Octavius arrives later."

"That sounds like a wise plan," Prisca agreed. "But first, let us pray for him."

Once the women had prayed, Valeria left with her mother. "I hope Octavius is all right," she whispered as they moved away from Eugenia's room. "But now I am going back to my room to wait for my husband. Will you send word if you hear anything?"

"Of course, my dear. And if Galerius returns before my messenger does, you do the same."

Though Prisca's words sounded confident, Valeria noticed her mother massaging her temples, a sign the empress was concerned.

Valeria turned and walked in the opposite direction, headed for her room to wait for her husband. She had been there only a few moments when Galerius arrived. At the sight of him, Valeria's concerns for Eugenia and Octavius dissipated, and when he gathered her into his arms and kissed her, she forgot them entirely.

"May I spend some time with you before I go see the children?" he asked.

Valeria nodded. She ran her fingers through his hair, still damp from his bath. Galerius reached up and removed her headdress and unpinned her hair. When it tumbled down her shoulders, he twisted his fingers around a lock of it.

"You have become a woman since I last saw you," he said, cupping her chin in his hand and gazing into her eyes. "I counted each clop of my horse's hooves on the long road home, dreaming of holding you in my arms."

Valeria smiled, surprised that Galerius' words brought the memory of Eugenia's concern for her husband. She had better ask about the situation before she forgot completely. "I am sorry to interrupt your homecoming," she said softly, "but—"

"Then do not," he commanded, lifting her in his arms and carrying her to the bed.

"I have dreamed of this moment every night you were away," she told him, stroking his face.

Later, when their passion was spent and she lay nestled in the crook of his arm, her head on his shoulder, she remembered the question she had been about to ask.

Valeria took a deep breath and plunged ahead. "Did . . . Octavius come to Vienna with you?"

Galerius flinched. "Why would you ask such a question when I have just returned to you?"

She turned her face upward toward his and ran her finger across his lips. "Because his wife is my dearest and closest companion, and she is frantic with worry that he did not return with you."

Galerius withdrew his arm and sat up on the side of the bed. "Octavius was a fool," he said, his back to her, though she could see the color rise in his neck.

Valeria's Cross

"Father had great respect and admiration for Octavius," Valeria reminded him, wondering why he had spoken of Octavius in the past tense. "He always said Octavius was a soldier to be trusted."

Galerius turned back to her, his eyes cold. "Octavius is dead," he announced.

Valeria gasped, the knife of disbelief piercing her heart. "No! It must not be true. It cannot be!"

Without hesitation, Galerius said, "It is absolutely true. And it was I who ordered my soldiers to execute him."

Valeria could barely speak, "How did he . . . die?"

"Octavius was beheaded and his body tossed into the sea for the sharks to devour."

Valeria felt her eyes widen in disbelief. How was it possible that the man she had finally grown to care for could do such a thing? "What are you saying? If it is true, then you are a barbarian!"

His rage contorted his face beyond recognition, and he grabbed Valeria's arm. "Perhaps I am a barbarian," he growled, "but you are a barbarian's wife, and you will not speak to me in such a manner. Do you understand?"

Valeria cringed. "You are hurting me. Let go!"

Galerius squeezed her arm tighter. "You listen to me. You will not defy me again. Is that clear?"

Fighting the tears that threatened to explode from her eyes, Valeria nodded.

Tossing her arm from his grasp, Galerius ran his fingers through his curls as he spoke. "Octavius was a pigheaded fool. He refused to follow my orders."

"His death had to do with his faith, did it not? Yet you knew he was a Christian when you asked him to join your legion," Valeria ventured, her voice trembling.

"But I did not know he was an uncompromising fanatic."

Valeria was terrified to speak, but she had to know. "Why
. . . would you have my friend's husband killed? You know
how much Eugenia means to me." Despite her best efforts,
a sob escaped before she could continue. "And Father loved
Octavius." As she stared at the man she called her husband,
the man who now faced her with such arrogance, she felt her
fear giving way to fury. How could he have done such a thing?

Galerius reacted with rage. His hands shook, and his face
turned crimson.

"I was right about you all along," she hissed, her voice gaining strength. "Before we were married, I believed you were a
monster." Sitting up and leaning toward him, she clenched
her fists, as all the anger and resentment she had felt over
Mauritius' martyrdom returned with a fury. "How could you?"
she demanded, striking his chest. "How could you? And how
could I have ever thought I was in love with you? I do not love
you at all. I despise you!"

Galerius grabbed her wrists, gripping her tightly, and
glared down at her. "I am going to forget this little incident."

"You are hurting me," she screamed, not caring who
heard her.

Galerius pushed her away, and she fell back upon the bed.
"I am going to see my children—alone." He shot her a look of
disgust as he threw on his clothes and then stormed out the
door, slamming it behind him.

Valeria stared after him, shock and anger warring for
dominance. Then she buried her face in the pillow and
screamed and cried until exhaustion got the best of her.
Spent, she sat up on the side of the bed, knowing what she had
to do.

*I must tell Eugenia. As hard as it will be, she must hear this
from me . . . and no one else.*

17

$\mathcal{V}$aleria swung what felt like legs full of lead over the side of her bed and asked her servant to fetch some warm water. She quickly washed her face and reapplied her makeup before dragging herself down the long hallway to her mother's room. When a servant answered Valeria's knock, she stepped inside.

"Octavius is dead," Valeria announced, restraining tears as she rushed into the topic at hand.

Her mother, resting on a divan, looked up, her eyes widening as realization spread across her face. Putting her book aside, she beckoned Valeria to her. "Are you sure?"

"I heard it from his killer."

Prisca gasped. "Not Galerius! But why?"

"The blood of another martyr, I am afraid," Valeria whispered, nearly choking on a sob. "Mother, when will it end? Can Father not do something about these horrible persecutions?"

Prisca grabbed her daughter's hand and held it between her own. "I am afraid Galerius has been a strong influence on your father. Despite our prayers, persecution is growing, and your father is not doing anything to stop it."

Valeria shuddered. "How could I have ever thought I was in love with that man? Is there anything we can do?"

"When we return to Thessalonica, I will arrange a conference with the priest. We must dedicate ourselves to prayer and study of the Bible."

Valeria recognized the look of concern on her mother's face. "I have heard from a reliable source that Constantius is a believer. Might we speak to him?"

Prisca's face paled. "Never! A woman never betrays her husband. We would be executed if we spoke to Constantius."

Valeria's heart froze within her. Surely this could not be so! "Father would never allow that to happen."

With the assistance of her ever-present servants, Prisca stood to her feet and pulled her woolen shawl around her shoulders. "Because of our faith in Jesus Christ, I feel that we are at risk. Galerius has convinced your father that if we want to save the empire, all Christians must die."

Valeria reeled as if she had been slapped. "Why does Father listen to him? Are believers not the best soldiers and servants in the empire? That was certainly the case with Mauritius and his valiant legion."

Prisca nodded in agreement. "True. But Galerius feels that every time a battle does not go exactly as planned, the Christians are to blame."

"How can this be? Their integrity is above reproach, and everything they do is done in excellence."

"Galerius has convinced your father that the gods are angry because the Christians refuse to make sacrifices to them."

"But that is a lie! It is the exact lie that convinced Father to have Mauritius and his men martyred for their faith. Besides, Galerius married me, knowing that I—"

"Knowing that you would submit to him and keep your faith private," Prisca interrupted.

Valeria felt as if her heart had imploded. "How different my life would have been if Mauritius had lived."

Prisca laid her hand against Valeria's cheek. "We do not know that for certain. Your father may never have consented for you to marry Mauritius."

"Love always finds a way. Did you not tell me that when I was a young girl?"

Prisca's smile was bittersweet. "So I did. But God has given you a higher calling. We simply must dedicate ourselves in prayer so that God will change the heart of your husband— and mine. Our faithfulness can literally change the world."

Valeria sighed. "Before Galerius changes Father's heart completely, you mean."

"We cannot change our husbands, but with prayer, God can do so."

"But we have been praying for a long time," Valeria protested, turning to walk toward the window. Gazing at the garden, she dared to speak her thoughts aloud. "At times I wonder if God is really there. It often feels that He has abandoned me altogether."

Prisca stepped up behind her. "Have you forgotten God's promises so quickly? *I will never leave or forsake you.*"

Valeria turned and smiled, feeling encouragement rise with her mother's words. "I shall never forget a single promise or scripture from our winter on Elephantine. I wish we were there now. I felt closer to God when we were in Egypt."

"God is still with us," Prisca said, her eyes soft with promise. "It is not that He was closer when you were on the Isle of Elephantine, but that you spent more time in the Scriptures and in prayer then. If you want to feel closer to God, you must spend time with Him once again."

Valeria smiled. "I am glad you will be here with me when Father and Galerius are away. Your discipline in your studies and prayer will be good for me."

"I can arrange for us to meet with the priest in Thessalonica," Prisca suggested.

Valeria brightened. "I have a better idea. Since Father has allowed you to live with me while he and Galerius are gone, we can return to Elephantine to study with the Bible scholars. I would especially love to visit Nanu." Valeria's distress turned to elation. "She and I could play with our babies together. In her last letter she told me that her baby boy looks more and more like his Uncle Mauritius. With the two of us, having loved and lost men of the Theban Legion at the martyrdom in Gaul, we could bring great comfort to one another."

Prisca raised her eyebrows. "Have you forgotten that your father is fighting a war in Egypt? It is no longer safe for us there."

Crestfallen, Valeria sank down on the divan, rocking back and forth. "What shall we do, Mother?"

Joining her daughter on the divan, Prisca embraced Valeria. "There is nothing we can do but pray."

Valeria pulled away and sighed. "You are right, of course." But for now, I can no longer put off my duty. I must go and tell Eugenia about Octavius before she hears it from someone else."

"I shall come with you."

Valeria smiled. "I appreciate the offer, Mother, but I am no longer a child. I want to do this alone. It is my duty." She stood to her feet, holding her shoulders back and her head high.

"This is true," Prisca agreed, looking up at her with obvious pride. "You go ahead and tell Eugenia, and I will join you soon."

As Valeria made her way down the long hallway, she almost wished she had accepted her mother's offer to accompany her. Reminding herself of her duty, however, she silently asked God for the appropriate words to say, and she prayed for comfort for Eugenia. Outside her friend's door, she stopped, her hand trembling as she knocked.

When a young servant girl answered, Valeria stepped inside and found Eugenia standing in front of the window, her eyes fixed on the road outside.

"I see you are feeling better," Valeria said, watching carefully to see how her friend would respond.

When Eugenia turned at Valeria's greeting, Valeria's heart sank at the sight of her friend's red and swollen eyes.

"Not really. I am watching for Octavius. Is there any news?"

Valeria paused and said, "We need to talk. Please, sit."

Unmoving, Eugenia hesitated, her gaze still fixed on Valeria. "Octavius is dead. I can see it in your eyes."

Valeria nodded and reached for Eugenia's hand.

Eugenia's face clouded over with pain, and she dissolved in sobs.

Valeria pulled her friend into an embrace, but the devastated woman slipped through Valeria's arms and collapsed onto the floor. Several servants rushed to Eugenia's aid, as Valeria knelt down beside her, fanning her with her handkerchief. Eugenia moaned but did not open her eyes. Valeria leaned over and whispered, "God will give you the strength to get through this. I do not understand how, but I know we can trust Him." Then she looked up to the servants and ordered, "Please carry Eugenia to her bed."

Valeria observed as the servants ministered to Eugenia. One of them brought some smelling salts in a handkerchief, while another brought a basin of water and a stack of muslin cloths.

They washed her face and fanned her, while yet another held the smelling salts under her nose. Before long, Eugenia's dark eyelashes fluttered open.

Valeria sat on the bed beside her friend and straightened the pillows behind her head. "Welcome back," she said softly.

Eugenia's face was emotionless as she asked, "How did Octavius die?"

Valeria swallowed and reached for Eugenia's hand. "He was . . . beheaded," Valeria admitted, surprised that the words were so difficult to say. It was not the horror of the act alone, but also the realization that she still harbored some sense of loyalty to her husband.

Eugenia fixed her eyes on Valeria. "Was it Galerius who ordered his execution?"

Distraught, Valeria could only nod.

"Do you know whose hand performed the hideous act?"

"I do not know whose hand held the sword, but I do know that Octavius died an honorable death . . . as a martyr."

"Galerius is a monster," Eugenia spat. "I loathe him. If I were not a Christian woman, I would cut out his heart and also the heart of the man who killed my husband, and I would feed them both to the buzzards."

Valeria's eyes opened wide, as she gazed at her friend in horror.

"I will not, of course," Eugenia added. "But I cannot help but wish that Galerius and whoever did this terrible thing would one day die horrible deaths themselves."

"Eugenia, you cannot mean what you say," Valeria protested. "You must beg God's forgiveness. If you curse Galerius and the man who killed your husband, something terrible could come to you. Galerius may be a monster, but we . . . you must allow God to avenge, just as you told me when I made these same threats when Mauritius died."

"Perhaps I was wrong when I said that to you. I know you understand—better than anyone. My tears are no greater than the tears you cried for Mauritius. Galerius killed the man you loved too."

Valeria swallowed, willing Eugenia to somehow understand that on some level, she still cared for Galerius, despite the awful sin he had committed. "As much as I loved Mauritius, it is different for you. Octavius was your husband. Now that I am married and understand the bond between a husband and wife, I know your grief cuts far deeper than mine. But I choose to forgive Galerius, and you must too."

Eugenia still studied her. "You have truly come to care for Galerius, even more than I realized."

"I admit that I have, to some extent. But I am also furious with him for killing the husband of my dearest friend, and I told him so." Valeria hung her head. "I am so sorry."

"I wish him dead," Eugenia declared. "The most horrible death."

Valeria cringed, wrestling with the understanding of Eugenia's pain, yet still feeling protective of Galerius. "Please do not despise him. You must forgive him, Eugenia, just as you told me that I had to forgive Father and Galerius. If Jesus could forgive His enemies after what they did to Him, surely you can forgive Galerius . . . with God's help."

Eugenia broke into tears. "I cannot even think of forgiveness at this moment. I do not know how I am going to survive without Octavius. What am I going to do?" She buried her head in her pillow and cried, "I want to die!"

Valeria put her arm around her friend and held her close while she sobbed. "I understand only too well how you feel," she soothed. "When Father told me the news of Mauritius' death, you will recall that I wanted to die too. But thanks to your encouragement, God became my strength and my refuge in my grief. Although I have never stopped thinking of Mauritius, I have learned to live again, and eventually, so will you. You will get through this, Eugenia. God will help you, and so will I."

After a moment, Eugenia rolled onto her back and lifted her bleary eyes to Valeria. "There is something you do not know," she said, her voice cracking from despair. "Something I have not told you."

Surprised that Eugenia had kept something from her, Valeria asked, "What is it? I thought we had no secrets from one another."

"Please do not be angry with me," Eugenia sniffled. "I did not tell you because I knew how much you wanted a child."

Valeria felt her eyes widen. "You are with child? You should have told me!"

"I did not wish to hurt you."

"Hurt me? Are we not like sisters? Oh, I am so happy for you! You must not die of grief now, for you have Octavius' child inside you." Valeria gently placed her hand upon Eugenia's belly. "What a blessing that you still have a part of your husband living and growing inside of you. Why, I can feel the sweet babe moving."

Eugenia's smile was weak and tore at Valeria's heart, even as her friend put her own hand over Valeria's. "Now this baby is all I have left of Octavius," she whispered, her smile fading. "The poor thing will never have a chance to know his father. What a fine man he was."

"Oh, but he will, for we shall tell him," Valeria promised, fighting back her own tears.

"Or her. It could be a girl, you know."

"A girl or a boy, what does it matter? Children are a blessing from the Lord!" Then Valeria grew quiet, as a new thought occurred to her. "Did Octavius know you were with child?"

Eugenia shook her head. "I had not told him. I only suspected I was pregnant a couple of months ago. I had planned to send him the news by messenger, but when the wedding was announced, I thought I would soon see him, so I waited. I wanted to tell him in person." Eugenia shuddered. "But now he shall never know."

"Perhaps if you had told him, he would have fought to live," Valeria mused, immediately regretting her words.

Through her tears, Eugenia's eyes narrowed. "It would not have mattered. My husband would never have denied his Savior."

"I know that. But I have heard that many of the Christian soldiers comply with the orders to make sacrifices to the gods by secretly making the sign of the cross during the rituals."

"Octavius was not a man of compromise."

"Perhaps if Octavius had known you were with child, he might have cooperated more."

"Cooperated? How dare you say such a thing? Do you consider making sacrifices to the gods being cooperative? What has happened to your faith, Valeria? You have weakened. Has your evil husband become as much an influence over you as he is over your father? Have you forgotten so soon what precipitated the martyrdom of Mauritius?"

Eugenia's accusations stung Valeria like a hornet, swelling her heart with grief. "What a cruel thing for you to say."

"It was not my intention to hurt you," Eugenia conceded. "But you have grown double-minded in your faith."

Before Eugenia could continue her tongue-lashing, Prisca appeared at the door. "I am deeply sorry, my darling," she said, rushing to Eugenia's bedside and gathering her into an embrace. "Is there anything I can do for you?"

"No. But thank you. I will be fine."

"Her baby will bring her happiness in her sorrow," Valeria said.

"Baby?" Prisca's face lit up. "What a great God we serve! I am so happy for you, dear Eugenia, even in the midst of your sorrow."

"It is difficult to rejoice when I have lost Octavius."

"But you are going to have his child," Prisca soothed, "and your baby will bring you great joy."

Valeria could stand it no more. Ashamed at the twinge of jealousy she felt toward her friend's pregnancy, she stood to her feet, wanting only to escape the emotional scene and return to her own room. "Will you be all right," she asked, "or shall I stay with you for a while longer?"

"Do not worry about me. You have a wedding to prepare for, so please go," Eugenia said. "The servants are here to care for me."

"I regret that we cannot stay, but there are so many last-minute details we must attend to since the wedding is tomorrow," Prisca said.

"Please give the young bride my deepest regrets that I am unable to attend."

"She will understand," Prisca assured her.

Once out of the room, Prisca and Valeria walked down the hallway in silence.

"I know what is going through your mind," Prisca said at last.

Valeria refused to look at her mother, knowing full well that her mother truly did know what she was thinking and praying, and that she was restraining her tears with great effort.

"You do not understand why God blessed Eugenia with a baby and not you."

Oh, why had her mother voiced those selfish words? The tears were moving from her eyelids to her cheeks as she answered. "I understand why God blessed her with a child. It is only right. The baby will be her comfort in her time of sorrow and will provide a will for her to carry on."

Prisca put her arm around Valeria. "Your time will come, my dear."

"First, I have to overcome these awful feelings I have toward my husband."

"God will give you the strength to do so. You must trust Him."

"Trust whom? Galerius?"

Prisca shook her head. "No. Your Father in heaven. You cannot put your trust in man, for he will always disappoint you, but God never will."

Valeria stopped at her doorway before going inside her room. "But he already has," she said, wiping a tear from her eye and turning away from her mother.

18

*V*aleria's own words sliced her heart like a spear. *God has disappointed me . . . many times! My whole life is a disappointment.* She slammed the bedroom door behind her and ran to her bedside. Overwhelmed with conviction she fell to her knees. For the next couple of hours, she cried out to God, begging His forgiveness for her lack of trust in Him. She then begged God to supernaturally flood her heart with love and forgiveness for her husband. She prayed for strength for Eugenia in her grief and for the marriage of her stepdaughter, especially for happiness on her wedding day. When at last there were no more tears, she felt the peace that only a restored relationship with God can bring.

The wedding is tomorrow, she thought, rising from her knees. *I must get a good night's sleep, as I will need every ounce of my strength to help my stepdaughter get through the ordeal.* Even more emotionally taxing, she knew she would have to face Galerius again, though she was sure he would not come to her chambers tonight, for she had angered him so.

Although Valeria had mentally forgiven Galerius during her prayer time, her heart still struggled with hatred for him over the death of Octavius. If Galerius did come tonight, it would be difficult for her to make love to him. Just the same, she hurried to the door to make sure it was unlocked.

A servant knocked on Valeria's door the next morning, awakening her from a sound sleep. Before she opened her eyes, she reached to the other side of the bed, but her husband was not there. Valeria sat up and saw that the covers were still intact. She was relieved that he had not slept in the bed, but her relief was mingled with sadness, her heart nearly as empty as her bed.

"Come in," she called to the servant, who wished her good morning and went about her tasks of opening the curtains, lighting the lamps, and stoking the fire. Soon the room was overflowing with servants, each assigned tasks in preparation for the wedding day.

Valeria quickly ate the breakfast they served her, and then, with their assistance, bathed and dressed, though not yet for the wedding. She planned to go to her stepdaughter's room to help her prepare, and then she would dress later.

As she passed Eugenia's room on the way to the bride's chambers, she felt compelled to check on her newly widowed friend. To her surprise, Eugenia was sitting up in bed, while a servant held a spoonful of food in her hand and coaxed the grieving woman to eat.

"How are you feeling?" Valeria asked, concerned at the sight of her friend's red, swollen eyes.

Eugenia's smile was weak. "I am better now that you are here."

Valeria approached Eugenia's bedside, hugged and kissed her, and then took the spoon from the servant. She sat down upon an ornately cushioned chair and tried to feed the oats to a reluctant Eugenia.

"You are now eating for two," she reminded her friend, "so you must not refuse this food. Come, now; open your mouth and take a bite."

"I cannot," Eugenia insisted, placing her hand over her mouth. "I feel nauseated."

"If you cannot think of your own well-being, then consider your baby," Valeria urged. "This bite is for him."

Eugenia finally opened her mouth and accepted the spoonful, though she quickly grimaced and gagged. Valeria jumped back, thinking her friend was about to be sick, and then ordered a servant girl to pour Eugenia some water in a goblet.

Valeria watched nervously as her friend sipped the water. When she asked Eugenia if she felt better, the woman shrugged and nodded. "It is not quite as bad as I thought."

"Can you force yourself to get a few more bites down? Do not think of your stomach; think of the baby growing inside you! Your son is hungry."

Eugenia laughed, though her eyes did not reflect any humor. "How can you be so sure this child within me is a boy? Perhaps it is a baby girl."

Valeria shook her head. "No. It must be a boy. He will grow into a mighty man of God. I am counting on him and Candidianus to grow up and put an end to the Christian persecutions." Valeria smiled wistfully. "Please, my friend, eat. Your baby will change the world, but you must provide the sustenance for him."

"I thought you were the one who was going to change the world," Eugenia responded. "The world cannot wait for this baby to be born and grow up. We need you, Valeria."

"But I am a mere woman," Valeria protested.

"Have you so soon forgotten the prophecy the Theban monks spoke on behalf of you and your mother?"

"I shall always remember and cherish those words." Valeria rose and walked to the window, gazing absently into the morning sunshine. "Every detail of the time we spent in Egypt will remain forever etched upon my heart. I carry every moment with me, wherever I go and whatever I am doing—especially the time I spent with Mauritius."

"Why do you torment yourself with the memory of Mauritius when you are married to Galerius? I thought you had grown to love your husband?"

Valeria shrugged. "There are things about Galerius that I find endearing, and one thing I am certain of is that he is in love with me. I can honestly say that I am devoted to him, but the relationship I had with Mauritius went far deeper. We shared the bond of love and the bond of faith. Galerius treats me as well as can be expected, but we are unequally yoked."

"Yet you want to have his child."

Valeria dropped her eyes. "It is the child I want so badly—not particularly *his* child."

Eugenia reached toward her friend, and Valeria returned to the bedside and took her hand in her own.

"My mothering instincts have grown stronger since I have Candidianus," Valeria said. "How I love that baby boy! And I have even grown close to young Valeria. I am on my way now to help her dress for her wedding."

"Do you fancy yourself her mother?"

"I consider myself more of an older sister. Galerius' daughter and I have walked similar paths. I sincerely believe that I have been called to comfort her in her marriage, especially on her wedding day."

"Comfort? I find it strange that you would use this particular word for such a joyous occasion. After all, a bride should be happy on her wedding day. Perhaps young Valeria is looking forward to her marriage." She paused. "I know you were miserable when you were anticipating your wedding, but you were not a typical bride."

"Surely I was not the first reluctant bride in this world."

"Have you asked the girl about her feelings regarding her marriage?"

"It is not necessary. She puts on a good pretense, but how could she be happy about marriage to such a haughty man? And what a bad disposition he has! Father does not care for him in the least."

"The child-bride confided in me that she was anxious to have his baby," Eugenia told her.

Despite her affection for her stepdaughter, Valeria felt her resentment rise. "If she becomes pregnant before I do, I think I shall surely die!"

"Still the dramatic one, I see," Eugenia commented, touching Valeria's cheek. "Does it bother you that I am pregnant and you are not?"

"I am envious of any woman who is with child," Valeria admitted. "But that does not mean I am not consumed with happiness for you. I praise God that He has given you a child to comfort you in your sorrow."

"The Lord gives, and the Lord takes away. Blessed be the name of the Lord."

Valeria marveled at her friend's statement of faith. "What a gift our heavenly Father has given you."

"And I am praying that He will give you the gift of a baby as well. But I believe that if this is to happen, you must first forgive your husband for killing Octavius."

"I have forgiven him . . . in my head, but my heart? God will have to do this."

"Did you tell Galerius that you forgave him?"

"I will."

Eugenia smiled, a hint of pleasure in her still-sad eyes. "Good. It does no one any good to hold resentment against him."

"Does this mean you have forgiven Galerius too?"

"It was not easy, I confess. But God has dealt with me to do what is right."

"You are truly remarkable, my friend."

"Not really. Like you, I am only human, but what good will it do for me to hate Galerius? Having resentment against Galerius would in no way harm him, but it would certainly destroy me."

Valeria's eyes grew misty at the thought, bringing a look of determination to Eugenia's face. "This is no time for sadness—at least not for you, the official mother of the bride. Now, please, help me feed this child who will change the world."

Valeria smiled and lifted a spoonful of oats to Eugenia's lips. Once Eugenia had finished the contents of the bowl, a servant wiped her mouth and gave her some water. Valeria lingered a moment longer to make sure Eugenia was going to nap, and then left to go to her stepdaughter's suite.

Valeria approached the heavily carved door to her stepdaughter's room and paused, suddenly transported back to her own wedding day. She shuddered at the memory of how frightened she had been on the morning of the ceremony.

Surprisingly, when Valeria had told the young woman that she was to be married, the girl had reacted with childish excitement. If she felt any resentment or fear today, Valeria wanted to assure her, just as her mother had done, that God would give her a supernatural love for her husband.

Dismissing the thoughts from her mind, Valeria took a deep breath and knocked.

A servant girl answered; standing behind her was Valeria's mother-in-law, Romula. Valeria saw the telltale signs of a fading beauty shining through the makeup caked over the older woman's face. Valeria forced a smile at the high priestess. "Good morning, Romula. How nice to see you on this joyous occasion!"

Without a word, Romula stepped close to Valeria and peered into her eyes. Valeria shuddered at the fear and hatred she saw mirrored there, but she stoically reached out to offer an embrace. To Valeria's dismay, Romula pushed her away. It was an awkward moment, as Valeria trembled at the presence of evil. It was obvious their spirits were in conflict.

"I have come to see the bride," Valeria announced, her voice pleasant. "Is there anything I can do to help?"

As if Valeria had not even spoken, Romula squinted her eyes and hissed, "I have heard from the servants that you did not join the others in the temple this morning for worship. I sense the gods are angry."

Before Valeria could respond, an unfamiliar male voice interrupted the confrontation.

"Nonna! Who is this beautiful creature with whom you have become so cross?"

When Valeria looked past Romula to the stranger who had spoken, her heart skipped a beat. A handsome young man with dancing eyes had joined the discussion and now stepped in between the two women.

"This is Galerius' wife," Romula said.

"Ah, the beautiful temptress Valeria. Your reputation precedes you. Although after seeing you, I must say there are truly no words in our language to adequately describe your beauty."

Valeria found the young man mesmerizing. He appeared to be about her age. His green eyes were flecked with droplets of gold, and his dark hair was sprinkled with sunlight. He was tall and lean, with a broad chest and strong arms. Dimples marked his cheeks, and his lips were full as they dripped words from a deep voice that was as soothing and sweet as honey.

"I am pleased to make your acquaintance at last," he added, bowing before her and kissing her hand. When he continued to hold it, Valeria became flustered.

"And who might you be?" she demanded, her voice laced with irritation and curiosity.

He laughed. "I am your stepson."

This time he leaned over and kissed Valeria on the cheek. Stepping backward, she tugged her hand away, disturbed by the emotions that swirled inside her. The young man was far too handsome for any woman to feel safe in his presence—stepson or not.

At that moment, the young Valeria appeared, her petti-coats rustling. "Leave Valeria alone," she ordered, and then swung around to face her grandmother. "And, Nonna, you behave yourself too. Valeria is my beloved stepmother and my most cherished friend." The beautiful bride-to-be turned toward Valeria. "I will not allow them to torment you," she announced, planting a kiss on each of Valeria's cheeks. "Now," she said, stepping back, "you deserve a proper introduction. This beautiful but highly irritating young man is my wicked cousin, Maximinus Daia, more commonly known as Daza."

"Daza may be your aunt's son," Romula interjected, "but he is also your brother. Have you forgotten that your father has adopted him?"

"Perhaps," Valeria huffed, "but he will *never* be my brother. Why, it would be shameful to have such an attraction to a brother!"

"As you have probably deduced by now," Daza said to Valeria, his green eyes twinkling, "I am the black sheep of the family. But I am told that a mother can love even the darkest sheep in the fold. Is that true . . . Mother? Do you love me?"

Daza's sister stepped between them. "Be forewarned, dear Valeria, that no woman is safe around this rogue's good looks and effusive charm."

Daza laughed. "It is one of life's rare privileges to make your acquaintance, dear Mother. I trust our paths will cross again soon." He kissed her cheek, this time with such fire that Valeria feared he had burned a hole in her skin.

"Come with me," the young girl said, snatching Valeria's hand. "I will protect you from this scoundrel."

Stepping away from Daza and Romula, Valeria was surprised to sense such a strange attraction to the man who had called her Mother. It was not the admiration or type of attraction she had felt when she first saw Mauritius, nor the affection she had developed for Galerius, but more of a strong animal magnetism that drew her to him. Her feelings both frightened and startled her, but she reminded herself that God would not allow her to be tempted more than she could bear. At the same time, if Daza had invited her to ride away on a white horse with him at that very moment, she might well have accepted.

The sound of Romula's harsh, raspy voice broke the spell, and Valeria nearly jumped at the interruption to her thoughts.

"Stay away from this woman who is your father's wife," Romula warned. "And you," she said, turning to point a gnarled finger at her granddaughter, "if you desire a happy life and fruitful marriage, I suggest you avoid her as well."

Stunned, Valeria wondered where Romula's hatred and venom had originated. Though she had made her disapproval of Galerius' marriage to Valeria known, undoubtedly because of her refusal to worship the pagan gods, the two women had at least been able to speak civilly to one another before this. Quite obviously that was no longer the case, and Valeria knew it did not bode well for her.

19

*V*aleria was unsure of where to turn or what to say or do, so she mumbled a polite goodbye to Romula and Daza, and followed her stepdaughter to help her dress for the ceremony.

"You have not seen the last of me," Daza called to her.

Valeria ignored him, but she was sure her stepdaughter had noticed her trembling.

"Are you frightened of them?" young Valeria asked when they were in the next room.

Valeria considered her answer before shaking her head in denial. After all, she was not really lying. It was not fear in the true sense of the word, but rather that she was unsure of herself and her actions because of her strong attraction to this man she had just met, though she knew she would never do anything to shame her husband or dishonor her God—or the memory of Mauritius. Yet Daza was a force to be reckoned with. How dare he march into her heart and life without warning!

"I am so sorry," her stepdaughter sighed. "They had no right to treat you that way. Nonna is not as bad as she appears, but she is highly superstitious, and she especially does not trust

Christians. And Daza—his good looks and charms have rotted him to the core. He believes he is the gift of the gods to
all women." She laughed. "Sometimes I fear he is right. He is
terribly handsome, is he not?"

Valeria forced a smile, not wanting to reveal her true feelings. "He is a charmer, but he is also obnoxious."

"For his sake, I hope Father does not hear how he tormented
you. I may be upset with Daza over his behavior toward you,
but I can assure you that my father would be furious. He would
not be too happy with Nonna either. Will you tell Father?"

"No."

The bride appeared relieved. "You are very generous.
Neither of them deserves your kindness, but I am grateful to
you, because Nonna and Daza are my family, and despite their
moral failings, I love them dearly."

Anxious to change the subject, Valeria smiled. "I am most
anxious to see your wedding dress."

The girl signaled to the servants to unveil the gown.
When they lifted the protective cover, Valeria gasped. "It is
magnificent!"

"Yes, it is. Oh, this is truly the happiest day of my life!"

Although her stepdaughter had accepted the news of
her betrothal to Maxentius with enthusiasm, Valeria had
been sure that once the wedding drew close, the young girl
would become apprehensive. Apparently she was mistaken.
"You are sincerely looking forward to becoming the wife of
Maxentius?"

"I do not know him that well," the young girl admitted
with a shrug, "but what I know, I like very much. He is so
handsome, do you not agree?"

"Why, yes, of course."

Young Valeria giggled. "Oh, when he kissed me for the first
time, I thought my heart would jump right out of my chest. I

loved him at once! I must confess, I am looking forward to my honeymoon more than I am my wedding."

Valeria smiled. "I am so pleased that you are excited about your marriage."

"I cannot imagine feeling more joyful," the girl sighed, "except for the day I hold my first baby in my arms. Now, that will be blissful! Maxentius has promised me that he will give me lots of children—if the goddess Diana chooses to bless us with the gift of fertility, of course."

Valeria winced, the mention of a pagan god piercing her heart like a dagger. In the brief time the young Valeria had been under her tutelage, she had tried to instill Christian teachings in her stepdaughter's heart. But, alas, old habits were difficult to break, especially after a childhood of pagan practices. Although Valeria felt greatly relieved that Romula had decided to live with her granddaughter in Venice rather than in Valeria's household, she knew it would be difficult for the girl to continue to practice her newly discovered Christian faith there. Prisca had encouraged Valeria not to worry but to pray for her stepdaughter, and that was exactly what Valeria was doing, but she found moments like this terribly discouraging.

She took a deep breath. "Have you forgotten so quickly what I taught you from the Scriptures?"

Young Valeria dropped her head for a moment before looking up. "I have not forgotten, but . . . just this morning in the temple, Maxentius and I made a sacrifice to the goddess Diana. Romula said—"

Valeria cut her off in mid-sentence. "Children are a gift from the Lord, not the goddess Diana."

"Then why are you not pregnant? You said you wanted a baby, and you believe in your God with all your heart, yet you have no child of your own."

Her words stung, and Valeria's hand flew to her chest in a futile effort to slow her racing heart. "In God's time, I will have a baby. Your father has been away a lot since we have been married."

"But how do you explain—?"

"Please." Valeria held up her hand to silence her stepdaughter. "This is your wedding day. Let us not speak to one another with hurtful words. After the wedding, we shall have to say goodbye, and my spirit is already heavy, for I shall miss you with all my heart."

The girl kissed her cheek. "And I shall miss you."

Valeria was touched by her stepdaughter's affection, but she was still reeling from the hurtful reminder of the pagan beliefs of her husband's family, as well as the reminder of her barrenness. For months, Valeria had struggled to hide her anxiety over her failed attempts to become pregnant before Galerius left for war. How could she bear it if young Valeria and Maxentius had a child before her and Galerius? Feelings of flight overwhelmed her, but she fought them, turning the conversation to Eugenia. "Have you heard the news that Eugenia is with child?"

"Oh, yes! Eugenia told me yesterday. Interesting that your God, who gave her a baby, also took her husband from her."

The knife in her heart twisted. "My God was not the One who had Eugenia's husband killed."

"It was my father, was it not?"

Valeria could only guess where this conversation was going, and she was not about to allow it. "I continue to pray that one day we will live in a world free from religious persecution," she said, choosing her words carefully.

"But despite your prayers, the persecutions are only getting worse, not better."

Though their conversation was private, Valeria sensed that the surrounding servants were listening, and that the Christians among them were praying for her, giving her hope and courage.

"You were taught to believe the scripture— *faith is the evidence of things not seen.* God is working in the situation at this very moment," Valeria declared. "When the circumstances are right, I can assure you that God will intervene."

"What a pity your God did not intervene in time to save poor Octavius. He was such a handsome man—a good man."

Valeria forced a smile. "But God has sent a baby to Eugenia to comfort her in her sorrow."

"And if your God were a loving and merciful God, why not both—a husband and a baby?"

"There are many things in this life that we do not understand, but we trust that God has a plan and a purpose. The greatest promise of the Resurrection is that one day we shall all be together again in heaven, and then it will be forever— no more tears, pain, grief, or sorrow, for Jesus will wipe away every tear."

"It sounds more comforting than the journey of death to the River Styx that Romula has taught me. If your scenario is true, it is a most beautiful thought."

"Of course it is true," Valeria assured her. "The holy Scriptures tell us so. And the Resurrection proves that Jesus was exactly whom He said he was."

The girl opened her mouth to answer, but one of the servants spoke up first. "You must hurry. There is not much time before the ceremony."

Valeria smiled, ending the conversation, and then stood by and watched as the staff dressed her stepdaughter. She was indeed a beautiful bride. As Valeria observed from a distance, she offered a number of helpful suggestions, though she could not help but think of the girl's real mother. Surely the woman had heard of the wedding and was even now grieving over her inability to be present as mother of the bride. And young Valeria was, no doubt, thinking of her mother as well, though she graciously did not voice her thoughts.

When the bride was at last dressed and ready, Valeria kissed her goodbye and excused herself, and then hurried off to get dressed. Before she could escape the suite, however, Daza stopped her at the door.

"Not so fast," he said, taking her arm.

Glancing around, Valeria realized that Romula was nowhere to be seen. Terrified at being alone with the handsome creature, she protested, "Please, I must go and dress or I will be late for the wedding."

"May I speak with you privately?"

Surprised that his voice seemed sincere and his eyes pleading, Valeria hesitated.

"I wanted to inquire about Eugenia," he said. "I understand that she is your closest companion."

Surprised, Valeria asked, "You know Eugenia?"

"I have met her a few times, but I also heard about her from her husband."

"Octavius?"

"Yes. He was . . ." Daza hesitated. "He was my closest friend. We both served as my father's lieutenants and fought side by side."

Valeria touched his arm. "I am so sorry. We are all deeply grieved over the loss of Octavius."

"How is Eugenia?"

"She is inconsolable, as one might expect."

"Then I must go and see her and tell her how brave Octavius was in his last hour. How long should I wait before I call upon her?"

"Any news of her dead husband would be of great comfort, so please make your request known to her servants right away."

"I shall. I begged my father to spare Octavius. There was no braver soldier in the Roman Army."

Valeria nodded. "I agree . . . but I really must go."

"Please wait. There is another matter that I must speak to you about."

"All right, but only for a moment," she said, trying to ignore the rapid pounding of her heart and hoping Daza would not detect her attraction for him.

He escorted her into the hallway and backed her up against the wall, as if to speak with her in private. "I wanted to beg your forgiveness for my behavior. I came on a bit strong when I first met you today, and I noticed that I made you feel uncomfortable."

"Your behavior was despicable," she said, trying to keep her voice firm yet matter-of-fact. "But if you are concerned that I am going to tell my husband about it, rest assured that I am not. You are forgiven."

"I am no fool," he answered, his voice low and husky. "I am aware that you are my benefactor's wife. What I want to know is, do you love him?"

Valeria was stunned. How could he be so insolent as to ask such a thing? "He is my husband."

"You have quite skillfully ignored my question. Will you at least tell me if he is in love with you?"

She felt on the verge of tears as she admitted, "I believe he is, yes."

"But you do not know that for certain."

Valeria opened her mouth to assure both herself and her interrogator, but no words came.

"It is common knowledge," he whispered, "that he still pines for his former wife. Since you are now raising their son, you must be well aware of that."

Wondering even as she spoke why she admitted such a thing to a virtual stranger, she said, "You must know that Galerius and I did not marry for love—at least not in the beginning. It was an arranged marriage, for political reasons, although Galerius has assured me that his heart now belongs to me. I am learning to love him, and I believe he is slowly forgetting his first love as well."

Daza scoffed at her. "You are naïve. The reason he no longer sees his former wife is that Diocletian has forbidden him to do so. And you believe it is because he no longer loves her?" He laughed. "In truth, Galerius has been threatened with death if he sees her again, so I can assure you that you do not have to feel threatened by her."

Valeria was stunned. She had no idea her father had intervened in Galerius' relationship with his former wife. "I am not envious of her. At times I even pity her."

Daza raised his eyebrows. "Not only are you young and beautiful, but you are compassionate as well. My adoptive father has done well for himself."

He traced the outline of her face with his finger, and Valeria trembled, though she did not trust herself to pull away.

Daza continued, his hand on her cheek as he leaned in close enough for her to feel his warm breath on her face. "I am sure it is not difficult for any man to love you. In truth, from the moment I saw you today, I loved you instantly, and I knew that I would surely die for you."

"That is preposterous. You do not even know me."

He laughed, his dark eyes lighting up and reaching into Valeria's heart. "Ah, but you are oblivious to the powerful effect your beauty and innocence has on a man. And your tenderness—it could melt anyone's heart, even a man such as myself, who has his pick of women."

His arrogance broke the spell, and she tore her eyes away from his. "You are quite impressed with yourself, I see."

"Not really. I am just stating the facts. Surely you know that you are beautiful and have a strong effect on men. In that same way, I know that women find me attractive."

"And though I am flattered by your effusive compliments, I am not taken in by them. Now, if you will excuse me, I must go to my room and dress for the wedding."

"Before you leave, I would like your permission to see you."

"What? And you think my husband would not object to that?"

"He would not have to know."

Valeria spun away from him, ready to race down the hall toward the safety of her room. "I can assure you, he would know!"

He grabbed her arm and turned her back to look at him. "Are you not aware that Galerius has his concubines?"

"Every woman knows that her husband has concubines. Except my mother, of course. My father will be eternally faithful to her."

"So he is. And since you possess the same qualities as your mother, I imagine that someday Galerius will be eternally faithful to you also—once you give him your whole heart. In the meantime, I know I could bring you great happiness. I can sense that you are hopelessly attracted to me. And why not? I am young and virile, and . . ."

"Insufferable, arrogant, presumptuous—"

Before she could finish her chastisement of him, Daza lowered his lips to hers and kissed her. At first she fought him, trying desperately to push him away, but soon her resistance melted, and she returned his kiss with abandon until at last he pulled back and gazed down at her.

"Forgive me," he begged, tracing her lips with his finger. "I never force myself upon a woman. I hope that I have not offended you, but I could not resist, and when I kissed you, your lips were drawn to mine." He shook his head. "Octavius' death has deeply affected me. Losing my friend has made me realize how short our time is upon the earth. I want to seize every moment of happiness that I can."

"But I am married . . . to your uncle, your adoptive father."

"Do you not know that the majority of the women in the court have their lovers while their husbands are away at war? Their husbands are aware of it too."

"Of course I know that. I am no fool. I have heard their whispers, and indiscretions are often common knowledge."

"Some of the women have affairs with their servants. Even when their husbands return, their passion is so rampant that they sneak away at every opportunity to be with their lovers. What do you think of this?"

"It is not my place to judge them."

"But have you not seen them with their lovers when their husbands are away at war?"

"Of course, but I have ignored them. Their business is their own."

"Then will you take me as your lover? I would be honored to satisfy your passions. Consider that you could have a prince for a lover, and not a slave. No one will ever know."

"My God will know. I am a Christian."

A look of surprise flashed in his eyes. "Is Galerius aware of this?"

Valeria lifted her chin and squared her shoulders. "Yes . . . to some extent."

"Everyone knows your mother is a Christian, but I thought you practiced your father's religion and were only sympathetic to those Christian renegades."

"I am equally as devout as my mother."

"Then it must be painful for you to be married to such a pagan."

Valeria felt the blood drain from her face, as tears pooled in her eyes and spilled over onto her cheeks.

Tenderly, Daza took Valeria in his arms and kissed her tears away.

"Please, stop," she begged. "It is wrong."

Daza released her. "How can you love a man like Galerius, who makes such a mockery of your religion and murders your fellow believers for their devout faith in your beloved God?"

"With God's help, I have accepted my fate."

Daza shook his head. "Then you are a stronger person than I. When I begged your husband to spare Octavius, he laughed at me for my compassion and accused me of being weak and cowardly. Galerius derived great pleasure in killing our friend. How can you share your bed with such an evil man?"

How can I indeed? she wondered, even as she sent a prayer to heaven for help. After a few moments she recovered. "Because I believe that one day I shall lead my husband to the Truth."

Daza roared with laughter. "I know of no other man as devoted to the gods, but I admire the naiveté of your faith."

"Are you not devoted to the pagan gods, as are Galerius and Romula?"

"My family is wildly fanatical, but I am the rebellious sort. I choose not to believe in any god. I am a Platonic thinker; I believe in myself. A man has to make his own way in this world."

"But the Lord orders a man's steps."

"Then maybe you can teach me about your God, and I will find Him."

Valeria knew he was toying with her. "I will pray for you, but God will send his laborers to you."

"But I want you to be my laborer."

"You want me for your lover. I am far too clever to fall for your machinations."

"You are very intelligent, a rare trait in a woman, and I personally admire it."

"Please, let me go now. It is getting late."

"Not until you agree to be my lover."

"I will never agree to that."

"But have the other women not told you that it is expected of you? No one will judge you. Galerius may be away for years at a time, and you are young, with healthy needs and desires. It is normal and acceptable for you to take a lover. Galerius and I have the same blood running in our veins, so consider that I could even give you a baby and he would never know it was not his. All the women—"

"I am different from the others."

"I do not believe it. Surely, you are not frigid. Your kiss was hot, flaming with passion and desire."

"I did not kiss you; you kissed me."

"Ah, but you returned my kisses, and I could taste your hunger. You desire me as much as I do you."

Valeria glared at him, unable to deny that his kiss had awakened a level of feelings within her that she had not experienced since Mauritius died and that she certainly did not experience now with Galerius.

"You must release me," she said at last, pushing his arm away. "I am a Christian, and I serve the living God, who expects faithfulness from me in my marriage. I could never behave like the others. Never!"

"If this is true, then why did you return my kisses?"

"Let me go!" Valeria ordered, determined not to cry so he would think her even weaker.

With one last look, he released her arm. "I will let you go this time, but I am not a man who gives up so easily. I yearn for you, Valeria . . . and I always get what I want."

"Not this time," Valeria snapped, and then hurried away before he could grab her again.

"We shall see about that," he called after her.

20

*O*nce Valeria was safe in her room, she fell upon her bed in distress. As rude and obnoxious as Daza was, she had to admit she had felt an irrepressible passion for him during their confrontation. Over the last few months, Valeria had accepted her fate—marriage to Galerius. And to her surprise, she had come to love her husband. Their lovemaking was full of passion too. But how could she sustain the love and passion she felt for him when he continued to execute Christians, especially those she loved?

Oh, how she hated the necessity of political alliances! Why could people not simply marry for love, rather than expediency? If she had been allowed to do so, she would not be married to Galerius—the very man behind the deaths of both Mauritius and Octavius—nor would she be fighting this irresistible attraction to Daza.

Her servants tiptoed around her bed and tried to comfort her, but she ordered them all away. Life was so unfair. To make matters worse, her father, whom she loved, was as much to blame for Mauritius' death as Galerius! Even her mother was not sympathetic to her dilemma. Prisca thought prayer was the answer to everything, but lately it seemed Valeria had seen little evidence to prove that theory.

A young servant girl gently nudged Valeria and reminded her that she would be late for the wedding if she did not get dressed immediately. Overwhelmed by guilt over her reaction to Daza, Valeria felt the need to bathe again, to wash away Daza's kiss from her lips and his touch from her face and arms. Though the time was short, she ordered the maids draw a bath, and she quickly scrubbed herself. Why had she allowed Daza to kiss her? What if he told someone? She shuddered at the repercussions. Galerius would be furious, and her behavior would bring shame to her parents. Perhaps Galerius would even order her execution.

Valeria froze. She considered Romula's hatred of her and what would happen if she suspected what had transpired between Valeria and Daza. She even wondered if Romula might have put Daza up to the mischief. If so, he was probably with Galerius at this very minute, telling him of his wife's unfaithfulness. But had she been unfaithful? No, it was only a forced kiss, one that she had resisted—at least, at first.

Of course, there was also the possibility that Daza could lie to Galerius and tell him Valeria had approached him. With that in mind, Valeria decided she must speak to her mother and tell her the whole story. Prisca would be angry with her—or perhaps not angry but definitely disappointed, which was even worse. But Valeria had to talk to someone she could trust, and Eugenia was busy dealing with her grief. Oh, what a terrible world she lived in! But before she could fall into complete despair, her servants reminded her that Galerius would arrive momentarily to escort her to the ceremony.

Though recoiling at the thought, she forced herself to slip into the simple turquoise silk toga she had chosen for her stepdaughter's wedding, and then stood as a servant girl fastened it at the shoulder with a large diamond clip. Matching diamonds dangled from her ears, and her hairdressers swept her long, sun-streaked copper curls into a simple but classic design atop her head.

"You look beautiful, madame," one of the servants told her, but as Valeria gazed at herself in the mirror, she realized that she was showing signs of stress.

"Are you not sleeping well, my lady?" her makeup artist asked, expertly dabbing makeup to cover the darkness under Valeria's eyes.

Valeria did not respond, for she did not want to admit that she often lay awake at night, grieving the loss of her happiness, and worrying, despite knowing that to do so was a sin.

Just as her dark circles were repaired, there was a knock at the door, and Valeria stood up to greet her husband. He entered and immediately came to her, kissing her cheek absently as he offered her his arm.

"Does this dress please you?" she asked, hoping to keep the conversation pleasant, as she knew he was furious at her for her outburst when she learned of Octavius' execution.

He nodded, but it appeared his mind was far away, possibly in another land to conquer. Or perhaps he was thinking of his former wife. This was a day the two of them had probably spoken of sharing together . . . the marriage of their beloved daughter. How cruel this world was to separate the couple! Now on Galerius' arm as he walked to his daughter's wedding was a woman who still longed for the man Galerius had killed, while Galerius no doubt thought of the mother of his children, wishing she could be there to share in this gala event. Life was indeed unfair and unkind.

As Galerius escorted his beautiful young wife to his daughter's wedding, his mind was on the exchange he'd had with Diocletian just minutes earlier. They had been standing together, conversing, when a messenger arrived with a trunk full of gifts from Narses, the ruler of Persia. Though it was customary for rulers to send gifts for a royal wedding, Diocletian had been suspicious.

"He is extending an olive branch," Galerius had assured him, but Diocletian had insisted that his spies within Persia had informed him that Narses was bent on destroying every trace of his immediate predecessors, erasing their names from public monuments, and could not be trusted.

"He is seeking to identify himself with the warlike reigns of Ardshir and his father, Shapur," Diocletian had explained, pacing in agitation. "And as you well know, Shapur sacked Roman Antioch and captured the Emperor Valerian, skinning him alive to decorate his war temple."

Galerius suppressed a shudder. "We have only been involved in a few skirmishes along the borders."

"Aye, you must invade Syria soon and attack the cities. Mind you, I cannot provide any reinforcements until we conclude the war in Egypt," the emperor reminded him.

"My men and I can easily handle the Syrians alone," Galerius boasted.

Diocletian raised an eyebrow, and then his lips curled into a smile. He put his arm around Galerius' shoulders and said proudly, "Only my son, Galerius, is brave enough to attack the feared Syrians."

The words echoed in Galerius' mind like an omen, even as he and Valeria entered the great hall in preparation for the royal wedding. He was well aware that the Syrians fought to the death. As evidenced by what they had done to Valerian, the last Roman emperor who had invaded their territory, they were feared far and wide as bloodthirsty barbarians in search of trophies. Galerius shuddered at the thought of becoming one of them, but it was time to put such thoughts behind him. There would be time enough to act on them later—if indeed it became necessary to do so.

✑

The wedding was magnificent. Galerius and Maximian had spared no expense in celebrating this powerful union. Rich foods were abundant, and fine wines flowed freely. Even though her stepdaughter's marriage was decreed for political reasons, Valeria had never seen the young woman so happy. The bride appeared positively giddy, and her husband was quite obviously taken with her. When Valeria saw the way Maxentius gazed at his bride, she was besieged with envy. Galerius seldom looked at her quite like that. She watched her husband as he spent most of his evening conferring with the two emperors, Diocletian and Maximian.

At least Valeria was able to enjoy the wedding festivities alone, relieving much of her anxiety, even as she relished her duties as mother of the bride. The lavish banquet had now ended, and the entertainment was about to begin. For the first time today, she felt relaxed. Her evening was close to perfect until she heard a familiar voice behind her.

"You look ravishing, Valeria. May I have the pleasure of this dance?"

Valeria whirled around to find Daza hovering like a vulture ready to attack its prey. "Thank you," she replied curtly, "but I am waiting to dance with my husband."

"Ah, but he is deep in conversation with the emperors. Surely, he does not have time for you, so as his son, I will entertain my stepmother."

Valeria hesitated, struggling to think of an excuse, but nothing came to mind. Finally she replied, "You must first ask Galerius for permission to dance with me. If he agrees, then I shall not refuse you. Otherwise you must promise that you will stay far away from me."

"As you wish. I should think he would be grateful to have me entertain you while he is deep in conversation about war strategies, but perhaps I am wrong. There is only one way to find out, so I shall ask him."

Nearly mesmerized, Valeria watched the handsome young man make deep strides in her husband's direction. She mumbled a quick prayer that Galerius would refuse his permission, thus resolving her dilemma.

Not one to give in to the pleasures of the flesh, she could make no sense of the strong attraction she felt for Daza. Yet she had never seen a man quite as attractive, who resembled a younger, far more handsome version of Galerius. Daza was taller and his eyes were the deep, dark green of the Mediterranean Sea, unlike the penetrating black eyes of Galerius. Daza wore his dark hair longer than most men, allowing it to curl erratically around his tanned face, an ideal frame for his perfect features. His body was strong and muscular, and he appeared as fit as an athlete.

For a moment, Valeria tried to relive how it felt to be enveloped in his strong arms earlier that day, and the thought made her tremble. She had never experienced such a strong physical attraction, even to Mauritius, but she had been a young virgin then and did not know what it was like to be with a man. Now, though her affection for her husband was certainly not all it could be, she had experienced some passionate pleasure with him. But it was nothing to compare to the pleasure of the kiss she had shared with Daza this afternoon.

Still, it was Daza's gaze that affected her most. She felt as if he were looking into the very depths of her soul, the most private part of her being. The fact that they shared grief over the loss of Octavius only increased their bond to one another. She was so affected that she had to force herself to look away, chastising herself for staring at him with inappropriate thoughts. After all, she was a married lady, the wife of a respected Caesar, and, more importantly, a Christian! Yet in Daza's presence, she behaved like a lusty harlot.

Valeria jumped when she felt someone slip an arm around her waist.

"Did I startle you?" her mother whispered.

"Yes," she admitted, blushing as she brushed her mother's cheek with a kiss.

There was great concern in Prisca's eyes. "I saw the way you looked at that young man."

Valeria's cheeks grew hot as she feigned ignorance. "What on earth do you mean?"

"A mother knows. I saw you chatting with him, and when he walked away, I watched you stare at him with hunger in your eyes. Who is he?"

"My . . . stepson."

"What?"

"It is true. Maximinus Daia is his name, though everyone calls him Daza. He is the son of Galerius' stepsister. Galerius is his uncle, but he has officially adopted him and is his benefactor—meaning that Daza will become Caesar when Galerius becomes emperor."

Prisca narrowed her eyes at Valeria. "I only hope I can trust you to behave yourself in your 'stepson's' presence."

Valeria drew herself up as if insulted. "I am married to his uncle and adoptive father, and I can assure you I would never even entertain any thoughts of—" Valeria could hardy believe the words that came from her lips. She had lied to her mother! *God forgive me.*

"Valeria, please. You must stay alert at all times. You are young and still so innocent. What worries me is that you are terribly vulnerable. You were forced into a marriage with a man you did not love on the heels of grief for your first love."

"Murdered by the man I was forced to marry, I might add."

Prisca ignored her and continued. "Now your husband has caused the murder of your best friend's husband as well—for no reason but that of his faith." Prisca lowered her eyes and did not look at Valeria as she spoke. "Under the circumstances, you would not be human if you did not harbor ill feelings toward Galerius."

"I am glad you can finally admit the tragedy of my circumstances, Mother, instead of repeating your usual positive statements, such as 'keep praying and God will give you a love for your husband.' I will not pretend anymore. Though part of me has grown to care for Galerius, another part of me is still very angry with him and struggling to forgive him. There are days I feel close to him, but there are also days when I do not even care if he ever believes in God."

"Valeria, how can you say such a thing?"

"Please do not pretend to be shocked. You had to know how I felt. I have tried to love Galerius. He is kind to me at times, but he also mocks everything and everyone that is dear to me—and to you. For that reason, I loathe him."

"May I remind you that just days ago you were glowing with love for your husband? These feelings of resentment will not hurt him," Prisca warned, "but they will destroy you. You must put these regrets and resentments to rest, once and for all. It is time for you to get on with your life."

"Eugenia said something similar earlier today, explaining to me why she had chosen to forgive Galerius for murdering her husband. I know she is right, and I, too, have chosen to forgive him. But that does not change my feelings." She sighed. "Still, I have been faithful to your words of wisdom, Mother. Each day I have prayed that God would give me a love for my husband. And I have prayed for Galerius, too— morning, noon, and night—that he will come to know our Father in heaven. Yet I see no evidence of any of this happening . . . ever."

"Evidence? What do the Scriptures say about evidence?" Prisca did not pause for Valeria to answer her question. " 'Now faith is the substance of things hoped for, the evidence of things not seen.' Not seen. What do you suppose the Apostle Paul meant by those words? And remember, the Scriptures also tell us, 'Do not grow weary in doing good!' "

"Mother, I can assure you that my faith is strong enough that I will not fall into temptation with this handsome young man."

"Then why do you look at him with such desire?"

"Is it that evident?"

Prisca raised her eyebrows, her expression saying more than words ever could.

Valeria shook her head. "I do not know why Daza has such a powerful effect on me. Perhaps there is a familiarity about him because he is so much like Galerius, and yet . . . younger, handsomer."

Prisca shook her head. "Fortunately, our days here are few. With his good looks and position, this young man is dangerous, especially if you consider that Romula raised him." Prisca watched him chatting animatedly with Galerius. "Daza is far too clever for you. Just stay by your husband's side; when he is unavailable, come to me. I will protect you."

"Do you really believe I need protection?"

"I most certainly do. Now I understand why God has sent me to live with you in Thessalonica. I am to be your protector so you will not destroy your life."

"Why do you worry? We do not even know if Daza plans to take up residence in Thessalonica. I am sure someone of his youth and physical stamina is an excellent soldier, much needed in Galerius' ranks."

"Just so you know, I will be watching you like a hawk watches a floundering rabbit."

"Well, your assignment is about to begin. Daza has gone to ask Galerius' permission to dance with me."

Prisca's eyes narrowed. "You will have no choice in the matter. You must dance with him if Galerius grants his permission, but I will be watching your every step."

"Would it shock you if I confessed that I desire to be alone with him?"

"No, it would not shock me, but you are such a foolish young girl to even say such a thing."

"Am I? Is it not common knowledge that most of the ladies in the court have indulged in relationships with their male servants while their husbands are away at battle? And no one thinks anything of it. So why can I not enjoy the same pleasure?"

"It may be a common practice among the court," Prisca hissed, leaning close to her daughter, "but it is not true of all the ladies. I have never been unfaithful to your father, nor was Eugenia ever unfaithful to Octavius. We would never give in to the desires of the flesh. We are Christians and are therefore held to a higher standard."

"But Father was a peasant, a soldier, when the two of you met and fell in love. You were allowed to marry the man you loved, but I was not. Have you no mercy for me, Mother?"

"Oh, my darling, I pray for you constantly. I know your circumstances are difficult."

"Difficult at best . . . and at times, unbearable. If I am forced to make love to my husband tonight, I will close my eyes and pretend he is Mauritius or Daza—anyone but Galerius."

Prisca's eyes flashed with obvious shock and anger, and then they softened as she lifted Valeria's hand and kissed it. "This is not the life I had dreamed for you, my precious daughter, but I do know that it is the life God has ordained for you. I wanted you to know the love of a man like I have enjoyed with your father, and I am confident that one day you will find deep and abiding love with Galerius."

Hot tears stung the back of Valeria's eyelids. "Something inside of me died the day Father told me of Mauritius' fate. Then today I met Daza, and I began to feel alive again."

"Hush," her mother whispered. "Here he comes. Just remember, I will be watching your every move—and his."

Daza was all smiles when he returned to inform Valeria that her husband had not only granted his permission, but he had also thanked him for escorting his wife. The arrogant young man took her hand, sending a charge through her body that made her tremble. On the dance floor, he swung her around and pulled her so close that Valeria could feel his heart beating in perfect rhythm with her own as they moved gracefully among the dancing throng.

"You are trembling," Daza whispered in her ear. "I feel your desire."

"I am trembling because my mother is watching us."

His face registered shock and surprise. "You told her . . . about us?"

"First of all, there is no 'us,' and I did not have to tell her anything. She sensed the attraction we have for one another, which worries me all the more."

"Ah, so you do admit that you have an attraction for me?"

Valeria blushed and ignored the question. "I fear that Galerius will sense it too."

"He is far too preoccupied with the affairs of the empire to pay us any attention."

"Turn around, and you will see that he watching us now."

He swung her around on the dance floor until he had a clear view of Galerius. "So he is, but I think he is admiring what a lovely couple we are together—or maybe what a beautiful wife he has." Daza nuzzled her cheek with his chin. "There is not a woman in this world as lovely as you."

"Nor is there a man . . ." Valeria stopped mid-sentence, shocked at herself for uttering the impulsive words. If only she could take them back!

"Ah, so you do not deny that you desire me!" He pressed his cheek closer to hers, but she jerked her face away.

"I cannot deny it, but alas you are forbidden fruit."

He pressed his hand into the small of her back and pulled her closer. "But your sister Eve eventually took a bite of the apple."

"I see you are familiar with the Scriptures."

"Octavius made sure of it. And for your love, I would gladly serve your God."

Valeria shot him a look. "What would your grandmother say about that?"

"I do not care what Romula thinks. I am not a mama's boy like Galerius. I am my own person. The woman has no influence whatsoever on me. I can protect you from her evil schemes."

"I cannot help but wonder if Romula has put you up to pursuing me so she can discredit me in my husband's eyes."

"Nothing would please her more, but I would not be a part of any such scheme. I am pursuing you on my own accord.

From the moment I saw you, I knew I could never live without you."

"Please do not utter those words," Valeria warned, placing her finger upon his lip.

He seized the opportunity to kiss her finger, and Valeria twisted her neck around to see if her mother was watching. Fortunately, someone had greeted Prisca and she had turned away momentarily. Valeria then turned her head the other way and was relieved to see that Galerius was deep in conversation with her father.

Daza held her more tightly and whispered in her ear, "I cannot . . . I *will* not live without you."

To her relief, before she could respond, the music stopped. Valeria politely thanked Daza for the dance, and then turned and hurried toward her mother without a backward glance.

21

$\mathcal{V}$aleria lay in her empty bed, staring into the darkness. She was not surprised that Galerius had not come to her room since her outburst over Octavius the day before. They had made the pretense of being the happy couple at his daughter's wedding, but for the most part, he had ignored her. Unless her father intervened, she had doubts that she would ever share a bed with her husband again. That also meant she would likely never conceive a child. Perhaps if she apologized he would return to her.

She considered how she had been drawn to Galerius the first time she heard him speak to an audience, his oratorical skills commanding nearly as much respect as his new position as Caesar. She also recalled every sweet detail of their delayed wedding night, when they had finally consummated their marriage. But no matter how hard she tried to keep her thoughts focused on her husband at his finest, he paled in comparison to Daza.

She shut her eyes and tried in vain to block out the image of the smile on the young man's handsome face when he had returned to claim his right to dance with her. With thoughts of Daza still teasing her mind, she admitted to herself that she was in no mood to apologize to Galerius and invite him back into her bed. Because it was not her husband she yearned for; she wanted his son in her bed. Had she not dreamed of having Mauritius by her side instead of her husband? And yet she had still managed to enjoy her marriage to Galerius.

It is because Mauritius is dead, she told herself. And our love was pure and good—unlike what I feel for Daza. Oh, why can I not stop thinking of that horrid man? I do not want to want Daza—yet I do, desperately! Help me, God! Forgive me and help me, please!

With her mind now focused on God, she hoped that, at least for tonight, she could remain faithful to her marriage vows, even within the privacy of her thoughts.

Eugenia was still in mourning, but it was the queasiness in her stomach more than anything else that kept her confined to her room. Valeria missed her terribly. How she longed to pour out her heart to her faithful friend, to confide in the woman who was so like an older sister to her! But how could she? Poor Eugenia had enough to cope with in her own life, and Valeria knew it would be unfair to burden her with anything more.

She had considered talking again to her mother, but she was afraid Prisca might go to the emperor or even Galerius in an effort to remedy the situation. Valeria could not even imagine what that could mean to family relations. No, it was best she handle it on her own, and with God's help, she was certain she could.

As Valeria sat next to Galerius at breakfast that morning, she attempted to win him back and forget about Daza. She stayed as near to her husband as possible, although he continued to ignore her. She toyed with the eggs in front of her, stirring them with a silver spoon but not interested enough to scoop any into her mouth. Even the bowl of peeled and sliced fruit that sat before her offered little temptation. She only wished her lack of appetite was due to the same reason Eugenia did not want to eat. Oh, how she ached for her friend's loss, but how she envied the impending birth of Eugenia's baby!

Of course, she had her stepson, Candidianus, and she grew to love him more each day. What a precious baby he was! Their bond was deepening, and she had to admit that she so looked forward to the day when he would call her "Mama." At the same time, Valeria could not help but continue to agonize over the pain the boy's real mother endured in the name of political expediency.

Her thoughts were interrupted as Galerius laid his hand on her arm and leaned over to kiss her cheek. "I must excuse myself. I will see you for lunch on the terrace."

Valeria nodded absently, knowing that Galerius was going to a strategy meeting with her father and some of the military leaders, who had gathered at the wedding. Perhaps she would have the servants fix something special for Galerius for later. If she busied herself overseeing the preparation, she would not have time to allow her thoughts to wander where they had no business going.

And then she saw him. Even as Galerius strode across the room to meet Diocletian near the doorway, Valeria was shocked to discover Daza standing right before her. When had he come in? How had she missed his entrance? And why now, just as her husband left her?

Oh, Father, she cried silently, *I am no match for this man's greedy seduction! Help me!*

"Are you all right, my dear?"

Startled, Valeria glanced up to her side, where Prisca stood, cool and erect, a sentry come to do her duty. Valeria felt herself relax.

"Thank You," she whispered, as much to her mother as to God. "I am fine . . . now."

Prisca nodded, her knowing gaze cutting through to Valeria's soul. For once she did not mind.

"I have already had my breakfast," Prisca said, her eyes darting from her daughter to the uneaten food on the table and then back again, "but I see you have not finished yours. I will join you, and we can have a nice visit while you eat."

The empress moved her eyes from Valeria to Daza; Valeria's eyes followed. The attractive young man's hungry gaze had changed to an innocent smile, as Valeria introduced him to her mother. Daza responded with effusive charm, but it was obvious that Prisca knew his intentions and was not impressed. He ducked his head briefly in Valeria's direction before turning to walk away, but she had not missed the promise in his eyes that he would be back. The thought froze her heart with fear, even as her blood ran hot through her veins.

❧

She did not have long to wait. Valeria was scarcely halfway down the hall on her way to see Eugenia when Daza intercepted her. It was as if he were invisible, or could blend into the walls. One minute he was not in sight—and then he was. It unnerved her nearly as much as the brazen look of desire on his face. How was it he could leer at her that way and feel no shame, knowing she was married to the man who was his adoptive father? What kind of man coveted the wife of the man who was one of his closest relatives and also his benefactor?

Worse yet, what kind of woman betrayed her husband in her mind, lusting after a younger, more handsome and virile man, even as she dared to call herself a Christian? For that was exactly what she was doing, as she stopped in her tracks, less than a foot from the man who lured her with his eyes and drew her with his passion. What a horrible person she must be to want him so!

"I am on my way to visit Eugenia," he told her.

"Then I will leave you two to visit and come back later."

He grabbed her arm and pulled her against him, brushing her lips with a quick kiss that promised more. "No, please join me. I fear my visit will be too emotional for Eugenia. It would be good if you were there."

Valeria hesitated, knowing she should rush away but unable somehow to move. "I suppose you are right," she said, telling herself she had agreed for Eugenia's sake.

When they arrived at Eugenia's room, their mutual friend was sitting up in bed. She smiled when they walked in. "Two of my favorite people! Please, come in."

Valeria kissed Eugenia, but Daza was much more affectionate. He gave Eugenia a bear hug, practically lifting her off the bed. He planted kisses all over her face and fussed with her pillows, making sure she was comfortable, and then took her hand and held it while they spoke.

"So the two of you have met," Eugenia smiled, dismissing Daza's exuberant and emotional display as she eyed them both.

Valeria blushed and nodded, hoping Eugenia would not detect her true feelings.

"I am truly sorry about Octavius," Daza said. "I believe I miss him nearly as much as you do."

Eugenia's voice shook as she asked, "Why could you not have stopped it?"

"I tried, but Galerius . . . he was determined to make an example of Octavius. The battle was not going well, and Galerius was convinced it was because his pagan gods were angry that the Christians were not making sacrifices. I begged Octavius to reconsider and make the sacrifices along with a sign of the cross, but he was adamant that he would not compromise. This time, Galerius was determined that Octavius would sacrifice or die."

"Was Octavius afraid? Did he suffer?"

"He exhibited amazing courage, even in his last moments. You would have been so proud. He was not afraid, but praised his God continuously. He asked me to tell you that his last thoughts were of you when he stepped up to meet his executioner. His death was quick, over in seconds. I daresay he did not suffer."

Eugenia bit her lip. "I am trying to forgive Galerius, but it is so difficult."

"Forgive him? That is impossible."

"Humanly, yes, but with God, all things are possible. He commands that we forgive, and He provides the strength to do so."

"You ladies serve a strange God." He looked at Valeria and shook his head, then turned back to Eugenia. "Is there anything I can do for you?"

Eugenia got straight to the point. "The greatest gift you can give to me and to the memory of my husband is to give your life to Jesus Christ, the One for whom Octavius died."

Appearing uncomfortable, Daza stood to his feet. "I will consider it." He leaned over to kiss Eugenia goodbye. "Take care of yourself and the baby."

"How did you know about the baby?" She glanced in Valeria's direction. "Did you tell him?"

Valeria nodded.

"I will look out for the boy, and one day when I am Caesar, perhaps I will adopt him as my own, so he too can be a great Caesar." Daza smiled. "But for now, I must go. We are preparing to return to the battlefield tomorrow."

"I will pray for you," Eugenia promised.

When the women were alone, Valeria asked, "Do you like Daza?"

"What is not to like? I adore him. Can you only imagine what a great leader he would become if he embraces Christianity? It was Octavius' greatest hope. There is no doubt that Galerius will make him his Caesar when he becomes emperor."

"But is Daza a man of character?"

"As much as is possible for a pagan."

"But he said he was not a pagan."

"True. He is more of a Platonic thinker, but their beliefs are far different from ours, spiritually and morally." Eugenia's eyes narrowed as she stared at Valeria. "The two of you have conversed, I see."

Valeria felt her face turn crimson.

Eugenia pointed a finger. "You must stay away from Daza. He is a good friend, but you are too vulnerable to resist his charms. And I know for certain that he is far too weak to resist your beauty."

"You are too late," Valeria admitted. "I must confess that I desire him more than words can say."

Eugenia's mouth flew open. "What? You have not—"

"No, but I have tasted his kisses and been sorely tempted. Please pray for me! The men are leaving tomorrow. If I can just resist him another day, I will be safe."

Eugenia frowned. "I am disappointed in you. Stay away from him, here with me in my room."

"I cannot. I have promised Galerius that I will have lunch with him."

"That is a blessing. Promise me you will beg Galerius' forgiveness."

"I cannot promise, but I will try. I am safe for lunch, but I have no doubt that Daza will seek me out. He has an uncanny way of finding me alone. And I cannot deny, I long to be with him."

"Then you must not be alone until he leaves for battle. The Scriptures promise that God will not allow you to be tempted more than you can bear. Please know that I will be praying for you."

Valeria nodded, and then hugged her friend and left. Outside Eugenia's door, she leaned against the wall to compose herself before going to meet her husband. She still had to walk from Eugenia's room to her quarters. *Will Daza be waiting for me around the corner?* Before she could shoot up a silent prayer, he appeared, placing his hands on the wall on either side of her and leaning in until he was only inches from her, his breath sweet and warm while his lips teased her with promise.

He is going to kiss me again, and oh, how I long for him to do so! But I cannot! "I must not—"

But he closed the gap between them and softly, gently pressed his lips against hers, silencing her and becoming more insistent when she did not immediately resist. Soon she was returning his passion, eagerly throwing her arms around his neck and pulling him close. She knew she was wrong, knew her actions were dangerous, yet she could not seem to stop. In truth, she did not want to stop. *Perhaps that is why it seems God no longer hears my prayers.*

When at last he pulled back, Valeria gasped for air as if she were drowning, and indeed she felt as if she were. *Do not stop,* she cried silently, and yet she clamped her lips shut so the words would not escape. *Oh, God, rescue me!* Hot tears pricked the back of her eyelids as she wondered if she truly wanted to be rescued.

As he leaned in for another kiss, voices at the end of the hallway jerked him back. Like guilty children they stood, stiff and waiting as Prisca and one of the servants came into view. The look on the empress's face changed from surprise to anger as she took in the scene before her.

"Valeria," she said, walking straight to her daughter and taking her by the arm, "I was just looking for you. Come, I will escort you to your room so we can talk."

Daring to sneak a glance at Daza, Valeria saw his disappointment. Though she knew she was in for a tongue-lashing, she would welcome it if it meant escaping the alluring clutches of the devious Daza.

Without another word, she turned from the man who only moments before had nearly consumed her with his kiss and hurried with her mother to the safety of her room.

22

$\mathcal{P}$risca remained with Valeria in her chambers, lecturing her about her behavior until Galerius appeared at last. When Valeria jumped to her feet to greet her husband, Prisca slipped out the side door.

"Come, sire, I have had a lovely lunch prepared for you on the terrace." Valeria took her husband by the hand and invited Galerius outside, making every effort to be an attentive wife.

Galerius ordered the servants to leave and then turned to Valeria. "I am touched by your kindness. Thank you."

Valeria nodded and clasped her hands before her, a contrite heart spurring her words. "Sire, I beg your forgiveness for my earlier behavior. I was shocked and deeply grieved over Octavius' death. I do understand the great burdens you have upon your shoulders. Can you please find it in your heart to forgive me?"

Galerius eyed her suspiciously as she dared to reach up and touch his cheek, praying she had not permanently alienated him. "It was not my place to meddle in your affairs. It will never happen again."

"Never?" He chuckled. "Now that would be a disappointment. I find it intriguing that my bride is filled with fire. An agreeable wife would surely bore me." He smiled, pulling her close. "Come here, my naughty girl," he whispered before kissing her.

"I was so looking forward to your return—counting the days—but I made a mess of things, and now you are leaving again." Valeria swallowed. "I also want you to know that . . . I forgive you for killing Octavius."

Anger flashed in Galerius' eyes, and his smile faded. "Forgive me? I did not ask your forgiveness, for I did nothing wrong. I was only doing my duty."

Valeria drew back, but he pulled her to him, his grip tightening and his eyes still fixed on her.

"Please do not be angry with me, sire," she begged.

Galerius studied her for a moment, and Valeria was certain she caught a flicker of regret in his eyes.

"I am sorry about Octavius, but I have an army to rule. If I allow one of my charges to disrespect the rules or me, it could lead to an uprising."

Forgetting her promise to stay out of his affairs, Valeria boldly asked, "But can you not leave the Christians alone? Let them worship their God, and you worship yours."

Galerius' smile was tight. "It is impossible for you to understand the complexities of war, my dear. But tell me, how is his widow?"

Valeria smiled as Galerius sat down on the divan beside the window. "Do I detect a genuine concern from my fierce warrior?" She poked her husband in the chest, and then plopped down on his lap and put her arms around his neck. "Do not tell me you have a soft heart hiding under that gruff exterior."

Galerius put his finger to his lips. "It is our secret. You must tell no one." When she nodded knowingly, he asked, "How did Eugenia take the news of her husband's death?"

"She is heartbroken, of course."

"Ah, but I am sure she knew all along that war is a widow-maker." His eyes took on a faraway look. "Would you be heart-broken if I were the one who had died?"

Valeria blinked in surprise, hoping he had not sensed her thoughts of Mauritius. "Oh, yes," she cried, immediately stretching to plant a kiss on his cheek. "I would be devastated if I lost you, Galerius. Please do not even speak about it." She placed her hand over her heart. The sincerity of her words and the miracle God had performed amazed her. "After living with you as my husband, I am not sure I could live without you." She nuzzled her head into his shoulder.

"I love you," he whispered in her ear, tenderly stroking her hair.

"And I love you," she answered, praying he did not recognize the limitations within her words.

"What are Eugenia's plans?" Galerius asked then, pulling back to look down at her. "Will she remain with you?"

"Of course, particularly now that she is expecting a child. I am convinced that God has sent this baby to comfort her in her sorrow."

A cloud swept over her husband's face as he mumbled, "What a stupid fool."

Valeria recoiled at the harshness of his response. "Whatever do you mean?"

The dark cloud disappeared as quickly as it had come. "I was not speaking of you or your friend, my dear. I was speaking of her dead husband. What sort of man willingly leaves his family behind by refusing to make a sacrifice to the Roman gods?"

"Octavius was unaware that he was about to become a father. Eugenia was waiting to surprise him with the joyous news upon his return."

Galerius sighed. "Still, it is impossible for me to conceive how a man can refuse to make a simple sacrifice when he knows the consequences—not only upon him, but upon his family."

Valeria swallowed her retort, wisely waiting for a moment before speaking. "Would you not die for your gods?"

"Why, of course. But my gods would never require martyrdom of me. Octavius served a selfish god." Galerius shook his head. "I will never understand Christians."

"But are they not your best soldiers?" Valeria knew she was walking dangerously close to the subject of Mauritius but she was determined to continue. "Father says their integrity is strong and their service impeccable."

"But they are also obstinate and opinionated—and hurtful."

Valeria raised her eyebrows. "This has not been my experience. Most of the Christians I have known are kind and loving. I have never known one to be purposely hurtful to anyone."

Galerius' eyes narrowed. "Unless you disagree with their beliefs."

"What are you saying?"

"When I was a little boy, my father worked as a shepherd. Each day I went with him to tend the sheep."

Valeria saw a hint of moisture in his eyes, and her heart softened, as she thought of the parable Jesus had told of the good shepherd and the lost sheep. It would be easy to tell Galerius of Christianity, for he would surely understand the concept of God's love and care for His "sheep." But she knew this was not the time. The Theban monks had taught her that everything must happen in God's time.

"We were a happy family," Galerius continued. "Then my father died, torn apart by a bear, as he tried to protect his sheep."

Valeria touched his face and kissed away the hint of tears at the corner of his eyes.

"Life became hard after he was gone, and we suffered greatly. There was little food or money, but my mother assured us things would soon change because a wealthy widower in our village had asked her to marry him."

"And did they marry?"

Galerius shook his head, and his eyes misted over once again. "Our lives would have been far different if they had. Instead, life became even more difficult."

"But the hardships you endured have obviously contributed to the great man you have become," Valeria reminded him.

"Perhaps," Galerius conceded. "Just the same, my mother, sister, and I never recovered from the shame and humiliation we endured at the hand of this man and his friends when he called off the wedding, and . . . married someone else."

Valeria was stunned. "What caused his sudden change of heart?"

"The man became a Christian."

Valeria raised her eyebrows, suddenly understanding her husband's hatred toward the Christians. "Did he try to convert your mother?"

Galerius nodded, his jaws twitching with unspoken words. "Oh, yes, but she refused for fear of angering the gods—or worse, losing her position at the temple. But even she was shocked when he deserted her."

"That is a very sad story," she conceded. "But you must admit that it is difficult for a man and woman of different faiths to be married," Valeria ventured, choosing her words carefully.

"It has caused no problems in your parents' marriage," Galerius pointed out.

Valeria took a deep breath, ignoring her racing heart. "Or in ours. Please, continue your story."

"My mother made a choice to remain faithful to her gods, and she could have lived with her decision. But then this man married one of the Christians, and she was insanely jealous of my mother and ridiculed her, making her life miserable."

"I suspect this woman was not a Christian and likely made a false profession of faith in order to marry this wealthy man," Valeria speculated.

Galerius shrugged. "Whether she was a false Christian or not, I cannot say. But one thing I know—she was an evil woman. Eventually she convinced her husband that my mother was a fanatical lunatic, and he mocked her, too, as did their Christian friends in the village." Obviously agitated by the memories, Galerius stood to his feet and began to pace.

"Romula must have been devastated."

"That is an understatement. Even though I was only a little boy, I remember how she cried, night after night. She was so deeply hurt, but it did not take long for her hurt to turn into anger, and then hate, and finally revenge. Eventually she devoted herself to her beliefs and worship of the gods, cursing all Christians. She vowed to do everything in her power to destroy them."

"And she taught you to despise Christians too?"

He stopped and stared at Valeria. "Christians are not difficult to despise."

Ignoring the retort that rose up inside her, she stepped to his side and took his hand. "Christians are not perfect." She took a deep breath. "There was only one perfect man, and He is Jesus." Though she wanted to say more, she sensed the need for restraint. She smiled and changed the subject. "Have you had an opportunity to spend time with your delightful son yet?"

"Our son?" He smiled. "I went to the nursery just minutes ago. He was sleeping, but the nurse echoed what I have already heard from everyone else—that you are a wonderful mother."

"I could not love that baby more if I had birthed him myself," Valeria admitted, blocking out the thoughts of her husband's first wife and the agony she no doubt still felt at being separated from her husband and children. "Candidianus is a joy to my heart. Thank you for giving me the privilege of raising him. And I . . ."

When her voice drifted off, Galerius frowned. "What are you thinking, my pretty one?"

She mustered her courage and, doing her best to keep her voice steady, said, "I hope you will consider my feelings before you murder another Christian or anyone else who is near and dear to me."

The look of stunned surprise on Galerius' face quickly faded, and he laughed aloud. When at last he regained his composure, he said, "You need not meddle in military affairs, my dear. That is best left to me; it is not your concern."

Valeria took a deep breath. "I understand why you despise Christians, but please consider that not every one of them is as cruel as the man your mother loved . . . or his wife. It is obvious you have sought revenge, but not all Christians behave like this. It is time to let it go."

His laugh faded from his eyes. "You are my wife, not my military advisor. Though I must admit, you amuse me." He lifted her chin again and kissed the tip of her nose. "And how can I amuse you, my love?"

Valeria smiled, determined to push past her lingering feelings of anger and resentment. "Give me a child, one that will be a part of both of us."

His face softened, even as his eyes sparkled. "Let us first enjoy the lunch your loving hands have prepared for me, and then I shall be delighted to accommodate your wishes."

23

ℬack in Galerius' palace and with the wedding behind them, Valeria and Prisca entertained themselves as best they could, overseeing the servants and the running of the large royal household, but also spending much time in prayer and study of the Scriptures. At last Valeria felt her spiritual strength returning, and though she often wished her husband and father would come home, she also enjoyed her ability to freely worship without concern about offending either of them.

Her greatest joy was watching little Candidianus seemingly grow right before her eyes. She also marveled at the miracle of life so obviously forming within Eugenia as her shape changed. Valeria missed her stepdaughter, but news from the girl was full of the joys of her newly married state, including an expected child.

Once again, Valeria's heart constricted with the pain of a barren womb, but she quickly asked forgiveness of her heavenly Father for any feelings of jealousy or envy. She was grateful for Candidianus and the love he brought to her life. In addition, she harbored the hope that she had become pregnant while she and Galerius were together in Venice.

This morning, as Valeria worked in the garden, she was thankful that she no longer had to contend with Daza. Surely, by the time the men returned and her husband's obnoxious stepson showed his face in her presence again, he would have recovered from his lust for her.

Even as she had. Yes, Valeria could now say that with calm assurance. No longing or desire remained in her heart for the handsome young man. God had used the physical distance between them, as well as her many hours in prayer, to deliver her from what would surely have been her destruction.

Hunger pains reminded Valeria it was lunchtime. She rose to her feet and brushed the dirt from her skirts and then her hands. Candidianus would be hungry. Though the nurse would see to the boy's needs, Valeria preferred to do as much as possible for the young child herself. She still ached to cradle a babe of her own, and yet she wondered if her love for her own flesh-and-blood infant could be any deeper than it was for the little boy who held her heart in his chubby hands.

Smiling at the thought, she stepped from the garden into the coolness of the palace to retrieve her son from his room. On her way down the hall, Eugenia stopped her. "I was just coming to the garden to give you this letter from Galerius."

Receiving the message from her friend's hand, she hurried to her room to read it and to freshen up before feeding Candidianus.

≈ ❧

Valeria was still in tears when Prisca came to her room later that afternoon. "What is wrong, my darling? Eugenia told me you received a letter from Galerius. Did it contain bad news?"

Valeria shook her head. "No, it was filled with declarations of his undying love for me."

Prisca raised her eyebrows. "I never took Galerius for a writer."

"I suspect Galerius' secretary embellishes my husband's words with his own flowery language. But I will admit the beautiful letter lifted my spirits."

"Then why on earth are you sad?" Prisca sat down on the divan beside her daughter and stroked her hair.

Valeria choked up again before confessing, "I hoped I might be pregnant, but I . . . have just discovered this afternoon that . . . I am . . . not."

Prisca took Valeria's chin and lifted her face toward hers. "Darling, I know how disappointed you must feel, but please do not work yourself up into such a state. You are very young, and there is still plenty of time for you to have lots of babies."

"But how can I get pregnant when my husband is thousands of miles away most of the time?"

"You just said Galerius wrote in his letter that the battle will be over soon. In the meantime, you have Candidianus—and what a joy that child is!" Prisca smiled and raised an eyebrow. "Perhaps God is delaying the desires of your heart. Consider that if Candidianus were older, a new baby would not have to compete with his charming older brother."

Valeria smiled through a veil of tears. "You always seem to have an answer. Of course it would be impossible for any baby to be as good-natured as Candidianus, and certainly not as smart or beautiful."

Prisca nodded. "Every child is special, but I agree that Candidianus is one of the most gifted and beautiful children I have ever known." She chuckled. "Although I would suggest that we break our habit of referring to him as beautiful. The lad is growing up so quickly, he will soon despise the word!"

Valeria smiled. "I shall call him my handsome boy." She paused as Prisca blotted her tears with a handkerchief. "I am sorry, Mother, but with the wedding behind me, the palace décor completed, Galerius away, and now no baby to prepare for, I am in the depths of despair."

Prisca smiled. "I have the perfect solution for you. Last week I made contact with a wonderful Christian priest in Thessalonica, a Greek scholar named Bishop Marcus. He has agreed to come to the palace three days a week so we can continue our study of the Scriptures. Our first lesson is Monday."

The news sent Valeria's spirits soaring. Although her days were spent caring for Candidianus, she still had an abundance of time on her hands. There was no way she would rather spend it than studying the Scriptures.

For the next few months, Prisca and Valeria dedicated themselves to their studies of the Greek language and the Scriptures, in addition to caring for Candidianus. They also attended the nearby Greek church and began worshipping with the believers there.

❧

A few months later, Valeria was sleeping soundly when urgent words penetrated the darkness and called her back to reality. She forced her eyes open and squinted at the outlined face behind the candlelight. Even as she recognized one of her servant girls, Valeria's heart leapt at the implications. Had something happened to Candidianus? To her mother? Or maybe her father or husband had been wounded . . . or worse, killed on the battlefield.

She bolted upright in bed and tried to steady her voice. "What is it?"

"Forgive me, madame, but Lady Eugenia is asking for you," the girl answered, her own voice quavering as she spoke. "The baby is coming!"

To witness the miracle of childbirth was a gift from God for Valeria. The squalling baby boy arrived in the wee hours of the morning, just as the first silver light of dawn began to peek over the horizon and invade the windows of the bedroom. By then Eugenia was too exhausted to do anything but sleep while Valeria held the tiny bundle in her arms and paced the floor beside his mother's bed, crooning to him while he alternately flailed and sucked his fists, frantically searching for nourishment.

"Soon, little one," Valeria whispered. "Let your poor mother rest a little, and then she will feed you as best she can."

"You are a natural."

Valeria started, turning toward the sound of her mother's voice, surprised to see Prisca standing in the doorway.

"I am very proud of you," Prisca said, approaching her. "The servants told me you were here for Eugenia throughout the night." She kissed Valeria on the cheek and then peered at the tiny bundle in her daughter's arms. "It is a boy, I hear."

Valeria nodded. "Octavius, after his father."

"Of course." Prisca looked up, still smiling but with a hint of tears now misting her blue eyes. "May I hold him?"

Gently, Valeria transferred the squirming infant from her own arms to those of her mother, who received him with the expression of an experienced mother, immediately smiling and cooing at him.

"Little Octavius," Prisca crooned. "So like your father already, with your dark hair and dimpled chin! What a joy you will be to your mother."

Valeria smiled. She had noticed the same characteristics the minute she laid eyes on the new arrival. Even Eugenia had commented on it before finally falling into an exhausted sleep.

"He looks healthy," Prisca commented.

"I thought so too. I am so glad. Eugenia needs a healthy, strong baby. I prayed for one."

Prisca nodded. "As did I. It appears our faithful Father has answered our prayers."

Eugenia moaned in her sleep, and the two women turned their gaze to her bedside. Valeria knew her friend still had a long, hard road ahead of her, but she was grateful to know she would travel it with Octavius' son at her side.

⟡

One morning, as Prisca and Valeria were on their way to a communion service, a messenger arrived with a letter from Galerius and another from Diocletian. Valeria tore into hers and began to comment as she read. "The Roman Army was victorious over the Egyptians."

Frustrated, she turned to Prisca. "What does Father's letter say?" Valeria stepped behind her mother and stood on her tiptoes to look over Prisca's shoulder.

"Excuse me. This is personal." Prisca slapped the letter to her chest, pretending to hide it.

"So Galerius is not the only soldier who has a secretary that writes poetic love letters," Valeria teased.

"Your father pens his own letters," Prisca retorted. "But before your curiosity kills you, Diocletian makes no mention of Syria." She smiled. "He is returning from Egypt and wants us waiting for him upon his return to the palace in Nicomedia."

"Perhaps Galerius will soon be victorious in Syria so he can join us in Nicomedia," Valeria mused. "I shall simply die if he is delayed!"

Prisca nodded. "But just look at you. How you have blossomed in that time from a frightened and reluctant young girl to a self-assured wife and mother. Your once slender, girlish body has developed into the voluptuous figure of a grown woman. I fear Galerius' eyes will pop out of his head when he sees you again."

Valeria laughed. "Oh, I hope so! That should help me get pregnant right away." Valeria patted her empty belly. "We must visit the dressmaker before the men return. I want an entire new wardrobe, one that will dazzle my husband when he returns from Syria."

"First we must pack for our trip to Nicomedia. When we arrive, we shall order our gowns from my favorite dressmakers there."

❧

"Eugenia is asking for you to stop in at her room as soon as you can."

The servant's announcement shot panic through Valeria's heart, as she and her mother rushed to Eugenia's side.

"What is it?" Valeria cried as they burst into her friend's room. "Is the baby all right?"

"He is fine," Eugenia replied, "but I need to speak to you before you leave. It is important."

The servants placed chairs at Eugenia's bedside, where the new mother held her hungry baby to her breast. When Prisca and Valeria were seated, Eugenia smiled at them.

"Thank you for coming." She paused and then plunged ahead. "As you know, we are living in uncertain times."

"What is it, Eugenia?" Valeria pressed. "Please, get to the point. Why did you call us here?"

"I am sorry, but I want you to understand why I have made this decision to leave."

"Leave," Valeria cried. "What do you mean? You cannot leave me!"

"But I must. I want to return to Nicomedia to live with my parents and raise my son among my sisters and the rest of my extended family."

"But, Eugenia, we are your family! You can raise your baby right here in the palace. He and Candidianus can grow up together."

"It is true that you are like a sister to me, but I fear it is not safe for Octavius and me here. Rumor has it that Galerius is pressuring Diocletian to reinstate the persecutions."

"That is rubbish," Prisca said. "My husband does not want any bloodshed."

"I pray you are right," Eugenia said. "But please understand that I want to devote all my time and energies to Octavius, and I believe I can do that better at home with my family."

"That I understand," Prisca conceded, "but I do not know how we will survive without you."

Valeria did not trust herself to speak, as tears trickled down her cheeks. She cried herself to sleep that night, unsure if her heart could withstand yet another loss.

24

Valeria was relieved to leave for Nicomedia with Prisca so she would not be at the palace in Thessalonica when Eugenia departed. Watching her dearest friend, her precious little son in her arms, walk out of her life was more than Valeria could bear.

A few days after Prisca and Valeria arrived in Nicomedia, Diocletian joined them by making a triumphant entry into the city. Valeria felt a mixture of disappointment and relief that neither Galerius nor Daza accompanied him. After her father had rested from his journey, Valeria joined her parents in their private chambers. She greeted her mother with a kiss, then bowed prostrate before her father. When a servant helped her to her feet, she rushed into his arms.

"Welcome home, Father! I am delighted to see you," she cried, hugging him tightly. She held his hands and stepped back from him. "Just look at you! You look wonderful—tanned and rested. Congratulations on your triumph in Egypt."

"After our victory I spent a few weeks at our palace on Elephantine to recuperate from the battle. Such a lovely place, and everyone there inquired about my beautiful wife and daughter. They wanted to know when you were coming again for a visit." He smiled at Valeria. "Ah, and you, my precious little rosebud, have blossomed into a beautiful woman while I was away."

Valeria blushed and kissed Diocletian on the cheek. "Thank you, Father, though I would like to hear those same words from my husband. When will he be returning home? How can I present you with a grandchild if my husband is never around?"

"Always full of questions, are you not, my dear?" He sighed and grew serious. "Galerius has been involved in border skirmishes until a few weeks ago when they invaded Syria. A messenger should arrive soon to apprise me of the outcome."

Diocletian chuckled then and touched his daughter's face. "You have my word that as soon as I hear from him, I will give you a full report."

"When do you suppose that might be?"

"Any day now."

"Why would Galerius invade Syria?" She could tell by the look on her father's face that he was ready for her to end her incessant questioning, but she was determined to push ahead until he grew weary and stopped their conversation.

"We had no choice, my dear. King Narses declared war on Rome. He first invaded western Armenia, reclaiming the lands delivered to Tiridates in the peace of 298. Narses has now moved south into Roman Mesopotamia."

"But why did you not join Galerius in Syria?"

"I plan to consult with him from afar because it is too risky for me go to Persia. If captured there, I could suffer the same fate as the late Emperor Valerian."

"But Valerian was defeated by the Persians."

Prisca quickly joined the conversation. "I am afraid I left out some of the gorier parts of Valeria's history lessons. I did not want our daughter to have nightmares."

"Selective history?" Diocletian chuckled. "Then I shall tell her." He took his seat on a divan and asked the women to join him. With his wife on one side and his daughter on the other, he began. "In the beginning of Valerian's reign, the affairs of the Roman Empire were in disarray. In the East, Antioch had fallen into the hands of a Sassnid vassal, and Armenia was occupied by Shapur I. Valerian and his co-regent, his son, Gallienus, split the empire between them, with the son taking the west and the father heading east to face the Persian threat."

"I thought Valerian conquered Antioch and returned it to the Roman control."

"You are correct." Diocletian touched Prisca's arm and winked. "You have taught her the history well, my dear."

Prisca beamed as Diocletian continued. "The year following Emperor Valerian's victory, the Persians ravaged Asia Minor, so Valerian moved his troops to Edessa. When an outbreak of the plague killed a number of the legionaries, it weakened the Roman Army's position. Shapur then defeated them in the Battle of Edessa. Emperor Valerian called a ceasefire so he could negotiate a peace treaty with the Persians, but Shapur double-crossed him and captured him."

Prisca added, "Valerian has the distinction of being the only Roman emperor ever captured by the enemy. Shapur kept Valerian invested in the purple to show the world that he had the Roman emperor in chains. Whenever Shapur mounted on horseback, he used the emperor as his stepping stool, placing his foot on the Roman Emperor's neck."

Valeria made a face. "How could the Roman empire stand by and allow their emperor to suffer such insults?"

"Oh, they tried to intervene," Diocletian assured her. "Shapur was offered an enormous reward for the emperor's return. In addition, the allies repeatedly advised Shapur to use Valerian as a token for peace instead of an object for insult. But Shapur was too busy gloating in his capture of the mighty Roman emperor. His ears were closed to reason."

"This is the perfect place to stop the lesson," Prisca protested, but Valeria was eager for her father to finish the account.

Diocletian complied. "Shapur flayed him alive—skinned him and then stuffed the skin with straw and formed it into the likeness of a human figure. It was preserved and is still displayed today in a celebrated temple in Persia—their 'monument of triumph.'"

"A far cry from the ornate marble and brass sculptures traditionally erected to the emperors," Prisca lamented.

Valeria winced. "And you allowed my husband to invade Syria?"

"Your husband is the fiercest warrior in all the empire. Someone had to go, and had I not believed Galerius could conquer the Syrians, I would never have allowed it." Diocletian paused for a moment. "But would it not make your life easier if you lost your husband in battle?"

Valeria gasped, stunned by her father's admission that the life he had chosen for her was far from easy. She was unsure how to respond, but before she could answer, the servants announced that dinner was served, so the conversation momentarily ceased as they gathered around the banquet table.

Diocletian's lieutenants requested permission to speak with him in the middle of the meal, falling prostrate before him. When Diocletian motioned them to their feet, the senior officer spoke. "My Lord, we have urgent news from the Syrian battlefield."

"If you ladies will excuse me," Diocletian said, rising from the table as he nodded to Prisca and Valeria. Diocletian then led the guards into the adjoining hall.

Valeria's heart raced, as she jumped to her feet and hurried to the door, against which she pressed her ear and listened. The words she heard made her gasp, and she felt the blood drain from her face.

"What is it?" Prisca cried.

Valeria turned from the door to face her mother, as she struggled to remain on her feet. "Galerius . . . has been defeated in Syria."

25

$\mathcal{D}$eeply troubled, Galerius paced the floor of his tent as he awaited Diocletian's arrival in Antioch. Never before had Galerius lost a battle, but only a few days earlier, Narses and his Syrian Army had sorely defeated their Roman opponents. Humiliated and tormented by the defeat, Galerius was forced to admit that he, and not his army, was at fault. The finest soldiers in the empire were under his command, but he had lost over half of them in the battle. Their blood was on his hands. The Persians had been lying in wait for them, a clever trap Galerius had not anticipated.

Diocletian had informed Galerius that he would wait in nearby Armenia and would also return to Nicomedia during the conflict. The emperor had chosen not to participate in the Persian battle, which thrilled Galerius, as it would be his first opportunity to shine without any involvement from his emperor. How he had boasted to Diocletian that he would advance to Persia and take care of the situation. To his utter dismay, Galerius now wallowed in defeat. How could he face Diocletian? He would soon find out because the emperor was due to arrive any moment, and Galerius had heard that

Diocletian was furious that his Caesar had made such a mess of things.

It was no secret that Diocletian had chosen Galerius as his Caesar for his exceptional military skills. With the loss, how would he now fare with his father-in-law?

Galerius stopped pacing and listened with dread. In the distance was the unmistakable sound of the royal procession, approaching his tent. Trumpets blared to announce the emperor's arrival. The people loved all the pomp and circumstance that Diocletian demanded wherever he traveled, but Galerius and the soldiers thought it ostentatious.

Now, surrounded by his lieutenants, Galerius swallowed hard and exited his tent to greet the emperor. Since Diocletian demanded that everyone, even his Caesars, fall prostrate before him, several of the servants had laid Turkish rugs in the dirt to accommodate the practice.

Diocletian stepped from his golden carriage and strutted around the prone soldiers, kicking some of them with his heavy sandals. "What have you done?" he raged. "Imbeciles! How could I have trusted you with such a crucial battle?"

Galerius knew the answer, though he would never voice it. It was Diocletian's cowardice; he feared the same fate as Emperor Valerian. Had Galerius won the battle at Mesopotamia, one of his goals was to return Valerian's body to be entombed in Rome. Now that would not happen.

Diocletian interrupted Galerius' thoughts by demanding that the prostrate soldiers stand to their feet. "We are taking the processional into Antioch, and you, Galerius, will walk ahead of my carriage with your soldiers following behind you. Now march onward!"

"But, my lord," Galerius protested, restraining his fury at the humiliating command, "I am dressed in the imperial purple. Surely you will grant me permission to change into a battle uniform."

"I will grant you no such thing," Diocletian bellowed. "You shall wear the purple. How else would you feel the full effect of the shame you so deserve?"

Galerius seethed, but without a word he fell into the royal procession and began to march ahead of the imperial cart, flanked by his soldiers. They were a mile inside the Roman city of Antioch, and people gathered along the way, mocking Galerius. Hurling insults, the citizens jeered, some even throwing garbage at the Caesar and his soldiers. Galerius held his head high. If the march was his payment for defeat, perhaps he deserved it, but one thing was certain—he would take his punishment like a mighty warrior.

After Galerius passed, the people fell prostrate for their emperor. By the time the procession reached the center of town, the dusty road had soiled Galerius' robes, but the people no longer paid him any mind for they were making such a fuss over Diocletian's visit.

That evening, a great banquet was held in honor of the emperor, during which Diocletian called a brief meeting with Galerius and his lieutenants.

"The defeat was not due to the failings of the empire's soldiers, but to the failings of their commander. You are to blame," Diocletian declared, pointing his finger at Galerius. "This defeat is unacceptable. You will remain in Syria until you can rally your troops for an offensive." With those words, Diocletian spun on his heel and returned to the banquet.

As Galerius and his men slunk back to their camp, Galerius felt the burden of defeat on his shoulders, and he knew he had to devise a battle plan to beat Narses and the Syrian Army. Foregoing sleep for the next three days, he worked on the plan, too humiliated even to write to Valeria. He was sure

267

she had already gotten an earful from her father anyway. Besides, she was so enthralled with motherhood that she would scarcely notice her husband was gone. Galerius could only pray to the gods that she would not make a sissy out of his son, Candidianus.

⚜

In the spring of 298, a new contingent collected from the empire's Danubian holdings had reinforced Galerius' army. Narses did not advance from Armenia and Mesopotamia, leaving Galerius to lead the offensive with an attack on northern Mesopotamia by way of Armenia.

Narses retreated to Armenia to counter Galerius' attack. The rugged Armenian terrain proved favorable to Roman infantry, but highly unfavorable to Narses' Sassanid cavalry. Galerius was also able to retain the aid of the locals, which surprised the Persian forces; in two successive battles, Galerius secured victories over Narses. During the second battle, the Roman forces seized Narses' camp, his treasury, his harem, and even his family, whom Galerius sent to live in Daphne, a suburb of Antioch, for the remainder of the war, serving as a constant reminder to the Persians of Roman victory.

Galerius then advanced into Media and Adiabene, winning continuous victories, most prominently near Erzurum, and securing Nisibis before the autumn of 298. Moving down the Tigris, he took the village of Ctesiphon, overlooking the ruins of Babylon. At last he had redeemed his loss and was able to return triumphant, sailing home on the Euphrates River.

Galerius smiled as he stood on the bow of the ship, heading home in triumph to his wife. *I am indeed the great leader.*

⚜

Galerius and Valeria had said a tearful goodbye following his daughter's wedding in Venice, but now he had returned a hero. As such, Valeria gave her husband a welcome that he would likely never forget.

Now there was a Syrian victory to celebrate, and Galerius was highly revered throughout the empire. Though Valeria missed her mother, who had returned to Nicomedia to be with Diocletian, it was a time of happiness for her and Galerius in Thessalonica, as she raised Candidianus and desperately but futilely tried to get pregnant.

A few weeks after Galerius' homecoming, a dark cloud descended over Valeria's happiness when Daza arrived. It seemed Valeria spotted him waiting in the shadows nearly everywhere she turned. As a member of Galerius' court, he was with the family frequently, especially for meals. Although Valeria had become immune to his charms, she found his presence a source of irritation. The sooner she could become pregnant, she reasoned, the sooner Daza would stop ogling her.

And then, after a few weeks of rest, Galerius announced that he must return to the business of the empire.

"You have spoiled me with your presence every day," Valeria complained, wondering how his absence might affect her ability to avoid Daza. "I shall miss you."

"Ah, but I am not the only one returning to work. Next week Narses is sending an ambassador for peace negotiations, and I want to extend our hospitality to him. Can I depend on you to be my gracious hostess?"

"It shall be a pleasure," Valeria replied, looking forward to her domestic duties and wanting to make Galerius proud of her.

Valeria and the chef worked long and hard on the menus for the banquet, and she also met with the servants concerning the table arrangements, while her social secretary consulted with her on protocol.

Upon the ambassador's arrival, his obvious captivation by Valeria's beauty and charm was quite evident. At dinner that night, he wisely included Valeria in the conversation.

"My lord," the ambassador pleaded, "I beg of you to return Narses' family. Our king does not sleep or eat. His heart is broken. Keep whatever riches you like, but I beseech you, Caesar, to please restore his family to him."

Galerius raised his eyebrows haughtily. "May I remind you of how your country treated Emperor Valerian? He was tormented and ridiculed, and ultimately tortured to death. I have been nothing but kind and respectful to Narses' wife, his children, his concubines, and even his slaves."

"Yes, Caesar," the ambassador conceded, "and my countrymen have compared you to Alexander the Great and his treatment of the family of Darius III. But will you not release the family to Narses?"

"No," Galerius snapped. "I have made up my mind. You may return to Syria in the morning and tell King Narses that we will discuss his family during the peace negotiations. In the meantime, they will remain my prisoners. But you can assure your king that they will be treated with the utmost respect. I will have some of centurions give you a tour of their living quarters, and you can speak with the ladies in the morning."

That evening, when Galerius came to Valeria's bedroom, he was beaming. "You looked ravishing," he told her. "I was so proud of you. What a charming hostess you were! The food was delicious, and when I complimented the chef, he informed me that it was you who spent hours researching and planning the menu. And the flowers were beyond compare. You left no detail unattended." Laughing with obvious delight, he scooped her up and twirled her around. "I am the luckiest man alive. How can I ever thank you?"

She smiled. "There is one wish you can grant me."

"Your wish is my command," he said, removing her emeralds and kissing the nape of her neck. "You have told me how much you want a baby, and I shall give you a child. Is there something more you desire?"

"I do not wish to meddle in your business. You had my word that I would not."

He grinned. "That is a relief."

Valeria took a deep breath. "But please consider how you would feel if it were I and Candidianus and our servants who were imprisoned by Narses."

Galerius hesitated. "I have refused to let them go. I will not be a double-minded Caesar."

Valeria nodded. "Very well. I can accept your decision."

"Do you hate me for it?"

"Of course not. I am aware that I cannot possibly understand all the intricacies of the wars and the peace negotiations. I trust you completely."

Galerius smiled. "Once the peace negotiations begin, I give you my word that I will take your wishes into consideration."

"And you will return Narses' family to him?"

Galerius roared with laughter. "If only you knew what an evil ruler Narses was, you would not make this request of me."

"But his wife and children are innocent victims."

"And I treat these innocent victims very well. But come, my love, do you want me to give you a baby or not?"

Galerius lifted Valeria again, and this time he carried her to their bed.

Peace negotiations with the Persians began in the spring of 299, with both Diocletian and Galerius presiding. Their *magister memoriae*, Sicorius Probus, was sent to Narses to present the terms of the peace treaty, which were stringent, with Rome securing a wide zone of cultural influence in the region. The fact that the empire was able to sustain such constant warfare on so many fronts was taken as a sign of the essential efficacy of the Diocletianic system and the goodwill of the army towards the tetrarchic enterprise. As a special gift to Valeria, Galerius returned the wife, children, and servants of Narses to the grateful king.

"This means more to me than all the jewels in Persia," Valeria declared.

With Galerius' victory over the Persians came an abundance of power and clout. He became rude and obnoxious, not to Valeria, but to Diocletian. Valeria assumed he was taking revenge for the humiliation Diocletian had forced upon Galerius when he was defeated in Syria. However, his treatment of Diocletian deeply hurt Valeria and Prisca, so much so that Valeria dared speak to him about it.

"Your father?" Galerius responded when Valeria told him of her concerns. "Syria was my victory. I earned it. It is time for your father to retire. How long must I be Caesar?"

"That is my father's decision and not yours," Valeria reminded him.

Galerius glared at her. "Whose side are you on anyway?"

"I take no sides," she declared, turning away. "Why can you not allow things to run their natural course?"

Galerius grabbed her arm and turned her back to face him. "Because I am king of the world," he declared, his eyes making it clear that he meant every word.

26

*F*ollowing the victory in Syria, the Roman Empire enjoyed a time of great prosperity and peace. Diocletian lived and entertained lavishly in Nicomedia, as did Galerius in Thessalonica. After his victory over the Syrians, Galerius became haughty to everyone else, though he was usually kind and loving to his wife. It seemed he appreciated her attentiveness and care for him, his son, and the members of their court. Valeria had written to her mother that her life was happy and fulfilling. The one thing she feared was Galerius' ambition, but she was uncomfortable expressing her sentiment in writing. With no one in whom to confide her fears, Valeria continuously prayed about the matter.

Valeria also enjoyed the responsibility of running her own household and the affairs of the palace, though she missed the close companionship she had lately shared with her mother and had shared with Eugenia. Overall, however, she was managing well . . . until the day Daza approached her in the garden, where she strolled with her new personal servant, Dorthea, who had replaced Eugenia.

"May I have a word with you?" Daza asked.

"Certainly," Valeria replied, hoping her fear was not evident.

"Alone?"

"There is nothing you cannot say to me in front of Dorthea."

"This concerns my father, and it is a private and sensitive matter. Will you take a short stroll with me?"

Valeria glanced nervously at Dorthea. "You may be dismissed. Wait for me on the garden bench at the pond."

When they were alone, Valeria turned to Daza. "What is this urgent matter concerning my husband?"

Without pause, Daza leaned close. "My sweet Valeria, I have missed you desperately. Since the day we parted at the wedding in Venice, I have thought of nothing but you. The sweetness of your kisses, your heart beating as one with my own—"

Valeria held up her hand. "The only reason I agreed to see you is that you said you had news concerning my husband. What is it?"

"I am sorry. With all my heart, I believed that you shared the feelings I have for you. I was in hopes that you still burned with the passion of our brief time together."

Valeria did not wish to be harsh, but she had to be firm in order to drive him from her. "We were never together. It was only a brief kiss . . . or two. It meant nothing."

"You can never make me believe that," he protested. "Your kisses were fueled with passion and desire. I know that you love me as I love you. While I was away in Syria, I thought of your sweet fragrance, the tender touch of your hand, the burning heat of your kisses, the softness of your—"

"Stop! You tempted me and took advantage of me at a time when I was weak in my faith and strong in defiance of my marriage. Shame on you, Daza! Never speak these words in my ear again. Never!"

But Daza seemed determined. "My sister has two babies at her breast, and your womb is yet empty. Surely I can give you the children you want. In their veins would run my father's blood, and no one would ever have to know they were mine. We can be discreet. Besides, your husband will not live forever. I will wait for you, and one day, we can be together. I will make our children Caesars, and they will rule the empire as a Christian nation."

The mention of children stung Valeria's heart and brought tears to her eyes. She clutched her chest as she answered. "Galerius has accepted my inability to give him children. He loves me unconditionally." Biting her lower lip, she added, "I love my husband, and I would never, ever betray him. Please go . . . at once!"

Daza touched her face, blotting her tears with his fingertips. "I am sorry, Valeria. I beg your forgiveness. Your tears have torn my heart. I did not mean to make you cry or to hurt you over the reminder of your barrenness, but I have known women who were barren but then birthed children with other men. I truly believe I can make you happy, not just by extinguishing the burning desire and passion you have for me so you will be satisfied, but to give you a lapful of children as well."

Valeria swallowed, fighting to control her breathing. "I admit I once had passionate feelings for you. I was tormented by them, but I have matured in my faith, and I am no longer tempted."

But even as she protested, the man's beautiful green eyes held her captive. Her heart began to pound so furiously that she became lightheaded. Daza had been unfair to tempt her with hope of children, the greatest desire of her heart. When she felt herself sway, she also felt Daza cup his hand around her waist to steady her. At his touch, and with his tempting words swirling around in her head—a baby, a Christian nation, her passions satisfied by a handsome and virile young man—Valeria felt weakened.

It was almost more than she could endure as he gently pulled her body closer to his, and yet, had God not promised in the Scriptures that no one would be tempted more than they could bear?

"Stop!" she begged, struggling to pull away. "Please."

He dropped his hand, and she nearly stumbled backward.

"I have my answer," he whispered.

A hint of irritation began to rise within her. "And what answer might that be?"

"That you still desire me."

"Why, you despicable, arrogant, boorish—" Valeria stopped mid-sentence, summoning all her determination. "Leave at once," she demanded.

Daza's jaw tightened. "I will leave as you say, but remember that I possess the power to give you the world."

"And what good is the world if I lose my very soul?" Valeria asked, her reply paraphrasing a verse of Scripture Father Marcus had taught her.

As Daza swaggered away, he called back over his shoulder, "Live for the moment, Valeria, my love. It is the only happiness you will ever find in this life and beyond. For one day all that will remain of you are a few particles of dust."

A battle raged in Valeria's heart, and she longed for her mother's comfort. As angry as Daza had made her, his enticing words and tantalizing touch had tempted her. In her weaker moments, she would muse, *Perhaps I could bear a child with him. No one would ever know.* She was well acquainted with the voice of Satan who whispered in her ear. Then, for the remainder of the day, she would be consumed with guilt over her considerations and justifications for sinning.

At night she refused any thoughts of Daza in her bed. When she lay down with Galerius, she focused only on her husband, concentrating on his every touch and pleasing him with hers. She refused to allow herself to fantasize that it was Daza making love to her, or even Mauritius, for that matter.

Sadly, Valeria did not have the power to lock Daza from her dreams. His face had replaced the face of Mauritius. From the time she fell asleep until the sun rose the next morning, he tormented her heart and mind. No matter how she prayed or thought on other things before drifting off to sleep, it was Daza who dominated her sleeping hours. Some nights she was so distraught that she refused to sleep, to the point that it was making her ill.

Galerius soon noticed Valeria's lethargy, commenting on her pale complexion and dark-rimmed eyes. Concerned, he called in the court's physicians to examine her. When they found nothing physically wrong, they told Galerius that perhaps it was her anxiety over her inability to bear a child.

"I am perfectly content with the way things are," Galerius assured Valeria. "I know how badly your arms ache for a baby, but truthfully, I do not have a burning desire to fill my quiver with children. My desire burns for you and your great passion and beauty. Candidianus and Daza are the best sons a man could ever hope to have. And Valeria Maximilla is a wonderful daughter, who has already given me two grandsons." He pulled her close. "I like having my wife's attentions focused almost entirely upon me."

Valeria was greatly comforted by her husband's words, but she also trembled, for if he knew the true genesis of her deep troubles, he would be furious and deeply hurt. Her infertility was a great part of it, but her passion for Daza tormented her more, especially since he had nearly convinced her that she would be able to have a child with him.

A few weeks later, when Galerius informed her he was traveling to Bithynia for a meeting with her father, who was wintering there with Prisca, Valeria insisted on going with him, secretly terrified of what she might do if left alone with Daza.

"But the journey will be too hard on you in your present health," Galerius said.

"A change of scenery, away from the day-to-day routine, would provide a refreshing tonic for my present ills."

"Very well. I will confer with the court doctors, and if they give permission for you to travel, I will consider it."

Later that day, Galerius told her he had received clearance from her physicians. Valeria was relieved, but then she was caught off guard when she ran into Daza in the hallway. Before she could protest, he pulled her into an alcove and pressed her up against the wall, his body nearly crushing hers as he whispered into her ear.

"Galerius leaves for Bithynia in a few days, and I have convinced him that I should remain at the palace in Thessalonica to look after his affairs here, including your care."

"But—"

He kissed her before she could say another word, and then moved his lips to her ear, though she still could not speak because he placed his hand over her mouth. "Soon, my love," he whispered. "I will come to you in the night and give you the baby you have wanted for so long." When he pulled away and looked into her eyes, he warned, "You must invite your husband into your bed every night before he leaves and when he returns, so there will be no suspicion whatsoever. Do you understand?"

Valeria opened her mouth to chastise him but instead went straight to the point. "I am traveling to Bithynia with my husband."

Valeria felt his body convulse with disappointment, mirroring her true feelings exactly. How she longed to be the recipient of the promises he had whispered in her ear!

He composed himself and said, "Then I shall wait my turn. Your husband cannot remain at your side forever. I do not care how long it takes; I will wait for you."

Without another word, he turned on his heel and walked away, leaving Valeria trembling and longing for his touch.

When Galerius and Valeria arrived in Bithynia, they were greeted with the usual fanfare. To Valeria's disappointment, Romula was in her father's court.

"I am surprised to see your mother."

"She is here at your father's invitation, not mine."

Valeria had sensed friction between Galerius and his mother of late over the name of Romulus. Since his victory at Syria, Galerius had wanted to take the name of Romulus, believing he was the actual god, but his mother had refused to give up the name for she too believed that she was the female goddess, Romula. She had argued that Galerius could take the masculine name while she retained the feminine version, but because of Galerius' boulder-sized ego, he had refused to share the honor. How Valeria despised the machinations of the pagans!

Curious, Valeria mused, "Why would my father desire Romula's presence?"

Galerius sneered. "Your father is timorous and obsessed by his fears of what tomorrow will bring. He constantly consults the gods on the future. My mother is the high priestess who assists him in the divinations that will supply Diocletian with the prognostic of events."

Valeria shook her head. "When I was a child, my mother shielded me from these sorts of things."

"Would you like to come to one of the ritual ceremonies with me to satisfy your curiosity about the divinations? There is one about to take place in the temple now."

"No, thank you," Valeria replied. "I am tired from our journey, and I promised the physician that I would get my rest while I was away."

Galerius' face clouded over, and a glint of determination shone in his dark eyes. "I want you with me. Afterward, we shall retire to the bedchamber and enjoy a long nap together."

Valeria tried to make excuses. "But I have not yet visited my mother, and I also have to pay my respects to the ladies of the court."

"You can do that later. I insist you come with me." He took her hand and led her downstairs where most of the members of the court had already gathered in Jupiter's temple. They no sooner appeared in the temple than Diocletian spotted them and hurried to their side. "Welcome, my darling," he said, planting a kiss on Valeria's cheek. "What a nice surprise that you would indulge your old father with your presence in the temple. Please, take a seat; the ceremony is about to begin."

Several servants rushed to pull out a chair for her, but in the midst of the warm welcome from her father, Valeria noticed one person who was not happy to see her—her mother-in-law.

Romula frowned, pointing a long, sharp fingernail at Valeria. "What are you doing here? Do you plan to take part in the sacrifices?"

Though Valeria knew Romula was trying to embarrass her, she declared without shame, "No. I am a Christian."

Many of her fathers' servants were Christians, too, and they glanced at her sympathetically. Valeria noticed that on each of their foreheads was the mark of the cross for their protection. One of them leaned in and consulted privately with her father, and then came and bowed before her, carrying a small pot of ashes to mark her forehead with a cross.

Galerius' face reddened, and he looked away.

The ritual commenced. The livers of the sacrificial animals had been removed and delivered on an ornate tray to the high priestess, while their carcasses were placed upon a great pyre and set afire as an offering to Jupiter. Romula then turned and handed the tray to the soothsayers before joining the dancers, who gyrated around the temple in their colorful garb, chanting and singing and carrying flaming torches that emitted incense throughout the room. Valeria squirmed uneasily in her chair. The sensual way the dancers contorted their bodies made her blush in her husband's presence. Valeria found the pagan rituals vile and debauched, a departure from the reverence of Christian services. She struggled to remain expressionless so as not to further displease her husband.

Galerius nudged Valeria and pointed toward the soothsayers, who whispered among themselves.

"What seems to be the matter?" Valeria asked.

"They are attempting to read the future in the livers of the animals, but there is a problem, just as there was in Antioch when the soothsayers were unable to find the wanted marks on the livers and entrails."

Galerius went to converse with the temple priests, who declared it was the presence of the Christians and the sign of the cross that blocked the readings. When Galerius rejoined Valeria, he explained. "It is believed that the sign of the cross chases away the demons—not just from the Christians, but also from the markings in the livers and entrails."

"Do you want me to leave?" Valeria asked, wondering why Galerius had insisted she come if he was already aware of the problem. Was it possible he had purposely manipulated the situation at her expense?

"On the contrary, let us wait and see what happens," he answered.

The soothsayers continued conversing among themselves, and soon they began to tremble.

"Why are they shaking?" a fearful Valeria asked. "What is going to happen now?"

"They frequently repeat the sacrifices, as if the former had been unpropitious."

Once more the sacrifices were made, but with the same result. Tages, the chief soothsayer, stepped forward and addressed the worshippers. "There are profane persons here, who have obstructed our rites."

Diocletian, his fury evident, stood to his feet and ordered all who were assisting at the holy ceremonies, as well as everyone who resided within the palace, to join in offering the sacrifice. "Anyone who refuses," he declared, "will be scourged."

"I should leave," Valeria whispered, and then stood to her feet.

Galerius held up his hand to block her passage. "You heard the order. Are you not within the palace?"

Catching sight of his daughter, Diocletian's voice boomed in her direction. "Sit back down," he ordered, and then turned to a servant. "Go fetch my wife and bring her and her servants to the temple immediately." When the messenger scurried away, Diocletian began to pace, stopping occasionally to confer with Tages.

Valeria knew her growing fear was evident, as Galerius slipped an arm around her shoulder. "Do not be afraid, my darling. Surely you made these sacrifices as a child. It is not so difficult."

Valeria knew better than to protest, so she sat quietly, her heart racing at the implications of what was being required of her by her own husband and father.

And then Prisca appeared and took a seat beside her daughter. "Please tell me what is going on. I was ordered to come here at once."

Galerius quickly explained the situation, at which point Prisca stood and summoned her husband to her side. "Surely you do not mean for us to make the sacrifices," she said, her voice calm but her eyes pleading.

"If you do not," Diocletian responded coolly, "then you must be scourged. There will be no exceptions. You must serve as an example to the others."

Valeria reached up and took her mother's hand, her words urgent but hushed. "Please, Mother, do not agitate him. Father has quite obviously lost his senses again."

Prisca did not respond but turned as if to leave, only to be stopped by four centurions blocking her way. She gasped, and then made an obvious effort to collect herself.

"You may find me in my quarters," Prisca said calmly, turning from her husband to her daughter. "Come, Valeria."

Her actions seemed to infuriate Galerius, who sprang from his seat and confronted Prisca, towering over her as he bellowed, "Valeria is my wife. She will follow my orders and not yours."

Valeria's stomach lurched, and she felt sick at the thought of choosing loyalties between her mother and husband—not to mention her Savior. Silently, she prayed for strength and wisdom.

The Christians were then taken to the great hall, with Galerius leading Valeria along with them. When the guards escorted a reluctant Prisca in to join them, Valeria nearly fainted with fright. What could her father and husband be thinking?

She did not have long to wonder, as Galerius took her arm and turned her to face him. "Do you still refuse to make the sacrifices?"

Nervously, Valeria glanced at her mother to garner her strength. "I do, my lord."

His jaw twitched as his eyes went cold. "Very well, then. You shall be first in line for the scourging."

Valeria's mouth flew open. Surely her husband did not mean to—

Galerius reached for one of the whips held by the executioner and shoved his wife to the center of the ring. "Do you want to change your mind?" he asked.

Dizzy with fright, Valeria shook her head no. Immediately the man she called husband, the man who claimed to love her, raised his arm and lashed her half a dozen times, until her blood seeped through her clothing and she thought she would surely faint from the pain.

When Galerius' fury had subsided and the beating ended, Valeria was lifted by her servants to be carried away on a litter to her room where her wounds could be washed and treated. Through a haze of tears and pain, Valeria caught a glimpse of her mother on the sidelines, awaiting her turn in the ring, weeping and crying out to her daughter.

Later, as Valeria lay in her room, bandaged and drifting in and out of consciousness, Dorthea told her that all the Christians in the court had been violently beaten, though many sang hymns and praised God even as the whip slashed and cut into their backs. When it was Prisca's turn, Diocletian had taken the whip from the executioner and flung it viciously over his shoulder, ready to inflict the punishment on his own wife, as Galerius had done. At the last moment, however, he had stopped the whip in midair, crying out, "I cannot do it. I cannot! Please, Prisca, go to your room, and I will deal with you later." And he had turned away and ordered everyone back to the temple to resume the sacrifices.

27

$\mathcal{V}$aleria moaned when she heard the door to her room open. Cracking an eye, she was relieved to see her mother rushing to her side, her face tight with worry. The servants who had been tending Valeria moved back and made room for Prisca to sit down in the chair beside her daughter's bed.

Prisca's eyes brimmed with tears. "Oh, look what that monster has done to you!"

"Do not worry, Mother. I will recover. I am far more concerned about Father. Galerius and his wicked mother have preyed upon his irrational fears in order to rid both his court and the army of any Christians."

"At least there will be no persecutions," Prisca announced. "I was with your father when he met with Galerius this afternoon. He was adamant that there be no bloodshed."

"But can you be sure of that, with Galerius and Romula so relentless in their quest to persecute Christians?"

"Oh, I am quite aware of their machinations. In most instances, so is your father. But he has long opposed Galerius' fury and fanaticism against Christians, especially persecution."

"But in the past Galerius has influenced Father to execute Christians in the army when they refused to comply with his orders for the sacrifices," Valeria reminded her mother. Tears sprang into her eyes as she thought of Mauritius. And then she thought of Daza. *I should have remained at home with him.*

Prisca squeezed her hand. "Those were isolated instances. When your father spoke to Galerius this afternoon, he warned him how pernicious it would be to demand bloodshed throughout the world, especially since most Christians consider it a privilege to die for their God."

The pain in Valeria's heart was worse than that in her back, as she asked, "What will happen to us, Mother?"

Prisca bit her lip. "Your father warned me that we have no choice in the matter . . . that we must participate in the sacrifices or pay the price."

"What shall we do?" Valeria cried, feeling her eyes widen.

"We must pray, of course, but in the meantime, we should seek wise counsel. I sent a messenger with a letter to Bishop Marcus requesting a meeting with him when we return to Thessalonica."

"But, Mother, you cannot leave Father alone. Without you by his side, I shudder to think what might happen. You are the only person who can reason with him. He listens to you."

❧

Valeria was grateful Galerius did not come to her bedchambers. The only comfort she found during her recuperation was her sinful thoughts of Daza. If only she had stayed in Thessalonica with him. It would have been a sin, but nothing could be as horrible as the suffering she had endured at her husband's hand. Lying upon her bed of pain, Valeria made her decision. When she returned to Thessalonica, she would give herself to Daza. It was wrong, but surely God would forgive her. Daza was her only chance at happiness in this life.

To Valeria's relief, she did not see Galerius again until she had recovered from her scourging and returned to her place in the court. Even then, he did not appear in the least remorseful. He was polite but indifferent toward her. It was obvious to both Prisca and Valeria that Romula had at last succeeded in poisoning Galerius against his own wife. The intimacy that had once flourished between husband and wife now crumbled like an old stonewall, replaced by an impenetrable barrier. Valeria was grateful that Diocletian and Galerius now spent much of their time in Bithynia, discussing the business of the Roman Empire, but the subject of persecutions was always at the forefront.

What Valeria did not know was that Diocletian soon found it impossible to restrain the madness of Galerius' obsession with the persecutions. After many days, Galerius had worn the emperor down, and Diocletian resolved to seek the opinion of his friends on the matter. Galerius and Romula cleverly convinced Diocletian that he should also consult the gods, so a soothsayer was employed to inquire of Apollo on the subject.

Apollo's response was, of course, to persecute the Christians . . . to burn them for not bowing down at the sacrifices. Yet even with the message from Apollo, Diocletian attempted to observe moderation in his punishment of Christians, wanting to avoid bloodshed. Galerius, however, demanded that all persons who refused to sacrifice be burned at the stake.

When Diocletian returned to Nicomedia, Galerius followed, insisting that Prisca and Valeria return with them so he could keep a watchful eye on them, making sure they complied with the sacrifices. The public demands the emperor and his Caesar made upon their wives served as a warning to all

Christians. No one in the Roman Empire would be excused from the sacrifices.

Just as the women had feared, Galerius continued to fuel Diocletian's paranoia with lies and reports of conspiracies against him. During their visit to the imperial palace, the structure caught fire from lightning, but Galerius seized the opportunity to suggest to the emperor that the fire was a plot carried out by Christians. He also succeeded in swaying the pagan priests to blame the Christians. Diocletian, highly susceptible to superstitions, fell for the ruse, but not to the extent that Galerius and Romula had hoped.

As a result, a determined Galerius had a second fire set and again blamed it on the Christians. Valeria watched from the shadows, but she was helpless to report it to anyone but her mother. Either no one would believe her, or she would be severely punished if she told anyone what she had seen. This time Galerius achieved his objective, as Diocletian went into a rage and had all the devoted Christians in his household, including the eunuchs, burned to death.

Taking advantage of Diocletian's fury, Romula suggested he choose an auspicious day, the festival of the god Terminus, celebrated on the sevens of the kalends of March, to terminate the Christian religion. When that day dawned, the prefect, together with chief commanders, tribunes, and officers of the treasury, convened at the church in Nicomedia. At the sound of the church gates being forced open, Valeria dismissed her servants and sequestered herself in her room.

"Oh, Jesus," she cried, collapsing on the floor beside her bed. These are Your people who are suffering! Please, Lord, intervene on their behalf, and stop this madness!"

But the heavens seemed as brass, and the reports of destruction continued to find their way to Valeria's ears. She soon learned that after the church gates had been demolished, the rampagers had searched everywhere until the Holy Scriptures were found and burned, and the contents of the church pillaged. The church, situated on rising ground, was within view of Valeria's room at the palace, though she refused to go to the window and watch its destruction. She later learned, however, that Diocletian and Galerius had no such compunction. In fact, they had stood, as if on a watchtower, viewing the church's invasion and disputing whether or not to set it on fire. They compromised, declaring the church would be taken down piece by piece by the soldiers with their axes. It was nearly more than Valeria could bear, and she thought surely she would die of a broken heart. A few days later, Galerius' ultimate thirst for fire was quenched when a Christian tore down the edicts against Christianity that Diocletian had posted on the church doors. In a fit of rage, Diocletian had the man burned, and then he had Christian men, women, and even children who had refused to sacrifice burned or thrown into the sea with millstones around their necks.

The Great Persecution had begun in earnest, and it seemed to Valeria that her prayers had made no difference at all.

❧

The morning after the invasion of the church, a messenger arrived with a letter from Bishop Marcus. It was addressed to Prisca, who was in her room at the time, with Valeria at her side. The women were relieved that the messenger had been able to reach them without being stopped, as the women's comings and goings were now being monitored closely.

Upon receiving the message, Prisca tore the ribbon off the scroll and unfolded it.

"What does it say?" Valeria asked.

"He has suggested we participate in the sacrifices but secretly make the sign of the cross," Prisca said as she scanned the letter. "He says we can do more good for Christianity in our positions as wives of the emperor and the Caesar than as martyrs."

Valeria was stunned. How could the good bishop suggest such a compromise when so many were giving their lives rather than deny their Savior?

Over the next few days, the women considered whether to heed the bishop's advice or choose martyrdom. But in the midst of their sorrow, Valeria discovered she was pregnant. At last, a child was growing inside her, and her joy knew no bounds, despite the horrible circumstances they found themselves in at the time. Even Prisca agreed this was indeed a sign from God that they should choose life.

"Perhaps this child shall be the Christian emperor who will one day change the world," Prisca told Valeria.

When Prisca sent Galerius the news of Valeria's pregnancy, he came at once, his happiness surpassing even Valeria's.

"My darling, why did you not tell me? I would never have taken the whip and—"

Valeria placed two fingers against his lips. "Please, do not speak of it. I did not know at the time, and besides, I forgive you. I understand that you had to make an example of me in front of the others. Let us put that behind us now and speak only happy things into our baby's ears."

Galerius took her into his arms. "Because you have made the sacrifices, the gods have smiled on us by giving us a baby."

Valeria flinched. She knew this baby was a gift from her God, but she dared not say so to her husband.

Galerius decided that he and Valeria should leave at once, while she could still travel, so the baby could be born in Thessalonica.

"This baby is already making a difference in the world," Valeria confided to her mother, who traveled with them to Thessalonica. "Galerius' preoccupation with this child has resulted in a definite decrease in the number of persecutions."

On the trip home, Valeria realized she no longer feared seeing Daza. Pregnancy had changed everything. She was so absorbed in the upcoming birth of her child that even the Christian persecutions were far from her mind.

Two days after her return, Daza knocked boldly at her door. Except for two of her servants, she was alone, sitting in her chair and doing needlework for the baby.

"May I speak with you alone?" he asked.

The two servants discreetly took their leave before she could protest.

With tears in his eyes, Daza professed, "When I heard Galerius had whipped you, I swore an oath I would kill him with my bare hands if he hurt you badly." He paused, drinking her in with his gaze. "Now I see that not only are you well, but you are with child and it becomes you. You have never looked more beautiful or tempting."

Valeria shushed him. Having lost all her Christian servants, she was unsure if the current ones might be outside the door, listening.

Daza drew closer. He fell to his knees by her chair and touched her growing belly. "I am truly happy for you, my beloved Valeria. I know how much you wanted a baby."

"Thank you," Valeria replied, moved by his selfless affection.

He leaned in then and whispered, "How I wish that this baby were mine!" He nestled his head in her lap, and then kissed and caressed her belly with such tenderness that Valeria felt powerless to stop him. She was greatly relieved, however, that she felt none of the previous emotion or desire for him.

This baby inside her had extinguished all traces of the passion that had once burned for Daza.

"I love you, Valeria," he whispered, "and I swear to you that I will love this baby as if it were my own, simply because it is a part of you."

His words touched a cord of longing in her heart, but she dismissed it as quickly as it came.

Daza stood to his feet then and stood gazing down at her, his devotion evident in his green eyes. "One day Galerius will be gone, and I shall be emperor. When that day comes, I swear to you, Valeria, I shall make you mine, and I will treat you as you deserve. You can worship your God as you please, and I will give you all the desires of your heart. For now, I must leave you. And as my gift to you and your baby, I give you my word that I will no longer torment you as long as you are married to Galerius."

When Daza left her room and the servants returned, she continued her needlework, pondering his words. With each stitch she prayed that Galerius would grow to love her and want to protect her and grant the happiness that Daza offered. What woman alive would not want to be loved in such a manner?

28

$\mathscr{V}$aleria's joy over her pending motherhood was short-lived. As she lay in bed with Prisca sitting faithfully by her bedside, they mourned together.

"I waited so long," Valeria sobbed. "And I wanted this baby so desperately! Why has God taken him from us? Why would He deny us such joy?"

Prisca's eyes glistened with tears. "I have no answer for you," she said. "There are some things we will simply not understand this side of heaven. But, my darling, you must never doubt that God loves you and grieves with you, even at this very moment."

Valeria desperately wanted to believe her mother's words, but the emptiness in her heart and in her womb were too strong to overcome. And she couldn't even begin to consider what this loss would mean to her relationship with Galerius. He had been so devastated by the blow that he seemed to have aged ten years in a matter of days. Though Prisca tried to console her heartbroken daughter with the hope that she and her husband would be able to conceive another child, Valeria somehow sensed that it was not to be.

And so it was. Though Galerius and Valeria continued in their relationship as man and wife, they were unable to conceive another child.

Meanwhile, when Diocletian celebrated his twenty-year reign as the Roman emperor, he decided to mark the celebration in Rome, and Valeria was grateful for the distraction. The family traveled together to the great city, where Diocletian and his co-emperor, Maximian, enjoyed the honor of a triumph, followed by festive games, but the mood of the citizens of Rome dampened their enjoyment. It was obvious that the people weren't as welcoming of their emperor as they had been in the past.

"The people no longer worship me," Diocletian complained on more than one occasion. Prisca and Valeria tried to reassure him, but he was so hurt by his subjects' rejection that he insisted on leaving Rome in the middle of winter. It was not a wise decision.

By journey's end, the emperor was so sick he had to be carried into his palace at Nicomedia on a litter. By the spring of 305, inaccurate rumors had spread through the kingdom that Diocletian had died.

"I must counter these falsehoods," he insisted when they were brought to his attention. Prisca did what she could to convince him to stay in bed and rest, but to her great surprise and delight, Diocletian rallied and soon showed himself in public. His subjects were stunned, not only at the fact that he was indeed still alive but also because his appearance had so deteriorated.

As word of the seriousness of Diocletian's condition reached Valeria, she was devastated and quickly convinced Galerius to take her to Nicomedia. Had she known that Galerius would use the opportunity to persuade Diocletian to abdicate, she might not have been so anxious to make the trip.

On the first day of May, at the very spot where, several years before, Diocletian had proclaimed Galerius as Caesar, he addressed his officers and court.

"My infirmities of age have warned me to retire from power, and to deliver the administration of the state into stronger hands," he explained, following with the proclamation, "Bow down before Galerius, your new Augustus."

The Roman people, especially the soldiers in the army, had fully expected that Constantine would replace Galerius as the new Caesar. The troops were stunned when Galerius announced that Daza would be his new Caesar, and then watched in amazement as Diocletian removed his own purple robe and placed it upon Galerius' stepson.

After the coronation of the purple, everyone cheered and saluted the old emperor as he and Prisca departed in a carriage to return to Nicomedia. Soon after, Diocletian left for Spalatum in Dalmatia, where he had built himself an extensive palace by the seashore for his retirement.

At the same time Diocletian abdicated at Nicomedia, Maximian, the emperor of the west, performed a similar ceremony at Milan, proclaiming Constantius as Augustus, and Severus as his Caesar, completely overlooking Constantine.

Both Prisca and Valeria rejoiced when Diocletian, in response to a request to try to reclaim his power, replied, "Were you but to come to Solano and see the vegetables which I grow in my garden with my own hands, you would no longer talk to me of empire."

The great Emperor Diocletian had indeed retired, and the Roman Empire would never be the same.

After Diocletian's retirement there was great upheaval in the Roman Empire. Emperor Maximian was betrayed by his son and died, smothered by his son's own hand. Severus, never having the respect of the soldiers, was deserted by his own troops and killed in battle.

Only then did Diocletian leave his retirement for the installation of the new emperor. He traveled to the palace in Nicomedia, where Galerius and Valeria had taken up residence as the emperor and empress.

When Diocletian arrived, Galerius told him that he planned to appoint Licinius, his closest childhood companion, to replace Maximian. Diocletian argued that Licinius was ill-prepared for the position, but Galerius' mind was made up. To appease Diocletian, he agreed to name Constantine as his Caesar.

Daza was so incensed with Galerius' decision that he approached Valeria, barging into her quarters without knocking and marching right up to her bed, where she was resting.

"You must speak with your husband on my behalf," Daza blurted. "He has humiliated and betrayed me!"

"I am sorry," Valeria answered, sitting up on her bed, "but you of all people should know I have no influence over Galerius, especially when it comes to the business of the empire. It infuriates him when I try to meddle in his affairs."

"Well, you must try. For the love of your son, you must do something. Galerius should have made me the emperor, and not Licinius. I would have named Candidianus my Caesar."

"But you are yet so young, and Candidianus is just a boy. Have patience, and your day will come. Will you not remain Caesar and serve under Licinius?"

"For now, yes, but for how long? I will be passed over again in favor of one of his sons eventually. And now Constantine is in the picture, for he shall be Licinius' Caesar. Even worse,

Constantine has promised his sister's hand in marriage to Licinius. Do you not see our family's power is weakening? I have heard a rumor that Licinius is just biding his time until he can be rid of me."

"Galerius would never allow that."

"But what happens when Galerius is no longer around?"

"You will succeed him."

"No, Licinius will succeed him. I do not think you understand the seriousness of this matter. Galerius' decision to choose Licinus could have dire consequences for both Candidianus and me. Mark my words . . . Licinius will never appoint Candidianus a Caesar. He will choose his own sons over him."

Valeria frowned, not wanting to believe what she heard. "But the intention of the tetrarchy is to have the sons succeed. Galerius will insure that you and Candidianus succeed him. Besides, Licinius is Galerius' closest childhood friend. They are like brothers. Surely, Licinius will honor Galerius' sons."

Daza shook his head. "If Licinius is named emperor today, Candidianus will never become Caesar."

Valeria felt a flash of fear. She was confident that Daza was strong enough to take care of himself, but Candidianus was still so young. "What can I do?"

"If Galerius will not listen to you, perhaps you can enlist the help of your father before he returns to Spalatum. I am positive he does not approve of Licinius' appointment. He must know that Licinius is a fool and a terrible soldier as well. Worse, he is a coward. Please, Valeria, ask your father to intervene."

"You must talk quietly. If anyone hears you, I tremble with fear for what could happen to you," Valeria said, touching Daza's hand, surprised at the feeling of tenderness she still carried for him.

Daza stood to his feet. "I am sorry. I should not have burdened you, but I have nowhere else to turn."

Valeria made up her mind. "I will do what you ask. I will speak to my husband and my father."

When Valeria approached Galerius, he scorned her fears concerning Candidianus.

"Licinius is like a brother to me. He will treat our son far better than Daza ever would," he assured her.

"But would it not be wiser to keep the titles in the family?"

"Licinius is my family."

Valeria sighed. There was no use in trying to change her husband's mind. She sat down at her desk and quickly penned a note to Daza, in which she promised she would speak to her father, and then she had it secretly delivered to him by a trusted servant.

Valeria asked Prisca to accompany her to Diocletian's quarters. When Valeria shared her fears with her father, he agreed that Licinius' appointment to emperor was a dreadful mistake, but he also told her there was nothing he could do to change it since Galerius was now the Augustus.

The coronation took place, but Daza defiantly refused to participate. He was incensed at the nomination of Licinius to the dignity of emperor, and he refused to be called Caesar or allow himself to be ranked as third in authority.

Weeks later, Galerius sent messages to Daza, pleading with him to yield to Licinius as the emperor, in reverence for Licinius' gray hairs. But Daza became even more insolent, insisting it was he who first assumed the purple; by possession, then, he had right to priority in rank.

Galerius was furious. Valeria heard him bellow about the despicable creature he had made Caesar and who forgot the great favor conferred upon him and impiously withstood the requests and will of his benefactor. Galerius, eventually overcome by the obstinacy of Daza, abolished the subordinate title of Caesar, gave to himself and Licinius that of the Augusti, and to Daza and Constantine that of sons of the Augusti. Some time after, in a letter to Galerius, Daza pointed out that at the last general muster his army had saluted him under the title of Augustus. Galerius, vexed and grieved at this, commanded that all four should have the appellation of emperor.

And so the empire continued, as did Valeria, tending her garden and raising her only child, Candidianus.

29

*W*ith Prisca visiting Valeria at the palace as often as possible, the two immersed themselves in prayer and study of the Scriptures with Father Marcus, including Candidianus in their devotional times whenever possible. But as the boy transitioned into a young man, Galerius quickly insisted he enlist in military service.

"How will I ever let him go?" Valeria fretted during one of Prisca's visits. "He's just a boy, my only child! Why must Galerius insist on his going off to war? Why can't he allow me this one joy, to keep my son here with me?"

Prisca held Valeria's hand as they sat side-by-side on the divan in Valeria's room. The two women had dreaded this day for months, but now it was upon them. Candidianus would leave in the morning, and Valeria was inconsolable.

"I know you think I offer you the same advice at every turn," Prisca soothed as she increased the pressure on her daughter's hand, "but I truly have no other answer for you. The truth is, my dear daughter, that once again we have no choice but to relinquish our desires and our fears to God and trust Him to do what is best for our loved ones."

Valeria locked eyes with her mother, determined to elicit a more specific answer. "And what does that mean?" she asked. "Do I give up my son, along with everything else I've given up in my lifetime, trusting God to bring him back to me when the battle is over? I prayed to that same God to bring Mauritius back to me so many years ago and look what happened! What if . . ." She could scarcely speak, but the terror burned in her heart and she had to say it out loud. "Oh, Mother, what if Candidianus does not come back to me either? What if my precious son—my only child—dies on the battlefield?"

Prisca's eyes filled to overflowing with tears, and her face softened as she answered. "Then you will know that he is with His Savior—and with Mauritius and so many others who have gone before. And when he rides away tomorrow, you can be grateful that we know for certain that Candidianus is committed to his Christian faith, and he is safe in his heavenly Father's care—wherever he is."

The truth of her mother's words washed over her, but they in no way eased the pain in her heart at the thought of losing the young man who had brought her so much joy through the years, from the time Eugenia first brought him to her until he grew into the handsome young man that he was today. But in that moment she knew she must relinquish him into God's faithful hands, for there really was no other choice.

That evening a knock at Valeria's door interrupted her prayers for her son. She smiled when Candidianus walked into the room.

"Mother, I have come to tell you goodbye," he said, standing tall and erect and looking very much like a soldier. "I know you will see me off in the morning, but we may not have much time to talk then."

Valeria choked back her tears, determined to put up a brave front for her son. "And you shall be the finest soldier in the Roman Empire."

Candidianus ducked his head and took a seat beside her. "I hope so, Mother, because I would rather die than disappoint Father."

"Do not say such words. You could never be a disappointment to us."

"Between you and me, I do not believe I am designed to be a great warrior. I would rather be a scholar."

"Ah, but it is your superior intelligence that will serve you well in battle and make you a hero."

Candidianus blushed. "Then I shall not disappoint you, Mother."

"Are you afraid?" Valeria asked bluntly.

"Not of battle, for I know I have God's protection, and if He has ordained my time, then I will relinquish my life to him. But there is one thing that frightens me more than death."

Valeria touched his face. "And what might that be?"

He blushed. "I have never been with a woman, and Father tells me he has arranged a marriage for me."

Valeria's mouth flew open. "I have heard nothing of this. You are too young! Who is he proposing that you marry?"

"I thought you knew. Please do not tell Father I told you, but he has arranged for me to marry Daza's daughter, Paulina."

Valeria relaxed. "Paulina is a beautiful child. She has her father's green eyes. And Daza is your cousin. He is like a brother to you. He will protect you once your father and I are gone. This is a good match."

"Perhaps, but I have much to learn about women. Father said he will enlist one of the concubines to teach me, but—"

"He will do no such thing. You and Paulina can learn together."

"But Father said—"

"Do not be concerned about that. I will take care of your father."

"What advice can you give me, Mother?"

Valeria took her son in her arms as though he were a little boy and kissed the top of his head. "My darling, Paulina will look to you to lead, so you must always put God at the center of your marriage, making choices based on your faith. Always focus on what is good and lovely in your relationship."

Candidianus stopped her. "Mother, the Christian monks and priests have taught me well in the basics of marriage, but I am asking you what I cannot ask them . . . about making love to my wife."

Valeria hesitated, touched that her son would approach her about this subject without a hint of embarrassment. She cleared her throat. "From my own experience, I can tell you that love between a man and a woman is a beautiful thing. The secret of success in a relationship is to focus on your wife's satisfaction before your own and then you will be blessed with abundant love and passion."

"Just as the scripture says, 'It is more blessed to give than receive.' So are you saying that the same is true in lovemaking?"

Valeria nodded. "It is true of almost anything in life."

Candidianus smiled. "Is there anything else you would recommend for a novice such as me?"

Valeria smiled. "Go slowly, and apply as much tenderness as you can when you are with your wife. If you do this, her heart will melt and she will respond to you with an undying devotion."

Candidianus let out a big sigh. "You make it sound so easy."

Valeria took his hand in hers. "You will be a wonderful husband, my dear, sweet boy. And I urge you to discuss this with your father."

He blinked in apparent surprise. "Father is such a warrior . . . and forgive me for saying this, but he is a bully too."

"Do not speak of your father in such a way."

"I only share this with you because you and I both know it to be true," Candidianus explained. "I just never imagined him as a great lover."

Valeria smiled. "He is the best. Talk to him."

It was her son's turn to blush.

Valeria kissed his cheek before continuing. "I cannot tell you how much it means to me that you have chosen to discuss this sensitive topic with me."

"But you are my dearest friend," he told her.

"Paulina is a blessed young woman," Valeria said with pride.

"I am blessed too. She is an extraordinary beauty, but she is fun and adventurous as well."

"Yes, she is a darling girl with a spirited personality. I believe the two of you will be quite happy together."

Candidianus stood to his feet. "I hope so. But for now, I have a war to fight."

Valeria stood and hugged him goodbye. When he was gone, she threw herself on the bed and cried. The pain of losing her son was so great, but she had not dared expose her true feelings because she wanted to keep the pathway open for him to talk with her about anything.

Dear God, please watch over him for me!

The final goodbye, though brief, was no simpler or less painful as Valeria stood in the cool morning breeze the next day, begging God to give her the strength to stay on her feet as she watched her son depart. How grown-up and courageous he appeared as he prepared to mount his horse and ride away— and yet what a little boy he still seemed to her when he stood in front of her one last time.

"I will miss you, Mother," he said, towering over her by nearly a foot. "And I will pray for you each day."

"And I for you," she whispered, unable to say more.

Candidianus pulled her into an embrace, nearly crushing her against his broad chest. "Please don't worry about me. I will be fine."

Valeria nodded, suppressing a sob and thinking how grateful she was that Galerius was not home to interfere with these last precious moments of farewell. She was grateful, too, that Prisca had graciously said her goodbyes the previous day and left Valeria and Candidianus alone this dreary morning.

The young man relaxed his embrace and pulled back so he could look down into his mother's face. Valeria could no longer hold back the tears, and she let them flow freely as she gazed up at the one who owned so much of her heart and desperately tried to memorize his every feature.

"May God watch over and keep us safe while we are apart," Candidianus said, "and bring us back together soon."

Before Valeria could answer, he kissed her forehead and then turned and mounted his horse and galloped away, leaving his mother to watch him as he disappeared on the horizon.

Galerius' hatred of Christians had not eased, and he at last succeeded in forcing his wife and mother-in-law to participate in the pagan ceremonies. Though Valeria and Prisca agonized over the decision, they finally came to the place of outward compliance, though they unobtrusively made the sign of the cross during the sacrifices, begging the Lord's mercy and forgiveness in the process.

But at night, when Valeria lay in the dark beside her sleeping husband, she shed silent tears, tortured over her compromise. *Mauritius would be so ashamed of me,* she thought, as she reflected on the ceremony she had been forced to attend just that morning. *He and his men went fearlessly to their deaths, singing praises to God and encouraging one another, while Mother and I have seemingly made a pact with the devil. I tell myself it is so we can live on to pray for the salvation of our husbands and others as well, but I wonder . . . is it really that we are cowards, that our first allegiance is not to Christ after all? Oh, God, can You truly forgive us our betrayal?*

The only sound she heard in response was the deep, even breathing of the man whose life and name she shared, but whose heart and beliefs were so foreign to her own.

Valeria and Galerius lingered over breakfast, discussing the latest news about Candidianus. He was reported to be a valiant warrior, though he, too, had been forced to participate in the pagan ceremonies that so plagued his mother and grandmother. Yet how could she expect him to do otherwise, Valeria wondered, since she had set such a poor example for him to follow?

But now a messenger appeared and their discussion of Candidianus ceased. When the courier left, Galerius turned to Valeria, the look on his face mirroring trouble.

"What is it? Please tell me the bad news does not concern Candidianus!"

He took a deep breath before answering. "Because she is so special to you and was once in our employ, one of the tribunes has notified me that your friend Eugenia and her son . . ."

Valeria's head felt light. Whatever Galerius was about to tell her, she sensed she did not want to hear it.

"They were . . . among a group of martyrs in Nicomedia who were . . . executed this morning."

Her heart froze. Eugenia? Octavius? Martyrs? How was that possible?

"Why was I not told?" Valeria cried. "Perhaps I could have stopped it!"

But of course she knew that wasn't true. Overwhelmed with yet another loss, Valeria escaped to her room, where she mourned in solitude for a month, allowing no one, not even her mother, to visit her.

At least Eugenia is reunited with her beloved husband, Valeria thought, as she knelt by her bed in prayer, pouring out her pain to the Lord. *And young Octavius has at last met his father, whose name he bore and whose courage he so obviously inherited. Perhaps they have even seen Mauritius and told him of my undying love for him.* Had it not been for her concern for Candidianus, Valeria would surely have preferred to fall asleep that night and never awaken. How was she to continue on after so many losses?

Ah, but I must, for I sense that my work is far from finished.

***

Eventually Valeria's life returned to normal, and she and Galerius miraculously reached a period of deep affection and respect in their marriage. But it was truly supernatural because

Valeria had to turn a blind eye to the persecutions taking place all around them. Ever faithful, she continued to pray for her husband's salvation. Their home was peaceful, although outside the gates, the kingdom raged with upheaval.

With Candidianus away, Valeria now spent most of her time in prayer and Bible studies. She was engrossed in her morning devotional when a sharp rap at her door interrupted her thoughts.

"Excuse me," the young male servant blurted the moment Valeria opened the door, "but your husband requests your presence in his quarters immediately."

Valeria frowned, as she considered Galerius' possible purpose for such a dire summons. "What is it? Is something wrong? Has something happened to Candidianus?"

The young man's distress was evident, as he stammered, "I am . . . not at liberty to say, madame. Please, come quickly."

Whispering a silent prayer for wisdom and courage, Valeria closed her bedroom door behind her and silently followed the anxious servant down the hallway toward her husband's room. She and Galerius had not visited one another's rooms during the day in many months now, though Galerius almost always came to sleep in her bed at night. The last few nights, however, he had not done so. His absence, combined with the fact that he had summoned her with such urgency, did not bode well.

The sound of her husband's moans greeted her as she knocked on his door. Without waiting for an answer, she flung it open and rushed to his bedside, where he lay prostrate on his back, his face white against the pillow.

"What is it, my dear?" she cried, bending over him to stroke his face, which was hot with fever. "You are ill."

Galerius opened his eyes and focused his gaze upon her, astonishing her with the level of torment she saw reflected there. Despite their many differences, her heart went out to him as she considered the seriousness of his pain, for she knew her husband did not take to his bed lightly.

Turning to the servant who had escorted Valeria to her husband's room, Galerius gasped, "My clothes—remove them, quickly."

Valeria was confused. Why would he issue such an order? Before she could ask, he bellowed at the obviously apprehensive servant, "Now! Get them off of me, now!"

Trembling, the young man removed Galerius' boots and then fumbled with his clothes, at last pulling his pants down and yanking them off his feet, even as his moaning increased. Tossing the clothes to the floor, the servant stood aside, revealing his master's nakedness.

Valeria gasped. "Dear God," she whispered, as her vision grew fuzzy and her head light. "Galerius, what has happened to you? What sorts of wounds are these? Who did this to you—and how?"

But she could not hear his response, as she slipped to the floor, welcoming the darkness that enveloped her.

*

The malady was unlike anything Valeria had ever heard of, and even the doctors were perplexed. Regardless of what remedies they attempted, the disease continued to progress. Her husband's entire body was soon covered in ulcers, and in his groin area the sores had burst and left a deep, cavernous hole, revealing his rotted guts. After Galerius noticed his genitals were swollen, he intentionally avoided Valeria, hoping the malady would heal. Within days the swelling and pain had become almost unbearable, forcing him to retire to his room and to summon his wife to come to his side.

And that is exactly where Valeria stayed, praying for her husband's healing but also for his salvation, for it was evident that apart from a miracle, the man could not last for long. Within a few days, an odious ulcer had begun to grow upon the grossly swollen genitals, and the physicians, aghast and helpless and scarcely able to stand the stench, informed Valeria that her husband's body was infested with worms. The doctors had no idea how to stop the onslaught of the infection. Though they were twice able to stanch his profuse bleeding, the man who was once so strong and regal in his bearing was soon reduced to one scarcely recognizable as human.

Galerius cried and begged for relief, but none seemed forthcoming, though he insisted that Valeria's presence gave him comfort and made the pain bearable. And so, despite the stench, Valeria stayed at his side, beseeching God for a miracle.

When some of the royal physicians complained about the odor and refused to draw near his bed, Galerius, stung to the soul with rage and pain, bellowed as a wounded bull—and then promptly had the hapless doctors executed. He then had physicians brought in from other areas of the kingdom, though few were able to endure the noxious odor of his decaying body. The doctors who refused to approach him were killed, yet even the people in Nicomedia avoided coming near the palace because of the hideous odor that wafted through its windows and into the streets. "Surely, the emperor is rotting!" they declared.

"It is hopeless," Galerius said at last. "Do you not understand, Valeria? Your God is not going to hear your prayers, nor will He answer them. It is He who is torturing me, punishing me for persecuting His people—Mauritius, Octavius, Eugenia and her son, even you and your mother, and thousands of others, so many I have lost count." He grabbed her arm and pulled her close, as if he wanted to confide in her. She leaned in, listening, as he whispered, "They come to me at night—the spirits of those I have murdered. They torment and torture me with the heat of hell itself, promising me that I will pay for all eternity for the evils I have done."

Valeria was horrified at the realization of the level of torment her husband had endured, even as he slept. "Oh, my darling, no," she crooned. "It is not the spirits of the martyrs who come to torture you, my love. It is the very host of hell, tempting you to believe that there is no way out for you. But it is not true, dear one. It is not true!"

Galerius' pain-ravaged body convulsed with sobs as he cried out, "Does that mean you can forgive me? And your God—can He forgive me as well? Is there any hope for me?"

"My darling, I have already forgiven you," Valeria spoke softly, soothing her husband's fevered brow with her hand. "The consequences of our actions are also God's gift to us because it allows us sinners a second chance to make things right with Him. I cannot promise you that by turning to God your suffering will go away, but I can assure you that you will not be lost in darkness forever, for God has already provided a way of escape from the eternal punishment we all deserve. God is saying to you now, 'Come unto me, all who are weary, and I will give you rest.'"

Galerius said weakly, "I need rest. I have not slept for days, and I am in agony. Yet you make it sound so easy."

"It is easy. God's salvation is a free gift to his children."

"But why would God give a gift to a man as evil as I?"

Valeria could see the confusion on his face and tried to explain. "God allows the physical torture of the body and spiritual burden of the heart because it gradually becomes the motivation for salvation . . . to have your sins washed away by the Blood of the Lamb."

"So despite this punishment, you are saying I can be saved?" Galerius' hollowed eyes grew wide.

"This punishment may be your road to redemption, but it is God's forgiveness that is the key that will unlock the gates of heaven."

"But how can I be forgiven with all I have done?"

"Consider that St. Paul was a great persecutor of Christians. God afflicted him with blindness and placed a great spiritual burden upon his heart, but Paul begged forgiveness, and he lived to do great things for God and the kingdom."

"I want to live," cried Galerius. "But I fear your God is angry at me for all the evil I have done! How can he forgive a sinner like me?"

"Jesus Christ has already paid for your sins and mine. This is why Christians want to honor and serve Him—not that we can ever repay Him for His sacrifice. But even if you do not live, you will go to heaven, which is a far greater kingdom than the Roman Empire. Why, the Scriptures tell us that the streets are paved with gold!"

"And even I can go there?"

"God says through the prophet Isaiah, 'though your sins are like scarlet, I will make them white as snow.' God wants us to understand that no matter how sinful we are, we can still be His children. Yet we have to repent in order to be redeemed by God. Then the balm of Gilead will soothe the pain in our soul."

"But my doctors have applied the balm of Gilead to my ulcers. It has not healed or helped me in the least."

"The true balm of Gilead is Jesus. He is the one who can grant us our salvation and our healing."

Galerius closed his eyes then, as he cried out, "Forgive me, Father, for I have sinned! If you do not spare my life, I want to go to this paradise."

The words were like honey to Valeria's heart, as she forgot about the reeking odor and leaned against her husband's breast, wrapping her arms around him while hot tears spilled from her eyes. "And so you shall, my darling! So you shall. Oh, my dear husband, I have prayed for this day for so long, but I never thought it would happen like this!"

"I never thought it would happen at all," Galerius sobbed. "But now that I have asked for His forgiveness, I must also ask for yours. I have tormented you and made your life miserable, yet you have been a loving and gracious wife to me—so much better than I deserved."

Valeria's heart constricted as she thought of the many times she had closed her eyes and pictured Mauritius' face, even as Galerius held her in his arms. She thought too of the fleeting moments of passion and temptation that had passed between her and Daza years earlier, and the guilt nearly crushed her.

"Oh, Galerius," she sobbed, "my beloved husband. My dear, dear husband . . . forgive me as well. You have been good to me and given me great love and affection."

In answer, he began to stroke her hair, and Valeria wept at the tenderness and vulnerability of his gesture, even as she sensed that her husband's time on earth was nearly over.

"Send for a scribe," he instructed her after a few moments. "I want to show my gratitude for God's forgiveness and in some meager way attempt to atone for my evil works by dictating an edict that will end the persecution of all Christians."

In her pending loss, Valeria rejoiced, not realizing that in a very short time her earthly protector would be gone . . . and her life would take such a drastic turn that she could not have imagined it if she had tried.

30

$\mathcal{F}$ollowing Galerius' death, Valeria immediately sent a messenger to Egypt to request a position for herself and her mother in Daza's court.

"Are you sure we would not be more secure with Licinius in Nicomedia?" Prisca asked. "After all, Daza has surpassed Galerius in his torture of Christians and Jews. Are you not afraid of him?"

With Daza ruling Syria and Egypt, Valeria had not seen him in many years. "I am unfamiliar with the man Daza has become, but one thing I know from our years of friendship and unrequited love, I can trust him to take care of us."

"Ah, but people change," Prisca cautioned. "And are you so naïve as to believe he will not want to quench his desires that have smoldered all these years?"

"Mother, Daza is a happily married man with a family. And do I need to remind you that his daughter is engaged to Candidianus? Besides, I am now a middle-aged woman, not the young girl he once lusted after."

"You are so naïve. You are more beautiful now than when you were young. He will still find you a great temptation."

Valeria rolled her eyes. "Once he gave up hope of being with me, a deep friendship ensued between us. I often privately advised him regarding Galerius. I can assure you Daza will allow us to grow old gracefully in his court with great respect and honor. And he always promised me I could worship as I pleased."

"But Daza allowed such bitterness and resentment to take root in his heart when Galerius first passed over him for emperor that I have heard his persecutions of the Christians and Jews are beyond imagining."

"Mother, have you forgotten that because of Galerius' edict, there is no more Christian persecution in the empire?"

But to Valeria's surprise, before her letter even reached Daza, he sent a messenger early one morning, proclaiming his undying love for her and begging her to come at once so they could at last consummate their unrequited love.

Valeria was indignant and quickly sent a return message stating that he knew her well enough to understand that she would never lie in bed with another woman's husband.

In great haste, Daza sent an apology. "Forgive me, my love, but you have misunderstood your passionate suitor, for this was not a request to share your bed without the benefit of marriage. It was a marriage proposal. I desire to marry you so we can be together as long as we both shall live."

This incensed Valeria all the more. Because of her status as Daza's stepmother, she responded with scathing frankness, ordering the messenger to "tell your king that I am unduly flattered by his marriage proposal, but alas, I am still clothed in my widow's weeds. My mourning for his father has not yet expired, so I am not at liberty to entertain any thoughts of marriage. Furthermore, I am shocked that Daza would make such a request of his father's widow when my husband's ashes are yet warm!"

The messenger soon returned with another heartfelt apology from Daza. "The king begs your forgiveness. He says that you may live in his court unencumbered until you feel sufficient time of your widowhood has passed, and then the marriage is to take place. In the meantime, he will set aside his wife, so you will not feel slighted and the emperor will be ready when you are, to marry, and together you shall rule the Roman Empire."

Once again, Valeria's response was anything but positive. "Tell Daza that I will never marry him or prostitute myself with him. He has acted impiously in proposing to divorce a faithful wife to make room for another, whom I fear in time, he might also cast off?"

This time Valeria's reply infuriated Daza. The messenger did not return to Nicomedia; instead a platoon of soldiers appeared at the palace one morning and arrested Valeria and Prisca. Their eunuchs and servants, and even their close friends, women of high station, were burned at the stake after unfair trials, where all the women were unjustly accused of adultery. Valeria and Prisca were forced to watch each act. When the last person who was dear to them had been tortured to death, Daza had the women banished to the deserts of Syria. As evil as he had become, it was apparent that he could not bear to have his beloved Valeria executed.

After their ship arrived in Ctiesphon on the Tigris River, Valeria and Prisca were marched across the desert for miles until they reached the place of their exile.

✑❦

The horrors of the desert were far more than Valeria and Prisca could have imagined. Valeria secretly forfeited a bag of her jewels to bribe a centurion to take a message of their plight to her father at Spalatum in which she described their fate and begged him to intervene on their behalf.

But Daza relished turning down the requests of the powerful old emperor. To celebrate this great achievement, he ordered that a fourteen-year-old vestal virgin, who resembled Valeria, be brought to him. When she rebuked him because of her Christian faith, he proceeded to ravish her body until he eventually tortured her to death with his own hand. Then he sent a messenger who forced Valeria to listen to every sickening detail of the girl's capture and ultimate demise.

On their trek across the Syrian Desert, the entourage surrounding Valeria and Prisca encountered countless snakes and lizards, as well as experiencing severe dehydration. Many of their captors died. One day the soldiers, who were unfamiliar with the desert, were remiss in recognizing the ominous sound of a saw-scaled viper, the deadliest of snakes of the desert. Except for one faithful servant, everyone gasped in horror as the fiery, copper-colored snake flew through the air and landed on Valeria, inserting its deadly fangs into her neck.

Thinking with great speed, the young servant yanked the snake's fangs from Valeria's neck and tossed the serpent behind her where the soldiers killed it. Like a vampire, the servant fell on top of Valeria and sucked the venom from her neck.

By nightfall the servant was dead but Valeria lived, although now seriously ill and delirious. Prisca held a prayer vigil at Valeria's side. When they reached the home of Prisca's friend Lydia, where they had been offered refuge, Valeria lay close to death for a month, consumed with grief for the servant who had given her life to save her. Still, when Lydia's husband, Cyrus, sent word of Valeria's condition to Daza, he refused to show mercy.

Somehow Valeria and Prisca survived in Syria for the next two years, during which time Diocletian continually implored

Daza to release them, though his pleas were in vain. Now, nearly two years later, Valeria sat at her dressing table in Syria, resigned to her circumstances.

This particular morning she had awakened with thoughts of Daza, and had reflected on the many difficulties she had brought upon herself and her mother because of her refusal to marry him. His love for her had metamorphosed into an even more passionate hatred, and she was powerless to stop it. It was so different from the love she had known with Mauritius, or even Galerius. Ultimately, she feared that Daza's love would destroy her and Prisca.

She frowned at her aging reflection in the mirror, then took a lemon from the blue pottery bowl of fruit. With a small silver knife, she methodically sliced the fruit in half and squeezed the juice into her palm, and then splashed it about her face. The remaining juice she rubbed between her hands.

"Lemons are wonderful." Her mother's voice interrupted Valeria's beauty regimen. Fresh from her morning walk, Prisca removed her cloak and came to stand behind her daughter, who massaged the juice into her cheeks with her fingertips.

"Did I not tell you that the best beauty provisions are sent from heaven above?" Prisca asked.

"My skin has never felt so soft." Valeria patted her cheek and then turned to reach up and embrace her mother. "You look happy this morning, Mother."

"I am hopeful," Prisca announced. "Lydia says news has come from Nicomedia. She is waiting for us on the terrace to fill us in on the details."

Valeria's heart leapt at the implications. "What sort of news?"

"I do not know, but Lydia was smiling when she summoned me."

Valeria did not bother to put her hair in a chignon but left it swinging about her shoulders as she and Prisca hurried to the terrace where Lydia waited.

Lydia smiled, motioning them to the opposite side of the table, where a servant pulled out two chairs for the ladies. From the curious expression on Lydia's face, it was hard to imagine what sort of news she was about to tell them. Valeria shut her eyes in anticipation of yet another disappointment—though she wondered what could be worse than their exile in Syria. She clung to her mother's hand as they waited.

"This is not yet confirmed," Lydia told them, "but this morning Cyrus said he heard at the marketplace that Daza is dead."

Valeria gasped, lunging forward on the edge of her chair. A mixture of happiness and sadness wrestled in her heart over the news, as she was transported back to a time when the two of them were young and hopelessly attracted to one another. But the joy of what this meant for her and her companions far outweighed any smidgen of grief she felt for the man who had become her late husband's adopted son and yet had persecuted Christians—including herself and her mother—unmercifully.

"When did this happen?" Prisca asked.

"Apparently, Licinius' soldiers had the emperor and his troops surrounded, so Daza drank a vial of poison," Lydia said, her lips curling into a smile. "But not before he signed a declaration that put an end to the Christian persecutions, adding to the edict already signed by Galerius before he died."

Valeria was speechless as she embraced her mother, remembering the day she had sat at her husband's bedside while he dictated the declaration to a scribe. How foolish she had been to think that edict would assure safety to all Christians! But now . . .

Lydia clucked her tongue. "Even this is not for everyone, I am afraid. Daza ordered the pagan priests executed because they advised him to attack Licinius." Lydia leaned in closer. "This could be good news for you."

Valeria jumped to her feet and looked down at Prisca. "Oh, Mother! Soon we too can go grow cabbages with Father!"

"What do you mean, child?" Lydia asked.

Prisca quickly described Diocletian's gardening to her cousin. This time, Lydia joined in the laughter.

"God has answered our prayers," Valeria exclaimed.

"Not so quickly," Prisca cautioned. "We have no idea what Licinius might do."

"But he was such a close friend of Galerius," Lydia protested, "and of Diocletian too! Surely he will allow you both to return home. After all, Galerius was his benefactor."

"They were boyhood friends too," Valeria added.

Prisca's voice was steady, her face unsmiling as she responded. "It does not matter. We must wait until we know for sure how Licinius will respond to us. Remember, we thought we were free to worship and proclaim our faith openly when Galerius signed his edict before his death. Unfortunately, we quickly found that it did not apply to us."

"Perhaps you will feel differently when you hear what else I have learned," Lydia said. They all took their seats at the table, and Lydia spoke in a whisper so the servants could not hear. They had learned to be very careful, never knowing who could really be trusted. "Before Licinius went into battle, he was rumored to have had a vision."

Valeria frowned. "What sort of vision?"

"From God. It came to him in a dream. Cyrus heard that when Licinius awoke the next morning, he made a commitment to go into battle with our Lord and Savior as his protector."

"Licinius, a Christian?" Prisca clapped her hands. "Then it is no surprise that he was victorious over Daza. We will likely be free to go home soon." She touched her daughter's face, and Valeria felt the strength of hope flow from her mother's touch.

"Oh, to see the coast of Solano again—and Father, of course," Valeria mused.

When she was a little girl, Valeria had often visited her paternal grandmother at Salona. It was a magical place, and when she and Galerius had visited the palace her father had constructed for his retirement outside Salona, Valeria thought it was more magnificent than any palace she had ever seen in Rome or Nicomedia.

"There are churches there too—churches where we can worship openly, now that the persecutions have ceased," Prisca noted.

As the women basked in the morning sunshine, allowing the implications of Lydia's news to settle deeply into their hearts, Lydia's husband, Cyrus, and one of their guards returned from the marketplace. As soon as the guard was out of hearing distance, Cyrus brought more news. "Apparently it was Constantine who pressured Licinius to go into battle with Daza."

"Why?" Prisca wondered aloud.

"Daza was the only ruler who ignored Galerius' edict to end all Christian persecution. As we well know, he did exactly as he pleased. And look at the trouble it caused the two of you!"

Cyrus glanced around and then took a seat beside his wife and across from Prisca and Valeria so the guard could not hear them. He leaned forward as he spoke, "A month ago, Constantine looked up at the sky and saw a cross. He analyzed the ruin of the Roman emperors throughout the centuries and realized the lives of the pagan rulers always appeared to end in death and destruction."

"Except for Father's reign," Valeria interjected.

Cyrus nodded and continued. "Constantine consulted the Christians in his army, who told him there was great power in the name of Jesus. Even speaking the name of Jesus made the demons flee. From that day forward, Constantine's army marched into battle with the symbol of the cross and the prayers of the Christian priests at the forefront."

"Mother, I believe you are responsible for Constantine's faith," Valeria exclaimed. She then explained to Cyrus and Lydia that Constantine had been raised in Diocletian's court as a young boy and was heavily influenced by Prisca's faith.

"Train up a child in the way he should go, and when he is old, he will not depart from it," Prisca recited. "Constantine also had a Christian mother, Helena, who faithfully prayed for him. Helena has had a great influence on my life as well. In my opinion, there is no greater Christian woman in the world today."

Lydia clucked her tongue. "Such a pity her husband divorced her."

"It was with a heavy heart that he did so," Prisca explained. "But he was forced to marry Theodora for political reasons."

"Now with three Christian sons as his Caesars, Constantine plans to rule the Roman Empire as a Christian nation," Cyrus explained, his big hand resting affectionately on Lydia's smaller one. "Especially after Licinius' oath to God and Daza's suicide."

Prisca smiled. "Helena will leave behind a great legacy when she dies."

Valeria stood to her feet, joy overflowing her heart. "Enough of politics," she exclaimed. "We are going home!"

"Not so loud," Prisca warned. "The guards are just outside the gate."

Valeria did her best to rein in her exuberance, but thoughts of returning to her father's palace kept a smile on her face throughout the day and into the night. It was only when she laid her head on her pillow after darkness fell that fear began to nip at her thoughts.

What if Licinius . . . ? The thought was so unbearable that she refused to let it take shape. Instead, after tossing and turning for hours, she got up and drank a potion to help her sleep. As her conscious thoughts began to blur with the images of her dreams, she drifted backward to a time when love had burst upon her with the joy and freshness of unfettered youth and an unchallenged future. How had the years passed so quickly . . . and changed things so drastically?

31

$\mathcal{B}$y the next morning, Valeria awoke to find that the Roman soldiers, who had guarded them during their exile, were gone. She and Prisca approached Cyrus, who explained that few soldiers were loyal in this political climate, quickly switching their allegiance to whatever leader held the power. Now that Daza was dead, they were scurrying like cockroaches to align themselves with either Licinius or Constantine.

"You can be sure some of them will return in anticipation of eliciting favor for your eventual release," Cyrus warned the women. "Meanwhile, we must work quickly. It would be best if you can escape while they are gone. I have tentatively arranged for your passage to Spalatum on a merchant's ship next Monday."

"But what about you and Lydia?" Prisca asked.

"That same ship will continue on to Nicomedia, so Lydia and I can travel with you."

"But would you not consider remaining with us in Spalatum? After all you and Lydia have done for us, Diocletian would welcome you into his court," Prisca assured the elderly couple.

Cyrus nodded appreciatively. "Lydia and I would be honored. We had planned to go into hiding with Lydia's family in Nicomedia for fear of what actions Licinius might inflict upon the members of Daza's court."

Prisca appeared concerned. "Will our departure not attract the attention of the soldiers?"

"There are hordes of Syrian merchants whose ships leave the harbor daily to travel up the Mediterranean coast and into the Aegean Sea, so our departure should go unnoticed."

"But such a trip will be costly," Prisca observed. "How will we pay for our passage? We have spent nearly all our money during these many months in hiding, and it will take time to find buyers for my jewels."

"Lydia and I have money, and you also have the chest of gold Diocletian sent for you when you first arrived," Cyrus explained. "I buried the chest for such a time as this."

Prisca flashed a smile, but a frown quickly replaced it. "Will we not be recognized?"

Cyrus winked at the ladies. "I have arranged for us to go in disguise."

"As whom?"

"I shall go as a priest, and you ladies should dress as nuns. I have secured the clothing from the local monastery, but will you look through your jewels for a masculine cross befitting my priestly garb?"

Valeria thought of the Theban cross that had once hung around Mauritius' neck and which she had kept with her all these years, though she wrestled with the idea of giving it up, even now. Before she could offer, Prisca hurried to her room and soon returned with a heavy gold cross with one large sapphire in the center of it.

Cyrus took it and went to his room. When he reappeared, his head was shaved and he was wearing a long black robe, adorned with Prisca's cross around his neck.

"I am leaving shortly to secure the final arrangements for passage on the merchant ship. I have arranged for one of the servants to take you on a supposed shopping excursion in the market at dawn tomorrow so you will have your pick of the fresh produce. Meet me onboard then," he instructed, while scribbling the ship's location and the owner's name on a piece of parchment, which he handed to Prisca for safekeeping.

"I have a message for Candidianus," Valeria said, offering Cyrus a papyrus letter that she had retrieved from her toga. "Will you send it to him for me while you are in the village?"

Prisca quickly snatched the letter from her hand. "No one, not even Candidianus, must know of our plans," she warned, clutching the missive to her chest.

"Are you insinuating that you do not trust my son?"

"We can trust no one," Cyrus interjected. "No one must know that we are traveling to Spalatum. Your letter could easily be intercepted."

"But I want Candidianus and Paulina to join us there," Valeria explained. "If Licinius proves to be disloyal for any reason, Candidianus and his fiancée should also have Father's protection."

"We do not know what our future holds," Prisca admonished. "We must take every precaution. One can never put trust in man—only in God."

Valeria stared at Prisca, concerned that her mother had become paranoid during their years of exile in Syria. After all, Daza was dead, and Licinius was Galerius' dearest friend. Valeria had convinced herself there was no reason to fear.

"Speaking of precautions, I want to leave some of the gold with you," Cyrus told the women. "And also the name of the merchant who has agreed to give us passage to Spalatum."

"Please do not talk like this," Lydia protested, as she embraced her husband.

Cyrus pulled away. "We cannot be too careful, my love."

Cyrus left for the village early the next morning, while it was still dark.

By nightfall, just as Cyrus had cautioned, the guards returned, complicating the women's plans.

"We must slip out tonight when they are sleeping, instead of the early morning hours," Prisca said.

"But will the servant not be suspicious if we ask him to accompany us in the middle of the night?" Lydia asked.

"Of course, but we know our way to the village," Prisca reminded them. "It is only two miles, so we can go alone."

Valeria trembled. "What about the vipers?"

"By now I know the scraping sound of a saw as intimately as I know my own heartbeat," Prisca assured her. "We shall know by their warning when they are near."

Even with her lingering misgivings, Valeria nodded. The decision was made.

Finding their way to the village in the middle of the night proved an obstacle course for the women. Fortunately, there was a full moon to light the road. The night was hot, and the road was dusty. To further complicate their journey, they had to drag their bags behind them, but the women kept going, trudging through the sand. Less than a mile from town, they nearly stumbled upon a large object stretched across the road several feet ahead of them.

Prisca yanked them behind a small sand dune. "Do not look. Close your eyes, and we will detour around the corpse."

"Corpse?" Lydia whispered, the alarm evident in her voice.

"I cannot say if it is an animal or a man, but my instincts tell me we should avoid whatever it is."

Valeria's heart raced. "But suppose it is a man, and he is still alive! How can we leave someone suffering and wounded in the middle of the road?"

"It is probably an animal," Prisca repeated.

"And it could be a trap," Lydia added. "Someone could be lying in wait for us."

"We should try to reach the village, and then send someone back to check on the body," Prisca suggested.

"Should we not at least check the pulse?" Valeria asked.

"If it will make you feel better, Valeria, I will go and get a closer look," Prisca said.

As Lydia and Valeria held hands and prayed, Prisca inched closer to the body. When she got near enough to see the remains, she quickly turned and raced back to her companions.

"It is—was—human, as we feared, but the body has been dismembered," she gasped. "The buzzards have already picked a substantial meal from it. Put a handkerchief over your nose as we pass by; the stench is unbearable. And do not look at it."

As they skirted around the corpse, Valeria ignored her mother's warning and stole a glance from the corner of her eye. The sight staggered her, and she scarcely kept from falling, as she spotted her mother's jeweled cross in what was left of the corpse's outstretched hand. She swallowed hard. Cyrus would not be meeting them on the ship or in Spalatum. Should she tell her mother and Lydia? No. If she did, Lydia, in her grief, might refuse to leave his body. Plenty of time later for the new widow to discover the truth.

Cyrus is dead. Murdered. The silent words blared inside her head, even as she realized their gold was gone. How was it possible that the thieves had missed the cross? Could God have blinded their eyes so it would remain as a sign to the women of Cyrus' fate?

She realized then that they too would likely have been murdered had they not traveled at night. Their escape was daring, dangerous, but what choice did they have? They had waited for two years, and not even her father had been able to rescue them. This was likely their only chance to escape.

The women reached the harbor just before daybreak, having stopped to slip into their nuns' habits just before entering the town. Having grown up on the sea, Valeria was delighted to see the coastline again, even in the darkness and despite the heaviness of grief she bore over the gruesome sight she had witnessed in the desert.

Valeria feared it would take time to secure their passage, so she was relieved that her mother had not argued when she suggested they go directly to the ship, despite the early hour. She wondered how Prisca and Lydia would react when they learned Cyrus had never arrived to pay for their passage. Thank the good Lord he had made the arrangements ahead of time and left enough gold with the women to cover their expenses!

Prisca went on board first, while Valeria and Lydia waited on the dock. When Prisca indicated that it was safe to board, Valeria watched her mother for some indication that she now knew Cyrus had never arrived to pay their passage. Prisca, however, said nothing, and Valeria decided her mother must be waiting until she could talk with Lydia alone.

Checking out the small vessel, Valeria quickly realized it was a far cry from the elegant royal ships on which she had sailed throughout her privileged lifetime. Her mother must have read her expression because she squeezed Valeria's hand and spoke reassuringly. "Consider the journey to Spalatum an adventure."

Valeria could only hope she was right, as they were greeted by the kindly merchant who owned the ship.

"Have you heard from the priest who arranged our passage?" Lydia dared to ask, as Valeria realized the woman had probably suspected Cyrus's fate all along.

The man shook his head. "No, I have not, but it is still a couple of hours before the ship sets sail. Perhaps he will arrive shortly." After the merchant introduced the women to the captain, he wished them a safe journey and disembarked the ship.

"Welcome aboard, holy sisters," the captain greeted them. He was a short, wiry man with eyes the color of the sea and hair bleached by the sun to the color of mahogany. Valeria thought his weathered and tanned face with so many lines on it resembled a road map. As he gave the women a tour of the vessel, he explained that their provisions, including water and wine, were stored in wooden casks, with brine to preserve the meat.

It was not long after the crew launched from the seaport that Valeria felt exhilarated. Never again did she want to set foot upon Syria's shore! It was the country that Galerius had defeated, the victory elevating him to the highest office, but it was difficult for her to feel any gratitude. Her time in Syria had been hard, particularly the isolation. For the first time since her husband's death, she felt alive. It mattered not how difficult the voyage would be; it had to be more pleasant than remaining in Syria. Her exhilaration was dampened only by the knowledge of Cyrus's death, which it seemed Lydia might well have anticipated.

When the noon meal was served and the three women were seated around the table, the captain asked one of the crew members to bless the food, and then the feast began, as the sailors grabbed their food by the fistfuls and the ladies watched in dismay.

In addition to salt pork and fish, there were olives, chick-peas, beans, lentils, olive oil, almonds, and cheese. The women also noted an array of sardines and cod, but filled their bowls with rice and a few almonds and olives, and their cups with fresh water. Valeria picked up two biscuits, but noticed one was infested with weevils and discreetly placed it to the side of the basket.

"Ah, holy sister," an older sailor commented, "these biscuits are hard, but if you dip them in your water, they will soften."

"But the weevils will drown," Valeria whispered to her mother, trying to suppress her laughter.

By day's end, the women were exhausted, and the captain led them below to their sleeping quarters. The men in the crew had bedded down in whatever space or crevice they could find, and the women stumbled over bodies as they followed the captain through the hold. They were surprised when they reached the door of the cabin and peeked inside. The tiny room looked as though it could accommodate one or two at most, but amazingly all three squeezed inside.

The berthing compartment was equipped with four cots fastened to the wall. Valeria insisted on taking one of the top berths, allowing the two older ladies to take the more easily accessible lower bunks. Two tiny portholes, one beside her bed and the other at the bunk below where her mother would be sleeping, filled the room with moonlight. A lovely Turkish rug covered the plank floor and added a surprising touch of elegance. In one corner a mirror hung above a pitcher and a basin for washing. The captain pointed out the built-in chests on the opposite side of the cabin, where he instructed them to stow their belongings, which had been taken below earlier by a ship's hand.

After the women were settled in for the night, they battled claustrophobia, but the captain had already warned them that anyone who slept topside had to lash themselves to the masts to keep from being swept overboard. As a result, they tossed and turned in their tiny quarters for hours before finally dropping off into a fitful sleep.

A few days later, when the women awoke and came up on deck for breakfast, they saw land in the distance, a sun-drenched island, glittering like a jewel upon the turquoise sea. One of the sailors explained that the boat was scheduled to stop in the village of Nicosia on the isle of Cyprus to pick up a shipment of oranges bound for Solano.

"Do you suppose those oranges will be delivered to Father's castle in Solano?" Valeria whispered to Prisca. Still weeks away from Diocletian's palace, she realized that they were one day closer to freedom. When the ship was at last anchored in port, the captain paid them a visit.

"The isle of Cyprus is one of the most idyllic places on earth," he explained. "We will dock here at the city of Nicosia around noon to restock our supplies and pick up several shipments, though I advise you not to go ashore, as we will be leaving again in three hours at most."

❧

Though the women lamented their inability to spend a few short hours on the incredibly lovely island, they realized the captain's advice was well worth taking. Instead of exploring the quaint shops and cafes of Cyprus or strolling the warm sands of its shore, they admired it from a distance and waited for the sailors to return from purchasing supplies for the remainder of the trip.

"It is hard to believe," one of the crew commented to another as they passed by the ladies after coming back onboard. "Do you suppose it's true? Could the old man really be dead at last?"

Valeria's heart lurched at the implications, and she cocked her ear to better hear the conversation.

"Could be," answered the other sailor. "After all, Daza and Galerius are gone, so why not Diocletian? He was the oldest of the three."

They were out of earshot by then, as Valeria pivoted toward Prisca, only to realize her mother had also overheard the exchange. The look of horror on Prisca's face mirrored what Valeria felt in her heart. Surely it could not be true!

In moments the three women had cornered the captain and asked if there was any truth to the rumor that Diocletian was dead.

"I, too, have heard the rumor," the captain admitted, "though I cannot say if there is any truth to it. No one seems able to confirm it." He frowned. "Forgive me, ladies, but you appear unduly upset over the possibility. I'm surprised, since Diocletian was known for his persecution of Christians. I should think you'd be relieved at the prospect of yet one more of your tormentors having passed on to his eternal reward . . . or punishment, as the case may be."

The reminder that if her father truly was dead he had most likely expired without first coming to faith in Christ nearly knocked Valeria to her knees. As she struggled to remain standing, she felt her mother take her hand, and she found strength in their shared distress.

Excusing themselves as quickly as possible, the ladies retreated to their tiny cabin, where they huddled together and prayed for mercy. Not only were they devastated at the possibility that Diocletian may have died without first receiving Christ as his Savior, they had to consider what his death would mean to their own chances of survival.

Valeria bit her lip and moaned. "What if Father truly has died? And if he has, do you suppose there is any possibility that he turned to Christ in his last moments?"

It was obvious Prisca struggled to speak as she answered. "Only God knows, my dear, though we must pray he is still alive and that we can reach him in time."

And so the women committed themselves to pray that if Diocletian weren't already dead, God would keep him alive until they could speak to him—or until someone else could lead him to repentance before he breathed his last.

32

$\mathscr{A}$ few days after leaving Cyprus the captain told the women at breakfast, "Tomorrow we shall arrive in Lycia."

"I seem to recall that St. Paul visited Lycia," Prisca commented.

"According to the Book of Acts," Lydia added, "Paul was on his way to Rome for his trial when his ship docked in Andriace."

"We never pass the harbor of Andriace without stopping for a load of lumber," the captain explained. "A large forest of cedars of Lebanon grows here. Today we are picking up lumber for a client, a coffin maker, and also some Turkish rugs for a merchant in Nicomedia. We will dock in Andriace for a day to load the lumber, so you can enjoy an excursion to the city of Myra."

As they approached the port, Valeria and her mother admired the magnificent beauty of Myra, a city perched high on a craggy mountaintop, dotted with surrounding islands tucked into romantic coves and surrounded by snow-capped peaks.

As they disembarked the boat, the captain called out to them, "Enjoy yourselves, but please make sure you return to the boat by dusk."

Off the boat, the women began to plan their day. "First, we should find somewhere to have breakfast," Valeria suggested, "and then we can get directions to the church."

"I would prefer to visit the church first," Prisca said. "Clergymen keep abreast of the political climate, so they will know if Diocletian is still alive. I am anxious to learn my husband's fate before we return to the boat. If he has died, we cannot go to Solano but must seek protection elsewhere."

"But where shall we go?" Valeria asked.

"We have lived most of our lives in Nicomedia and have an abundance of friends there who can help us until we can approach Licinius to ask for protection in his court."

Valeria had not allowed herself to consider the far-reaching implications of her father's death. The women would be at the mercy of an Augustus again. Thankfully, Licinius and Galerius had been as close as brothers, so she felt confident that the newly named Augustus would welcome them into his court.

The women settled into a carriage pulled by donkeys that would ferry them up to the city. Valeria's eyes climbed ahead of the donkeys, settling first on a magnificent amphitheater carved from the stone, and then the tombs on the cliff above, set into the mountain. It was a fascinating gravesite with one tomb more elaborate than the next. When her eyes reached the tip-top of the mountain, she tried to see the city, but it was hidden behind a palm-lined promenade that snaked along the edge of the cliffs. The rising sun glistened off the sea below, and the snowcapped mountains surrounding the city lit it with such brilliance that it appeared to be on fire.

Once they reached the mountaintop, they exited the carriages at a magnificent temple. The attendant explained, "This is the Temple of Artemis, the most magnificent structure to the Greek goddess anywhere. Lycia is the birthplace of the goddess, the daughter of Zeus and Apollo's twin sister."

When the attendant paused, Prisca asked if he had heard the news of Diocletian's death. When he replied that he had not, Valeria's heart sang with relief.

As they meandered over the cobblestone paths, they enjoyed Myra's lush green landscape, set against an artist's canvas of blue skies that appeared to have no end.

Valeria's rumbling stomach soon interrupted their search. "I am famished. Can we eat before looking further?"

Prisca agreed, and the group serpentined the city's deserted streets. It was still early morning, so the Lycians were just beginning to stir about in the market. The women quickly found a charming restaurant that overlooked the sea. There on the terrace, they enjoyed a bountiful breakfast of eggs, fish, and pancakes. They also sampled a variety of plump, juicy fruits indigenous to the area—pomegranates, oranges, figs, and grapes.

Just as Prisca had predicted, the locals were eager to answer their questions and tell them tales of Lycia, including answering their queries about Diocletian. No one in the restaurant had heard of the former emperor's death, so the women were greatly encouraged.

One young couple visited with them for a time and told them a tragic tale about Lycia's history.

"When the Persians, under the rule of Cyrus the Great, invaded Lycia in 540 B.C., the Xanthosians put up a heroic fight," the man explained, "but most of their warriors were slaughtered in the battle. The survivors chose for their wives and children to die by their own hand rather than surrender. The Syrians then ruled Lycia for hundreds of years until the Greeks, and then the Romans, finally overtook them."

The travelers thanked the couple for the sad history lesson and got up to leave, but Valeria turned back to inquire if the couple knew where they could find the church.

The man told them he did, and then explained, "Bishop Nicholas was released from prison after the death of Daza. Just last month, he and some of his parishioners reopened the church."

"What can you tell us about the bishop?" Valeria asked.

"There is not a finer man anywhere. Bishop Nicholas was born in this very country in the city of Patara. He was orphaned at an early age, but he inherited a large sum of money from his parents, who died in the epidemic. Remarkably, he kept none of it for himself, but gave most of it to the poor."

"Apparently, he is a man who follows Jesus' command to sell all he had and give his riches to those less fortunate," Valeria commented. "How old is he?"

"He is yet a young man, but he has become legendary for his generosity. There were three young ladies in Lycia whose father could not afford a dowry. Without one, the young women were doomed to a life of prostitution until Bishop Nicholas threw three bags of gold into the window of their home."

The wife added, "The bishop came to their rescue, so the girls had ample gold to marry the best of husbands. The girls and their families still live in Myra."

At that moment, a younger man stepped up to their table. "Pardon me, but I could not help overhearing your conversation. I am a Christian—and what a miracle that I can say this now!"

Valeria's heart leapt, but she was cautious in her response. "How severe was the Christian persecution in Lycia?"

"It was dreadful. Our leaders gave generous rewards to any citizen who would turn in their Christian friends. Once they were arrested, the Christians were either imprisoned or exe-cuted. There were many martyrs here. But enough of this. If we go now, you can partake in the communion service at the church. I can take you there."

Eagerly accepting the young man's offer, they hurried off, but Prisca took Valeria's arm and pulled her aside while Lydia kept their young guide busy with her chatter.

"You are very trusting, my dear," Prisca whispered, "but please consider that many clergymen are corrupt. I have wit-nessed priests turning in their own congregation. Be very cau-tious when we meet this bishop."

"May the Lord lead," Valeria said, as she made the sign of the cross.

✍

Although the Eastern Church in Myra had been abandoned for several years, Valeria was moved as the building came into view. Its former beauty still shone through the peeling paint and weatherworn façade, and when they walked inside, the congregants, who were still milling around in the vestibule, greeted them warmly.

After a few minutes, the music began and the bishop appeared from a side door. A handsome man with piercing blue eyes, the bishop's snowy white hair fell to his shoulders. Although young, his beard and mustache had also turned prematurely white. When the bishop began to speak, Valeria turned her attention to Jesus.

Following the service, the bishop stood in the vestibule to greet his parishioners. When it came their turn, Valeria requested an audience with him.

Behind closed doors, Valeria dared to reveal their identity.

"Your Holiness," she began, "I . . . we . . . are not whom we have led you to believe."

Bishop Nicholas frowned, obviously confused. "What do you mean? If not nuns, then who are you?"

Valeria swallowed and looked to her mother for support, but it was obvious Prisca did not approve of her daughter's decision to risk everything by revealing their secret to this man they did not know. But what other choice did they have?

Valeria took a deep breath and plunged ahead. "I am . . . Valeria," she said, "daughter of Diocletian and wife of Galerius." She cut her eyes toward her mother and then Lydia before returning her gaze to the bishop. "This is Prisca, wife of Diocletian, and our friend Lydia." Afraid to say more, she waited.

The bishop responded with disbelief. "Why have you come here?" he demanded at last, his face growing red and his eyes bulging.

Valeria began to tremble. Had she made a terrible mistake? Had her mother been right after all? Would the bishop feel obligated to turn them in to the Roman authorities?

Seemingly wary of his famous visitors, the bishop rose and walked around to the front of the desk. Standing before the ladies, he explained. "I have just been released from prison. You must understand that in my position, I cannot hide you in the church and betray the Roman emperors."

Prisca glared at Valeria, who received the silent message that it had been a dreadful mistake to reveal their identity to the bishop. Outside the heavy cedar doors to the bishop's office were his assistants. Another door led to the outside courtyard, where dozens of parishioners milled around the terrace. Escape appeared impossible.

"Your Holiness, please hear us out," Valeria pleaded. "We are not seeking asylum. We have sailed from Syria for home, and Myra just happens to be a regular stop on the ship's itinerary."

"Ah, so the emperors have released you from your exile in Syria?"

Valeria hesitated, not wanting to lie but only to survive. "Not exactly. After Daza died, the soldiers who guarded us became lax in their duties. Some of them ran away, abandoning their posts. Others fled the country to declare their allegiance to the new emperors. Lydia's husband, Cyrus, suggested that we seize the opportunity to return home."

"Yes," Lydia spoke up. "My husband arranged passage for us, but he was murdered just before we set sail."

Valeria jerked her head toward Lydia. So she, too, had disobeyed Prisca's warning not to look at the corpse in the roadway.

The bishop's voice brought her back to the present.

"Are the Roman emperors aware of your escape from Syria?"

Valeria hedged. "Why do you ask? Have you heard that they are searching for us?"

The bishop rubbed his beard. "There has been no news of you since your exile."

"Then we have become insignificant," Valeria surmised. "They no longer care about us, or they assumed that we could not survive or find a way of escape without a man to help us."

The bishop smiled, visibly relaxing a bit. "One should never underestimate the power of a woman. You are both highly esteemed and loved throughout the empire. Many are aware of your Christian faith." He turned to Valeria. "Is there truth to the rumor that Galerius made a profession of faith on his deathbed?"

Valeria nodded, smiling slightly. "I was by his side."

"I would assume that it was your faithful prayers and kindness that ultimately brought your husband to this decision."

Valeria blushed, thanking the bishop for his gracious words, even as she sensed they could trust him after all.

"How may I help you?" the bishop asked then. "Is it money you need?"

"Oh no, Your Holiness, we have sufficient funds to last us until we reach our destination," Valeria assured him. "We have come to you in search of answers."

"But what can I tell you? No one can predict how the emperors will react to your escape. I am guessing the news from Syria has not yet reached them. What are your plans?"

Valeria's eyes filled with tears. "My father repeatedly pleaded with Daza to release us to him, but the devil's spawn relished denying his former emperor's request. Now that Daza has died, we are fleeing to my father's palace in Spalatum." Her voice cracked. "However, when we docked on the island of Cyprus recently, I heard a rumor that my father . . ." Valeria's voice broke. "That my father was dying . . . that he might even be dead by now. Do you know if this is true?"

"I am sorry," the bishop replied, his voice kind. "I thought you knew."

Cries of pain and disbelief escaped the women simultaneously, and Valeria rushed to kneel at her mother's side. They embraced, weeping, until Valeria looked up at the bishop and asked, "Do you know any details?"

"When Constantine and Licinius were in Milan, they concluded that Diocletian had to die in retribution for the Christian persecutions. Diocletian, though already quite ill, got wind of their plot and chose to die by his own hand. He drank a vial of poison."

Outraged, Valeria cried, "My father was their benefactor! How dare they betray him?"

"I understand why you are upset," the bishop soothed. "There were many men more evil than Diocletian, but with Galerius and Daza gone, Diocletian was the only surviving ruler of the persecution era, and therefore the sacrificial lamb to pay for all the innocent bloodshed."

Anger warred with sorrow in Valeria's heart, as she demanded, "Why could they not allow him to live out his life in peace? I will not argue that the persecutions were horrific, but consider all he did for the Roman Empire. Had he not divided it, there would be no Roman Empire today."

"The politicians are speculating that Licinius felt threatened by Diocletian."

The statement seemed to breathe life back into Prisca, as she protested its veracity. "Threatened? But my husband was sixty-six years old, and it is no secret that he was ill when he retired to Solano over six years ago. He was no threat to anyone."

The bishop's voice was gentle. "When he died, Diocletian was still revered by the military and respected by the Romans. He wielded a great influence in the empire. Licinius was insecure in his power and feared Diocletian would reemerge and propose another leader, or at least appoint a coleader for him."

"Father was never keen on Licinius' appointment as Caesar," Valeria conceded, "but Galerius insisted upon it since he and Licinius were boyhood friends. My father did not want to usurp Galerius, and so he agreed. I am afraid he should have allowed his instincts to rule."

Valeria's thoughts then turned to their own immediate plight. "What will we do?" she asked at last, turning her gaze toward her mother. "Father is gone. Where shall we go?"

"I am outraged," Prisca said, "but I clearly understand the reasons why the power-hungry Licinius perceived Diocletian as a threat. But you are the wife of Galerius, Licinius' longtime friend and benefactor. I cannot imagine that Licinius would not take us into the protection of his court. We are three help-less women. How can we be a threat to anyone?"

"Have you not heard of the fate of the women and children in Daza's family?" the bishop asked.

When the women indicated that they had not, Bishop Nicholas explained. "The church tried to intervene because we vehemently oppose the slaughter of innocent women and children, but Licinius had everyone in Daza's court executed."

The women gasped. A sudden realization crept upon Valeria, and she cried out, "My son, Candidianus? He was betrothed to Daza's daughter Paulina. Surely he—"

The bishop smiled. "I have good news for you on this account. Licinius spared Candidianus and welcomed him into his court."

"And his fiancée?" Valeria asked, as relief washed over her.

"Sadly, the young woman was executed."

Valeria's joy was tempered by the news, but she took hope in the safety of Candidianus. "I knew Licinius could not turn away the family of Galerius, his beloved friend. Licinius will surely have mercy on us as well."

Prisca nodded and rose from her chair. "I agree. We should go to Licinius at once and request his protection."

"Not so fast," the bishop warned. "Licinius can be unpre-dictable. Perhaps it would be wiser for you to wait in Myra, at least until Candidianus can approach Licinius and request permission for you to return to Nicomedia."

"I agree Candidianus should approach Licinius on our behalf," Prisca concurred, "but we have many friends in Nicomedia, and I believe we should go there at once."

"I wish I could convince you to wait," the bishop argued. "There are many Christian families in my parish who would gladly take you into their homes until you receive word from Candidianus. I can make the arrangements."

Prisca shook her head. "If Licinius has invited Candidianus into his court, then we should travel to Nicomedia at once."

"Mother," Valeria argued, "did you not hear the bishop's warning?"

But Prisca was already at the door, reaching for the gold handle, when the bishop sighed and said, "Very well. May the Lord bless and keep you."

33

The captain greeted the women warmly when they returned to the ship.

"Our plans have changed," Prisca informed him. "We will not be stopping in Spalatum, but we have received orders from the church that we are to travel on to Nicomedia."

The captain seemed genuinely pleased to earn the extra cash for their extended voyage, explaining that in a few days they would enter the Adriatic Sea.

"Then I will feel at home at last," Prisca replied, though her smile was tinged with sadness. "I grew up on the sea."

"This sea is far different from the one of your childhood," the captain warned. "Seaborne goods, ranging from cloths and rugs to wines and agricultural products, cross the Black Sea every day and night. Roman fleets are constantly scouring the waters in search of pirates and the enemy."

"Enemy?" Valeria frowned. "But we are at peace."

"Yes, but despite its Roman occupation, Syria remains a constant threat. The pirates, of course, are the real threat. In the dark of night, they quietly row their boats to the side of the ships and then sneak aboard and take them over so they can steal their goods."

"What happens to the passengers?" Lydia asked.

The captain chuckled. "You are safe with us. Throughout the night, I assign two men on watch." The captain then wished them a pleasant night's sleep and headed for the bow to help his crew launch the ship into the dark waters.

That evening Valeria tossed and turned in her tiny bunk. Haunted by the belief that they should remain in Myra under the bishop's protection, she was unable to sleep. Why had she not been able to convince her mother to stay, at least for a while, until the political climate settled a bit? As much as she longed to see her son, she felt it far too dangerous to head for Nicomedia.

The other thought that tormented her was that her father may have died without turning to Christ. When she had voiced her concern to her mother, Prisca reaffirmed her faith that only God knew Diocletian's heart—and that He did not make mistakes. Valeria had matured enough in her faith to accept that, but it did not lessen the pain of losing her father.

At last Valeria gave up on sleeping. The seas were calm, so she dressed and tiptoed out of the tiny cabin, escaping to the bow of the ship. Her heart crowded with forbidden worry, she sat under the starry sky as the sailors worked around her. But after an hour under the heavens, the beauty of the night served as an excellent tonic, and she began praising God for the magnificence of His creation. The joy in her spirit remained and even multiplied over the next days, spreading to Lydia and Prisca as well.

The captain soon announced that they would arrive in Solano the next morning. "We have just one load of textiles to pick up, so we will not be staying long in the port. I am afraid there is no time for you to go ashore."

"It is truly a blessing that we cannot disembark there," Prisca confided to Valeria and Lydia. "Being there without Diocletian would be far too painful."

"But we can stand on the bow and see the place of Father's birth . . . Dalmatia," Valeria said wistfully.

Very early the following morning, Valeria was awakened by pounding on the cabin door.

She stole a look out of the porthole, confirming that it was still dark outside. Looking to the other two bunks, she was relieved that her mother and Lydia were asleep. She crept to the door, but instead of asking who was there, she responded with a different ploy. "Please, you must go away," she whispered. "The other two ladies are ill and burning hot with fever."

"It is your captain, madame. I am sorry to hear that your companions are not well, but the Roman soldiers are on board and would like to have a few words with you."

"With me?"

"With all of you," came another male voice, obviously belonging to a Roman soldier. "Would you please open the door?"

The captain added, "Soldiers are checking every ship that sails into the harbor of Solano, searching for the wife and daughter of Emperor Diocletian. It was reported that the empresses escaped from their exile in Syria. I tried to tell them that you are holy women and not royals, but they insist on seeing for themselves."

Valeria's heart dropped. Her instincts had been right; they should have stayed with the bishop. Beads of perspiration broke out on her forehead, as she tried to think quickly. "But I fear the sisters' illness could be a danger to anyone who comes near. It would be better to answer your questions through the door."

As she awaited their response, she eavesdropped on their conversation.

"You mentioned these women are elderly nuns," one of the soldiers commented.

"Aye, sir."

"Who arranged their passage?"

"An elderly priest."

"What is their destination?"

"Nicomedia. But I can assure you these women are nuns and not the women you seek. They are truly holy women and not royals. They even eat from the table with the crew."

"Ask her to step outside the door," the soldier demanded. "Perhaps she can answer our questions satisfactorily without disturbing the other two."

The captain pounded on the door again, this time awakening Prisca and Lydia. Valeria put her finger to her lips in an effort to keep them quiet. Then she motioned for Lydia to remove her sleeping cap and took it from her.

"Would you please step outside?" the captain called.

"Please give me a moment to find my robe."

Prisca quickly tied a pillow around Valeria's waist to further disguise her and make her look heavier. Valeria slid her arms into her dark robe and tucked her hair under Lydia's cap. Prisca then dug deep into her traveling bag and found a vial of kohl. She patted a bit of the dark powder under Valeria's eyes to make her look tired and older, maybe even a bit ill. At last Valeria took a deep breath and opened the door.

When the captain saw her, he gasped. "Are you ill too?"

"I am tired, for I have been up all night caring for the others, although I fear I could come down with the illness soon." She held her linen handkerchief over her mouth, pretending she was trying to protect her visitors from germs; this gesture also helped disguise her appearance. She directed her muffled questions to the captain and a group of five Roman soldiers. "How may I help you?"

"Your captain has already told us you were traveling from Syria," one soldier observed. "We are searching for two empresses, also traveling from Syria."

"Can you describe them?" Valeria asked.

One of the soldiers held out his hand. In it were two Roman coins, one inscribed with Valeria's face and the other with Prisca's.

Valeria gasped. "The empresses? When we were in Syria, one of the women in our priory had seen them. She said they were very beautiful, so you should have no problem picking them out in a crowd."

The soldier closed his hand around the coins and stuffed them back into his pocket. "But you have not seen them?"

Valeria shook her head, remembering how, when the coins were minted, she had been outraged. The image, which the artist had sculpted, looked nothing like her. The nose was long and pointed and her chin jutted squarely. Now she was grateful because the false depiction had likely saved her life. *All things work together for good*, she mused.

"How long were you in Syria?" asked the soldier who had shown her the coins.

"Just a few months," Valeria answered, making a face as she turned up her nose. "We were sent there to spread the gospel. Ah, but it was such a desolate place that we are happy to return to Nicomedia." She held her breath, praying silently that God would forgive her deception. Their two years in Syria had seemed more like two centuries, so why not shorten the truth to a few months?

His pregnant pause frightened Valeria. The soldier squinted at her, and then ordered, "Step aside. I will not disturb your sisters, but I must make a quick inspection of your cabin to confirm that you are not hiding the empresses."

Lydia greeted them at the door as they entered, and Valeria had to suppress a giggle when she caught sight of the woman's white hair, usually coiffed into an elegant bun but now flying to and fro. Clothed in a white robe, Lydia appeared pale. Her eyes were hollow and wide, and she spoke in a nasal tone. "Bless you, and you, and you," she said to the soldiers.

Another soldier walked to Prisca's bunk, and threw back the covers. When Valeria saw her mother pretending to sleep with her mouth opened wide and snoring loudly, she thought Prisca's acting had even surpassed Lydia's masquerade.

"Very well," one of the soldiers quipped. "It is obvious we have not found the ones we seek." He turned on his heel, and the other soldiers followed.

After the soldiers left the cabin, the women listened through the door. When they overheard one of the soldiers quip, "It is obvious those old hags were not empresses," it was all they could do not to burst into laughter.

But inside their cabin, they soon became solemn when they realized they were being hunted. Even more caution would have to be taken in Nicomedia before they could present themselves to Licinius and ask for protection in his court.

"Bishop Nicholas must have turned us in," Prisca commented.

"I do not believe that," Valeria protested. "He offered to help us. The guards in Syria must have reported our escape. If so, it is to be expected they would be checking every ship in Father's port."

The remainder of their journey to Nicomedia was uneventful, but the knowledge that the Roman authorities were searching for them, coupled with their grief over the death of

Diocletian and Lydia's loss of Cyrus, made for a very sad journey into the unknown.

ℒ❧

When they were but a day away from the city, the women discussed their plans.

"We should go directly to my sister Lucia's villa in Nicomedia," Lydia suggested. "They will not likely look for us there, since they are unaware I am traveling with you."

"Lydia has a point, Mother. We can stay there and send a message to Candidianus and request that he come to see us before we make any decisions about our next move."

Prisca agreed, and when they arrived at Lucia's villa, the servants went to tell their mistress that there were three nuns waiting at the door to see her. The women's disguises were so effective that when Lucia came to greet them, she did not recognize her own sister or the royal visitors. When Lydia leaned over to kiss Lucia's cheek, she whispered her identity into her ear.

Lucia gasped, and fear sprang into her eyes as she hurried them into the library and closed the door behind her. "You cannot stay here," she said. "They are looking everywhere for you. Licinius has issued an order that anyone who hides you will also be executed."

Valeria was stunned. "Licinius has ordered our execution?"

"He has also posted an enormous reward for your return."

"Can you allow us to stay until morning?" Valeria asked, trying to absorb the news.

Lucia shook her head. "Please understand that I cannot subject my family to such danger."

Prisca, appearing sympathetic, pleaded with Lucia to allow them to stay until they were able to make contact with Candidianus.

"You obviously have not heard the news," Lucia responded. "Licinius has sentenced Candidianus to death as well. He is now in prison in Thessalonica, awaiting execution."

Valeria's hand flew to her mouth. "No!" she cried. "It cannot be!"

"How could he?" Prisca cried. "Candidianus is the son of Galerius, Licinius' benefactor. We are the widows of the men who put him into power, and this is how he shows his appreciation?"

"I am sorry. I agree it is unfair," Lucia said. "And it is unfair of me not to help you. But I cannot take the chance; you must leave at once." She turned to Lydia. "But you, dear sister, may stay."

"I cannot abandon my dearest friends," Lydia protested.

Prisca hugged Lydia. "You must. We will be fine. Pray for us."

"But where shall we go, Mother?" Valeria protested. "Night has already fallen."

"We cannot send them into the streets at night," Lydia argued. "Can they please stay until morning?"

Lucia sighed. "Very well, but you must leave promptly at dawn. I will tell the servants you are from a convent. And, Lydia, you should pretend to leave, and then come back dressed as a lady, rather than a nun. Take one of my togas with you to change into, and when you return, ring the bell at the gate. We will pretend you have just arrived for a visit."

Lucia retrieved a toga from her room and gave it to Lydia, who stuffed it under her robe. Lucia then escorted her to the front door and loudly bade her goodbye so the servants would know she was leaving.

Lucia then informed the servants that one of the nuns had to leave, and she asked them to prepare the guest room for the other two sisters, who were staying overnight. None of the servants reacted with suspicion, and Lucia showed Valeria and Prisca to their room.

An hour later, the bell at the front door rang, and Lydia was welcomed to her sister's home. After dinner, Lydia secretly came to the guest room to see her friends.

"What will you do?" she asked.

"I have friends who will give us shelter," Prisca assured her. "We will stay in touch, I promise."

The following morning Valeria and Prisca found themselves on the street unsure where to go. Desperate, they stopped at the villa of Cornelia, Valeria's oldest and dearest friend, who had been in Egypt when Valeria first met Mauritius. Cornelia was delighted to see them, and she agreed to let them stay until her husband, a wealthy merchant who was traveling, returned. In a more somber tone, she explained that the Roman soldiers had already come looking for them.

"We probably have some time since they were here just days ago," she explained. "They will not return any time soon, unless they become suspicious for any reason."

Dressed in their church habits, Valeria and Prisca were careful not to reveal their identity while staying at Cornelia's villa; neither did they venture outside, except to attend the church service each day.

A few days before it was time for Cornelia's husband to return, the women left, wandering for hours until they finally found refuge in a nearby church. They told the priest they had come from Syria, and he invited them to stay for a few days. When they heard from one of the women in the kitchen that the soldiers were searching the churches, they left early the next morning. That evening the only place they could find refuge was an abandoned cave.

"We should return to Lycia," Valeria advised. "Bishop Nicholas said he would help us."

"Do you not find it suspicious that the Roman soldiers began looking for us soon after we left Lycia? I suspect the bishop turned us in. Self-righteous priests often believe it is their Christian duty to turn in fugitives, instead of taking pity on them."

"He offered to help, and I believe he is a man of his word," Valeria disagreed.

"It does not matter anyway," Prisca sighed. "We do not have enough money left to return to Lycia anyway."

"But what about the gold . . ."

"Cyrus carried the bulk of it, leaving us only a portion in case of an emergency. He believed we did not need much money since we were going home to Diocletian."

By morning, Prisca decided to approach another close friend, a widow named Appia, and ask for refuge. Thankfully, Appia welcomed them into her home. For six months Prisca and Valeria lived there in relative peace, until one morning, a dozen Roman soldiers besieged their friend's villa. Fortunately, Prisca and Valeria had gone to a communion service earlier that morning and were still at church. A servant found them and told them that Appia had been arrested and the soldiers were waiting for them at the villa. The servant had somehow managed to sneak their bags out of the house and bring them to the women.

For the next few days, the women sought refuge at the church until a member of the congregation offered to take them into his home. A few weeks later, Prisca and Valeria were devastated to learn that Appia had been executed. Licinius had soldiers all over Nicomedia looking for them.

It was no longer safe anywhere in the city. They approached another friend who could not allow them to stay in her home for more than a night, but she provided money for them to go to another province. Valeria begged her mother to sail to Lycia to ask Bishop Nicholas to help them, but Prisca still harbored a mistrust of him, so they agreed to go to Thessalonica instead.

34

They arrived in Thessalonica under cover of darkness, and Prisca and Valeria immediately sought shelter in a church. The next morning, they sent word to Bishop Marcus, the priest who had taught them the Scriptures for so many years, seeking his help. Having risen to a high position in the church, he sent his regrets, saying it was probably too dangerous to meet with them. Instead he sent them a substantial sum of money and news that a mutual friend, Anastasia, had agreed to have them as guests in her home.

Anastasia immediately sent a trusted servant to retrieve them. The servant explained that their hostess's husband was traveling in the provinces and that his mistress had invited the "nuns" to visit while he was away.

It was a joy for the women to see Thessalonica again, but when they passed the castle, Valeria's heart ached. How much she had lost! This was the home where she had lived her happiest years with Galerius, the years when Candidianus was first brought to her.

The next two weeks at Anastasia's home were pleasant, but the following Monday night, Valeria was plagued by a disturbing nightmare. In her dream, she felt herself being pulled from a pit—deep and dark, thick with sludge. Another force tried to suck her back into the vortex of the dark abyss, but she refused to let go. Suddenly, everything began to spin out of control. Her leg jerked violently under the light blanket. Drunk with dizziness, she cried out, "Where am I?"

Awakened by her own voice, Valeria sprang up in bed and glanced over at her mother, who still slept. Valeria clasped her sweaty palms over her heart, which pounded erratically against her linen nightgown. "Jesus, have mercy on me," she whispered. She breathed in deeply, speaking the name of Jesus, and then breathed out slowly until her lungs were empty of air. After a few breaths, she lay down again and drifted back to sleep.

"Valeria! Valeria!" Just above a whisper, a man's voice called to her.

Valeria was sure she recognized the voice, but as a series of distorted faces whirled through her mind, she could not identify it. So many voices of the past, but this one seemed more recent.

"Valeria!"

"Who is there?" she demanded in a whisper as she sat up in bed.

Besides her mother, she was alone.

"What is wrong?" Prisca asked.

"I had a nightmare. I sense we need to leave Anastasia's home immediately."

"But it was only a bad dream."

Valeria shook her head. "No. It was more than a dream; it was a premonition . . . a warning from God. I am sure of it."

"We will discuss it in the morning. If we are going to run again tomorrow, we are going to need our rest. Go back to sleep."

Reluctantly, Valeria agreed, and soon the women were asleep once again—until the pounding began.

"Prisca! Valeria!" It was a woman's voice this time, frantic and terrified.

The door swung open just as Valeria and Prisca sat up in bed. Anastasia stood in the hallway, holding a small lamp that cast a red glow over the room. "Come quickly," she insisted, stepping into the room. "The soldiers are at the gate. You must go to the church in the old square. There is a crypt beneath the church, where the priests are buried. You can enter it from the side door. No one will find you there. I have packed some oil, food, and water for you. Take this lamp—and this money as well. Hurry!"

Prisca and Valeria stuffed their meager belongings into their bags, as Valeria felt her spirit plummet to an all-time low. Was there no hope for them, no deliverance?

"Hurry, please," Anastasia warned, intruding on Valeria's thoughts. "With the soldiers at the gate, you must leave immediately."

There was no time for modesty now. Valeria fastened a toga over her nightgown and pulled on a hooded cape, and then slipped her feet into a pair of heavy sandals for walking, even as Prisca did the same. Allowing themselves to be rushed from what they had hoped would be their home for at least a few more weeks, Valeria's heart cried within her as they stepped into the night.

The women hurried down the street, darting into the shadows every time they heard a noise or saw even the slightest movement. Roman soldiers were posted everywhere, their voices echoing in the stillness of the night.

Finally they reached the church. Skirting around to the side, they maneuvered through the overgrown bushes until they found the entrance to the crypt. Cobwebs spun by industrious spiders stretched across the frame of the wooden door. With the soldiers close behind, the women realized there was no time to brush away the cobwebs. Valeria grasped the door handle and pulled. To her surprise, the decaying wooden door opened on the first try. She dropped her bag down the opening, and then tossed her mother's in and waited until she heard the soft thumps on the dirt floor of the crypt.

"That was a long drop," Valeria worried, hesitating.

"Hurry," Prisca urged. "The voices are getting closer."

Valeria took a deep breath and slid her foot into the opening, searching with her toe for the steps that lead downward. Carefully she made her way down the rotted ladder through the dangling cobwebs.

Prisca was right behind her and suggested they leave the door cracked to capture what little moonlight shone down from the otherwise dark sky.

Groping their way downward, they swatted both real and imagined spiders. Every rickety step took them deeper into the darkness, but considering that the soldiers might be just a few feet outside the entrance kept them moving. At last Valeria felt the spongy earth beneath her feet and sighed with relief.

"We must be at least thirty feet down," Valeria noted, as she reached up to help her mother down from the last couple of steps. "What do we do now?"

"We will need to find a place to sleep."

Valeria raised her eyebrows. "We are supposed to sleep here . . . with the coffins?"

"Right now I am so exhausted I could curl up in the coffin with a decaying priest."

"How can you have a sense of humor at a time like this?"

When they turned around and stepped further into the crypt, odors of gases from rotted bones and flesh assailed them, sending a wave of nausea through Valeria's body. Gagging, she grabbed her stomach and her mouth, as her body jerked with dry heaves.

Prisca shoved a handkerchief saturated in perfume under Valeria's nose.

"You think of everything," Valeria gasped.

"Keep moving," Prisca suggested. "Perhaps we can get inside the church to sleep."

Valeria held the lamp high and looked for a door. When she backed into something, she turned around and gasped, standing face-to-face with a coffin full of bones with lingering bits of dangling, rotting flesh, draped in a robe. Covering her mouth with her hands, she swallowed a scream.

Unsure of which direction to take next, Valeria turned slowly until she spotted a rock wall, covered in vegetation that had snaked its way inside through the crumbling mortar. With Prisca following, Valeria ran her right hand along the wall to prevent bumping into another forbidden terror.

The lamp flittered and dimmed.

"Where is the oil?" Valeria whispered.

"We should preserve it; keep moving with what little we have."

Taking baby steps, Valeria led her mother through the crypt.

"Perhaps it is a blessing that we cannot see well," Prisca commented.

"Imaginations can conjure up visions far worse than reality," Valeria responded.

Valeria kept moving until she came upon some stairs that led to an iron gate. She pushed it with her hand and then her shoulder, and finally her bag, but years of neglect had rusted it shut. She even kicked it, but no matter how much force she used, the gate would not swing open.

Exasperated, Valeria whimpered, "It is hopeless," and the women scooted back down the tunnel in search of another door.

Unable to find one, Prisca finally said, "We should stay right here. Spread a toga out on the floor."

Valeria sighed, too exhausted to argue. "Tomorrow we must try to reach the harbor and return to Lycia. It is far away from Licinius. He does not have many soldiers stationed there, and I believe the bishop will help us."

"I still suspect Bishop Nicholas is the person who turned us in. I know you do not agree, but—" She paused and sighed, and Valeria suspected her mother had resigned herself to trusting the bishop, as they no longer had any other options.

A loud crash from the opposite direction of the crypt prevented either of them from pursuing the thought further.

"Someone dropped down through the entrance," Valeria whispered as they strained to hear voices.

"It sounds as if there are at least three others inside the crypt," Valeria speculated.

"Soldiers," Prisca worried.

The women huddled together silently, trembling, as loud voices began rising in the tomb.

"Tear down the ladder," one of them ordered. "But first anchor a rope above in the ground."

Another voice rang out in the darkness. "I will search for another entrance to make sure they do not get away."

"How did they know where to find us?" Valeria whispered.

"They probably tortured Anastasia until she told them."

Heavy footsteps padded toward them, and Valeria's heart raced with each footfall. Springing into action, she hid their bags under some of the relics in the tunnel, keeping only their velvet bags of jewelry and Mauritius' Theban cross, which she fastened around her neck and tucked underneath her clothes.

She grabbed her mother's hand. "Come, we must find someplace to hide."

"But did you hear him? They are going to trap us down here," Prisca whispered, her voice nearly frantic. "They are destroying the ladder. We are trapped."

"Did Jesus not teach to be concerned only for the day?" Valeria grabbed her mother's hand to lead her back through the labyrinth. This time they went in another direction that led to the right instead of straight ahead. Finally Valeria saw another door. When she quietly jiggled the handle, it opened, leading them to a narrow stairway that veered upward. They shed tears of relief as they tiptoed quietly up the stairs. Once again God had spared them and shown them the way, but their spirits fell as they reached the top and saw yet another door. Valeria turned the knob.

"It is unlocked," she whispered, momentary relief washing over her.

Passing through the door, they were shocked when they found themselves standing in the bedroom of a snoring priest.

The priest stirred when the two women crept out the door into the hallway. They followed the winding hallway until they reached a door that led outside, but when they peered through it, they saw Roman soldiers everywhere.

"We must sleep inside the church until morning," Prisca suggested, "and then try to escape to the harbor before dawn."

"Will that not be obvious? Do you not think they will be checking every boat that puts out to sea?"

"As you said earlier, my dear, let us just be concerned with one day at a time. We will deal with tomorrow when it arrives. For now, let us find a place to lay our heads."

They tried several doors and discovered the one to the sacristy was unlocked. There they found ample room to lie down and sleep. They also found fresh-baked loaves nestled in baskets for tomorrow's communion service.

"Perhaps I should go back for our bags," Valeria suggested once they were settled.

"We have our valuables, so we should not take the risk," Prisca cautioned. "Leave the bags behind."

The next morning they feasted on the bread and then ventured out of the church to try to make it to the harbor. Heads down as they walked, they had nearly made it through the marketplace when they looked up to find that dozens of Roman soldiers with swords had surrounded them.

"It is finished," Valeria whispered, glancing at her mother.

Prisca sighed. "Yes, the chase has finally ended."

35

*S*ince Licinius had already signed the death order, a centurion informed the women that their executions would take place the following morning in the marketplace.

"My son, Candidianus. Is he here?" Valeria asked. "Will he be executed with us?"

The soldier averted his gaze but nodded.

Though heartbroken at her son's fate, Valeria somehow found a poignant comfort in knowing they would be together at the end.

"May I see him?" she pleaded. "Please! Just a word with him, that's all."

But her captor denied her request. Two jailers then grabbed her arms and dragged her down the dismal hallway toward a cell, as Valeria strained to look back at her mother.

"Wait!" Prisca cried out. "Please, may I share a cell with my daughter?"

Valeria's guards did not respond, but the man who stood guard over Prisca, whose rank was obviously superior to Valeria's captors, appeared to have a more compassionate nature.

"I am sorry, madame," Valeria heard him say. "We have our orders."

"Sir, please," Prisca begged, her words tearing at Valeria's heart. "May I please have a few last words with her?"

Prisca's guard hesitated and then nodded, ordering Valeria's captors to halt so the two women could have a final moment together.

When mother and daughter stood face-to-face, they clung to one another as Valeria wept.

"Do not be afraid, my child," Prisca crooned. "Remember the Scriptures: *You can do all things through Jesus Christ who strengthens you.* God will sustain us through this trial, and soon we will be with Him in paradise. Remember the words of the Apostle Peter: *Beloved, do not be surprised at the fiery trial when it comes upon you to test you, as though something strange were happening to you. But rejoice insofar as you share Christ's sufferings, that you may also rejoice and be glad when his glory is revealed.*"

The guard pulled Prisca away then, but she called back to Valeria, "I love you, my precious daughter. Soon we will be together in paradise."

The jailer unlocked the heavy iron door to Valeria's cell, and it creaked loudly as it swung open. He shoved her inside with such force that she fell upon the cold stone floor. The other guard unlocked the chains from around her wrists. Her arms ached, and she was grateful when the man helped her ease down onto the floor before he exited her cell and the door clanged shut behind him. With a heavy iron key, one of the jailers locked her inside, leaving two centurions posted outside her door.

Inside the cold, dank cell, Valeria sat and faced her death alone, which made her situation nearly unbearable. Chilled to the bone and trembling as much from fear as from the cold, she dropped her face into her hands and wept. She had not allowed herself to feel any emotion for a long time . . . until today. Now she felt nothing but terror. She attempted to pray, but no matter how she tried, she could not find peace.

"Where are you, Lord?" she cried, looking up toward the heavens.

No answer came. Valeria wept again, as she examined her arms and wrists, bruised and sore from the capture. Licinius was determined to kill everyone even remotely connected with the old tetrarch. It mattered not to him that Valeria and her mother were Christians; as part of the old regime, they had to die for the sins of Diocletian and Galerius.

Valeria berated herself. Why should Licinius believe that she and her mother were Christians? Had they not participated in the pagan sacrifices when Licinius was a guest in their home? Her earthly father had not been able to save her. Would her heavenly Father intervene? It seemed unlikely, now that the moon was shining down from the sky outside her cell and she was to be executed at dawn.

As Valeria pondered her fate and that of her mother and son, she could not help but wonder if indeed they were suffering persecution as Christians or if this was judgment from God for the sacrifices in which they had ultimately been forced to participate. How differently might things have turned out if they had refused to compromise their first allegiance! And what had their compromise accomplished? They would now be martyred after all.

As she communed with God, the memories of her past began to unfold, taking her on a bittersweet journey and bringing a smile to her spirit. Her life had been a good one, a blessed one. As it did so often, Valeria's mind wandered to her first love, Mauritius. When she remembered that she had fastened his cross around her neck, she fingered the precious memento of her beloved, allowing herself to dwell on the thoughts that had comforted her so often throughout the years. Tonight was no different. Her short time with Mauritius had been the happiest of her life. After they had spent the summer together in Elephantine, Mauritius had said goodbye. From there, he had gone to his martyrdom with such courage and faith, unlike her cowardly husband, Galerius, who was terrified of what would happen to him after his death.

But had she not loved Galerius too? Yes! God had given her a miraculous, supernatural love for her husband. Valeria had to admit that her life with Galerius was as happy as could be expected, under the circumstances. Her purpose as his wife had been to pray for his salvation, and her prayers had been answered, her desires fulfilled. Although Galerius had not accepted Jesus as Lord until days before his death, and then mostly out of fear, Valeria's years of prayers had been rewarded. What comfort there was in remembering how she had witnessed Galerius cry out to God for mercy to save his soul. He had even signed the edict to end the persecution of Christians. Just as the monks and others had predicted, her purpose had been fulfilled, and she had indeed been used to change the world.

But somehow, Valeria had believed God's plan for her on earth was not yet finished. The greatest desire of her heart had been to see her beloved son become emperor, like his father and grandfather before him, except her son would be a Christian emperor. Now that would never happen.

Hope deferred makes the heart sick. The scripture echoed in her mind until her head spun, and she felt sick and weary. She had not noticed until now that darkness had invaded her cell, extinguishing the last rays of sunlight. She lay down on the cold, hard floor, but she could not sleep.

She stood and looked out the tiny window into the night, and she knew the clock was moving toward her death. She could see nothing but the night sky. As she watched the stars, she thought of David, the young shepherd boy, sleeping outside with his flock of sheep, and she pondered his words in the Psalms: *"Lift your eyes and look to the heavens: Who created all these? He, who brings out the starry host one by one, and calls them each by name. Because of his great power and mighty strength, not one of them is missing."*

She thought of how Mauritius must have felt when he met his death. Valeria was certain that he did so trusting the God of the universe, who flung the stars into the heavens. She prayed that she would do the same, and at that moment, the burden lifted.

As she once again lay down on the cold stone floor, she noticed the light of the moon shining through the window, and there on the wall was a perfect outline of a cross above her.

Valeria cried out with joy to her heavenly Father, "I am not alone!"

When the centurions looked inside her cell, she repeated her declaration. "I am not alone. Christ will never leave nor forsake me."

They shook their heads and looked at her as though she had gone mad, but Valeria did not care. She marveled at the work of grace God had done in her heart over the years, and then she closed her eyes and drifted off to sleep, dreaming she was at last with her beloved Mauritius and her Savior.

36

When morning came, Valeria awakened filled with a sense of peace. The Holy Spirit had ministered to her throughout the night, and when the centurions came for her, she offered her hands to them to bind in chains. Once the iron door to her cell was swung open, she smiled and went willingly.

Outside the prison, she cried tears of joy as the guards allowed her to briefly greet her mother and son before the three condemned prisoners were led to the middle of Thessalonica, where a platform had been constructed for the executions. Upon arriving in the town square, Valeria was aghast when she beheld the large crowd, but she was surprised and pleased to see familiar faces among them.

As she scanned the spectators, her eyes stopped. Her body froze. Even the guards were unable to budge her.

"Mauritius!" she cried.

All eyes turned to the spot in the crowd where Valeria stared. There, on the front row, he stood—tall, tanned, and healthy—gazing back at her. When she recognized the compassion in his dark eyes, she tried to lift her hand but was stopped by the heavy chains that bound her.

"But Mauritius," she cried, "I do not understand. They told me you had died, but you were here all along."

The man appeared puzzled, but neither did he turn away.

Confused, Valeria turned to her mother. "It is Mauritius," she insisted.

Prisca appeared confused but said nothing.

Is Mauritius only an apparition? Valeria wondered. *Or is it possible I am hallucinating?* Her heart skipped a beat as another thought flitted into her mind. Had Diocletian lied to them about Mauritius' death? Or were she and Prisca simply getting an early glimpse into heaven?

The guard pushed Valeria forward. Not wanting to appear as if she were fighting her execution, Valeria did not resist, but her eyes stayed on Mauritius—or the vision of him—until she could no longer see him in the crowd.

Thoughts conflicted in her mind, even as emotions warred in her heart. If Mauritius had lived, then she would not see him today in paradise. At the thought, Valeria's heart filled with great sadness and disappointment. And yet the confusion remained.

The guards pulled her up the steps onto the platform. Now she could search the crowd for Mauritius again. Her heart soared as she moved to the center of the platform and her eyes fell upon Nanu, the beautiful Egyptian who had almost become her sister-in-law. Nanu stood quietly weeping and clasping the hand of a handsome Roman soldier, most likely her husband. Valeria had heard that Nanu had moved to Thessalonica, but the two of them had lost touch soon after Mauritius' death and the martyrdom of the Theban Legion.

But wait! There was Mauritius standing beside his sister! Valeria had been so stunned at seeing Mauritius that she had not noticed Nanu next to him. But as she beheld them, she became even more confused. Nanu was older, her hair streaked with gray, yet Mauritius was young. Of course! The man who resembled Valeria's beloved was the toddler she had once loved, Babafemi. He was the image of his uncle!

Valeria looked over at her mother and cried, "He is Babafemi, Nanu's son."

Light dawned in Prisca's eyes, and she nodded at her daughter, who turned to smile at Nanu and her family. The trio waved back in an encouraging but heart rending acknowledgment.

Valeria continued to scan the crowd then, her eyes stopping on Lydia and her sister, Lucia, who had obviously come to lend the only support they could—their reassuring smiles. Valeria felt their love and nodded at them.

A Roman guard grabbed Valeria by her left arm then, hurting her, though she dared not complain. Instead she bit her lower lip until it bled. He pushed her out in front of the crowd, and she held her head high while another Roman soldier read a list of her crimes. These were not her crimes, but those her husband and father had committed against Christians, yet she was to die for their sins. At that moment she felt such close kinship to her Savior, knowing she was partaking in His suffering. Saint Peter had experienced such intimate fellowship with Christ, as had Paul—and Mauritius.

Unable to lift her hand to make the sign of the cross, Valeria continued to hold her head high, her eyes searching. Many in the square said it was as though she sought someone with the courage to step up and save her. But no one did. The vigilant guards watched the crowd carefully, waiting to arrest anyone who dared protest or interfere.

Next the guard pulled Prisca out in front of the crowd. How Valeria wished she had the power to save her mother from this public humiliation! Prisca did not deserve this treatment, as she had done nothing but good things for the Roman Empire. Yet her list of crimes far outnumbered Valeria's.

Though Valeria had promised herself she would not cry, seeing her mother humiliated caused her to lose control, and she sobbed openly.

Her beloved Candidianus was next. He was a handsome young man, and the courage he exhibited as he stood before the executioners was obviously admired by everyone in the crowd.

One by one the doomed trio was offered an opportunity to speak last words to the crowd. Candidianus was first. He chose to say none of his own words but quoted from the Scriptures a verse that Valeria had taught him when he was a little boy: "I have fought the good fight, I have finished my course, I have kept the faith."

Valeria was next. "I am innocent of all charges, my only crime being born the daughter of Emperor Diocletian and being the wife of Emperor Galerius." She closed with a verse from the Book of Revelation: "*And God shall wipe away all tears from their eyes; and there shall be no more death, neither sorrow, nor crying, neither shall there be any more pain; for the former things are passed away.*"

When Prisca took her turn, Valeria thought her mother regal in her response. "I have served my Savior and the Roman people with great love and honor. May God have mercy on our souls."

The centurions stepped forward and unlocked the prisoners' chains, prepared to blindfold them and bind their hands with strips of muslin. When the guard placed the blindfold around Valeria's eyes, she refused it. "Sire," she whispered, "the cross I wear belonged to the uncle of the young Egyptian soldier on the front row. Will you remove it and give it to him, please?"

The guard hesitated, looking in the direction of his superior officer, and then without a word, quickly unfastened the gold chain from around Valeria's neck and slipped the cross into his pocket before binding Valeria's hands.

When the guard left the platform to take his place in the crowd, Valeria watched him discreetly transfer the Theban cross into the hands of Mauritius' nephew. After receiving it, the young man looked up at Valeria and smiled. She returned his smile, turning her eyes then toward the guard, questioning his kindness.

Without a word, the centurion knelt down before her and drew a cross in the sand. Valeria immediately understood.

A priest now stepped onto the podium to administer the last rites to the prisoners. *Focus on his kind eyes*, Valeria told herself. To her surprise, when she did so, she recognized him. It was Bishop Marcus, who had taught them the Scriptures at the palace in Thessalonica. Smiling at her, he leaned down and whispered words of encouragement within the hearing of the condemned trio, quoting from the Book of Romans.

"Who shall separate us from the love of Christ? Shall tribulation, or distress, or persecution, or famine, or nakedness, or danger, or sword? As it is written, For your sake we are being killed all the day long; we are regarded as sheep to be slaughtered. No, in all these things we are more than conquerors through him who loved us. For I am sure that neither death nor life, nor angels nor rulers, nor things present nor things to come, nor powers, nor height nor depth, nor anything else in all creation, will be able to separate us from the love of God in Christ Jesus our Lord."

The bishop administered the rites to each of them, and then he prayed. Next the guards ordered the condemned trio to kneel and place their heads upon the wooden headrest before them.

Valeria turned her head to see her mother, and then her beloved son. They had also refused to wear blindfolds, so they were able to speak their final goodbyes with their eyes.

At last Valeria kept her gaze fixed upon Candidianus. The young man should be a Caesar now and soon an emperor, but instead, his life would be cut short, not because of the decisions his father made but because of those he chose not to make. If only Galerius could have seen into the future, he would never have made the fateful decision to trust Licinius with his son's life. Now Candidianus was betrayed. Worst of all, Galerius was betrayed by the man he considered his most trusted friend.

When her executioner suddenly appeared and stepped onto the platform, Valeria's thoughts were interrupted. Her gasp at the sight of him was so loud that the people in the square heard her and winced. The man was so large that with each step he took, the platform shook. Some of the women in the crowd cried out as he took his place beside Valeria.

For a brief moment, Valeria's courage escaped her as she gazed upon the man clad in black. He looked as Valeria imagined Satan himself would appear. Leather straps bound his calves and forearms, cutting into his skin. Behind a black mask, his dark, menacing eyes darted from the top of her head to the tip of her toes as if to determine how strong a blow he should wield with the heavy axe he carried in his right hand. That he was strong and muscular comforted Valeria, for she had heard that with weaker men in this position it sometimes took three to four blows before the head came off the victim. The pain was more than Valeria could imagine.

Because Candidianus was to her right, he would be executed first. His executioner appeared as evil as her own.

What could be worse for a mother than watching her son die?

Valeria refused to watch the brutal blow to her son, but she let out a small cry when she felt the warmth of his blood splatter upon her face and hands. As she glanced down and saw the hem of her white robe stained red from blood that poured from Candidianus' body, she moaned and squeezed her eyes shut.

Valeria did not have to endure the horror of her son's death for long. She felt her executioner step closer. There was no hesitation as he swung the mighty axe behind him. Valeria prayed aloud, so that many people heard her last words: "Into thy hands I commend my spirit," and the sword came down swiftly upon her neck. A single blow and Valeria was decapitated. Her extraordinary turquoise eyes fluttered for another two or three seconds, still appearing to search the crowd for her rescuer to appear. When the stored oxygen in her brain had expired, the eyes stared vacantly like two blue sapphires.

. The witnesses who had gathered to watch the spectacle marveled at the smile that remained on the face of the doomed empress. When it was over, a lone voice in the crowd declared, "Surely this day our beloved Empress Valeria is in paradise with the blessed Savior."

Epilogue

Following their beheading, the bodies of Valeria and Prisca and Candidianus were tossed into the sea off the coast of Thessalonica.

Licinius subsequently quarreled with Constantine, who defeated him in 314 and forced him to cede all of his European territories except for Thrace. War resumed in 324, and Constantine defeated Licinius at Adrianople and Chrysopolis. Constantine, as he had hoped and schemed, became the sole emperor of the Roman Empire. His sister, whom he had given in marriage to Licinius, pleaded with her brother to spare her husband, so initially Licinius was imprisoned. Constantine eventually had Licinius put to death in 325, and then ruled the Roman Empire as a Christian nation until his death on May 22, 337, in Nicomedia.

Glossary

PEOPLE:

Diocletian—Emperor of the Roman Empire, known as the greatest persecutor of Christians in the history of the world. He put an end to the disastrous phase of Roman history known as the "Military Anarchy" or the "Imperial Crisis" (235-284). He also established an obvious military despotism and was responsible for laying the groundwork for the second phase of the Roman Empire, which is known as the "Tetrarchy," the "Later Roman Empire," or the "Byzantine Empire." His reforms ensured the continuity of the Roman Empire in the east for more than a thousand years.

Prisca—Empress and wife of Diocletian, mother of Valeria.

Valeria—Daughter of Roman Emperor Diocletian and his wife, Prisca; the wife of Galerius. She assumed the title of empress when her husband Galerius became emperor after her father's retirement.

Galerius—General in Diocletian's Army, who became Diocletian's adopted son and husband of Valeria, daughter of Diocletian. Galerius was appointed Caesar and co-emperor under Diocletian and later became the Roman emperor after Diocletian abdicated.

Valeria Maximilla—Daughter of Caesar and Roman Emperor Galerius; wife of Maxentius, son of Maximian, emperor of the Western Roman Empire under Senior Emperor Diocletian.

Maximian Caesar—Diocletian's counterpart, whom he assigned as emperor of the western half of the Roman Empire.

Maxentius—Husband of Valeria Maximilla, daughter of Galerius by his first wife, and son of Maximian Caesar, emperor of the Western Empire under Diocletian.

Candidianus—Son of Galerius, adopted by Valeria as her own son. He was engaged to marry the daughter of Maximinus Daza, the son of Galerius' sister and the adopted son of Galerius.

Maximinus Daia—Nephew of Galerius, the son of his sister. Maximinus Daia, often called Daza, served in the army as a *scutarius*, *Protector*, and *tribunus*, and was adopted and appointed Caesar by Galerius.

Bishop Nicholas—This bishop, with the white hair and beard, later became known as Santa Claus, for he was always leaving secret gifts at night at the homes of the needy, especially children.

PLACES:

Nicomedia—Turkish city, where the palace of Roman Emperor Diocletian was located. Subsequently, it also became the city of Galerius and Valeria's second palace.

Thessolonika/Thessalonica—Greek city where the first palace of Galerius and Valeria was located.

Solano—Croatian city, known as Split today, where Diocletian built a magnificent palace for his retirement.

Elephantine—Egyptian island, where Diocletian built a palace and a Roman fortress.

Theban Region—Egyptian area, home of the world's most renowned Bible scholars and the Theban Legion, composed of some of the greatest soldiers in the Roman Empire.

Afterword

The amazing and inspiring story of the Theban Legion is cited in Foxe's *Voices of the Martyrs: 33 A.D to Today*.[1] Though definitive argument exists that this story was only a legend, the remains of 400 men have been found in the area, lending credibility to the account. In addition, the Catholic Church recognizes the event as fact.

Portions of *Valeria's Cross* are fictionalized, loosely based on historical dates and events. The authors took the liberty of adjusting facts so that Captain Mauritius and Valeria could meet and fall in love. The remainder of the story is closer to the historical facts, with events embellished since this time period is not well documented, especially concerning Emperor Diocletian's daughter, Valeria. However, it is quite possible that the young woman was involved in a romance when her father ordered her to marry a pagan, General Galerius.

Some historians also argue that Prisca and Valeria were not really Christians but only sympathetic to them, based on the fact that they eventually took part in the pagan sacrifices of Rome. However, other historians affirm the women's faith because at that time the large majority of Christians, who felt they were not called to be martyrs, participated in these sacrifices by making the sign of the cross as they did so. As for the women's exile and death, those events are well documented.

---

[1] John Foxe and The Voice of the Martyrs, *Foxe: Voices of the Martyrs: 33 A.D. to Today* (Orlando, FL: Bridge-Logos, 2007), pp. 63-64.

Discussion Questions

1. What would you consider some of the greatest points today's Christian women could learn from Valeria and her mother, Prisca?

2. The story of the Theban Legion, which is recounted in the *Foxe's Book of Martyrs*, is considered a legend by many scholars but absolute truth by others. Whether true or legendary, how did the story of their lives and their deaths impact you, and how does it speak to you today?

3. What surprised you most about the life and times of this era? Had you read much about it before?

4. The Romans were not known for their morality, so how do think Christian women coped with the lifestyle? How can you apply their coping mechanisms to your own life and culture today?

5. What do you see as the greatest challenges for Valeria and Prisca being married to such devout pagans?

6. After Galerius' demise, were you surprised that his friends and family members did not remain loyal to his family?

7. Diocletian went mad a couple of times in his life. What do you believe were the causes?

8. Of the two rulers, Diocletian and Galerius, whom do you believe was more evil? Why?

9. What is the greatest lesson you learned about life and history in reading *Valeria's Cross*?

10. What aspects of the royal life would you have most enjoyed during the rule of Diocletian and Galerius? The least? What do you think you would have done had you lived as a Christian during this time?

11. The Theban Legion were Christian martyrs. When you were reading this book, you must have asked yourself what you would have done had you been in their place. Would you care to share those thoughts?

12. What would you have done in some of Valeria's situations? Do you think you would have behaved in a similar manner or differently?

Want to learn more about authors
Kathi Macias and Susan Wales and check out
other great fiction
from Abingdon Press?

Sign up for our fiction newsletter at
www.AbingdonPress.com
to read interviews with your favorite authors, find tips
for starting a reading group, and stay posted on what
new titles are on the horizon. It's a place to connect
with other fiction readers or post a
comment about this book.

Be sure to visit Kathi and Susan online!

www.kathimacias.com
http://kathieasywritermacias.blogspot.com

www.susanwales.info
http://ladysusanwales.blogspot.com